ADAM MANSBACH's books include the number one international bestseller *Go the Fuck to Sleep,* the California Book Award–winning novel *The End of the Jews,* and the cult classic *Angry Black White Boy.* His work has appeared in *The New Yorker, The New York Times Book Review, Esquire,* and *The Believer,* and on National Public Radio's *All Things Considered.*

Praise for *Rage Is Back*

"A hilarious revenge thriller . . . like watching a Quentin Tarantino film or listening to a Wu-Tang Clan album—perhaps simultaneously. This is a great thing. Mansbach, best known for the runaway bestseller *Go the F**k to Sleep,* is, more importantly, one of hip-hop's great novelists. *Rage Is Back* has humor and horror and humanity and is altogether fresh. It should rest in the pantheon of hip-hop classics along with Henry Chalfant's film *Style Wars* and Martha Cooper and Chalfant's companion collection of photographs, *Subway Art.*"   —*Chicago Tribune*

"Flashing bits of brilliance like a beautifully burned train clacking over a few minutes of elevated rail . . . Mansbach can write with real talent, maybe crazy talent. His social criticism can be gleefully clever."
                                            —*The New York Times Book Review*

"In Dondi, Mansbach has created an unforgettable narrator who combines elements of Holden Caulfield, Oscar Wao, and even a hint of Ignatius J. Reilly. But Dondi is no simple amalgam. He's a straight-talking smart-ass who wins points for his brutal honesty, urban worldliness, and sympathy for the honorable criminal. Mansbach's wild ride will likely earn cult-classic status—and deservedly so."   —*The Boston Globe*

"Mansbach has clearly had a play date with Michael Chabon and Junot Díaz, and his fresh, witty novel is one that hip readers will relish. Laced with zaniness and cultural bling, it's a nostalgic tribute to the glory days of street art, back when New York City had character. In the sweet and obscene voice of mixed-race Dondi, Mansbach has created a sharp commentator on the persistent nervousness of our integrated society. And who knows, his swirling descriptions might entice you to pick up an old can of Krylon. . . . But even if you never go out bombing with your crew, you'll consider just what we gave up to keep our subway cars clean—and dull."   —*The Washington Post*

"*Rage Is Back* does for graffiti what Michael Chabon's *The Amazing Adventures of Kavalier and Clay* did for comic books. A rollicking, frenetic, and hilarious jaunt through the (literal and figurative) New York City underworld, *Rage Is Back* is a nostalgic love letter to the city and the golden age of graffiti. At turns wise and immature, stubborn and magnanimous, Dondi mashes up disparate linguistic registers with an effortlessness that brings to mind Junot Díaz's perennial narrator, Junior . . . but beneath all the weed and spray paint, it's a warmhearted story about a son searching for his father and for himself, a trip through the past and present of an American art form that fits surprisingly well within the confines of the novel."   —*San Francisco Chronicle*

"A bracingly funny book, largely due to Dondi's magnetic narration . . . Mansbach gets Dondi just right. But for all his fine comic writing, Mansbach doesn't neglect the more serious aspects of New York City's battle over graffiti in *Rage Is Back*."   —*The Miami Herald*

"As language, [*Rage Is Back*] has the feeling of something new and exhilarating."   —*To the Best of Our Knowledge,* National Public Radio

"A virtuoso stylistic performance."   —*Toronto Star*

"At once a very true story and a very fictional one. Amidst bits of magical realism, *Rage Is Back* is still about a very real conflict and takes place in an accurate depiction of Fort Greene [that] would certainly ring true for many locals. There's no denying that a boy who switches from the *The Odyssey* to Nas in seconds, as Dondi does, is scarcely found in literature. And yet, his voice is very real."
—*The Local, The New York Times*

"A muscular ode to New York City's 1980s art underground . . . Combines a poet's touch with the wild sparks of a subway train speeding through a graffiti-splashed tunnel."   —*Elle*

"The book will surely be called 'gritty' and celebrated for its street ethos and Junot Díaz–style colloquialism, but it's the sporadic elements of the supernatural that set it apart. There also is a surprising moral complexity here. . . . Mansbach has clearly thought through these issues, and he addresses them artfully. *Rage Is Back* is a wild and enjoyable ride, bumpy as the C train and loud as the headphones on the kid sitting next to you."   —*Newsday*

"*Rage Is Back* continues [Mansbach's] hyperarticulate, authentic blend of hip-hop culture, street art, and youthful disillusionment. One of the most refreshing aspects of Mansbach's story is the hyperdetailed drug trips and supernatural streak of magical realism in an urban landscape."
—*The AV Club*

"By about the third time that Adam Mansbach's narrator refers to himself as 'your boy here,' Kilroy Dondi Vance will have utterly endeared himself to even the most out of it reader when it comes to contemporary culture. Mr. Mansbach's reverent insight into the little known world of authentic graffiti artists is both the most compelling aspect of the novel's multilayered narrative and a stunning achievement unto itself. Dondi's narration skillfully features more similes than in the oeuvre of a rapper who's been in the game for over a decade . . . [and] serve[s] to imbue Dondi's storytelling skills with 'greatest-of-all-time' status in the who's-your-favorite-rapper discourses. *Rage Is Back* also soars through the underbelly of the city. For aficionados of underground concepts in literature, Mr. Mansbach's craftily constructed underworld will not disappoint. . . . *Rage Is Back* will surely become the substance of graffiti lore for the foreseeable future."
—*New York Journal of Books*

"It's the great American graffiti novel. The golden era of New York hip-hop and graffiti lives—on the shelves of bookstores."
—*The Brooklyn Paper*

"*Rage Is Back* is a funny, macho-but-vulnerable coming-of-age-story. It's seeped in New York nostalgia and narrated in bright and vulgar prose that succeeds in hinting at no small quantity of swagger and soul. As Dondi says, 'it's not easy to talk from your heart and out your ass at the same time.' Delightfully, *Rage Is Back* manages to do both."
—*The Daily Beast*

"A wild tale with surreal twists, both comic and moving, that bring to mind the works of Michael Chabon and Jonathan Lethem."
—*New York Daily News*

"You're rewarded immensely with a twisted and colorful tale of retribution . . . don't be surprised if you get sucked into this engrossing tale."
—*Vancouver Weekly*

"An elegant contraption of a book, *Rage Is Back* is held together and made to run because of the remarkable voice of the narrator . . . breathtakingly ornate. Enjoy the ride. There's much instruction and delight along the way." —*The Buffalo News*

"Two years after a joke propelled him to the bestseller list, [Mansbach] proves he belongs there with his excellent new 'Great American Graffiti Novel.' *Rage* uses graffiti as less a setting than a central character in and of itself: Mansbach loves the form too deeply to grant it anything less, loves it so much his writing reads like graffiti looks—big, colorful, dense, often profane, occasionally impenetrable. But, like any great (or Great) novel—like *Sleep*, even—*Rage* is also vastly bigger and deeper and more valuable than the sum of its (many, moving) parts: not quite easy, but not quite meant to be." —*East Bay Express*

"With its hyperverbal view into the hip-hop culture near to the author's heart, *Rage Is Back* is masterfully verbose." —*Boston Phoenix*

"The book's pulsing plot mimics the rhythms of hip-hop, with rapid verbal exchanges . . . a rambunctious ride through graffiti culture, filled with magical moments and outlandish situations . . . makes you wonder whether Quentin Tarantino might consider a movie adaptation."
—*Austin American-Statesman*

"A fierce and funny thrill ride through the train yards and back streets of the graffiti underground. Mansbach writes with splendid rhythm and intensity." —*San Jose Mercury News*

"It makes sense that Mansbach would write a novel that intertwines graffiti artists with a story about family . . . because hip-hop culture, race, and family are three of the overarching themes in all of his work. What is evident as soon as you start reading *Rage Is Back* is that Mansbach is one of the few writers capable of taking those subjects and writing something that comes off as organic and fun to read. Like Lethem's *Fortress of Solitude*, Mansbach's latest has bright flourishes of urban magical realism. And also like Lethem's book, you can clearly hear the characters' voices as you read through *Rage Is Back* . . . you find yourself finishing the book and realizing *Rage Is Back* is totally not what you expected, and that's one of the things that makes the book so wonderful to read." —*Flavorwire*

"Dondi is a hip-hop Holden Caufield. . . . He's got a bright, acerbic, cynical adolescent outlook that's a treat to read. The caper that fills the second half of the book is big, weird, brash, and riddled with history and supernatural juju, and his ride through it is vastly entertaining, right through to the last page. This is a tremendously fun novel."
—Boing Boing

"A cacophonous love letter to the old dirty, pregentrified New York."
—*New York Post*

"Gels in a most satisfying way as fractured relationships are mended and old friends hatch—and splendidly execute—a plan to exact careful revenge on the man who long ago split them apart. Read it on the B train."
—DailyCandy

"Unfolding like a fever dream of an impossible return to graffiti-era New York, Mansbach's *Rage Is Back* delivers a mind-bending journey through a subterranean world of epic heroes and villains, and is already being called the great American graffiti novel. A must-read for the literate hip-hop head."
—Okayplayer.com

"Through gripping prose, Adam Mansbach puts the reader in the thick of the graffiti underground."
—*AM New York*

"*Rage Is Back* is a gutsy act of cultural nostalgia, full of longing for a vanished New York, a chaotic, colorful city full of graffiti and guerrilla art. Adam Mansbach is a fearless, funny, and thoroughly engaging writer."
—Tom Perrotta, author of *Little Children* and *The Leftovers*

"Adam Mansbach's new novel is a trip! A trip through dimensions, drugs, and even an ingenious time machine. *Rage Is Back* is hilarious and insightful, tender and surprising, but best of all it's a tribute to the old heads, the bombers and taggers, and the glory of writing in all its forms."
—Victor LaValle, author of *The Devil in Silver* and *Big Machine*

"Adam Mansbach's *Rage Is Back* is a profound reminder of why fiction matters. A riotous and propulsive read, this darkly poetic novel took me places I could never get to with my own two feet, and introduced me to souls living colorfully outside the mainstream. Behind its street boy pose is an ambitious novel about family, friendship, and the ties that bind. Mansbach makes it look easy."
—Attica Locke, author of *Blackwater Rising* and *The Cutting Season*

ALSO BY ADAM MANSBACH

*Genius B-Boy Cynics Getting Weeded
in the Garden of Delights*
(poetry)

Shackling Water

Angry Black White Boy

*A Fictional History of the United States
with Huge Chunks Missing*
(editor)

The End of the Jews

Go the F**k to Sleep

Nature of the Beast
(graphic novel)

RAGE IS BACK

Adam Mansbach

P

A PLUME BOOK

PLUME
Published by the Penguin Group
Penguin Group (USA) 375 Hudson Street,
New York, New York 10014, USA

USA | Canada | UK | Ireland | Australia | New Zealand | India | South Africa | China
Penguin Books Ltd, Registered Offices: 80 Strand, London WC2R 0RL, England
For more information about the Penguin Group visit penguin.com

First published in the United States of America by Viking,
a member of Penguin Group (USA) Inc., 2013
First Plume Printing 2013

P REGISTERED TRADEMARK—MARCA REGISTRADA

Drop caps on the first page of each chapter by Blake Lethem

THE LIBRARY OF CONGRESS HAS CATALOGUED THE VIKING EDITION AS FOLLOWS:

Mansbach, Adam, date.
Rage is back / Adam Mansbach.
p. cm.
ISBN 978-0-670-02612-8 (hc.)
ISBN 978-0-14-218048-8 (pbk.)
1. Fathers and sons—Fiction.   2. Graffiti—Fiction.   3. New York (N.Y.)—Fiction.
I. Title.
PS3613.A57R34 2012
813'.6—dc23
2012019123

Printed in the United States of America
10 9 8 7 6 5 4 3 2 1

PUBLISHER'S NOTE
This is a work of fiction. Names, characters, places, and incidents either are the
product of the author's imagination or are used fictitiously, and any resemblance to
actual persons, living or dead, businesses, companies, events, or locales is entirely
coincidental.

RAGE IS BACK

1

hen Ambassador Dengue Fever told me that
Billy wasn't dead after all but half alive and
back in town, skulking through the Transit
System's blackened veins feral and broken and
scrawling weird mambo-jahambo on the walls
with chalk—chalk! as if spraypaint never
existed—I pretty much just shrugged a what-
ever shrug and kept on selling hydroponic sinsemilla to stainless
steel refrigerator owners living in neighborhoods that had just been
invented, and hoping Karen would let me back in the apartment
soon, me being her son and all, even if I had been expelled from
fucking Whoopty Whoo Ivy League We's A Comin' Academy on
account of some Upper Eastside whiteboys' inability to keep my
botanical enterprises, of which they were the major beneficiaries,
on the low.

Dengue was blind as Lady Justice, and so fat now that his eyes
wouldn't have done him much good anyway, obscured by slabs of
blubber when he laughed or even spoke. He dressed like an African
tribal chief in a Hollywood movie, or a hip-hop backup dancer circa
1989: voluminous kente-cloth, chestload of polished wooden beads,
an ankh-handled staff that had evolved from prop to crutch. The
nation-state for which he served was a graffiti crew called the Immortal Five, the name long smudged with irony: Amuse murdered, Sabor

dead by his own hand, Cloud 9 incarcerated, Dengue having fallen asleep one night with perfect vision and awakened from a nightmare permanently sightless, and my father, Billy—Rage—Billy Rage—a fugitive, missing in action, last seen sixteen years ago, last heard from almost twelve and incoherent even then.

"I don't want to hear another rumor," I told the Ambassador from my bed, his couch. "Matter of fact, I'm not sure I wanna hear shit about Billy even if it's true."

"Jus' cool, bredren. That yuh father yuh chat 'bout, yunno." Dengue's from the Patterson Projects in the Bronx, but for serious matters, he tends to favor the brimstone gravity of Rasta-speak.

"Tell *him* that," I said.

Dengue reached into a kitchen cabinet, wrapped his palm around a small bottle and twisted the cap between his thumb and finger. An orange spurt of hot sauce roped into the pan and sizzled. Only when the Ambassador cooked did a decade's worth of model-glue fumes dissipate, or seem to. I'd never been able to unravel whether his dependence on the braincell-popping odor was the by-product or the genesis of his obsession with constructing "Battle Alphabets," huge, three-dimensional versions of the spike-tailed guerrilla letterforms he'd once painted on subway trains. He built them from industrial plastics, scrap metal, wood. Whatever people brought him, for Dengue never ventured outside his apartment.

Tiny tubes lay everywhere, squeezed flat. I'd seen him rub the toxic adhesive into the arm of his chair before sitting, bend laboriously forward and apply it to the rug between his house shoes. The crib was only five hundred square feet, a rent-controlled fourth-floor walkup in the East Village that Dengue had occupied since New York was America's War Zone and real estate was priced accordingly. Four hundred and change, if you subtracted the space occupied by squadrons of armored letters, many mounted atop remote-control cars to form a mobile infantry.

I'd been crashing with the Ambassador for three days. I sat as close as possible to the window at all times, scattered *Village Voice* pages atop the carpet before going to sleep. My headache was constant. The fact that Dengue's mind still worked at all was staggering.

I hadn't knocked on his door until my second banished month, after two full four-day rotations through the homes of every other hospitable person I knew. I was being very careful to maintain most-favored-houseguest status with them all, because there was no telling how much longer I'd have to do this. With all the money I'd blown treating my hosts and hostesses to breakfasts and flowers and weed I could have rented my own place, but no landlord who hasn't been sniffing glue himself hands the keys over to an eighteen-year-old with no documented income, regardless of how much cake the kid flashes. Not even if he's Banana Republiced up, pants fitting right and everything.

Plus, I still expected Karen to stop tripping.

Dengue divided the skillet's browned contents between two plates, seventy-thirty. "Faith," he said. "Yuh mus' try an' feel it, Dondi. The universe vibratin' different, seen? Big tings ah gwan."

"Remember a few years back," I asked, "when that one kid was all over the graffiti chatrooms, swearing he saw a new Rage piece on the Staten Island Garbage Barge?"

Billy and Amuse had hit the boat, famously, in '85, during the day it was docked off Manhattan for maintenance—some freak once-a-year shit they'd researched and timed out. The pieces ran for months, and the *Post* even published a photo, making my old man and his partner the uppest dudes of the year. A fat new jewel in the crowns they already wore.

When the rumor surfaced, I hopped a ferry over to New York's forgotten borough and watched the barge slide by, stacked high with filth New York was running out of places to pile. The sides were blank. I hadn't believed the story to begin with. If Billy had bombed the vessel—if Billy were still Billy—he'd have put Amuse's name up too, honored his dead.

If Billy were still Billy. That was back when I still acted like I knew him. *Felt* like I knew him, I should say, the way little kids feel like they know the swashbuckling righteous-crusader assholes we cram down their throats the minute *Goodnight Moon* gets boring. Stand Billy between Sherwood Forest's Prince of Thieves and Gotham's Masked Avenger—neither one a family man, I might add—and the luster paints itself on with an elephant brush. Your boy here led grade-school Brooklyn in somber nods for six years running. *He had no choice,* I'd tell myself, pumping my chin at some irregularity in the pavement. *He had to leave.* Good old head-not-the-heart Dondi, thinking his way free of the pain. I kept that up until autumn 2000, when Karen started letting pigeons shit the monument, at which point the secret door to a whole new magical kingdom of fuckeduppedness swung open like, "bring your ass in here, young man, we've been expecting you." But later for that.

The Ambassador fell into his recliner, plate in hand. "Dis nah di same," he said, and shoveled a mound of plantain, potato, egg and pork into his mouth.

"I know this dude," he elaborated, un-Rastafarianed by the swine. "And he knows Rage."

"Let me guess. Some dirty white bum was spotted wandering around a train yard, mumbling to himself. Quick, call Fever, must be Billy Rage. Never mind the fact that painting subway cars in 2005 makes your source delusional to start with. Like the buff doesn't exist? Like anybody's gonna see his piece except a couple work bums and maybe a guard?"

"You too young to understand nostalgia, D."

"Yeah, right. I spent my childhood surrounded by grown-ass men who still call themselves Donk 202 and Blaze One and shit, trading train flicks in Karen's—oh, I'm sorry, Wren 209's—living room and arguing about who kinged the 2s in '76 and who rocked the Flying Eyeball character first, Kid Panama or Seen. I know more about nostalgia than anybody my age should, man." I took a final bite, and dropped my fork. "That was delicious, by the way."

"When you lose one sense—"

"The rest get sharper?"

"—you eat all the *bloodclaat* time. You want to hear what Sambo said, or not?"

"You know somebody called Sambo?"

"Sambo CFC. Crazy Fresh Crew. Old-school Queens cat."

"I don't even know what race to hope he is."

"It means 'curly-haired' in Spanish. Creo que homey es Peruano."

"That's fuckin' muy ignorante. Nobody beat him down for writing that?"

"It's just a name. You finished being indignant?"

I nodded. Like he could see me. Maybe he heard it, or felt the displaced air.

"Sambo was at the Coney Island Yard, our old homebase. He saw a dude in the tunnel wearing one of those Mexican blanket things. You know, Eastwood keeps the sawed-off tucked underneath in all those Sergio Leone joints?"

"A serape."

The Ambassador snapped his fingers. "Serape."

"They cost ten bucks at army surplus, Dengue. You don't have to go to Mexico to get one." He and Billy had said their goodbyes at the Southern border. All these years later, the slightest whiff of nacho cheese stoked Fever's optimism.

"Sambo said it took this guy an hour to walk the last fifty feet to the yard, because the whole time, he was writing on the walls. Nobody just walks the tunnels. You got the third rail, live trains, no light—you could get killed. Sambo called out to him, and dude turned and ran."

"Unless the walls said *Rage Rage Rage* or *Fuck You Bracken,* I'm emphatically unconvinced."

"There's a book in here called *Ritual and Religion of South America* or something like that. Big hardcover I boosted from The Strand. You see it?"

I found the tome steadying the base of a three-foot wildstyle Z, barbed arrows and chunky mechanical bits pinwheeling from it. Z is one of Dengue's favorites. He believes a letter's power is a function of its angles, the more and the sharper the better. Get him going on letter theory and you better clear your day. He'll take it back to Egyptian hieroglyphs, the ancient Hebrews' Unspeakable True Name of God with its mystery vowels, the science by which Franciscan monks illuminated the opening letters of each chapter in their hand-scribed Bibles. You thought Taki 183 and Julio 204 were old school, forget about it.

I freed the book. It was enormous. Graffiti writers can steal anything. Now the art supply and hardware stores lock all the paint inside glass cabinets and make you show ID, but racking was a way of life during the train era, the first thing you learned how to do. Some guys built reps just for "inventing" cans. It's ridiculous how much I know about this old man shit, I realize, believe me. Kid Panama painted the Flying Eyeball first, by the way, in case you were dying of curiosity.

Dengue finished eating and slid his utensils neatly to one side of the plate, as if a waiter were going to come and clear our dishes. "There's a flick in there of these juju priests down in the rainforests who cover everything in symbols to ward off evil. They use all kinds of shit. Blood, vegetable inks, chalk."

I flipped until I found it. Three wizened, bark-brown men, eyes clear and deep in their skulls, mouths slack where teeth had been, standing before a thatched hut in the jungle, staring at the camera, every inch of their bodies painted in arcane patterns, symbols, slash marks, the dyes dripping down their chests and thighs. The hut, the ground, even the trees were covered. It reminded me of that Keith Haring self-portrait, where he's standing naked on a bed screaming, his body and the room done up in black-and-white designs. Except that these men were not posing. They looked defiant and serene, like people waiting for a storm.

Don't ever mention Haring to a graffiti writer, by the way, or Basquiat either. Not unless you're ready for a tutorial about how those guys were chumps, never hit trains, didn't hang out at the Writers' Bench on 149th and Grand Concourse, only painted where it was safe, fronted like they were real heads and made millions while the real heads are real broke heads, some of them with real broke heads.

Dengue listened to me eye the picture. "The whole tunnel looked like that," he said. "All the way across the ceiling, in some places. Chalk and red latex house paint with mashed-up berries in it, those poisonous ones that grow in the park. Sambo walked through two stations, and it was still going when he turned around." Dengue's hand darted from his lap to the windowsill, and closed around the neck of a Wray & Nephew bottle he kept there.

"I sent some kids out last night for a look," he said, swigging the last of his overproof Jamaican rum. "This stuff is in tunnels all over the city. Somebody's putting in *work*."

"The letter Billy sent from the Amazon was years and years ago, Dengue. And it was gibberish. He said they were teaching him to talk to trees."

The Ambassador wedged the empty bottle between the over-stuffed pillows of his thighs and leaned forward.

"Kilroy Dondi Vance. Listen to your uncle for once in your life. Billy's here. Mi nah overstand wha' condition di bredda in, but I-an'-I cyan *feel* him."

I torqued myself off of the couch, started to duffel up my clothes. "Yeah, great. I'm leaving a sack of weed on the coffeetable. Catch you later."

"Yuh feel 'im too, K.D. Yuh jus' doan reca'nize it, cuz yuh nah remember wha' Billy's presence feel *like*, seen?"

"Whatever, Dengue. May the force be with you."

By the time the door shuddered into its locks I was down the first flight of stairs, phone drawn, scrolling through names for somebody to crash with next. Sometimes you feel like a nut and sometimes you don't, to quote a candy bar commercial I never saw but Karen grew up loving.

The Ambassador was spot-on correctamundo, of course, but you probably guessed that. Why else would I start the story here, right?

reeloading is exhausting. All conversation, no alone-time, and for the only child of a single mother like your boy here, solitude is the base of the mental health food pyramid, the grain-and-bread group of not losing my shit rather than the occasional, Chili Cheese Frito-esque indulgence some people seem to find it. When I do get some quiet, it's in the dead-sober middle of the day, when regular citizens are out getting paid or educated, and I fritter it away shaking my fool head at the parade of unsound ideas and irresponsible people I've spent my life in thrall to—a great word, thrall; sounds like a monster's gullet—while normal kids were busy soaking up all types of valuable knowledge from their square-ass parents.

I speak mainly of the Uptown Girl (Billy Joel, whaddup?), my girlfriend until some twelve hours after the expulsion. But also the general cast, or caste, of Whoopty Whoo Ivy League We's A Comin' Academy. I'm pretty sure none of my classmates' mothers would've considered a son who sells narcotics a dream come true, any more than they themselves would have concluded that bopping around town holding the ripcord to an incarceration parachute was a reasonable way to earn a little cash—since, unlike your boy here, none of them needed to turn his classmates into customers so he could call his jealousy disdain.

The last thing I want to sound like is one of those black conservative TV pundits they're always trotting out to declare that racism hasn't existed since 1965 and the black community's in tatters because of unwed mothers and rap music. Or a character from an early John Singleton flick, back when he gave an earnest fuck and wrote the same "it takes a man to raise a man" speech into every script. Or a whiny little punk. I haven't sidestepped all the other hood clichés just to blame my problems on skewed values in the home, or a dearth of positive male role models. But the fucking path to success can be a little hard to discern when you're walking around bent over double, dragging a cauldron bubbling with a four-part blend of molten anger—for those keeping score at home, that's anger at Billy, anger at Karen, anger at not knowing how angry I should be, and anger at my inability to claim my anger—plus a full fondue set to spoon it up with.

The assiduous consumption of *Cannabis sativa* has proved useful in reducing the flame. Where there's smoke, there's no fire: I figured that out a hell of a lot earlier than perhaps I should have. If stress had sent Karen foraging for Häagen-Dazs, I'd probably be wearing a fat-suit right now. Instead, I've got the lungs of a coal miner. Fuck it. Everybody self-medicates. Or maybe it's just me. How should I know? Who am I, Auguste Comte (1798–1857), the father of sociology?

It was Saturday afternoon, and I couldn't think of a single person I could bear to kick it with. Tomorrow I was scheduled to housesit for Nick Fizz, one of Karen's homeboys from the High School of Art and Design, a real graffiti hotbed back in the early eighties that had funneled a lot of kids right into the shortlived gallery scene. Karen had gotten a trip to London out of her fine arts career, and sold one canvas, for enough money to cover her inaugural semester at City College. It was a big aerosol portrait of this old-school rapper named Melle Mel, and she'd be the first to tell you that it was hideous and is almost certainly locked away in a storage unit now, regardless of the coked-up pricetag.

Fizz, meanwhile, was the exception to the rule, a graff success story. He'd been smart enough to sidestep the crack epidemic that turned forty percent of New York's writers into dealers and another forty into fiends in the mid-eighties, had sufficient foresight or small enough cojones to retire from trains before the buff started decimating the best lines in 1986, forcing everybody to crowd onto the Js, Ms, Bs and Ls like emergency rafts and then killing the scene entirely, eternally, by '89. Weird that all these so-called hip-hop heads consider '89 the heart of the "golden era," when it was also the year graffiti died.

Anyway, Fizz decided it was graphic design he loved, not vandalism, and started an ad agency. Now he's right back on the trains, all-city via the cheesy banners lining the insides of every car— saturation-bombing at its most annoying, except that instead of some teenager's messy mop-tag repeated and repeated and repeated, it's "Now You Can Have Beautiful Clear Skin! Visit Dr. Jonathan Zizmor M.D.! As Seen On TV!"

Fizz's crib was bright and spacious, decorated with the kind of pink-fur-Kangol flair only a gay Puerto Rican b-boy can pull off. Better yet, Fizz lived on 108th and Broadway, half a block from the best Dominican restaurant in the city, La Rosita, which I discovered through this older chick from Whoopty Whoo Ivy League We's A Comin' Academy who was my Peer Mentor when I started there in ninth grade and who actually took the concept seriously and schooled me on which teachers to avoid like the zombie death plague and which like the common cold, what culinary options the neighborhood afforded, how to restrain myself from smacking the tonsils out of some ignorant rich kid at least twice a day, that sort of thing.

She was the only black girl in her class, which is why the administration hooked us up, although in her case the struggle was not attending Manhattan's third-most prestigious prep school under the auspices of the coveted What the Hell, Let's Give a Clever Young Colored Boy a Chance to Transcend His Race Scholarship like me, but being the daughter of Tom Petty's attorney, caked up to her clavicles and yet still presumed a welfare case. She graduated and went on to major in art history at Columbia, and until I got a girlfriend the big-sister/little-brother thing endured and I'd cross town and eat lunch with her sometimes, always at La Rosita. I can't explain why a simple plate of yellow rice and red beans and a side of yucca con ajo should be so much better there than at the other three hundred spots just like it, but there you go. So I could hardly wait to get to Fizz's spot and breathe air and eat good and sleep in a bed and jerk off in peace.

Fuck it, I thought, why wait for tomorrow when you can have tomorrow today. I hopped the 2 Express to Dumbo, which is this stupid yuppie acronym meaning Down Under Manhattan Bridge Overpass, like hardy-har, we live in a flying elephant, and made my way to this one particular building I discovered a little more than a year ago.

I'm not going to say exactly where it's located, although I guess you could figure it out by process of elimination if you spent long enough in the neighborhood—which was not a neighborhood at all a few years back, just a wedged-in ghost town of moldering factories and deserted cobblestone alleys. I haven't bothered to find out what the building was before they gutted and condominiumized it. If I were a different type of kid I'd have visited some windowless city planning office, claimed I was doing a school project and gone down to the basement and unrolled a set of decomposing blueprints beneath a flickering yellow lamp and had some kind of revelation.

Your boy here, I figured out as much as I needed to know and then left it alone. I'm crap at science to begin with, so if there's some monumental discovery about wormholes and the rending of space-time to be made, I'm not gonna be the guy who makes it. Nor am I foolish enough to run my mouth and blow my own spot, end up getting my foot run over by Stephen Hawking's wheelchair or some shit.

Sorry, I don't mean to be mysterious. The deal is this: if you enter the stairwell of this building at lobby level and walk all fourteen flights of stairs—which nobody would, since there's a very nice elevator tricked out with mirrors and wood paneling and it always seems to be idling right there, doors open no less—you emerge on the top floor having traveled exactly twenty-four hours into the future.

And no, smart guy, you can't walk down and go back. That would be hot, obviously. You could make a fortune, like the dude in *Back to the Future Part II*. It was the first thing I tried.

I'm going to say this once and then I promise I won't come back to it, or even address the reader in the second person anymore, which I can see getting annoying very quickly, seeing as most people want to lose themselves in stories, not open a book and have a finger pointing at them all the time, unless it's a pop-up book. If you're already frowning and thinking I'm an unreliable narrator, or going "oh goody, I love magical realism," then you should cut your losses and go read *Tuesdays with Morrie*, before I get to the really wild shit later on. Skepticism is an admirable trait, but so is asking yourself if you're really such a fucking Master of the Universe that things might not be happening beneath the surface of your world right now without you knowing. Or even in midair when your back's turned. I mean, hell, they didn't discover the duckbilled platypus until 1896, and then everybody thought it was a hoax because mammals aren't supposed to lay eggs, you feel me?

I've thought about it a lot, and as far as I can tell, there's very little to be gained by jumping one day forward. It seems like there should be, but really you're behind. You missed work, school, you don't know if the Yankees won. Also, whenever I get my H. G. Wells on, I step into the future with a queasy stomach, spangly vision, a general desire to curl up and die that lasts an hour, maybe two. It didn't happen the first time, before I knew what I was doing, so possibly it's not travel sickness but some psychological aversion to flouting cosmic law, giving physics the finger.

The whole thing reminds me of this game I used to play with my boy Cedric in sixth grade, where we'd invent these doofus superheroes. Like, The Salamanderer, who has the regenerative powers of an amphibian: if you cut off his arm, it grows back, weaker and smaller, in about six weeks. Or Diner Man, who's totally invincible, but only in diners, and spends all his time trying to convince supervillains to grab some pie. Or this dude we never got around to naming, whose power was that he could fly six inches off the ground. We used to convulse on the floor of my bedroom, laughing at this stuff. It wasn't until recently that I realized it was a metaphor for something. And only as I write this does it occur to me that Graffito The Elusive should have been on the team: will go to any extreme to save the innocent, unless they're his relatives.

The reason I didn't take the elevator up to fifteen to begin with is that I figured the stairwell in this yupster breeding tube would be as good a place as any to pinch a bowl out of my customer's bag and get zooted. You can't risk smoking on the street these days, not if you're young and brown—Karen's genes are the dominant ones, at least in my complexion—and especially not with a messenger bag full of seventy-dollar eighth-ounces of bomb O.G. Kush in miniature mason jars slung across your chest. Plus, unlike most people my age, I only smoke from glass pipes. To me, blunts are disgusting. You can't even taste the weed. That might be the point if you're smoking bullshit from the local herbgate, but to roll Cannabis Cup–caliber marijuana in some filthy, stale Dutch Masters cigar and then seal it with your own rank slobber is an insult to everybody who took the time to plant, grow, dry, smuggle and distribute it.

I'm also unusual in that I like to exercise when I'm high. Pretty much only when I'm high, actually. It motivates me or something, I don't know. Fourteen flights sounded like fun. So I blazed, climbed, slammed open the stairwell door all out of breath, and gave a discreet little rappety-rap on the door of Penthouse A.

People think weedheads are spacey and laid-back, but not when they're waiting for their nuggets and worried that the delivery service isn't going to come through. Which they seem to be every time, even if I've been providing quality service for a year. So right away, it struck me as odd that this guy—his name was Patrick; he was a stockbroker or a financial analyst or a hedge fund manager or something, one of those money jobs where my eyes glaze over as soon as I hear the first syllable out of the person's mouth, and unlike most custies he'd never invited me to smoke with him, which was why I'd thought to take preemptive measures—would leave me standing in the hallway for so long.

I knocked harder. Maybe he was tore up already, and I was bringing by the reinforcements. Another few seconds ticked away, and then from deep inside the condo came the irritated bray of a man who's sitting around in his underwear, or worse, and has no designs on being disturbed.

"What? Who is it?"

"Hey," I called. "It's Mike, from Organic Produce Delivery?"

The door swung wide and Patrick faced me, hands pocketed in some raggedy and no doubt hastily donned sweatpants. I'd only seen him in his just-clocked-out gear before: necktie balled up in the pocket of his suit, bottled beer in hand, top two dress shirt buttons undone, white T underneath—*I Hate My Job*, by Calvin Klein. Seeing Patrick like this, I felt a little pang of sympathy. He looked like he'd worked out in college, and didn't have the time to anymore.

"You kidding me? You guys were supposed to be here yesterday."

Now, I'm high as shit here, keep in mind. As a matter of fact, from here on out, assume that unless otherwise specified, I'm probably high as shit. But in a charming, articulate way. Naturally, I assumed Patrick the square-ass stockbroker was trading in hyperbole, so I flipped open my cell phone and confirmed that yes, okay, I was running fifteen minutes behind, whatever, old Pat's more of a dick than I thought.

"Sorry, man," I said. "Train was running weird." Standard New Yorker excuse, totally unverifiable.

Patrick crossed his arms over his chest. "You fucking with me?"

That right there should have given me pause. The only time a stumpy white twenty-nine-year-old *Wall Street Journal*–reading spaz like Patrick will act even the slightest bit aggro toward a six-foot mocha teenager is when there's a formal hierarchy in place to back him. He'd have no problem loud-talking a waiter or cursing out the mailroom guy at work, but he won't say shit if he gets jostled on the subway, you know what I mean? The power structure that's had his back throughout his life isn't enough. He's gotta see it practically in writing.

I adjusted the strap of my bag, and spread my legs a little. "Why?" I said. "Do people fuck with you a lot, Patrick?"

He leaned forward without uncrossing his arms, and addressed me in the tone and speed of voice a junior high school teacher might use with her thickest student, about a week before giving up forever and applying to business school.

"Buddy. It's *Tuesday*. I called for a delivery on *Monday*."

"Well, then," I said, "one of us is crazy."

I looked at my phone again, and goddamn if it wasn't the next day, and I wasn't twenty-four hours and fifteen minutes late. I had eight missed calls, too. Three from my boss, five from Karen.

Whatever was happening, I wasn't going to recruit Patrick to help me figure it out. "Wow," I said, "I'm really sorry—I guess my phone is on the fritz. I just got the message an hour ago." I ran a hand over my dome. "You still need?"

Patrick stared a second, then nodded. "Yeah, sure. Come in."

I sold him his weed, and Patrick flipped the script and offered me a rip from the glass bong he kept on his coffeetable. Swear to God, if I ever get to be his age and pot paraphernalia is occupying a place of honor in my living room, punch me in the throat.

I had no desire to get further stoned, but there was the matter of precedent to consider, so I obliged. Ben Franklin or Hitler or somebody once said something to the effect of "if you want a man to like you, don't do him a favor, ask him to do you one." And by the same token, I guess being a deranged, incompetent asshole had endeared me to Patrick.

I thanked him, hustled down the stairs, and checked my phone in the lobby. Still Tuesday. I turned around and started trudging back up, holding the cell in front of me like a compass. I'll say it again: fourteen flights is a lot of stairs. The moment I stepped across the top floor's threshold, my digital display flipped from *Tuesday, 5:50 PM* to *Wednesday, 5:50 PM,* and I threw up on Patrick's doormat.

Karen was livid when I got home. She'd called the hospitals, the morgue, even the police—and in our family, you don't involve the cops in anything, for anything. Before I got to Whoopty Whoo Ivy League We's A Comin' Academy and started kicking it with rich kids, I never even realized you *could* call the police, unless you were calling them *on* somebody.

There weren't a lot of plausible places I could have disappeared to for forty-eight hours without answering my phone, and me and Karen were on decent terms then—as close to trusting one another as we'd been since the cataclysmic autumn of 2000, when we'd sort of crossed paths on the road to adulthood, traveling in opposite directions with knives to our backs. If we had put that year behind us, it was by centimeters. Karen still kept her hospital bracelet on her nightstand. I never unlocked the door of our apartment without steeling myself to find my mother gone, and a neighbor I barely knew waiting for me in the living room.

So I told her the truth, which she did not for one second believe. I asked her when I'd ever lied, and offered to take her to the building right then and prove it, and Karen sucked her teeth and said she couldn't force me to tell her where I'd been, but if I was going to start pulling vanishing acts and talking crazy like my father, then

I could go sleep on Dengue's floor like he had, or take my weak shit to 79th and Madison and see what kind of reception I got from the Uptown Girl's legendary parents, and was that clear?

It was. I went to my room, passed out, never brought it up again. That didn't stop Karen from treating me for the next month like the guy in the zombie movie who says he hasn't been infected, but he's lying. As if I might turn into Billy at any second, and she was going to pump me full of buckshot at the first clear sign.

That was a year ago. I hadn't come back to this building until Karen tossed me, but since then? Shit, I'd hoofed the stairs seven or eight times, skipped ten percent of my days. Gained nothing, and learned less. Wherever you go, there you are. It was an addiction without a high, just one more stupid thing I watched myself do again and again. You ever fast-forward through a movie, trying to skip past the boring parts or find some tits, and all of a sudden the credits are flying up the screen and you're like *damn, I played myself?*

I banked past the elevator, flung open the stairwell door and started climbing. Maybe Karen was right, and I was turning into Billy. I wondered how I'd know. My actual memories don't amount to much, and they've been beat-matched and blended with everybody else's so many times that I've lost track of what's lived and what's received.

I only knew the dude for two years and change, and even before he left, Billy was a man of absences, the type of guy whose attention was thrilling because you could never take it for granted. I remember the glee I felt when he came home and scooped me up and airplaned me around the room, and the tantrums I threw every time he bounced. Or maybe I don't remember those things at all. I was about to say something regarding a sense of grim determination about him, a kind of permanent, distant fury, a perpetual thousand-yard-stare, but those are all ridiculous things for a toddler to notice unless he was born on leap year day, and I was not.

July 1, 1987, baby. 8:09 P.M. Seven pounds and eight ounces of funkadelic soul. A Cancer, and don't think I don't know it. No fault of your boy's, but the night I was born was also the night everything started falling to shit. Karen's maternal fam is Trini, and apparently her grandma, rest in peace, had spent months cautioning the happy couple (not for long) against speaking the baby's name out loud when he was born, or remarking on his being cute or perfect or anything like that. Your first comments were supposed to be negative and misleading, *what an ugly girl,* because otherwise the various spirits would get jealous and have your 411 to boot and bam, start fucking with you. Maybe Rage and Wren should have taken that to heart. My mother's certainly mused on it a few times in the years since, joint in hand usually.

Three hours into my earthly existence, Billy went bombing, because that's what a fiend does. Triumph and tragedy are met identically. Boredom too. Something happens, or nothing happens, and you need a fix.

He kissed us both, left me snoozing the snooze of the innocent on my mother's chest, swung a backpack containing spraycans, a sketchbook, and some just-in-case bolt-cutters over his shoulder—yup, he brought it to the hospital; that was Billy's version of a maternity bag—and bullshitted his way past his parents and Karen's mom. He scooped Amuse, his ace, the Immortal Five's only other whiteboy, half-Jewish just like Billy, from the hospital lobby. The two of them rode the iron horse out to the Coney Island Yard, the city's biggest, and met up with Dengue, Cloud 9, and Sabor, the three of whom popped out from behind a work shed to surprise Billy with champagne, cigars, good wishes, and ten tabs of Donald Duck acid, two hits to a man. Billy took one. Faint stirrings of parental responsibility, perhaps. Amuse had three.

I was gonna do this as a footnote, but I think it's disrespectful to make a motherfucker rove his eyes all the way down to the bottom of the page and up again—plus, if the words matter, print them in a font I can read, you know? It occurs to me that a lot of people peeping this might already be like "Fuck that narcissistic, no-account asshole. Fuck him in his neck." I'm not disagreeing. But: I didn't say Billy had to bullshit his way past Karen, did I? Naw. The Train Queen of Fort Greene was like "Have fun, kill it, I love you so much, save some of the Baby Blue Krylon." Don't cry for Wren 209. At least, not yet. And also: the last twenty times somebody in your life gave birth, you found out about it by opening your inbox, right? *Mother and child are resting comfortably*, vital stats, kid's name (pretentious), one to three flicks?

Well, this was '87. What you call a mass email, my parents called hitting trains.

The Immortal Five unpacked their special-occasion stashes, out-of-production colors you had to trade for or hoard (or, if you were Cloud 9, spend a day boosting from dustcovered hardware stores in Virginia): Krylon Hot Raspberry and Aqua Turquoise and Icy Grape, Federal Safety Green and Sandalwood Tan Rustoleum, Bermuda Blue Red Devil. The lysergic diethylamide dissolved on tongues and swirled into bloodstreams, chased by the bubbly and then a couple six-packs of Bud tall-boys. Few sticks of weed to keep things copacetic. Toasts every few minutes, to me and Wren and fatherhood and family, as the squad lined up and commenced to bomb the living hell out of a lucky F train.

Billy rocked a wildstyle window-down whole car, KILROY DONDI VANCE, with the Cheech Wizard holding a bassinet next to the *K*, and then for dessert he caught a top-to-bottom: IT'S A BOY in silver blockbuster letters, with CAN'T BELIEVE IT—I'M A DAD! and 7 LBS 8 OZ and I LOVE YOU KAREN in True Blue script. Cloud and Dengue split the next car down and put up WREN 209 and HOT MAMA. Sabor, short on paint, helped with the fills, then bailed Amuse out on the IMMORTAL 5 ALIVE car he'd started before the tabs hit him full-on and he decided, googly-eyed, to sit down for a while and watch. On that much acid, the smallest sounds became a symphony; your senses were fizzing over, flowing into one another, and all you could do was breathe every-thing in. Especially since (who knew?) the rhythm of your own personal inhalation turned out to be the ordering principle of the entire universe.

Two tabs, though, was a time-tested burner-painting dosage, and for the next couple of hours the *pssht* and *clicka-clacka* of paint-cans sufficed for conversation as Billy, Sabor, Dengue and Cloud got down. Amuse had the crew camera, and the few flicks that aren't of his thumbs—not on some *oops* shit, but because homeboy developed a profound interest in the delicate ovaline swirls of his fingerprints that night, and spent most of the roll trying to do them justice—provide excellent evidence in support of the argument that the Immortal Five, whether at the top of their collective game or fried out of their collective brain, were some of the illest mother-fuckers in the history of the movement.

Naturally, there are any number of qualitative criteria by which to evaluate graff—how crisp are the cuts? how architecturally sound and imaginative the letterforms? how hot the color combos? does the shit flow?—but I don't give a fuck about all that. You either connect with art or you don't, right? Who cares why Nas is nicer than Jay-Z, or even why he's nice at all? He just is, so fucking enjoy it.

I once said as much to this woman who taught tenth grade art history at Whoopty Whoo Ivy League We's A Comin' Academy, accused her mid-slideshow of robbing me of my ability to dig art. She told me I'd dig it more if I knew why I was digging it, and I said that implied there was one proper way to dig something, or that hers was better than mine. I brought up this interview with Bran-ford Marsalis I'd just seen on PBS, where the host says all this smart-sounding crap about why Branford's last album was a trio recording instead of the usual quartet, and Branford nods and nods, smirk plastered across his mug, then says "actually, what hap-pened is that Kenny missed his plane," and next thing I knew me and Ms. Art Appreciation were discussing the metaphor of the cave in Plato's *Republic*, me claiming I'd read it even though I hadn't rather than letting her slay me with the bullshit trick of citing something the other person doesn't know to win the argument. We went back and forth until the bell rang, and the upshot of it all was that I got an A for the course without doing diddly-squat to earn one, so in the end she recognized game and is okay in my book.

Four, five in the morning is every writer's favorite time. The city's as quiet as your apartment right after the refrigerator cycles down. Nobody's alive except you and your boys and your recently completed joints, voluptuous and razor-sharp, vibrating and bulging with the struggle of containing their own energy. You're backstage grinning at the newest-freshest, knowing that soon you'll be home asleep and the burners will roll out on their maiden voyage. Civilians will try to read the words and get lost in the style, while your name pops off the lips of those who know. The heightened alertness of the mission has smoothed itself down to a glossy pride, and you're enjoying your last few minutes with an oblivion-bound creation you're never gonna see up-close again. Maybe you're doing some touch-ups or taking a few tags on the insides, or passing a final roach. For sure, you're talking late night trash, trading lies and war stories, or else an early morning spasm of sincerity has gripped the crew, and love and loss and life and death are on the table.

I don't know which it was. Dengue retains only flashes of that night. What Billy told Karen doesn't help—it's mystical, confused, impressionistic. There's nothing in his letters. And Cloud got an extra year tacked onto his grand larceny bid for the beating he threw a fellow inmate who asked him what really went down, legends aside.

This much is indisputable: if anybody had a bigger hard-on for graffiti than the writers, it was the NYPD's Vandal Squad. They were almost like writers themselves. They stayed up on who was hot, read wildstyles the average person could never decipher. They took train flicks, even brought cans to the yards and crossed out people they particularly hated. They wanted fame as bad as any new-jack thirteen-year-old, and they got it. Everybody knew Curly and Ferrari from Queens, Ski and Hickey from the Bronx, Tom and

Jerry from Manhattan. Writers made reps by putting in work, inventing style, hitting five hundred cars in six months, splashing color through the city's hardened arteries. For cops, it was busting heads and taking down prize bucks.

Most times you got popped, it happened after the fact. The police sat in their car, watched you sneak in and out of the yard. They caught up with you later, at a bar or in front of your building, tapped you on the shoulder just when you thought you'd gotten away with it but before you'd scrubbed the paint off your hands. They knew better than to match speed and wits with kids who, if they didn't outrun you and vanish through some escape-hatch you and your partner never even knew about, might very well turn around and knock your fat twelve-sandwich-eating ass the fuck out. A lot of distinctions blurred in the yards; a badge didn't shine as bright there. The boys in blue only invaded in pursuit of big game, and always in big numbers.

And so it is written that on July 2, 1987, at approximately the asscrack of dawn, fifteen po-pos rode down on the Immortal Five, with Officer Anastacio Bracken, the biggest asshole in the history of cops and robbers, leading the charge.

Surprise, niggers.

Due diligence is never getting so fucked up that you can't run. It's never entering a yard without having an emergency route mapped, plus a backup and a place to hide. Coney Isle was the I5's living room; all that was second nature, even on a double-dose of Donald Duck, and they played it by the books.

Billy heard the footfalls first, lots of them, pigs on the creep but coming fast. He shouted a warning, grabbed Amuse by the armpits, hoisted him onto his Pumas. A heartbeat later, the Immortal Five was in the wind. Billy and Amuse sprinted north, toward a ladder leading to a street grate a hundred yards inside a tunnel. Sabor and Dengue ran south, weaving between rows of trains, doubling back toward the entrance the cops had used and knowing that if it was blocked they could hide behind the work shed, or lay low underneath a car. Cloud 9, who loved paint as much as any writer dead or alive, wasted thirty seconds dumping cans into a pair of paper shopping bags, then shimmied up the side of a car and hauled ass eastward, leaping from the roof of one train to the next.

All good ideas, but not tonight. When Billy reached the ladder, he looked up and saw two cops smiling down at him, hands hipped, *hello sweetheart*. Sabor and Dengue couldn't get clear either; the Vandal Squad was everywhere. They had to reverse course, head for the street grate themselves. Bracken went after Cloud, the two of them racing across the cars—Bracken knowing exactly who was in front of him and chugging along with a stiffy, no doubt, at the sight of Cloud's skinny black ass.

A gunshot pinged against metal, and everybody froze—even the cops, according to Fever. Bracken had actually squeezed off at Cloud, tried to pop him in the back. No fair, no fair, no fair. Rules of the game were they could beat you silly when they caught you, but to draw a gun was crazy. Everybody kinda-sorta knew Bracken was a little nuts, but no one appreciated the extent until that night.

The Immortal Five were among those with a claim to stake about making him that way. Bracken had arrested Amuse back in '79—no big deal from a legal standpoint, since Amuse was a minor, plus lucky enough to get bagged taking street tags. Tons of guys were active then, so a dorky fourteen-year-old Heeb with one spray-can in his possession meant nothing to Bracken. He never suspected Amuse had been ripping up the 2s and 5s for eighteen months—didn't even ask what he wrote, just smacked him around and brought him in. Pop goes the cherry.

Amuse never forgot his first time. He was a real late-breaker on the puberty tip, thickly bespectacled and kind of soft, having been under Cloud 9's considerable protection from jump. Amuse and Billy were junior crew members back then, high school classmates of Cloud's little brother Finster. Too talented to leave off the team, but not yet ready for Cloud, Dengue and Sabor to party with after an evening's bombing was complete.

Nobody had ever laid hands on Amuse before, probably, but more to the point was that Bracken had disrespected him by not knowing who he was. I also suspect that getting arrested was a badge of honor—some quintessential whiteboy shit, right there—and Amuse didn't want to let it go when the city cut him loose eight hours later, so he declared jihad on his arresting officer.

Going after the cops who were coming after you was a graff hobby, pen versus the sword and whatnot. You dedicated pieces to them on the catch-me-if-you-can tip, dissed them on the insides—OFFICER BRACKEN AMUSE FUCKED YOUR WIFE. EAT A DICK UP AND HICCUP ANASTACIO—brilliant, witty commentary like that. Amuse took it a giant step further, off the trains and into Bracken's neighborhood: covered Bay Ridge with BRACKEN RAPES BABIES and the like. A year later, crazy angel-dusted Drum One caught Bracken asleep in his patrol car outside the Ghost Yard with the window down, woke him up and knocked him out. Robbed him for good measure, in one of the most celebrated incidents in aerosol history. The taunts became BRACKEN GOT HIS ASS KICKED and DEAR BRACKEN, WHERE'S YOUR BADGE? LOVE, AMUSE, and dude got upgraded from just another dickhead member of the Pork Patrol to a certified psychopath, tireless and hate-driven, a cop even other cops despised. A guy unhinged enough to shoot a kid in the back for vandalism.

He fired and missed and Cloud dropped flat, rolled off the car, hit the ground running. Bracken pulled up into a marksman's stance, feet planted, both hands wrapped around his revolver, and tracked Cloud through the narrow corridor between the trains.

More shots. Cloud sprinted for the mouth of the tunnel, shopping bags swinging from his fists and banging against his knees, and then blammo, Bracken put a hole through a can of Krylon Pastel Aqua and a geyser of depressurized paint exploded against Cloud's gut and he thought he'd been hit, started hyperventilating, couldn't understand how his legs still worked. By the time he figured out that human blood is not the color of swimming pool water, an adrenaline-fueled burst of speed had carried him out of Bracken's range, and all five Immortals were in the tunnel.

The only thing to do was keep going. See who gave up first, hope not to get hit by a train in the meantime, pray there wasn't a second unit waiting at the next station. They could hear Bracken charging after, calling out their names so that they'd know he knew. Up ahead was blackness, utter and engulfing, the kind in which you can't tell if your eyes are closed or open. Far scarier than actual blindness, according to Dengue, who would know.

If you've ever been on acid, you know that the last place you want to be on three fat tabs is trapped inside a sensory-deprivation chamber with your heavily armed worst enemy afoot and an indiscernible number of rough hands yanking at you while strange, breathless voices demand you run for your life.

Amuse lost his shit. He wrenched away, screaming, throwing wild punches through the air, catching Cloud in the stomach and freaking when he felt the sticky wetness. They tried to orient him, *Amuse, it's us, we're your friends, come on, we gotta go.* More flailing and incomprehension and the crunch-and-slap of cop boots coming closer, the crazed black tragicomedy of four sightless men trying to corral a fifth. Amuse had assigned his boys new paranoid-delusional identities by now; they were demons or goblins or who-knows-what. He started trying to bite them.

"You cocksuckers got five seconds to stop running, then I swear to Christ I'm emptying my clip."

That's an actual quote, according to Dengue, and this is where the frame would freeze and the voiceover would begin if The Death of Amuse were a Hollywood movie: Bracken with his gun cocked, snarling; Sabor, Billy, Cloud and Dengue pushing Amuse forward like he was the flagpole and they were those Iwo Jima motherfuckers. And . . . fade to white. I would say something like *This is where the story starts to come apart.*

Dengue might or might not have banged his toes against a hard flat metal edge, reached down and felt around and pulled a manhole from its mooring and felt a gust of hot rank air. Maybe the I5 dropped into an unmapped chamber, twisting their ankles when they came down on the decayed pilings of a long-abandoned train line. Maybe Amuse landed on his feet, or maybe he landed wrong and cracked open his skull.

Maybe none of that happened and they kept running and Amuse broke free and scrambled the other way, straight into Bracken, and got shot in the chest. Or maybe the cop fired blind, and some grudge-bearing god grabbed his bullet like Aphrodite in the Trojan War and pulled it through Amuse's dome. Maybe Sabor found a door, and they hustled down a staircase to a lower tunnel and Bracken followed—with five other officers behind him, their names lost to history. Maybe the I5 decided to turn and rush the Vandal Squad, on some last-stand shit, and in the blind insanity Amuse drowned facedown in a puddle, or the stress and the hallucinations were too much and he busted a ventricle all on his own. Maybe the crew inhaled noxious trapped gasses in that lower chamber, passed out, and woke up four instead of five.

I'd heard all those versions, plus versions of those versions. Every graff vet had a different story, and Dengue's memories kept changing, or he forgot what lies he'd told me last and made up new ones. The notion of stumbling upon a lower tunnel came up enough that I figured there was truth to it, the way anthropologists know there really was some kind of catastrophic, ancient flood because every society's got one folded into its mythology.

Somehow, the Immortal Five-minus-One got clear and surfaced above ground. No record of how or when or where, not even a snarl of competing stories, just an infuriating and impenetrable *somehow*. Maybe they regrouped outside the yard, rancid with panic but still hoping Amuse would pop up magically unscathed, *hey guys, looking for me?*, and they'd all have a laugh, gloom and horror flash-melted, disbelief turned inside out. Maybe they propped each other up, each man refusing to let the next think the worst, and fanned out to their parents' apartments to wait in vain for his call, straining to imagine the jubilant escape story Amuse would whisper from inside his bedroom closet, or the jailhouse check-in he'd mumble through aching, swollen jaws.

I think they knew, though. Whatever happened and however they got free, I've always had the sense they saw and heard and felt him die. I see them sprawled across a curb, keening hysterically at the dawn sky, sucking down long shuddery drafts of air as if oxygen were comprehension. Staggering home numb and weak, vomiting on their own stoops, waking up in bed unable to remember how they got there.

The remains were "found" in the tunnel the next day, by Bracken. Amuse had been run over by a train—got high and passed out on the tracks, that was the story. *A tragic accident,* Bracken called it in the NYPD's press statement, *and a lesson to those who persist in glorifying a criminal activity and downplaying its risks.* Amuse was described as *a career vandal, wanted by police for inflicting hundreds of thousands of dollars' worth of damage to MTA property.*

It's practically a cliché now, cops killing writers. Happens in every graffiti movie, even that German one. The police are always evil incarnate, menacing the ragtag underdog crew from the margins and then showing up when the dramatic arc starts sagging and taking somebody out, accidentally-on-purpose. All the adolescent shenanigans screech to a halt and the remaining characters reevaluate their lives and either pay tribute to their fallen comrade with a major artistic accomplishment or decide to get out of the game and go legit.

In real life, motherfuckers just lose their minds and destroy everything around them.

When I was younger I used to fantasize about killing Bracken for what he did to Amuse—and by extension to Billy, to Dengue, to Karen, to me. I'd imagine everything from elaborate kidnap-and-torture scenarios to simple ruses where I'd pretend to be hurt or demented and get his guard down, then cast off my infirmity and pull a weapon. The last thing I always did before slitting his throat or click-clacking the rifle or pressing the trapdoor button was reveal my identity and watch his eyes register the knowledge that yes, this kid had every right to end his life.

I gave it up when I started high school, on a hunch that the guidance counselors at Whoopty Whoo Ivy League We's A Comin' Academy would consider Obsessively Plotting Filial Revenge a poor extracurricular activity. And also after staring myself down and admitting that I wasn't really that guy.

Instead, I started casting around for a way to grant Bracken and his porcine brethren some humanity, out of a desire to preserve my own. I mean, look: exterminators kill roaches. That's their job. To them, roaches are vermin. They need to get got. When the exterminators go home at night they aren't fretting about all the bugs they've gassed. They've got kids and wives—the exterminators, that is, although I guess the roaches too—and they drive them to swim meets and oboe lessons and tuck them into bed at night and all that.

You see what I'm getting at. Vandal Squad cops don't view writers as anything more than a problem to be solved, and if you can accept that they see it that way, and that they lack the imagination to see it any other, you can let them off the hook. Except, that argument would exonerate Nazi death camp guards, and also exterminators don't lie awake visualizing what they're gonna do to the roaches when they catch them, or circulating lists of the Top Five Most Wanted Insects among themselves so everybody can be on the same page, poised for the stomp-out.

I was better at letting Billy off the hook—when it wasn't his eyes widening in moments-to-live recognition instead of Bracken's, anyway. A one-man judicial system, your boy here. Judge, jury and executioner. Prosecution and defense. All varieties of witness: star, character, hostile, expert, discredited.

When grandiosity seemed like it would play, I told the court my father had faced the same choice as every hero for millennia, and made the same decision: to lay aside all he held dear and go to war. That it was some epic, Odysseus-type shit to backburner his new-born son and loving common-law wife and take up arms. Except that the wily King of Ithaca, on whom we spent the better part of a semester my sophomore year, pretended to be batshit insane so they'd leave him and Telemachus and Penelope the fuck alone, hitched his plow up to a mule and an ox and sowed his fields with pebbles. And when Agamemnon called his bluff, O got on a ship and waved farewell and sailed off to chuck spears and reap glory. Whereas my father ran his war, if you could call it that, out of our apartment.

Billy went bombing. That's what a fiend does, all he knows how to do. The objective was simple: broadcast the truth, bring Bracken down. It's not as naive as it might sound. When you're an outlaw to begin with, and your outlaw best friend's been killed by a cop, all you've got is your word. Justice doesn't come and ring your doorbell. The DA's not trying to build a case. The police, forget about it. You'd be a fool to even show your face.

All you've got is your word. The word. And paint.

No more trains for Billy Rage. No more wildstyles, no more festivals of color, no more leaning over a blackbook, souping up his name until it flew, chased its tail, spat flame. No more art, or sleep, or lust for fame. Now it was about size and visibility, placement and relentlessness. Results.

On July 3, 1987, Billy embarked on what is widely considered the sickest run in planetary history. It would take me pages to catalog the spots he hit, some so implausible that dudes are still trying to divine his modus operandi. The medium wasn't the message anymore, the message was the message, so sometimes spray-paint was the delivery system and other times he used regular latex house paint and a roller, wore an orange jumpsuit and hid in plain sight, just another schmuck humping it out. Except an hour later he'd be gone and the brick wall or the billboard would be covered in ugly squared-off letters twelve feet tall and visible from a half-mile away:

7/2/87
NYPD'S ANASTACIO BRACKEN
MURDERED ANDREW 'AMUSE' STEIN
IN COLD BLOOD

Some nights he dressed in rags and sloshed himself with gin, staggered around Soho with a bum-sack full of cans and marked each square of sidewalk with a homemade stencil:

OFFICER BRACKEN KILLED AMUSE
DEMAND JUSTICE!

He rocked every concrete overpass—what writers call heaven spots or hangovers—above the FDR freeway on Manhattan's east side. He tagged a goddamn polar bear with the BRACKEN KILLED AMUSE stencil, red paint on white fur. I shit you not, a Central Park Zoo polar bear that not only could kill you with one paw-swipe but spends its whole life fantasizing about doing just that.

Billy got half the other animals up in the piece, too: all the goats and sheep from the petting farm, two monkeys, a penguin. Went up to the Bronx Zoo a month later and wrote an essay in Flat Black Krylon on the see-through wall that separates the guests from the gorillas:

ANDREW 'AMUSE' STEIN'S DEATH ON 7/2/87
WAS NOT AN ACCIDENT! AMUSE HAD
TAUNTED OFFICER ANASTACIO BRACKEN
FOR YEARS WITH GRAFFITI MESSAGES AND
BRACKEN SHOT HIM OUT OF HATE!! I KNOW
BECAUSE I WAS THERE. END THE COVER-UP—
DEMAND AN AUTOPSY!!
TRY BRACKEN FOR MURDER!!!!

He hit the wild boars, too: scrawled PIGS AGAINST BRACKEN across their coarse-haired flanks. So there is some evidence that he allowed himself a little fun.

A little rest? A smidgeon of fatherhood? Doubtful. Billy worked a typical graffiti day-job as a bike messenger, earned just enough to cover bills on the rent-stabilized Fort Greene apartment Karen had grown up in, hers since her mom left the city for New Rochelle. In theory, my mother was watching me during the day, with Billy taking over at night so she could finish her degree at City College and become a literary agent or an editor. Suffice it to say that Karen got incompletes for her whole fall semester.

You can imagine the fights. Or, rather, *I* can imagine the fights. Hell, I might even remember them. According to most childhood development experts—Whoopty Whoo's tenth grade Health and Human Development class is no jizoke—parents shouldn't argue in front of their kids, because trauma stays in the body, like THC. It's a good thing they don't screen for it; can you imagine what a vial of trauma-free piss would cost?

My mother claims she never threw Billy out—that on the contrary, she looked up one day and realized *I guess he doesn't live here anymore.* I tend not to believe it. Karen's the throw-a-motherfucker-out type.

What I do believe, though—what she's always said, both during the era of tightlipped equanimity and the post–autumn 2000 era of talking shit—is that if Billy had demonstrated anything less than total obsession, Karen would have had his back. She loved Amuse like family, and she was a trouper—not a graffiti-groupie or a girl whose boyfriend put her name on trains, but a hardrock, down by law. She'd rolled with grimy crews, counted Drum One as a homeboy, once kicked a toy in the nuts for disrespecting her at the Writers' Bench. Sure, she'd outgrown graff by then and gotten on with her life, but when she fell for Billy it was because of his passion, not despite it. Half their courtship took place underground; I may or may not have been conceived atop an army blanket on the floor of an out-of-service R Train. She got him cans and fatcaps for his birthdays—*got*, not *bought*—and until she was six months pregnant, Billy and the crew were still cajoling Karen into the occasional night of mayhem. One of her alternate names, which writers take the way a dude in Africa takes a second wife, to show he's wealthy enough to support one, was Immortalette 1. Forget halfway; Karen would have met my father on her own ten-yard line.

The way she tells it, all she really asked was that he stop and grieve. He said he couldn't stop, and that he *was* grieving—this was how he grieved. She called bullshit, told him he was afraid of what stillness would bring and that the longer he put off facing it, the harder it would hit him when he did. But by then he was too far out of earshot to respond.

What, one might wonder, were Dengue, Cloud and Sabor doing while Billy was razing the city in Amuse's name? Were they, too, devoting every minute and muscular decussation to bringing the hand of justice down?

They were not. Sabor crumbled into a depression so severe he didn't leave his house for weeks. By the time Cloud and Dengue made it up to Washington Heights to see him he was barely speaking, and his mother Esperanza was making plans to take him back to Santo Domingo, where his grandparents lived, for recuperation. I say depression, but she thought Sabor had been cursed. The only thing to do was put it in the elders' hands. His grandpops knew a brujo.

Maybe Sabor was too American for the healing rituals of his homeland to take hold, or maybe Esperanza misdiagnosed her son. Sabor left in October, and in January word came back that he had killed himself. Hired a cab to drive him to the seashore, brought his cousin's pistol, didn't leave a note.

Billy blamed Bracken. *Now he's killed two of us,* was the way my father saw it. Dengue accepts that logic, even now. I suppose it's easier than reconciling yourself to suicide, to the notion that tall, wavy-haired, Valentino-handsome Sabor, who'd bring huge

Tupperware containers of his mother's arroz con pollo to the yards and tell everyone *you gotta try this, bro*, Sabor who juggled three women at a bare minimum at all times, as a philosophy, one always scandalously older and one dangerously young and one who lived within walking distance of his crib, Sabor who rapped Spanish lyrics over salsa records and swore it would be the next big thing, Sabor who called himself Sabor the Saber and Sabor the Savior, who once painted a whole car reading WHITE GIRLS CALL ME FLAVOR, had decided that taking his chances with oblivion beat spending another day alive. It didn't seem to fit. Maybe it never does.

Billy was living with Cloud by then, in a loft on 139th and Lenox. It was near Karen's campus, and she'd drop me there before class, making Billy and whoever else was hanging out—a couple of writers if she was lucky, a six-pack of Cloud's criminal running buddies if she wasn't—swear to keep the baby away from all species of secondhand smoke. She'd spend the next four hours spaced out, imagining the unsavory activities being planned or executed in the loft and worrying that Billy would sling me across his back and go out bombing. Again.

What if you'd been caught, she'd demanded, when she found out. *They'd have taken our son to Child Protective Services. You ever think of that, you asshole?* He'd protested that it hadn't been risky, just some roller-work from the window of an abandoned building, but Karen didn't let him see me alone for a month, and if you're waiting to hear from the defense, you can keep waiting. Ain't shit to say on this one that can't be articulated by a middle finger swaying in the air.

From what Dengue's said, the reason he and Cloud didn't participate in Billy's campaign was simple: it seemed like a waste of time. It was some whiteboy shit, to think anybody else would care about your dead. As if New Yorkers were going to rise up at the bidding of some anonymous vandal who used too many exclamation points? The same people who'd authorized a parade of douchebag mayors to blow three hundred mil in taxpayer revenue fighting not homelessness nor crime but the graffiti plague?

The quest betrayed a lack of understanding about the means through which power operated and survived, how and who the police were, what they existed to protect and serve. When one of your homeboys got killed you rocked a memorial mural on the wall of the bodega nearest to his crib, got drunk, and tried to move on, regardless of the circumstances and how bizarre or infuriating they might be. For all Billy's hard-thumping heart, all the creativity and technical proficiency he'd demonstrated and the all-city mega-upness he'd achieved, Cloud and Dengue found the shit depressing. Seeing Amuse's name everywhere, with Bracken's never more than a few words away, made them sick. And even though it came as no surprise, so did New Yorkers' capacity not to care.

Three or four things happened in quick succession around that time, in the spring and summer of '88, all of them presumably set to a soundtrack of Big Daddy Kane (with whom Cloud had played a year of varsity basketball at Sarah J. Hale High School in Brooklyn), Boogie Down Productions (Dengue used to swap KRS-One graffiti outlines for nickel bags on the Patterson Projects' playground) and Rakim (who was from boondocksical Wyandanch, Long Island, and thus the rare rapper nobody could claim to have known back when he wasn't shit).

Some of the chronology is fuzzy, but the first thing to go down was that Cloud got serious about armed robbery. He had a four-man crew, him and two of his uncles and some cat named Sour Patch, and they were into everything, from hijacking cigarette trucks en route from Maryland to smash-and-grab jobs at jewelry stores down in the Diamond District to petty bodega holdups. One time Cloud donned a ski mask and robbed the pizza parlor on the first floor of his building, where he ate probably five nights a week. Went back an hour later, knocked off a meatball sub.

Cloud robbed like he wrote: not for the crown but for the fuck of it—to show the world he was a fly dude who could do anything and do it with style. Maybe losing Amuse and Sabor made him reckless, or maybe it turned him grim and grown. Either way, graffiti got deaded except for the part he loved best: stealing absurd quantities of paint. So Billy never hurt for supplies.

My father put his head down and kept bombing. Walled off a bedroom of sorts by stacking boxes of soon-to-be-fenced stereo components around his mattress, the better to sleep off the all-night missions. The messenger gig slipped away after one blown shift too many: goodbye income, farewell civilian world. Cloud stepped in and gave Billy work as a stock boy, inventorying merchandise and working out percentages and wholesale-resale differentials—pure charity, since Cloud could do it better in his head than my father could manage with a calculator.

With his days free, Billy branched out into fake-permission walls, the new game in town as the train scene came sputtering to a halt. You chose a spot you wanted to piece and did it in plain view, with a crowd watching, made a big all-day production of it. In your back pocket was fake paperwork signed by the building's fake owner, stipulating that he was paying you such-and-such amount to beautify his property. At the bottom of the contract was a fake name and a buddy's phone number that a nosy beat cop could call for fake verification: "Yes indeed, Officer, I appreciate your concern, but this young fellow is most certainly in my employ. And a jolly fine artist he is, too."

I don't even have words to express the sheer perversity of painting an unreadable fifty-can wildstyle BRACKEN KILLED AMUSE mural on a downtown corner. Billy did dozens. Maybe he missed making art.

Or maybe he was going nuts. Swinging-dick spots came next: the Brooklyn Bridge, the Statue of Liberty, Gracie Mansion. Maybe he thought landmarks would generate publicity, or maybe he'd gotten so used to being ignored that he felt like he could get away with anything.

What boggles the mind is that my father never once thought to pick up the phone and tell the press what he was doing. Nowadays that would be thing-the-first, but '80s motherfuckers had the media savvy of sea snails. Granted, there are libel-related reasons a newspaper isn't going to suggest a cop's a killer just because somebody writes it on a polar bear, but there were angles Billy could have played. Whatever, not like it matters now. And soon enough, he had more attention than he could've imagined, all of it the wrong kind.

November 1988. The Jungle Brothers dropped *Straight Out the Jungle*, everybody bought African medallions, and Transit Authority spokesman Charles Robicheaux announced that after an exhaustive search it had hired a new Chief of Security, selecting Detective Anastacio Bracken from the ranks of the NYPD's Vandal Squad. Bracken's long record of distinguished service and his administrative experience in coordinating a highly successful task force made him ideal for the position.

The Immortal 3 caught the press conference on TV, melting into Cloud's leather sectional as Bracken bellied up to the podium in a dark suit and a paisley tie, his thinning squid-ink hair combed back from his forehead and a modest civil-servant smile curling up around his bulbous drunkard's nose.

No wonder the fucker hadn't been heard from in so long: busy improving his prospects. But it didn't add up. Bracken was a low-level sadist with a high school education. Who the hell would make him chief of anything?

He adjusted his tie, looked straight through the screen at Billy, and announced that his first act as chief would be the introduction of a new tactic in the war against the vandals. Although the ongoing campaign to eradicate graffiti from the subways was experiencing success, an undesired side effect was that the criminals were coming above ground. *Like rats fleeing a ship.* Chuckle-chuckle-chuckle. To better combat the graffiti scourge, the city was going to begin prosecuting vandals in civil court, to the fullest extent of the law.

For example, he harumphed, pretending to consult his notes, *there is the case of a vandal who has recently done grave damage to historic sites including the Statue of Liberty and the Brooklyn Bridge. I'm not going to give him the satisfaction of mentioning his name, but this sociopath has cost the taxpayers of New York considerable money, to say nothing of the psychological effect his crimes have had on residents, tourists, and international visitors to our great city. This will not stand. That is why the City of New York, in addition to pursuing criminal charges, is also suing this individual for damages in the amount of two million dollars. We have built our cases carefully for months, and we intend to win.*

Why don't you tell them what he wrote? Cloud screamed at the television. *Why don't you tell them what it said on the goddamn motherfucking bridge?*

Billy didn't speak. For all I know, relief was blooming in his belly like some nasty flower. Here was a giftwrapped excuse to abandon everything he couldn't handle, and maybe he'd been waiting for one all along.

My father slipped away that afternoon, eased into exile. For what it's worth, he tried to stay close, ghostwalking the five boroughs and checking in by telephone, blending fact with fiction to keep eavesdroppers guessing. Every week, Cloud left him an envelope full of money at a Harlem jazz bar. Billy picked it up more often than he didn't. He forwarded most of the cash to Karen, folded inside long, apologetic letters that he asked be read to me when I was old enough to understand. I found them in Karen's dresser a couple of years ago, when I was looking for Zig-Zags. They were infuriating from the grammar on up: you could almost hear the bugle fanfare playing behind his words, see Billy striking a chest-puffed pose before vanishing into the night to continue the crusade for truth, justice, and the American way. The next day, I asked Karen why she'd never showed me, and she rolled her eyes up from her book in super-slow-mo and said *I was waiting until you were old enough to understand. Did you understand?*

Not like he probably hoped.

She turned back to her book. *Mmm-hmm.*

The money and the letters stopped when Cloud got knocked. Seems the boy Sour Patch felt the rest of the crew had violated kindergarten principle #1, share and share alike, cut him out of an afternoon's action and a corresponding chunk of cash. Cloud, being Cloud, told Sour Patch to suck his motherfucking dick. Next day, the local precinct got an anonymous tip about some stick-up kids hunkered down with guns and stolen merch, and an hour later Cloud was being stuffed into a squad car. Guess who was waiting for him downtown, ready to cut a quick deal if the vandal-cum-larcenist provided information about the whereabouts of a certain old friend?

Cloud, being Cloud, told Bracken to suck his motherfucking dick, and got a vicious closed-door pistol-whipping just in case fifteen years of felony charges hadn't packed sufficient sting. I always imagine Bracken crouching over Cloud's bloodcaked body and growling *I shoulda did you when I did your boy Amuse*, but that's just too many cornball movies tentacled around my brain.

It was the summer of '89 when my father left—late August, Dengue thinks, because the new BDP album had just dropped. In Billy's absence, the civil judgment had gone against him full force, two million smackaroonies—probably would have come down by a decimal point if he'd stood trial, since two mil is absurdly inflated for the removal of a few thousand hits unless you're painting over everything with liquid gold and using stegosaurus-tusk-handled brushes, but what did it matter? It was money Billy didn't have and the city would never see cent-the-first of even if he hit three lottos.

There was nothing left to do but get out and start over. That, or go to prison and start over ten years down the line as a wage-garnered ex-con, never mind what horrors of incarceration might await an unaffiliated whiteboy who'd never done dirt worse than coloring outside the lines. Even I can't fault Billy for jetting at that point. Just for every decision he made in the twenty-six months leading to it.

Rage rang Fever from a payphone around two in the morning,

told him it was time. The Ambassador grunted, swung a gym bag over his shoulder, shuffled to the street. He fired up the windowless white jump-out van Cloud had bequeathed to him before heading upstate for ten to fourteen Christmas Eves, and rolled to the pre-determined pickup spot, an all-night diner on West 5th. Billy hopped in, smelling not just sweaty but deeply, darkly unclean. The rosacea that sometimes turned his face and scalp an irritated, scaly red was in full flare, worse than Dengue had ever seen it. Destination, Mexico.

Why not Canada, you might ask, where people mostly spoke English and they had that delicious bacon? Because Billy thought passport control, and everything else, would be tighter to the north. Why take chances among drunken moose hunters and Royal Mounted Police when you could stroll right into a country every third *pendejo* was indenturing himself to the mob to sneak out of?

Nice logic, asshole.

3

robably you forgot that I was hoofing fourteen flights of stairs in Dumbo. My bad. Flashbacks are like heavy drinking. It's easy to start, easy to keep going, hard to wake up the next morning knowing where you are. I tried coming straight out of it, like a DJ slamming the next song over on the snare instead of bothering to blend, on some "Nice logic, asshole. I reached the top of the last flight and opened the door . . ." but it seemed like a lot to ask. I've never done a book before, as you've no doubt guessed, and a lot of little technical things I didn't even notice as a reader are already kicking my ass. Old-timey writers had it easier; a couple hundred years ago you could just lay it out, like "Chapter Three, In Which the Explanation of Why Billy Left (Such as It Is) Has Concluded and Our Faithful Narrator Reaches the Top of the Last Flight and Opens the Door." Nowadays, forget about it. Everybody's busy trying to prove how smart they are. As if that counts for something. Fuck writers.

In biology class, they tell you sight is our quickest sense, because light travels at 186,000 miles per second and sound a paltry Mach 5 or 3 or something. Nobody bets on the olfactory. But smell is a sleeper, cheating the starter pistol and sprinting straight at you, and when it hits you it can knock you down. Especially when that smell is a festering mélange of shit and piss and puke and panic, a toxic bouquet of everything a human being can secrete and reabsorb.

You experience an odor of this magnitude maybe once a year; it's only found haloing the farthest-gone of the unhinged and homeless. The hallway throbbed with it, and I threw an arm over my face and buried my nose in the crook of my elbow as I peered down the corridor, toward the source.

A man was slumped beneath the window at the far end of the hall. His legs were horseshoed out in front of him, arms at his sides, chin touching chest. An inverted forest of matted hair hung to his beard, obscured his face. The clothes were a mass of torn rags, layer atop layer, hints of the original colors showing through the greasy black filth like one of those drawings you make with Cray-Pas and a paperclip in a third-grade art class. On his feet appeared to be a pair of Converse All-Stars, but one sole was attached only in the middle of the shoe, front and back bowed down away from it, and the other sole was gone.

I took a step forward, eyes narrowed against the stench, and as I gained a better angle on the hallway, I saw the walls. All around the low corner in which the man sprawled were broad thick smears of red paint, applied to the beige wallpaper with bare hands. It looked as if a person had scooped himself out and spread the viscera into an ornate warning before his body understood it had been gutted and collapsed. Or like the mathematical proof of some impending planetary doom, worked out in great haste by a madman writing in the language of a savage alien race. It did not look like the shamanic symbols in Dengue's book but a corruption of them, a diseased and desperate mockery.

Nine long strides and I stood over him, waiting for the chest to rise and fall. It didn't. Not that I could see. I found myself counting my own breaths. To inhale even through the mouth was disgusting, so close to that smell, maybe even worse than through the nose because you cut the nasal cilia out of the action and their job was filtration, whereas mouth-breathing entailed gulping the microscopic shit-particles straight into your system.

I sucked down five lungfuls, and then the dude's leg twitched and I jumped back, startled, and kept watch for maybe a minute more, still seeing no evidence of respiration but at least sure he was not putrefying on the penthouse floor. Were I a clearer thinker, maybe I would have wondered how he'd gotten there, or where all that paint had come from, but all I really did in those sixty seconds was sack up for the possibility that this rancid motherfucker was my father.

"Billy?"

No response. I said it louder. Nothing.

"Billy!" I was shouting now, bent to his ear. "Yo! Rage!"

The head flew up. The eyes sprang open, animal with fear. And then his body shot up like something on marionette strings and he slammed me back into the wall. His forearm pressed across my windpipe, hard as bone, and he jammed the vampire-nails of his other hand into my gut. Animation could illustrate the feeling better than words: if we'd been cartoon characters, his arm would've disappeared into me until its shape emerged from my back, stretching my skin like rubber. I wondered if it was possible to throw up when you couldn't breathe.

I tried to speak, managed a strained "Billy" that only made him press the arm more violently against my neck. His eyes, inches from mine, bulged with panic and nothing more: no internal scramble to make sense of his situation, only the shock of the moment and the instinct to survive. This dude, Billy or not Billy, was feral. He was adrenaline and the wasted shell through which it coursed, rallying strength.

Or trying to. There wasn't enough, not even for the ninety seconds he would've needed to choke me out. I understood that before I had time to get scared. He was stink and bones, probably delirious with hunger.

I looked down at his smudged, leathery face and bloodshot

ice-blue eyes and had to admit that yes, this could be Billy. Then I lifted my leg and kneed him in the nuts, and he howled and collapsed into a puddle on the floor.

I reared back and kicked him again, hard in the soft parts. He balled up, clutching at himself, eyes clenched, and I gave him another, heel to vertebrae. The stink was inside me now, pushing its way back out through my pores.

The ugly truth is this: I stomped the everloving shit out of that man, with a fury I'd never been able to wrap my hands around before, a fury that had been floating through me for years in wisps and rumors. I stomped him for being Billy and for not being Billy. For his trespasses, and so that if my real father ever returned, I'd already have offloaded my hurt feelings on this doppelgangly cocksucker and could, I don't know, roll out the crimson rug and give the man a hero's welcome.

Tears and snot were pouring out of me and spattering onto him. I'd switched legs, the right fatigued, the left awkward and ineffective. Which might have been the idea, if there was an idea. I suppose I knew that when I stopped, I'd have to make some kind of decision: to walk away, to help him up, to find out—how's the song go? *Who is he, and what is he to you?*

He didn't make a peep throughout the stomp-down—further provocation for your boy, a final round of silence-as-guilt and judgment-in-absentia. It must have been my own subverbal utterances or the slap of rubber against flesh that brought good old stockbrokin' Patrick out into the hall, crinkling his cute little button nose and demanding to know what the hell was going on.

I stepped over the body and loped toward him. It took Patrick all of three seconds to announce that he didn't want any trouble, and reach for the door he'd just heaved wide.

I thrust my shoe against the jamb just in time and there we stood, slivers of me and Patrick visible to one another and the kind of smell people like him pay big dough to avoid wafting right into his sanctuary and nestling in the fibers of his Restoration

Hardware couch. Patrick yanked stupidly at the doorknob. If anything, he should've been trying to kick my foot away.

"Get out of here," he said. "I'll call the cops."

I'd been planning to nice-guy him, but when a cat like Patrick starts invoking the police, your best bet is to play to expectations, become the thug he sees rather than confuse him with politeness.

In case this all sounds calculating and calm-under-pressure, let me assure you that I was a quivering wreck in need of a hug and two-and-a-half thorazines, and alpha-maling Patrick was like kicking a cat after you've been ass-raped by a gorilla. Yes, I'm from Brooklyn, and yes, I do illegal things and threaten to smack people and harbor homicidal revenge fantasies. But until that day, the only beatdowns in which I'd ever partaken had been intellectual, or as recipient. I'm no hardrock. I'm a nerd with swagger, one of those rodents or moths or whatever who knows how to secrete a pheromone that tricks predators into thinking I'm something else and deciding there's probably a dude farther down the late-night train car who's more muggable than me.

I pushed my way inside the condo, grabbed the cordless off the marble kitchen countertop, and ripped the battery out of the back.

"No cops," I said. "Give me your cell phone, Patrick."

His eyes saucered. "How do you know my name?" I could see the home-invasion nightmare centrifuging into his cerebellum like a movie newspaper. As if anyone would take the trouble to go unwashed for months just for the sake of luring this schmuck into the hallway and jacking his plasma screen.

"What, all black people look the same to you? I'm your marijuana delivery man, jerkoff. Now help me out here."

He peered at me. "Mike? Jesus, what the fuck?"

"What the fuck is, I gotta get that guy out there cleaned up. Help me haul him to your bathroom."

To his credit, Patrick didn't answer right away. He thought about it, weighed the options, saw he had none.

"Who is he?" he said at last. "How'd he get here?"

"I have no idea. He was here when I came. But he might be my father."

"What are *you* doing here?"

Time traveling, dickface. "I had another drop-off in the building. Figured I'd see if you needed anything, long as I was in the neighborhood."

Patrick leaned into the hall. "*That's* your father."

"Like I said. Maybe."

"You were—"

"I know what I was doing."

"You're not gonna hurt him any more, are you?"

"I'm done. Come on."

I could have borne the weight myself, but I didn't want Patrick alone in his apartment, growing the balls to lock or rat me out. We draped the dude's arms over our shoulders, hustled him inside, and lowered him into the bathtub. His eyes fluttered open once when we lifted him, once when we set him down. Otherwise, he was dead to the world.

"Turn it on, turn it on, save us," Patrick shouted into the towel he'd wrapped around his face.

"Okay, but I'm warning you, he might spaz out. No telling."

"I don't care. *I'm* gonna pass out if I have to smell him any longer."

"You got anything to eat? He could probably use some food."

"All I've got is beer. But I can order something. There's a new Thai place on Water Street that just opened. It's supposed to be—"

"Dude!"

Dude as a complete sentence is one of the best things I've learned from white people. It shut Patrick up, and I stared at him until he bumbled off to reconstruct his telephone and contemplate whether the fucked-and-filthy prefer prawns or chicken in their curry.

I don't know how long I sat on Patrick's toilet, staring at the bum in the tub. The fact that I'd attacked him had become incomprehensible; finding that anger now was like searching the ocean for a broken wave. The fortitude to do what lay ahead—to touch this man, strip him of his rags, meet his naked body with my eyes—was unfathomable. My body begged for sleep, that most reliable of cop-outs, and I felt my eyelids dip to halfmast. Unbelievable. A lifetime of wheedling information and poring over blackbooks, and *this* is the moment I choose to decide nah, forget it, my daddy ain't shit, I got nothing to say to dude, our business here is done? What kind of fucking punk was I, if I couldn't man up for this?

I stood, rifled through Patrick's medicine cabinet until I found a pair of scissors, and cut from the waist to the neckline. Three layers of fabric gave with ease, so soft I could have torn them with my hands. I stepped back, realized I was holding my breath, exhaled. Took another one, and held that too.

There was a travel-pouch strapped to his sunken, sunburned chest, the kind paranoid German tourists tote their passports around Times Square in. I crouched, sliced it off him, retreated to the toilet and tried to work the zipper. The metal was full of grit, so I just slit the whole thing open and shook the contents onto Patrick's floor, covered in tiles so tiny and white they looked like baby's teeth: a dozen miniature cut-glass bottles full of different-colored saps and powders, amber and pale-green and gold, and a Ziploc bag, the contents wrapped in a shred of checkered fabric.

I stared down at all of it awhile, then forced myself back over to the tub. I tossed away the scraps of his shoes, grabbed the jeans by the cuffs, and yanked. They slid easily off his hips, and his tan came with them; below the waistline he was paler than Darth Vader's head. I glimpsed the snarl of pubic hair, turned before I saw more. Spun both faucets until water chugged into the tub, opened a bottle of liquid hand soap sitting on Patrick's sink and emptied it into the stream. An army of bubbles rose up around the body, like grass around a badger's corpse in one of those time-lapse nature films.

I sat crosslegged on the floor and started twisting open bottles and sniffing their strange, earthy contents. Tried to pretend I was browsing a curbside cardtable on the Fulton Mall manned by one of those Kufi-rocking cats who always push the blackest shit they've got—"here, smell this one, brother, it's called Super Nubian Kemetic Zulu Musk, the sisters love it"—and steer any whiteboy who comes along toward the Coolwater and Polo knockoffs, somehow failing to understand that white dudes who wear oils want the Super Nubian Kemetic Zulu Musk or that what I want is to smell like Polo for five bucks, not the lead djembe-thumper in some wack Central Park drum circle.

The baggie inches from my toe was obviously a better place to look for hard evidence, so I ignored it for as long as possible, spent the next five minutes thinking about the night I ran into Ravi Coltrane at Ben's Pizza on 3rd and MacDougal, around the corner from the Blue Note.

If you're wondering how I recognized him, it's simple. In addition to being a tenor saxophonist like his old man, Ravi happens to be John's spitting image. I'm talking doubletake-level resemblance. I watched him go to work on his slice at the next table over—they have these high circular ones that customers stand at—and imagined Ravi growing up with *A Love Supreme* and *Impressions, Blue Train* and *Africa/Brass*, but not his father. John checked out in 1967, when Ravi was two. Liver failure. I read a biography; Trane is my man.

Word, I thought. This is a cat I should be friends with. I'd just smoked a bowl. I finished my pizza, walked over, and said, *You're Ravi Coltrane.*

He looked up, checked me out, and said *yeah* through a mouthful of cheese and pepperoni.

My name's Dondi. My dad, he was a painter—he's not as famous as your dad, but people who know his stuff think a lot of it. He died when I was two, so I know him mostly through his work.

He saw where I was going, and nodded.

So I just wanted to ask you, and if it's too personal I apologize, but do you feel like you know your father from listening to his records?

He dabbed his lips with a napkin. *I know him as a musician through his records. But what I know about him as a man, I know because of my mother.*

We talked for a couple minutes. I asked whether he liked any of the various books about his dad and he shrugged, said they were all okay except when they tried to make John into someone he hadn't been—someone political, someone angry. I asked who Ravi was playing with tonight, and he said Elvin Jones: his dad's old drummer, seventy-plus now, full of stories about John that he mostly didn't tell because he still missed him so badly.

I wondered aloud what it was like for Elvin to look over from the drums and see Trane's son where his father had once stood. Ravi shook his head, said he wondered that himself. He glanced at his watch, crumpled his paper plate into a ball, and said he had to get back, then asked if I'd like to check out the second set. I said I would, very much. We walked across the block together. Ravi nodded at the doorman and we slipped inside.

I ordered ginger ale for fear of getting carded, and watched the show from the bar. Elvin played the greatest drum solo I'd ever heard in my life, as good as anything he'd laid down forty years earlier on any of the CDs I owned. But there was something about watching Ravi that unsettled me. He wasn't bad. Not at all. But he wasn't John. And yet he looked so much like him. It bothered me throughout the set, in some way I couldn't define, and so did the fact that I'd described my dad as dead.

I cut the water, opened the Ziploc. And just like that, he was alive.

Grinning from atop the stack of snapshots in my hand was Wren 209, sun-faded and begrimed and looking all of seventeen: her hand a jutting peace sign, her hair a peace-out natural, her earrings huge gold doorknockers. Of course the Karen Billy chose to carry with him would be a Karen he hadn't yet fucked over, a Karen unaware of the bullshit he'd soon pull. I had the urge to press a thumb to my mother's eyes, shield her from both of us.

Patrick appeared, handed over two Pad Thais, then had the class to make himself scarce. I sat on the toilet lid, shoveling spongy noodles into my mouth and waiting. Billy Rage nestled beneath his blanket of water, did his corpse impression. It wasn't until I'd devoured everything including that little mound of bean sprouts they always give you that I caught him peering out from his thicket of dreadlocks.

I pretended not to notice; I'd fucking done enough. Once or twice, my father shifted his lips and swallowed a mouthful of bathwater. Otherwise, nothing. Just eyes in the primeval forest, like this shit was a Joe Conrad novel. In the next room, Patrick fired up his Xbox or his PlayStation or whatever and the sounds of carjacking and cop-killing wafted through the air.

Half an hour ticked away before Billy's fingers slithered out of the water and his talons curled around the scalloped edges of the tub. The bald mountain peaks of his knees disappeared as he leveraged himself upward, inch by shaky inch. Finally, and with great strain, he managed to raise his entire mossy, dripping head above the surface.

"Será este lugar el infierno?" His voice was sludgy with disuse, but calm. I had no idea what he'd said.

"Dígame," he whispered. "Es el infierno?"

"Mi español es muy mal," I told him. "You remember how to speak English?"

Billy laughed, if you could call it that: a dastardly, low rumble like the sound of a kid falling down a flight of stairs.

"I should have known," he said, skull falling back against the porcelain with a dull knock, "that they'd speak English in hell."

"There'd be no bathtubs if this was hell."

His arms slipped out of view, and some part of him beneath the water made a swishing sound.

"This is Brooklyn," I offered.

Billy parted the curtain of his hair with his left hand, and before it fell back over his face I caught a quick freeze off his eyes.

"Don't fuck with me. If this is hell, say so."

"It's Dumbo. Have some Pad Thai."

A grunt, a squelchy sound, a flash of limbs, and then Billy was on his feet, looming tall and gaunt as filthy water sloshed over the bathtub's sides. I was eye-to-dick with my father. His was the same as mine. I'm talking Ravi-John identical. Except for the color.

Before I could grant that fact the proper scrutiny, Billy threw back his head and bellowed a stream of syllables, in a language I had never heard.

I didn't need to understand to feel its power, the same way you see a ceremonial mask in a museum and know it was used for some diabolical shit before reading the info plaque. These sounds were an incantation, or a prayer—what you'd say to the devil if he offered you some lunch, I guess. The veins of Billy's neck engorged and he clutched his stomach with both hands, like he was trying to push the noise out. Or hold his guts in.

Not for nothing? I felt like blood was going to start trickling from my nose. There was an echo in the chant of that eternal, animal *now* I'd seen in Billy's eyes when he'd attacked. As if these sounds did not come from but through him, my father's body the amplifier for some ancient dirge.

Billy lost his balance and the sound broke off—or perhaps it was the other way around, the incantation all that had been holding him upright. He latched on to the cheap plastic shower curtain, trying to break his fall. It ripped free of its metal rings, cloaked itself around him as he crumpled back into the tub: big splash, small rustle, silence.

I checked to make sure he was okay, or as okay as he had been before his aria, then decided to give him some alone time. I draped Patrick's bathrobe over the toilet, balanced Billy's Pad Thai on the edge of the sink, and stepped into the living room.

Patrick paused his game, picked up his bong. He took a practiced rip, aimed a train of smoke at the ceiling, and thrust the
blown-glass monstrosity toward me, fist wrapped around its neck.
I flashed on a pocket universe in which Patrick and I were roommates and this was just a ho-hum weekend at the crib, then
declined a hit and dialed my phone.

"The fuck your punk ass want?"

And hello to you too, Mom.

uring the eighties, everybody making movies had mad coke and no patience, so they conveyed the passage of time—a boxer training, a romance blossoming, a teenaged werewolf partying—by splicing together a bunch of four-second scenes denoting incremental progress and setting them to peppy power pop. Like the decade's other defining concepts—greed, crack, arms for hostages, the religious right, new jack swing—it was crude and tasteless, but effective.

I'd love to montage my way past the ordeal of nursing Billy back to what some might call sanity, drown the tedium and the frustration in a rockin' Tears for Fears jam and pick up a week down the line, when he started to do more than sleep and eat, and things got interesting. You might think there'd be some instances of high drama in between, but the truth is that they mostly happened in my head. Take the moment when Karen first laid eyes on Billy, lugged across her threshold by your boy here, my father's limbs stuffed into a too-small ensemble of stockbroker chinos and blue oxford buttondown. Wow, very emotional stuff, seeing him after all these years, right? Plus he's totally fucked up and incoherent? Presumably anger and relief and fear are playing double Dutch inside of Karen as she stands gripping the doorknob, with love and hate and fifteen other

feelings waiting for a chance to jump in too. It doesn't sound like
the kind of scene you skip, I realize that. But you don't know my
mother.

Karen said "Oh my God" and one huge sob jumped out of her, like
the first dude to leap from the North Tower. Then she cupped her
hands over her nose and mouth, took a deep breath, and turned
away. Stalked into the kitchen, slammed her teakettle onto the
burner, called "put him in the guest room" like I was delivering a rug.

And that was that. The fact that Karen didn't kick me out meant
I could stay. We discussed neither Billy's presence nor mine. Not
then, and not during the five days Billy spent sleeping, scanning
the walls with the uncurious, vacant expression of a senile old man,
and jamming food into his mouth, half-vegetable and half-animal.
That Karen didn't have a breakdown was good enough for me.
Once you've watched your mother lose her shit you never stop waiting for it to happen again, no matter how strong she might look. So
if Karen needed to handle this by ignoring both of us and keeping
her routines, that was fine by me.

She'd always been a creature of habit: up by quarter of eight and
out by quarter-past, Monday through Friday, bodega coffee ("light
and sweet, Ismail," as if, after a decade, Ismail had to be told) on
the way to the C train, a buttered breakfast-cart bagel and a second
coffee ("light and sweet, Sanjeev") when she resurfaced on 23rd.
Food devoured, left hand free to flip the bird by the time she passed
the construction crew perpetually not-working on the corner of 9th
Ave, with their gutbusting bacon-egg-and-cheese sandwiches and
reliably ass-related compliments. Coffee cool enough to drink by
the time her fêted hindparts met the nubby fabric and peekaboo
foam of a swivel chair on the second floor of the townhouse that
was Authors' Inc., a second-tier literary agency whose most bank-
able client was Madeline Mannheim of *Horse/Shoe Crew* fame.

In case you happen not to be a twelve-year-old girl, it's a book-
franchise-cum-TV-series that brilliantly cross-stitches female-
tweener passions for equestrianism and shopping. A new volume hits

the shelves every six months, outlined by Mannheim and written by somebody—anybody—else. Karen penned one herself, when I was ten. *The New Boy*, it was called. Paid seventy-five hundred dollars, flat fee, no rights and no credit. Took her a year of nights and weekends, then another month of rewrites because she'd inadvertently given all the choice lines to Missy Silver, the token black chick.

Karen had been an assistant agent then, and she was an assistant agent now. Authors' Inc. gave her a four percent annual raise, and on Fridays they ordered sushi for the whole office, and unlike the actual agents, she was under no pressure to sell. These were the things that kept her at a job she loathed. That and the fact that she had keys to the building, which allowed her to run her Friday writers' group undetected.

I can't prove the workshop kept Karen on an even keel, but the math checks out. It was insane by design, my mother at her most perverse. The off-the-books loot it brought in wasn't insubstantial, but it wasn't the point.

I'm not sure what the point was, why Karen chose to spend an evening a week amongst the Tri-State Area's most hopeless literary aspirants. Every day at work, she read through the dozens of unsolicited query letters and manuscripts and book proposals that streamed into Authors' Inc., in case amid the turds lay a diamond, or a marketable turd. Her first year, she handed one package up the ladder, a short story collection she thought was beautiful. The boss passed: no hook, no market. On the sly, Karen began compiling a file of the looniest letters. She'd whip out the folder when her college friends came over and read a few aloud.

Dear Ms. Spondrey,

Often I have thought of the daunting amenities of materials consumed. Some were a welcomed fancy and others a dose of unsavoury medicine of lament and righteousness. Though both are important components to which we live our lives, all of which that defines relevance. With this long-since digested epiphany, I have been convinced to surrender the charge for composing the vehicle of such to the liking of balderdash to some, knowledge in others, that to which we have so cleverly labelled as "book." As you are dealer of this so celebrated meal to the minds, I should like to present you an offering for the palette of mankind's favour.

Valence, The Unexamined Life is just such the feed for relevancy and influence, two of the most important elements that lend definition to our stay. Most of my twenty-some years of existing among life's queerisome travels I have sought after the values, influences, and forthcomings of others. It's a primal inhibition we so often indulge. Even arrogance is chided whilst hiding behind the cloak of darkened deceit in hopes of harvesting the lessons of one other's lot. The fictitious state of Valence is an exact presentation of these rudimentary values. It offers a window and synopsis of life's offerings of obscure randomness. Valence is ordinary. She is dangerous. She is loving, caring, deceiving and evil. She offers the grace of God. Her people are everyone you know, love and hate. Growing up in a household of Morticians, corrupted politicians, educators, gays/lesbians, and clergy, I have benefited life long insurance of roundness certainly in the least. No, it's more complicated than 'roundness.' I have survived a twisted and curved road of values that have been tested, re-tested, and then redefined by rules created by those who live without rules. Which is a good thing (to vernacularize). A broad thing, certainly. Valence holds the best of these interests, pleasures and tragedies. She develops their potentials and unfolds them into useful satire to the followers of her tarry. A publishable tarry—I shall leave to your regard.

Thank you,
Samuel Ward-Corman

TO WHOM IT MAY CONCERN,

I, Jacob Navidad, I have written two stories, one is about me on the ships, the name of the story is the name is <u>Journey of a Seaman</u>. The other story is about a white pigeon flying from Europe to A America, the name is <u>Coming to America</u>. I have some photos of the white pigeon and some squirrels is in the story, I need a Agency to help me to Publisher the stories.

Jacob Navidad

Dear Sir or Madam,

The bloodthirsty dogs drove the three boys deeply into the woods. The mayor and sheriff were seen tying up the two frightened men. They pleaded for their lives, but betrayed their secret oaths. Now death would be their gift. They strung them up and watched. All those dogs, all sizes and colors, attacked the men. Slowly, they were devoured. The birds of prey picked at their remains, eating their flesh, picking it clean to the bone.

Scott wanted to find his father. He had left him. There was talk that he was living with Abby Smith, the town tramp, at the edge of the woods, near the railroad tracks. Scott, Jack and Joat were relentless in this quest.

The ring Joat wore brought back memories. It was Charles. He had been brutally killed along with his lover, Bruce. They were both only 15, too young to die. Their homosexuality was known throughout Concord. The residents had made a vow for their demise.

On that early spring morning, the two young boys were beaten by the group, then laid across the cold steel tracks. The train was right on time, like usual. Their bodies were scattered for miles. Nobody cared, except Scott. He knew that once he found his old man, things would come out. Scott fought off the attacks by the dogs. He ignored death. Life itself was cheap. Death took a holiday. What Scott didn't know was that the killer had been with him all the time.

I have written many plays. I recently had a poem published called "April." Your agency is excellent. It brings the reader to the finest fiction, to be read and enjoyed. I have read your credentials in the Directory of Agents. I believe this book will be a number one bestseller. My proposal to you is I am offering you 70% of the commission of sales, and I will take 30%.

Sincerely,
August Chong

Query Letter

I'm not some big time graduate from Harvard University nor am I some well-known author. I'm just the new kid on the block wanting to do something that I like to do best, write. During my college days I took a few creative writing classes. I also wrote many of the term papers for my friends. I like to sit and write short fictional stories about any and everything. I can relate to one of the characters in my short story "Caught Up." Her name is Lisa. She is married to a man who loves her very much but he decided to tell her one night that she was not sexy enough for him. Of course, she started working out at one of the popular gyms in her area. She became so caught up in what she looked like that she forgot about her family at home. She has this one friend from high school that seems to try and sabotage everything she attempts to do, but she keeps her around anyway. This time her friend persuades her to go out with the new aerobics teacher at the gym and a few others guys and she gets caught up. I can relate to this young lady because I too was in a relationship like that. I was not married to the guy but I was very much in love with him.

I guess you can say that my self-esteem dropped lower than what it already was when he told me that I was not sexy enough for him. I began going to the gym hoping that I could tone up for him and I even changed my style of dressing. I was beginning to dress more with the latest trends. I too was caught up beause I liked the way the guys were noticing my new look. I ended up being hurt by those guys, with my new look. The moral of the story, if someone loves you they will only mention little tidbits to enhance you, not hurt you.

In conclusion, I decided to choose you guys as my literary agent because you deal with a wide range of fictional and non-fictional stories. I would like to take some pass events in my life and come up with a great fictional story. The character names that are portrayed are not necessary the real characters in my life.

Yours Truely,
Trina F. Kinney

Halfway through my freshman year, Karen picked eight of her favorites and wrote to them on agency stationery, explaining that while their work was not yet polished enough for representation, it showed sufficient promise to merit acceptance to the new Authors' Inc. Workshop for Emerging Writers. For three hundred dollars, they could enroll in an exclusive ten-week course, run by a publishing professional.

Seven ponied up. Two weeks later she was face-to-uncontrollable-facial-tic with her first group of students, and well on her way to learning the answer to the question she'd often posed, rubbery with laughter, after giving a dramatic reading of a jaw-dropping query letter: *who the fuck* are *these people?*

Sure, she was stoking their hopes for shits and giggles and cash. But as Karen liked to point out, if it was a crime to teach writing to people whose failure was assured, every professor at every MFA program in the country would be as guilty as she was. Each Friday, she came home flushed with anthropological delight. Being surrounded by people so wildly off-base about themselves, their craft, in some cases reality in general, Karen said, was like walking into one of those paintings of dogs playing poker. She meant it in a good way.

When the course ended, my mother retained two favorites, hooked a new batch, and did it again. I warned her that she'd soon be no better than the disaffected hipsters overrunning Williamsburg and Whoopty Whoo Ivy League We's A Comin' Academy, decked out in T-shirts emblazoned with slogans they didn't understand and buying albums by bands so bad they were good and generally getting caught up (as Trina F. Kinney might say) in the tornadoes of their own smug irony. *The whole thing is mighty white of you*, I'd add if I really wanted to start trouble. Karen usually responded by flipping me the bird, or a look that was the same as the bird, or by shrugging her shoulders and saying that if I felt that way she'd be sure not to spend any of the dough on me.

It was probably for the best that Billy chose a workshop night to rejoin the world in more than flesh; who knows what would have happened if he'd segued into lucidity with Karen nearby. Besides which, one more day of playing Florence Nightingale and I might have spazzed out and stopped feeding his ass.

The irony of taking care of a father who'd never taken care of me is so obvious I'm loath to dwell on it. When you're responsible for somebody with whom you've got so much unresolved shit, you've either gotta find the inner strength to make each act a tiny gesture of forgiveness, or else spend every stagnant, housebound hour pulsing with resentment.

Your boy here, I opted for the latter. The problem, as always, was how to throw darts at an invisible man. I could only measure the stone of Billy's absence by the water it displaced, the ripples shuddering across my life—convict him not just in, but *of* absentia. I kept circling back over the same memories all week: that autumn 2000 chain of events that made me realize how narrow life's margins were, how easily the simplest shit could snowball if you didn't have the right support, until your whole reality got yanked out from underneath.

It all jumped off a couple months into eighth grade at MS 113, when I started getting these dizzy spells. My vision would go sort of smeared, and I'd have like these hiccups in my brain, as if a loose wire were giving off electrical bursts—which makes no sense, as I learned a year later in biology, because the brain doesn't have the right kind of nerves to feel anything. It only happened two, three times a week, and looking back now I can't fathom why I told Karen, since I was in the throes of puberty and all kinds of equally incomprehensible and frightening crap was also happening to me, such as unprovoked rock-hard erections lasting upwards of forty-five minutes.

Like a responsible parent, Karen took me to a doctor, who scheduled an MRI or maybe it was a CT scan, and told me to stay up for twenty-four hours beforehand, and not eat anything for twelve. Karen all-nightered with me. We rented a bunch of movies, made a party of it. In the morning I went in, drank a glass of mysterious thick pink shit and lay down and let them slide me into one of those pod things for about three minutes so they could look at my brain. The nurse or technician or whatever seemed surprised I'd stayed awake and fasted, as if that part had been a joke. When it was over, Karen took me to Junior's for breakfast and let me order cherry cheesecake.

For your boy here, the whole thing was mildly troubling, quickly shrugged off. I had high school applications to write, b-ball tryouts looming, girls to ponder. Not only did I forget we were waiting on the test results, I was too absorbed in my own shit to notice that Karen was trying to hide something from me—and my mother wears her heart on everybody else's sleeve, so that was some major-league obliviousness right there. I don't know how or when she decided I had a brain tumor, but after that all-nighter Karen pulled three or four more, consecutive and unintentional.

They say sleep deprivation is a form of torture, and that

information acquired through such means is unreliable because a motherfucker will say whatever she thinks might stop the pain. But what if you're torturing yourself? When Karen's diet of terror and exhaustion started to yield results even my dumb ass couldn't miss, the most prominent was honesty, unfettered and raw. The unspeakable became small talk. It was like one of those old cartoons where somebody's shadow achieves consciousness and starts moving independent of the body. Nothing good ever comes of that.

On the fourth night, I awakened to find Karen sitting on my bed, talking. I don't mean *hey, Dondi, wake up*; I mean it was two in the morning and she was in the middle of a speech, describing what she would do to me if I turned into a man like my father and illustrating the case against Billy with a litany of *I should have known then* examples of selfishness and misplaced loyalty, spanning from the teenage dawn of their relationship to the very day of his departure—all of them new to me, which you've gotta understand was like happening upon a Biggie Smalls bluegrass album, or a new book of the Bible in which the various exploits of Jesus, God, Methuselah, et al. are revealed to be an elaborate fairy tale dictated by Hasaan the Joker to his manservant Sparkles during a fortnight's binge at an Assyrian opium den.

Maybe it seems weird of me to put such stock in the ramblings of a woman spiraling toward delirium. But I knew Karen well enough to understand that this was the realest she had ever been, even if I couldn't put together why. And besides, people don't wake you at the darkest hour of the night to lie. The Billy-as-Batman posters came down off the walls of my psyche then and there, leaving me with nothing to stare at but the faded paint beneath.

The next day, when I got home from school, Reggie from the fourth floor was sitting in the living room. There'd been an incident that morning at Authors' Inc. Karen was in the hospital. I was supposed to stay with him.

An incident, I said, trying not to panic. *What does that mean, an incident?*

She'd attacked a UPS guy with a letter opener, he told me. Her coworkers had to pull her off. Nobody knew why she'd done it, Karen included. She'd sounded pretty out of it when she'd called, said they'd given her something to calm her down. Been under a lot of stress, something about some test results.

Can I see her? I asked.

He shook his head, dreadlocks skritching against an orange corduroy buttondown, and told me to pack up what I needed for the night.

No offense, I said, *but why would she call you? Why not my grandparents?*

Reggie rubbed his hand against his stubble, like he was having trouble staying awake, and said *That's, um, are their names Joe and Dana?*

Yeah. My dad's folks.

She probably don't want me telling you, but what the fuck, you grown enough. Your mom's afraid if they find out she's in the psych ward, they'll bug out and try to take you away.

I think I nodded. "Grown enough" and "test results" and "psych ward" rattled around inside me, and I knew that this was my fault. My faults. And Billy's.

The eventual diagnosis was a psychotic break catalyzed by exhaustion, but once you break you're broke and it's not as simple as just catching up on Z's and clocking back in. It took them three weeks to get Karen stabilized and rested and all that. Which made me a long-term resident of Reggie's apartment.

Longer than Reggie, as things turned out.

He had a three-bedroom—the same layout as ours, which really banged home the whole different-world-inches-away thing. It was one of those dynasty apartments you'll find close to any college campus. Got handed down year after year along a line of descent that included Pratt students, graduates, and drop-outs affiliated with Sigma Phi, this co-ed artsy-druggy-hippie frat some knuckleheads formed in the sixties as a way to score campus housing, back when there was some.

Reggie seemed really charged about the crib's history: the bands that had formed there, none of which I'd ever heard of, the illustrious alumni, the fact that every year it was a stop on Sigma Phi's twenty-four-hour initiation ritual, a psychedelic tour of Brooklyn they called the Epic of Gilgamesh. How all the furniture and artwork marked different epochs, and past residents often dropped by to smoke a joint and make sure their Bob Marley wall hanging was still tacked over the couch or whatever the fuck.

His pride struck me as kind of misplaced, since Reggie himself was totally off-brand—not a Pratt guy or a Sigma, not even an artist. He'd moved in as a summer subletter, and become permanent when some chick left unexpectedly that August. Listening to him talk reminded me of the time I went to Passover dinner at my boy Greg Weiner's house and his Scots-Irish aunt lectured everybody about the amazing resilience of the Jewish people for three hours.

Reggie's roommates were a pair of luxuriously dreadlocked musicians, Twenty-Twenty and Knowledge Born, the former a recent Pratt drop-out from Massachusetts who was still cashing his student loan checks, and the latter the homey of the former, source of income unclear, arrival date recent, Five Percenter name uncorrelated to lifestyle. The two of them were always referring to "the studio," which I soon realized meant Twenty-Twenty's room. They talked music all day, but in highly technical terms: how to quantize a drum loop or filter the lows out of a sample. Reggie would chime in and bring the discourse to a dead halt, which made me feel sort of sorry for him.

Nobody seemed fazed by the random thirteen-year-old sleeping on the couch. Which makes perfect sense in retrospect, because two thirds of the population was busy gearing up for war, and whatever went on in Reggie's mind had nothing to do with me.

A couple days into my tenure, Reggie drove upstate for the weekend, to visit some people he worked with every summer at a kids' camp. Five minutes after he left, Twenty-Twenty and K-Born charged into his room and commenced drawer-dumping and mattress-flipping like they had a motherfucking search warrant, in pursuit of evidence that he'd jerked them out of some money on a phone bill.

I couldn't really follow the particulars, and they weren't too keen on making sure I understood, but that was just the flashpoint anyway. Reggie had been under suspicion of plenty more, for plenty long. Sue, the girl who bounced unexpectedly the summer he moved in, had done so after a couple hundred bucks went missing from her bureau. She was a willowy young stoner chick, not the type to confront anybody and especially incapable of stepping to Reggie. Not just because he weighed two-forty but because he worked with kids and had a pretty smile and was Your Friendly Neighborhood Dread, the kind of black dude who made white people feel super-awesome about themselves. To accuse him of stealing would have filled her with guilt and shame even if it was true, so instead she just mumbled something about bad vibes and left, and a year later when she was good and toasted at a Sigma Phi party she told Twenty-Twenty all about it.

Then there was the fact that Reggie dated white women exclusively—that is, the women he dated four at a time were exclusively white—and according to Twenty-Twenty and K-Born all his homeys were white too, which is definitely how you roll if you're a shady black dude looking not to get your card pulled; that's a no-brainer. Also, he really liked the Wyclef Jean album, and he couldn't play chess for shit, and he was always incredibly proud—*gleeful*, K-Born said, *like, holding up his palm for high fives and shit*—whenever he two-timed one of his waifish, non-rocket-surgeon-ass girls with another.

They tossed his room, and just like that some petty-money stern-talking-to shit became a beef you could legitimately disfigure a dude for. What they found (aside from a bunch of nasty porno mags which, oddly, featured nothing but black women) was a nightstand drawer crammed with the kind of overdue-rent notices they slip under your door when you're seriously fucking up. Month by month, the debt increased by Reggie's share of the rent. As the ranking member of the apartment, he made it his job to collect K-Born's and Twenty-Twenty's checks. He'd been mailing them in; he just hadn't been writing his own. They owed eight thou and change, and E.B. Holding Company claimed to have initiated eviction proceedings. Why they'd even been this patient was a mystery—until K-Born discovered the lease itself, in a shoebox on the top shelf of Reggie's closet.

I have no idea how E.B. Holding Co. managed to botch a simple document so badly, but it suggested that real estate might not exactly be their bread and butter. Reggie's surname was Troutman, but they had it as Fuentes—the dude whose room Twenty-Twenty had taken over. K-Born, government name Kemmit Bannon, was listed as Karriem Banwon, a definite improvement. Twenty-Twenty wasn't named at all, but one of the original dynasty dudes, a trumpet player named Joel who'd been living in Brazil since the early nineties, was still a leaseholder. His was the only name typed right.

Maybe you're wondering what kept me from jetting, when my apartment was right downstairs and my ace dude Cedric lived on Greene and Vanderbilt and Billy's parents were an easy subway trip away. I guess I wanted to prove I could hold down my square, to myself and to Karen. Keep the secret, and the faith. Besides which, there's nothing like other people's drama to make you forget your own.

Being present at the fact-finding mission made me a mascot, if not a co-conspirator. When Reggie's room had been thoroughly swept, the three of us convened in the living room to pore over the mess of papers red-stamped with PAST DUE and FINAL WARNING and EVICTION PENDING, marveling at the thought of Reggie early-morning tiptoeing to the front door to retrieve the notices, and puzzling over why he'd kept them. K-Born lit a blunt, started to pass it to me, then had his doubts and froze, arm half extended, eyebrows raised, cheeks pouched with smoke. I nodded. He handed it over. A star was born.

Remember when he told us he made that painting? said Twenty-Twenty, using the blunt to point. Across the room, balanced against the metal fire-escape door, was a small watercolor rendering of the door's latticework. That might sound dumb but it was actually pretty cool, kind of tied the indoors to the out.

You know Chynetta, who used to live here? I ran into her at Frank's Lounge one time, and she was like "That painting of the fire escape grille I did, is that still in the apartment? I'd like to get it back." I said yeah, come over whenever, I'll put it aside for you. So I went home and took it down, and Reggie was like, "Nah, nah, she didn't paint that, I did. There's two versions." And he got me. I was like, "Okay . . . if you say so. Can't see why you'd lie about that." And I put it right where it is right now.

We all stared at it for a while. Some people claim they didn't get high the first time they smoked. I can't see how that's possible.

Yo, remember the zip drive? K-Born turned to me. One day, Reggie comes home from the Y and he's like "My boss said I could borrow this zip drive. Can you use it?" Keep in mind, this fool doesn't even own a computer. I said no. Then, two days later, he's like "My boss said I could keep it, you know anybody I could sell it to?"

See, man, said Twenty-Twenty. He had this off-kilter, adenoidal voice, badly matched to his enormous head and regal mane. *That's that squeaky clean shit. If you boosted a zip drive from your job, just say, "Yo, I boosted a zip drive from my job." If the lease is botched, just say, "yo, the lease is botched, y'all wanna stop paying and ride it out as long as we can?" Don't try to play me like one of your white girls.*

Maybe he thought paying two thirds would keep them quiet, I offered.

Maybe he's a pathological liar, said Knowledge Born. He pressed a finger to the lease. *Look. The rent is eighty dollars more than he said. There's no angle to that.*

He's gotta be out, said Twenty-Twenty. *Whatever it takes.* K-Born nodded. Twenty-Twenty looked at me, and I guess I nodded too.

I don't know how I ended up with what might be the only copy of "The Truth," the song they made using sampled snippets of the beatdown. Twenty-Twenty had a portable tape recorder running on the window ledge, so that whatever Reggie said he couldn't unsay. They laid the track the same day, before the blood on the lamp-shades was even dry.

I'm listening to it right now, on a Maxell cassette labeled in black marker. Part of me admires the fact that they turned an ugly thing like kicking a dude's ass and making him homeless into art, but it's some pretty ugly art. You can hear the rawness in their voices, the attempt to tell a story that hasn't yet been processed, the bravado layered over something rappers are supposed to pretend doesn't exist, maybe shame.

The song starts with Twenty-Twenty and Knowledge Born trading off, line for line. K sounds amped, like he took a quick time-out from the fight to drop a verse. Twenty-Twenty sounds exhausted.

> *You got treated like family*
> *Uncannily, I got suspicious*
> *The truth shall set you free*
> *But if you lyin' we turn vicious*
> *Extended, the benefit of the doubt*
> *And heard you out*
> *Your facts don't correlate*
> *Grab your shit and fuckin' bounce*
> *Before we go upside your head*
> *to change your mindstate*
> *When I find snakes*
> *there's no mistake*
> *I'll see you at the wake*
> *I peeped the moves you made*
> *Plus I know the girl you date*
> *She told me everything . . .*
> *That's how I know you fake*

When Reggie came home, the three of us were waiting in the living room: Knowledge Born on the couch, a baseball bat stashed beneath him, Twenty-Twenty leaning on a metal cane he'd found in the back of the hall closet, and your boy tucked well out of the way, over by the fire escape.

Sit down, Twenty-Twenty said, as scripted. *We need to talk.*

Reggie parked himself on the futon. *What's up, fellas?*

I called Verizon, Twenty-Twenty said, hand on his hip. *There's no such thing as a reinstatement fee. You owe me sixty bucks.*

It wasn't a reinstatement fee, dude, it was the money we owed on the bill, plus they said they had to charge us for basic service in advance because we didn't pay. Reggie looked around the room, then raised his voice a little, slapped his palms against his knees and bowed his arms out from his sides. *What, you think I tried to rip you off?*

My heart was bucking, and if Reggie had so much as made eye contact I might have jumped out the fucking window, but it was interesting to see how fast he played the wounded-indignation card. I could see why it had been effective in the past, with people like Sue: it forced your hand, flushed any inner doubt up to the surface. And at the same time, there was a current of intimidation running below it, like *even a righteous man will rise up to defend his honor, and lest you forget I happen to be a large bearlike motherfucker.*

The plan was to pick Reggie apart point by point, get him to cop to the small offenses before they raised the major stuff, but that opening statement killed Twenty-Twenty's patience. He dipped into his room while Reggie was trying to clarify the phone situation, came back with a stack of papers.

Call Verizon right now, man. Ask them if we—

Twenty-Twenty flicked the latest overdue notice into Reggie's lap.

You know what? Fuck the phone bill. Why are we eight thousand dollars in debt?

I gotta give Reggie credit. His face fell, but he picked it right back up and tried to turn the tables.

What the fuck were you doing in my room? he demanded, rising a few inches off the couch.

Knowledge Born sprang to his feet, bat in hand. *We about to get evicted! You better tell us something!*

I can explain! Reggie yelled, finally starting to appreciate the situation.

Explain, then, from Twenty-Twenty. Reggie sputtered for a second, just long enough to not explain, and then Knowledge Born hit him in the shoulder with an aluminum Louisville Slugger left over from some departed dynasty king's softball league of yore. Reggie doubled over, and Twenty-Twenty brought the cane down on his back.

They both backed off, and Knowledge Born yelled, *Why we getting evicted?* and Reggie, still doubled over, said *Fuck you, when's the last time you even paid rent?* and got hit again.

I'll give them this: they kept it civilized. Two on one, with weapons, you could easily kill a man. Nobody hit him in the head except once, accidentally, ten minutes in, after countless starts and stops and fruitless demands. Reggie was punch-drunk and leaning back against a wall while Knowledge Born shouted the same questions and swung the bat in the air to keep him at bay. For some reason, Reggie walked into the swing, and got clipped in the forehead. His eyes rolled back and he buckled at the knees, but even then, the dude never went down.

He never admitted anything either, except lying about that watercolor. Twenty-Twenty threw it at his feet during a lull, *Who painted this shit?* and he looked up, groggy-eyed from being beaten, and said Chynetta's name.

Getting him out of the apartment was harder than it should have been. At first, he kept trying to bolt for the door, but they weren't done and he couldn't get past. By the time they were ready to toss him, though, Reggie would not be moved: *This is my fuckin' house! You guys get out!* That was when Twenty-Twenty grabbed the butcher's knife. Reggie went wild when he saw it, lifting up his tattered shirt and yelling *You gonna fuckin' cut me, Twenty-Twenty? Huh? Go ahead then, fuckin' cut me!*

Twenty-Twenty, in his goofy nasal voice, said, *Naw, man, I'm not gonna cut you, I'm gonna take your locks. You don't deserve them shits no more*, and for maybe the first time, some kind of fear jumped into Reggie's eyes. They wrestled him down, no easy feat, and yanked each and every last dread out of his dome, Knowledge Born yelling some crazy shit about the Sword of Justice all the while. Reggie was wrenching back and forth, bellowing *Take them! Take them all!*, and when they let him up, he took off running.

You know a man has pulled some foul shit in his life when you kick his ass and throw him bald and bleeding into the street, and the person he runs to calls you and instead of yelling *what the fuck!* she sighs and says, *What did Reggie do now?* That's what Christine, his ex-girl from up the block, inquired of Knowledge Born an hour later. He ran it down, and she asked if Reggie had cheated on her while they were together. *Hell yes, he did.* With that girl Barbara? *Among others.* And Christine gave him the boot, too.

Even now, I still expect to run into Reggie, or hear something, or get jumped on my way home and stomped to death. That was it, though. He never even came back for his clothes. Knowledge Born took over his room, and a guy named Roam the Wanderer, another rap star in the Sigma Phi constellation, filled the vacancy before the sun set. The leather couch was smeared with blood, so I moved to the futon. Twenty-Twenty gathered Reggie's locks into a Dutch Masters cigar box and left it on top of the refrigerator—whether deliberately or forgetfully I don't know, but it stayed there.

The next day I was back to school like Rodney motherfucking Dangerfield—school, and an algebra midterm I'd forgotten all about. I caught a dizzy spell halfway through, sat with my thumb-knuckles pressed to my eyelids for five minutes, never quite recovered. Ended up with what your man George W. Bush would call a gentleman's C. A month before, it would have been my biggest problem. Biggest I'd admit, anyway.

I had another spell the next day, soon as I woke up. What was equilibrium, in a crib like that? I felt dizzy even when I wasn't, just from the combo-stench of blood and misjudgment hanging in the air. It was astonishing how quickly those guys turned a good thing, a rent-free life, into a hot mess. They saw it as an opportunity to concentrate full-time on their music—so far so good, right?—and to that end Knowledge Born quit his part-time bar-backing gig, and Twenty-Twenty one-upped him by canceling his already-theoretical job hunt. I never knew what Roam did; his primary skill appeared to be passing out in midsentence, with a lit blunt in hand or a fork frozen halfway to his mouth, and holding the pose through eight hours of slumber. Made me feel like I was in one of those movies where some asshole has the power to freeze time, waking up to that shit.

The studio never opened for business until nine or ten at night, when everybody was good and bent. I did my homework then, with the goal of falling asleep before they resumed their living room salon. The TV jabbered all day long, and K and Roam and Twenty stayed parked on the couches, talking over it, too broke to do anything else. They somehow managed to pull together six dollars for a nickel bag and two Optimos every few hours, but the process was rife with bad feelings and caustic remarks and compromise. It was like watching a Senate subcommittee debate a bill on C-SPAN, only with profanity and black people.

I anted up for smoke when I was asked, but that wasn't often, because nobody wanted to sponge off the mascot. You can't freeload when nobody's paying, so I no longer felt particularly indebted, either. I was torn between trying to stay unobtrusive—hard when your room's a futon—and this unspoken thing of wanting to be around K-Born and Twenty-Twenty all the time because we'd been through some fucked-up shit together and it needed talking through, or communal ignoring. I still hadn't been to visit my mother. I didn't even know which hospital she was in, because by the time I'd thought to ask, Reggie was gone. I pushed all that away—the new Karen, the new Billy—with a vehemence and a rigor that shocks and saddens me, when I look back at it now. At the time, I guess I called myself growing up.

A week later Twenty-Twenty pawned his eight-track, and the

studio shut down for good. Knowledge Born was furious, whether he had a right to be or not, and the two of them nearly came to blows in the living room. The beef got drowned beneath a fifth of gin Roam sprang for, but by midnight Knowledge Born was two hours into a drunken talking jag, oblivious to the fact that nobody wanted to hear a word he had to say, and Twenty-Twenty walked across the room and knocked him out. Didn't utter a word, just swung that big right meathook, dropped him from the couch onto the rug. He was still there when I woke up the next morning. Everybody acted like it hadn't happened.

The three of them lasted another eleven months in there, ran the tab past thirty grand before E.B. Holding finally got it together and threw them out. What they lived on, how they ate, I don't know. I didn't visit. Twenty-Twenty bugged out when the eviction finally came—got drunk, broke back into the apartment the next night and smashed every window in the place with that same baseball bat. The cops showed up and hauled him off, with half the building watching. I have no idea where he and Roam and Knowledge Born are now.

As for my dizzy spells, they went away about a month after Karen came home, all on their own. Go fucking figure.

ll that history was pressing down on me with a particular weight the day Billy started talking, because my big morning activity had been appropriating Karen's prized chef's knife and sawing my father's locks down to a reasonable length. The pile of hair-ropes on the floor looked like a litter of newborn rodents, but as Twenty-Twenty had taught me and various Rastas real and pseudo had since reconfirmed—in particular my former herb-game boss, Jafakin'-ass Abraham Lazarus, and the posse of bobo yardie motherfuckers who spent their lives in his Crown Heights apartment watching cricket matches on cable and chanting down Babylon— severed locks were to be disposed of carefully, if at all.

A bluish twilight was creeping across the ceiling when I looked in on my father. He'd just put the finishing touches on a six-hour nap, and he was sitting up, rubbing his thumb against the blunt cross section of a dread. I'd clipped his nails and buzzed his beard a few days earlier and he hadn't even appeared to notice, so this seemed like a good sign.

"Billy," I said, sitting on the bed's edge. He turned his head without dropping the lock, looked at me through the cracks between his fingers.

"You know who I am, right?"

He blinked.

"I'm Dondi, man. Your son."

"Dondi," he repeated. Whether it was awe or stupor that robbed him of inflection, I couldn't tell, didn't know him well enough to judge.

"How did you die?" he asked.

"How—what?"

"I killed myself," my father whispered. "I did it with a rope." His hand swept toward his neck and halted inches away, as if it were too sore to touch.

I'd forgotten his questions about hell, written them off as rhetoric or gibberish. Now, I realized they were neither.

"Listen, Billy. We're not dead. This isn't hell."

He laughed, poked me in the arm like I had told a good one.

"It's not heaven, either."

His face closed up.

"Follow me, here," I said, not wanting to give Billy time to reflect on what he'd just lost. If you're under the impression that you're chilling in the afterlife, problem-free, lying on clean sheets and being groomed and waited on and drifting peacefully in and out of consciousness and then *blam! Uh-uh, pal, welcome back to earth,* that could kind of break you. Re-break you, whatever.

"You came to New York, alright? Dengue drove you to Mexico sixteen years ago, and I don't know what happened after that, but now you're home. I found you a few days ago, but you've been back longer. You were writing stuff in the tunnels. Do you remember that?"

He shook his head.

"What's the last thing you do remember?"

"Putting the rope around my neck."

"So you don't know how you got to the States? Or how you wound up on the fifteenth floor of a building I just happened to be at?"

He swallowed, and then, ever so gingerly, touched the fingertips of his right hand to his throat, and winced. I realized I was asking the wrong questions.

"Why were you trying to kill yourself?"

Billy closed his eyes. After a moment, his hand moved from his throat to his forehead.

"Who's still alive?"

I knew what he meant. "Just Dengue and Cloud."

"Bring them here."

"Cloud's locked up. And Dengue's blind. He doesn't leave his house."

Neither fact seemed to surprise. "So we'll go to him. You know where."

"Of course. He's the guy I ask about you."

Billy straightened, looked me in the eye. "And what does he say? What do you know?"

How do you answer that? How do you even try?

"What do I know? I know I grew up without a father. I know there was nobody here for me when—"

Billy cut me off, and not with a sob or an apology. "What about Bracken?"

It was unseasonably hot that day, every window open wide and saying *Aaaah*, and just then crazy-ass Rockwell, wandering the handball courts in the park across from our building, cawed his trademark salespitch. The most indiscreet dude in the history of illegal business, Rockwell distinguished himself from the competition by shouting "I got crack for sale" at the top of his lungs, like a human Mister Softee truck.

I used it as a chance to count to ten, the way they say you should when you feel anger welling up. Who *they* are, I don't know, but I'm glad I didn't buy their book, because that shit doesn't work at all.

"What *about* Bracken?"

"Is he still—is he powerful?"

"He's Transit president. Running for mayor."

"Oh, God." The back of Billy's skull thudded against the headboard. "Oh, Jesus Christ. Please, get me to Dengue right now."

He reached for his pants. I went and brushed my teeth. Ten

minutes later, we were on the train. It was the first time my old man and I had ever been out together without one of us carrying the other.

The ride was quiet—standoffish, I'm tempted to say, but a standoff takes two. Your boy here, I was trying to keep hold of my dignity: ask no questions if he had none for me, show no further emotion until Billy flashed some of his own.

Dengue buzzed us in, and by the time we reached his landing the Ambassador's body filled the doorframe, backlit by the glow of a reading lamp he must have turned on for our benefit. Glue fumes wafted down the hall. Normally, he'd have been more cautious about letting them escape.

"Billy motherfucking Rage," Fever boomed, lifting a Wray & Nephew bottle in salute. "Welcome home, brother. Get over here and give me a hug." Billy walked into his arms and disappeared, like an insect enveloped by a Venus flytrap.

I couldn't believe how easy it was, or how angry that made me. But if you look at anything for long enough, it gets complicated, becomes more than one thing. The hug stretched on, and the second thing revealed itself as fear, and I felt better. Dengue and my father did not want to let go because everything that followed this embrace would be harder and more painful. The questions and the answers, the ordeal of accounting for all that time.

Eventually they shuffled inside, elbows hooked around each other's necks. Dengue palmed my father's face, then flopped down on his throne.

"You look like shit, brother," he said, resting the bottle on the windowsill and plunging his hands down the chair's various cleavages in search of errant glue tubes. "Now. Talk to me." His hands reemerged empty, and he snatched up the rum. "K.D., get us some glasses. He's a prince, your son. Much respect to Wren for that. K.D., what a' gwan wi de ishen? You holding?"

"Yeah," I said from the sink. Every vessel in the house was filthy. "But I'm not sure he should be smoking. Or drinking."

Dengue reclined and spun the bottlecap back and forth in its grooves with his thumb, loosening and tightening. "Of course he should. Find some papers and roll up. None of your glass-dick hippie shit tonight. You in the presence of kings." He grinned. "Billy Rage. What the fuck, nigga? What letter you wanna be?"

I bent to look at Billy through the space between the rangetop and the cabinets. It was clear he had no idea what the Ambassador was talking about.

"R."

"No doubt." Dengue heaved himself up and turned to face the industrial shelving unit lining the wall. He ran his hands over a dozen alphabet racers, reading the giant letterforms glued to each vehicle like b-boy braille, and stopped when he found *R*.

"I'll take . . ." The Ambassador's fingers fluttered. "A." He placed the two cars on the ground and switched them on, then located their remote controls and tossed one at the couch.

"First one clockwise around the room wins. See if you can beat the blind man. Your son can't."

Billy picked up the controller, fisted the lever, and pushed it forward. The *R* car's monster tires spun against the carpet and took off. Dengue's truck pursued. The Ambassador navigated by sound; the vehicles had a particular pitch when they were stuck, another while cruising close to the baseboards or the furniture, a third when they were marooned out in the middle of the floor.

Billy's face brightened with attention and delight as his racer careened around the room, slamming against Dengue's machine and dodging obstacles. For a minute, the two of them were twelve again. Younger, actually, since at twelve their playthings had already been giant steel monsters.

The *A* sideswiped the *R*, knocking it over, and Dengue, cackling, cruised to victory. I deposited three glasses on the coffeetable, which was a sheet of fiberglass laser-cut into the jagged shape of the wildstyle piece painted on it, and supported by three sawed-off portions of a parking meter leg. These things had once sold for mid-four figures, during the '90s graffiti-design renaissance—or had been on sale for that amount, anyway; who knows if anybody ever bought one. Dengue had traded for his. Owning it constituted legal proof of blindness.

The Ambassador splashed rum into and around the glasses. The toast went unspoken. We drank. Billy's eyes roved over Dengue's floor-to-ceiling collection of art, junk, ephemera. I wondered what he thought of it all, but that was low on the list of things I wondered.

Looking at Billy was like watching a steak thaw. I realized I should've brought him here right off the bat. It was Dengue who'd seen my father off, after all, not Karen. Served me right for being a fucking romantic.

I balanced a Les McCann album on my knees—I have perhaps failed to mention that Dengue was once known as DJ Fever Funk, and thus long winding snakes of LPs buttressed the stereo cabinet, with Count Machuki leaning against Count Basie and the Lafayette Afro Rock Band rubbing up on Millie Jackson—and began breaking apart a nugget of Blueberry Clusterfuck. Dengue sniffed the air and nodded approvingly, then turned to Billy.

"I want the whole story," he said. "Everything, from the time you stepped out of my van to when you walked in here just now."

Billy rolled his glass between his palms. He'd only nipped at the rum. "There's a lot I don't remember. I sent some letters, didn't I?"

"Yeah," I said. "At first. You were working your way south. Said you wanted to get to the Amazon and see the rainforests. Last letter I'm aware of, you'd gotten there and you said the plants were sentient beings, and you were going to learn how to cure diseases and shit by communicating with their 'higher energetic selves.'"

Billy nodded. "Their spirits."

The way he said it, I knew sarcasm wasn't the appropriate response. But it was all I had. I grew up with my mother.

"How'd that work out?"

Billy placed his drink on the table. "It almost killed me. I thought it had. But . . . it was amazing."

He dug into his pocket and pulled out the travel-pouch I'd cut off him at Patrick's, rolled thin. He unfurled it, dumped six of those cut-glass vials on the table, opened each and smelled the contents. Five went back into the pouch. The last he handed to me.

"Drip half on there. As evenly as possible."

"Drip what where? In case y'all forgot, I don't see so goddamn good."

"I can fix that," Billy said.

"What, you learn optometry too?"

"I just need the right plants."

"No shit?"

"Billy," I said, "what am I dripping on the joint, and why?"

"It's an entheogenic resin made from the essences of four different plants cooked together. Plus my blood, and ash from burnt pieces of my hair. The recipe was given to me by a shaman who received it from a very wise tree called El Purga."

Entheogenic is a word you probably don't know, but I do because the shit is Greek, which is not to say that I'm smarter than you. *En* meaning in, *theo* meaning God. The god within. The ancients used it to compliment writers and artists so dope they seemed divinely inspired, like my boy Homer. We use it to mean a substance on which you will trip balls.

"And why?"

"Because I can't remember everything important, but the resin can. It will show you."

You recall a few chapters back when I was popping all that junk about *skepticism is an admirable trait, but so is asking yourself if you're really such a fucking Master of the Universe that things might not be happening* blah blah blah, something about the duckbilled platypus? Well, that shit is difficult to put into practice when your father's talking about getting psychedelic cooking tips from a tree, even if you found his ass atop a magical staircase and consider yourself willing to entertain whatever.

I'm taking the time to acknowledge this out of respect for you, the reader, because I hate stories with fuzzy internal logic. Kids who've grown up on Harry Potter don't know any better, poor schmucks: the people in those books are constantly doing things that were impossible five minutes earlier. In a few years, you'll see. The Rowling generation's going to be the most fucked up yet. Whereas you could break into George Lucas's house right now, traipse into his study, and say, "Hey George, what exactly is a parsec?" and as soon as he finished taking his bong hit, he'd be able to explain. Probably before security arrived. Or take Tolkien: not only could J.R.R. have told you why they didn't just ride those giant fucking eagles straight into the heart of Mordor instead of walking, he'd have done so in High Elvish, or the Tongue of the Woodland Realm, your choice.

I opened the vial and let the green-brown resin ooze onto the cannabis in a thin, honeylike trail. Twisted up a bone and offered it to Billy. He shook his head.

"It's for the two of you."

"Ambassador?"

Dengue made a peace sign, and I lodged the joint between his fingers. He brought it to his lips, sucked when he heard the *flick-whoosh* of the lighter, then leaned back and puffed until smoke encircled his dome like clouds around some bulbous mountaintop.

You had to be vigilant, blazing with Dengue. He hit a spliff until you stopped him or his fingers burned—got lost in the experience, forgot the protocols. This time, though, his head lolled after the third hit, one palm covering his eyes and the other resting on his rising-falling stomach, joint forgotten between two knuckles and a trail still twirling from the tip.

I leaned over and extracted it, then mean-mugged Billy.

"You and me," I said, "after this, we've got some shit to sort out."

I'd been going for *don't think you're off the hook*, but I failed to tough up the inflection, and instead it came out more like *you're gonna call me, right?*

"Travel willingly and well," my father said, and made one of those palms-pressed-together prayer-bows, which I fucking hate. Corny on old white yoga dudes, peace-and-blessings-type Negroes, and everybody else who buys weed from me.

"I'll try," I said, and took a wicked draw.

The smoke hit the back of my throat, and right away I knew this was different from any drug I'd ever fucked with. I pulled again and felt as if every organ and muscle, every molecule in my body, wanted to simultaneously shit and puke and come.

Just so you know, I did plenty of research in anticipation of committing these events to paper, went so far as to email my former Whoopty Whoo Ivy League We's A Comin' Academy faculty road dog, David "D-Fine" Feingold, and read every drug book he recommended: Tom Wolfe on Ken Kesey, Hunter Thompson on himself, even old A-Hux strolling through the doors of perception. I was hoping I could jack somebody's approach.

But first of all, with all due respect to the 1960s and LSD and ether and mescaline and Timothy Leary, none of that synthesized domestic product can carry the jockstrap of a single vial Billy brought back from the rainforest. With acid and MDMA, the chemicals sort of drape themselves over your consciousness, and you peer through them at the world. This was another thing entirely—world-obliterating, world-creating—and it was coming at me fast.

And second of all, I don't get what's supposed to be so great about Hunter Thompson. His shtick gets old about fifty pages in, if you ask me. *The Electric Kool-Aid Acid Test* was better, but it didn't give me anything I could steal, since a) it's pretty clear that Tom is sticking to what they taught him in journalism school, i.e. "get as close to your subject as possible by listening and talking and observing, but under no circumstances zonk out together in a Day-Glo school bus crawling with venereal diseases, no matter how tempting it may be," and b) as expressive and zeitgeisty as his punctuation is, it's not the kind of thing you can bite without looking like a biter. Only one person per grammatical system is allowed to express psychotropic euphoria by writing shit like psycho::::::tropic !!!!freaking::::::eu—pho—ri:::::: a::::a::::a!!!!, and it kind of reads like a cheerleading routine even when he does it.

I went shuddery and weak and closed my eyes, trying to go with the feeling, get beyond it, breathe deep and steady. I don't know how long I did that, but it seemed like forever, and when I opened my eyes again the sensation had passed and everything was pitch black. All around me was a huge vibrating sound, a constant hum that if you listened to carefully you began to understand was made up of the rustling of plants in the breeze and the rush of the breeze through the air and the syncopated drip-splash-evaporation of water droplets and the buzz of insects and the call of parrots and the dart of lizards and the decomposition of dead leaves and the growth of trees. And yet it was all one web of sound, so harmonious that if you didn't concentrate on listening it disappeared, became like silence.

I listened for maybe half an hour, isolating and digging on different parts the way you might check out the drums, then the bass, then the piano. Light started to suffuse the world, a little at a time, as if the sun was rising, but I knew it was midday and my vision was coming back. I saw what I'd heard—and heard so well that seeing it was no surprise. That made me trust the resin, whose choice it must have been for me to listen before I looked.

First were the trees, so lush and massive they canopied the sky. Then great shafts of mottled light, beaming through them like reverse searchlights and playing over the fluorescent, spongy moss and loamy earth. And finally the countless layers and levels of green that lay between, intertwined and restless and alive: with birds, with bugs, with monkeys I heard but could not see, and most of all alive with itself, as if Life were—I don't know, maybe this sounds stupid, but as if Life were this string of energy extending from each plant and animal and connecting each of them to all the others in a pattern so complex it formed a web like the web of sound. To be somewhere so peaceful and chaotic and unbent by human desire was to understand how dead and colonized most of the planet is. And also to glimpse something of the circular eternity of an experience we only see as a straight line, running from birth to death.

As I stood thinking these thoughts, a new sound, strange and foreign, imposed itself over the others. I turned toward it and saw three men, a hundred feet away, walking in single file. They followed the course of a path so faint I never would have picked it out. But now, tracing the distance between us, I saw that I was standing on it. I braced myself to be seen, and just as quickly realized I would not be, understood that although I saw and heard, I did not *stand*, would not follow them by *walking*. I was not here bodily, but in some other way. I knew that one of those approaching was Billy, and that whatever I experienced was what the resin—or the consciousness behind it, which was and was not his—deemed essential.

The first man came upon me: brown-skinned and black-haired, with eyes like polished onyx. He was clothed in two strings of red and white beads, one laid diagonally across each shoulder to form an X over his chest. A thin cord encircled his waist, and his foreskin was attached to it by a small clasp—so he didn't flop around when he walked, I guess. Through his septum ran a copper rod; hammered silver-dollar circles of the metal sat in both earlobes. His chest was flat, his body smooth and faintly muscled. He walked neither slowly nor fast, looked not at the ground before him but at the tops of trees and the flight paths of birds, as another man would scan a newspaper. I might have put his age at fifty, and been off by a decade in either direction.

The next man walked twenty paces behind. He wore the same beads and cord. A copper rod pierced each cheek like a set of whiskers. He was younger and taller, with the same teardrop-shaped eyes, and he sang to himself in a high, flutey voice, so quietly that the jungle swallowed up the song the instant he passed.

Last came Billy, thin and haggard, in cutoff jeans and sneaks, the straps of a rucksack digging into his bare shoulders. His hair was pulled into a wisp of a ponytail, his face scarlet and scaly-raw beneath his tan. He glanced up from the path and our eyes met, or at least I stared straight into his, and in that instant I went from thinking Billy's skin looked like it hurt to feeling the sting myself—and also knowing that it was the farthest thing from his mind, which was muddled by deprivation and electric with excitement, fear.

Getting delirious and lightheaded is a bitch when you're not even there. But that's what Billy felt, so the sensation hit me too, and I had to retreat a little ways into myself to keep my shit together. My father could barely put one foot in front of the other, and if the Dickclip Brothers noticed, they didn't seem to care. For a few seconds I felt helpless, irate, and then I kind of reached into Billy's consciousness, and realized I was wrong. Billy's state was deliberate, necessary, a preparation for the ritual to come. The knowledge bloomed inside me, the way the light had spread across the rainforest. I no more questioned it than I had the gift of vision.

Each moment, Billy's mind and body were becoming more and more my own. Following him along the path involved no choice. Knowing what he knew required no exertion. He was an apprentice to the men leading the way, and under their supervision he'd undertaken *La Dieta*, the diet: forsaken salt, sugar and human contact for months, made himself like a man wandering the desert so that his ego might recede and the spirits he sought to know would respond to his body's calls for help.

The path led to a small clearing, a spot where fire had burned back the jungle. The shamans were seated on a fallen log. Billy crouched before them, slid his backpack to the ground, unzipped it and removed a plastic kid's mug festooned with pictures of Gobots. The poor fucking Gobots, man. It was perfect, somehow. I don't know if you remember, but Gobots were the wack American-made answer to Transformers. Even their names were stupid. The leader was called Leader-1. The helicopter was Cop-Tur.

Billy passed the elder shaman a plastic bottle, half full of murky liquid. The man held it up to the light, uttered a few jungle-bitten syllables, and the word *bazaguanco* passed into my mind: from his lips or Billy's brain, I don't know which. My father trickled some bazaguanco into the Gobots cup and swirled it around, heart thudding in his/my chest. It smelled of warm, vegetative decay, like the garden compost bin at Karen's married-to-a-doctor homegirl's place in Woodstock, where we used to spend weekends once in a while until they got divorced.

The bazaguanco tasted like it smelled, and Billy gulped it down with eyes squeezed shut. I remembered what he'd said about the recipe for the resin, and as the brew bubbled in the cauldron of Billy's gut and the shattering of this reality by the next grew imminent, I decided it made sense. There were a gazillion plants up in this motherfucker. Which three or four could be combined into drugs or medicine was not the kind of thing you puzzled out by trial-and-error.

I'd like to keep coming up with fresh ways to describe the sensation of getting knocked dick-in-the-dirt by unfathomable rainforest drugs, but honestly, I don't even know where to begin. I read up on bazaguanco later, and what every new age gringo seeker and traditional-yet-Internet-savvy herbal healer and psychopharmacology doctoral candidate seems to agree on is that if there is a God, this is the shit that gets *Him* high.

People drink it and fall down energetic wormholes into fiery hells; they float through internal eternities as specks of light and then return to earth with the worst hangovers of their lives and no more pesky heroin addiction, no more crippling lifelong depression. No more cancer. They write lengthy accounts of interdimensional sojourns and terrifying confrontations, talk about vomiting up the dark matter of their deepest fears and traumas, poking at the goo with a stick the next day unable to discern what it could be. They fucking ramble on and on, and even if you've taken bazaguanco yourself, or smoked some other crazy shit and done the virtual tour, these accounts read as half amazing, half gobbledygook, which is why I'm dancing around all of it like that fucking dude Britney Spears married who tried to rap.

The younger shaman took a thin mat from the pack and unrolled it on the ground. Billy lay down. The elder leaned toward him, elbows on his knees.

Now our teachers will be yours. Billy nodded, exhaled a long, shuddery breath, and closed his eyes. As scared and *dieta*-diminished as he was, I sensed relief. He'd had his fill of these guys, these middlemen.

And then the bazaguanco took over and we were falling through blackness—and I mean fast, none of this tra-la-la trippy float-falling you see in movies, I'm talking a straight plummet like somebody threw us off a rooftop. Flailing, windmilling, bracing to hit bottom any second and pancake, and all the while it was getting colder and colder until breathing hurt, the lungs too tender for the harsh air. From the depths came a fast-rushing sound and then bats were everywhere, thousands of them shooting past us, their stink and screams filling the emptiness, the bright yellow malevolent streaks of their eyes all that was visible.

We fell through them and then everything slowed down. The air grew warmer, thicker, turned gelatinous. Instead of falling we slid through it, slower and slower and then not at all, and it oozed into every orifice, filled our noses and ears and assholes, our mouths and eyes, the most invasive and unpleasant sensation you can imagine. I could hear my teeth grinding, or rather Billy's—this snot-air conducted sound the way water does, amplified and nuanced it. You know what I mean if you've ever cracked your knuckles while lying in a bathtub, ears submerged, and skeeved yourself out at how calcified and loud and brittle the bone-on-bone grind sounds.

A rhythmic pounding shook the world, and for an instant I imagined us from the outside, if there was an outside: we were slivers of orange rind suspended in a giant Jell-O mold, and somebody,

Bill Cosby probably, was banging his fist against the table. *Boom. Boom. Boom.* Each reverberation loosened the mucus for a moment and we slid, stopped, slid again. Suddenly we were through it, free of the awful suck and squelch. I'd imagine being born felt something like this, except instead of blinding hospital lights and sweat-drenched maternal ecstasy there was only greater panic because we were underwater and whereas before, mollycoddled by snot, we had somehow been able to breathe, now we most certainly could not.

The water was clear, tasted like river—subtle hints of stone, lichen and mud, a sweet finish that lingers on the palate, pairs well with poached salmon and death by drowning—and it was writhing with snakes, yellow-and-black striped, above and below us, a goddamn commuter highway. The name *naka naka* popped into my mind, *poisonous* hot on its heels. And still the *boom, boom* tremoring the water, riling the snakes. We swam toward it. My/Billy's lungs burned. Any second they were sure to forfeit, fill with water and doom us to a mossy riverbed demise.

And then a great thick tree trunk came into view, shape vague through snakes and silt, the distance to it impossible to gauge, and the *boom, boom* became *buh-boom, buh-boom,* as if to say *I see you too* or maybe imitate our heartbeats. With each stroke the tree loomed larger, until it was massive and we threw ourselves upon it, arms and legs spread wide, fingers scrabbling against the rough bark. Billy's body surged with a relief I didn't understand, since as near as I could tell we were still drowning.

Buh-buh-boom. Buh-buh-boom. Light began to penetrate the water, pushing deeper with each moment. The surface of the river seemed to fall toward us, welcome and yet terrifying. It felt as if the weight might crush us, like a French press coming down on coffee grinds.

Billy breached the water. Or rather the water breached him, and settled at the level of his heaving chest, still flush against the trunk. Fifty feet above his head, the tree flared into a crown of limbs and leaves. They overhung the body in wild arcs, like the trails of spent firecrackers falling back toward earth. The trunk itself seemed to erupt from the river, like a launching rocket. No other life was visible: there was only water in all directions, and this regal giant speared straight through it like a toothpick dropped by God.

Gracias, anciano sabio, my father whispered. *Creo que te conozco. ¿Se llaman El Purga, verdad?*

The response was spoken not out loud, but inside Billy's head. *Do not embarrass yourself with Spanish. It is no more my language than any other. Yes, some know me as El Purga. You can call me the Undisputed King of the Broadway Line, son.*

Billy gaped up at him.

Just kidding, motherfucker. Now fall back. This river is my friend. She will support you.

Billy dropped his arms and legs, let the water take him. He drifted a few yards from El Purga and bobbed there in a standing position, nipple deep, two-thirds less buoyant than Jesus.

Let's have a look at you, El Purga said, and from the tree's highest boughs shot seven beams of light. One hit Billy between the eyes. Another bored into the center of his chest. A third touched down atop his head. Others were directed at points submerged; I could see them cutting through the water, pure white, like a series of thin ropes connecting Billy to the tree.

You ever go to the barber and get buzzed with the clippers in that one small spot behind the left ear that feels mad good, almost sexually so, and your eyes float back in your skull and you wonder if that's where your endocrine gland is located and also if dude knows what he's doing right now and whether there's some kind of unspoken homo undercurrent to the whole haircutting ritual and that's why everybody in black barbershops stays talking about broads and politics and boxing all the time? It was like that: warm, jangly and electric. But much longer, and all up and down the center of the body, and far more intense.

I felt it, but for the first time since I'd seen him, I was locked outside of Billy's mind, reduced to watching. Every few seconds my father would twitch, or moan, eyes closed and eyeballs roving beneath the lids as if he were having a nightmare. I started to notice dark specks of matter floating up the beams of light, toward El Purga. They seemed to be coming out of Billy, and soon the shafts were full of them and the expression on my father's face had become one of intense pain.

Halfway between my father and the tree the seven slim rays fused into a single thick one. The specks clustered together, like metal shavings drawn to a magnet, with more still coming out of Billy. Soon there was a huge black column of them, slow-turning like a rotisserie. Then the beams cut off and Billy's eyes popped open and he thrashed as if drowning.

El Purga's voice sounded inside his head: *Rage!* Billy's head jerked up and he screamed, because the black column was a black column no more but a subway train, a lifesized New York City F to be precise, and it was chugging toward him at full speed, barreling down invisible tracks but making real life noise, hellacious quantities of it. Slapped across both sides were burners and they read KILROY DONDI VANCE and IT'S A BOY and WREN 209 and HOT MAMA and IMMORTAL FIVE ALIVE.

You might, at this point, ask: Oh, it's like *that*, El Purga, you sick bastard?

Yeah, it's like that. And that's the way it is.

The train plowed into Billy and he disappeared into the river, plastered to its grille. Then I was underwater with him, father and son standing inside the lead car as the train shot straight down, tunneling through blackness. And in the middle of the car, oblivious to us, a younger Billy and a very young Wren 209 fucked on the floor, wrapped up in a rough green blanket with her on top, cowgirl style, titties bouncing, head thrown back, palms pressed to his chest, and out of everything I'd seen thus far, this was the shit I really, truly wish I hadn't. Billy stood and watched, dumbstruck and sad, but not for long because behind us came a voice, *Yo, nigga,* and he whipped around.

Dengue?

It was the Ambassador, all right, circa 1987, young and sighted, in an Adidas jumpsuit and matching yellow-and-green-when-it's-time-to-get-ill shelltoes.

Yes and no. Well, no. You've got some serious chakra blockage, you know that? There is much healing to do.

El Purga?

Tell me what you hope to learn.

I want to heal myself, and others.

A shock of pain, a flash of white, and then I/Billy was on the ground, staring up at Anastacio Bracken.

Don't tell me what you think I wanna hear, shitstain. Up came the nightstick. Blammo, right across the ribcage. *You wanna learn to kill me, don't you?*

Billy heaved for breath, squinted down the length of his body.

I don't know.

Bark began to grow over Bracken's boots, and then his legs. I knew I'd never use the expression "treed up" again.

I could teach you that. It was El Purga's voice now. At least, it was the voice he had first used, the one Billy'd heard inside his skull.

But by the time I do, if I do, you will no longer feel the need. Rise.

Billy obeyed, and as he stood, the train split open and a jet of water, a geyser, propelled him to the surface of the river. He floated on his back and listened to his heart, his breath. El Purga loomed above him, motionless and silent. Greasy black globules, the consistency of chicken fat, bobbed to the surface, one after the next, and spread across the water.

High in El Purga's branches, a faint light shone. The tree's voice was a whisper now.

I will give you a Karos, Billy Rage. A song. Memorize it. Use it to summon me. Later, you will learn other karos, for other teachers. Or you will not. I cannot tell with you, and usually I can.

The melody El Purga sang was spare and beautiful, ten notes

that sounded torn from nature: a bird's song, a waterfall's descent. They sang it together, Billy and the tree, a blissful smile on my old man's face. Once through, twice, and by the third time the world around me was sunspotting and fading, and I felt a tingling sensation and thought maybe the resin had run its course. I tried to fade too, closed my eyes and hoped that a few seconds later they'd open in Fever's living room.

Instead, I dropped into what felt like one of those accidental-but-incredibly-deep five-minute naps that leave you twice as tired as before, and woke up in a darkness rank with jousting smells: unwashed humanity and fermenting vegetables, charred animal meat and sweet, cloying smoke. It was a combo that didn't necessarily rule out Chez Dengue, if he'd ordered goat roti and sparked some cheap incense while I was gone, but as the Ambassador did not live in a candelit mud-and-straw hut swarming with mosquitos and subject to hundred-degree swelter, I quickly ruled the possibility out.

The Billy Rage who sat before me, crosslegged and hunched over a wooden table, was a different man from the one I'd left harmonizing with the spirit of a tree in the middle of a river, a bazaguanco trance, and La Dieta.

He'd been grubbing his ass off, for one thing. Gone were the sunken eyes and jelly-limbed frailty, usurped by a gut that overhung the plastic waistband of the ratty athletic shorts comprising his attire. It pained me to think that he would lose that weight and more by the time we met. The muscles of his arms were lean and ropey, and his skin bore no trace of rosacea red. He seemed like a man who had overcome something, emerged on the other side. And though I was a mere observer now, it seemed clear what that was.

Around the hut's perimeter stood jars and bottles, three and four rows deep, casting long flickering shadows on the walls. Clumps of drying plants hung from the ceiling. I watched Billy rise and walk to a corner. He bent at the knees, unscrewed the top of a container and withdrew a fragrant palmful, then returned to the table and sprinkled it over a bowl. He repeated the process twice more, moving with the confidence of a photographer in his darkroom. On the third trip Billy hesitated, furrowed his brow, sang a string of notes into the heavy air. He finished and stood waiting, then nodded as if to a reply and selected his next ingredient.

I saw the man standing at the hut's mouth before my father did. It was the younger of the two shamans. He'd out-aged Billy in the intervening years, and there was a bunch more crap sticking out of his face—a triangular rod through his septum, three more straight ones through his earlobes. Maybe it was based on status or ritual or something, I don't know, but the extent of his adornment seemed poseurish. He reminded me of those gutter-punks you see sitting in front of the big monument on Astor Place, with their studded leather dog collars and face tats, everything orchestrated to look reckless and boss—and it would, except that if you watch for more than two seconds you'll catch them flicking their eyes at every passerby, desperate to be scorned, feared, judged, whatever. Or my "spiritual" custies, who aren't satisfied unless you notice that they're wearing cruelty-free jeans and brewing fair trade coffee.

"Billy!" He said it a little louder than necessary, like a gym teacher.

"Esteban."

"It is time. Are you not ready?"

Billy poured a brown juice into his bowl, gave the potion a sniff and a stir, then emptied it carefully into a jar and nodded. The shaman watched with an impatience bordering on fury. It was unclear whether Billy moved so deliberately to irk him or because that was the way he did things now.

"You should never have been entrusted with this responsibility."

Billy screwed a lid onto the jar, tucked it beneath his arm, brushed past.

I'd expected a village outside. Instead, there was only a vegetable patch, and a fire pit enclosed by stones. The swarm and teem of the jungle was shouting distance away, huge and dense and sudden. Perhaps Billy wanted to live near his teachers. The dim, massive shape of a tree that might have been El Purga dominated what little I could make out. As my eyes adjusted to the darkness, I realized trees that might have been El Purga stood everywhere. I wondered how many Billy knew.

He and Esteban walked in silence. After a few minutes, the jungle opened onto a clearing the size of a basketball court. A wide circle of torches blazed, and by each one stood a man, bare to the waist, painted in red designs. In the center, surrounded by four more torches, lay a pyre of wood, and on the pyre was a man, a dead man. The old shaman.

Esteban held out his hand, and Billy gave him the jar. He took a gulp, and passed the brew around the circle. Billy drank last, and when he finished Esteban strode into the middle, bowed before the corpse. The men grew still.

"Tonight we rejoice as your spirit flies free. We ask that you continue to protect and advise us, dear teacher, as we honor you by returning your shell to the dust."

He uprooted each of the four torches, and used it to light a corner of the pyre. The flames shot forward, met. The men watched silently, and soon the drink kicked in. Some wandered a few steps before falling to the ground. Others crumpled where they stood. Soon, Billy and Esteban were the only men left on their feet. Neither looked as if he would remain that way for long.

With what appeared to be great effort, Esteban rolled his eyes toward Billy. His head followed after a slight delay.

"You will leave, now that he is gone."

Billy stared into the flames. "He wasn't what kept me here."

Esteban's smile was cruel. "Ah, but he was."

Now Billy looked at him. "Others protect me. I'm well past being afraid."

"Such arrogance! You're only a guest here."

"The teachers decide who they will teach."

Esteban took a step toward my father, moving as if knee-deep in mud. "I know your mind, gringo. You will take this knowledge away, to misuse where no one can see you. You are not a healer. You seek power. A fucking brujo in training!"

"And what are you, Esteban, with your jealousy and threats?" The words dripped from Billy's mouth in slow motion, as if he were drooling honey. "Who have you healed? Not even yourself." And with that, my father plopped straight down onto his ass. His hands fell into his lap. His head attempted to join them, and got as far as his chest.

Esteban lowered himself to the ground inch by inch, then crawled toward Billy until he was close enough to speak right in his ear. "You don't know who you're fucking with," he said in English, and collapsed onto his back.

The night collapsed with him. Imagine the world is a big sheet of paper and you're a little doodle-person right in the center, and the artist, let's call him Shitbag Larry, decides to start over, so he crumples up the sheet and the last thing you ever see is the edges of the universe beginning to furl in, like you're a black hole and the nature of light and matter is to pinwheel toward your stomach in a pure-white maelstrom. Those two images might not quite mesh, the crushed doodle and the black hole, but you know what? I don't fucking care, I'm sick of trying to describe all this oogabooga-ass drug shit in lucid terms. That was what it felt like to me, and if you want to quibble with my descriptions when I'm trying to recount some essentially unfathomable shit then once again, *Tuesdays with Morrie* might be more your speed. Over twelve million copies sold. Published in fifty countries. Called "as sweet and fresh as summer corn" by *USA Today*. No? All right then.

I think the resin knew what I could handle and what I couldn't, because my final experience under its guidance was just a flash. The blinding white of the imploding cosmos narrowed and focused, resolved into a shaft of noontime sunlight shooting through the broken slat of a cheap wooden curtain and terminating in a blotch of yellow that sat defiantly on a hotel room's scabrous concrete wall.

Cockroaches, broken glass, and congealing vegetative sludge covered the floor. The bed was a jumble of shit-spattered sheets, the narrow mattress teetering halfway off its metal frame. A ceiling fan's blades meandered through air like rancid butter. Beneath them sat a chair, and on the chair a coil of rope, and only after seeing all of this did I spot Billy, shivering in a corner with a blanket around his shoulders, hair matted and snarled.

He looked up, quick and scared, as if he'd seen a ghost. We locked eyes and boom, I was inside his mind again. Only now it was a place of devastation, a bombed-out city swarming with ghouls and pulsing with the terror of the final, demented survivor—as though someone had severed each and every fiber tying Billy into the web of life, connecting him to other living things. My father was alone, truly and hideously alone, as only a man trapped in a universe of his own devising can be. And yet the trap was so malicious and meticulous that only another person could have wrought it.

All I wanted was to escape—to abandon Billy before whatever had ruined him infected me. I had no time, no strength, to contemplate the path he'd traveled to this place. He had been attacked and bested, that was all that mattered. And though I knew he would not die, that right now he was sitting on a couch in Manhattan waiting for his son's return, I didn't want to see what happened next. Not even if it meant solving the mystery of his survival.

The choice, of course, was not mine: I would see what I was shown. Billy rose, staggered to the middle of the room, picked up the rope. A loop was knotted into it already. He pushed his head through, the image strangely birthlike. And there my father stood, motionless, the rope trailing down his body like a gruesome necktie. I knew he was not searching for the courage to kill himself, but rather the physical coherence necessary to perform the act. He was in too much disarray even for that.

We were only three feet apart. Without intending to, I began to breathe with him. It was effortless; I had inherited his lungs. Billy

fell into the chair and shut his eyes, then lurched forward and
opened them and saw me.

I know that doesn't make a lick of sense, but his face went quiz-
zical and unbelieving and he stood and squinted and raised a hand
as if to run it through the air and test whether I was real or just the
latest in a long line of delusions. Then the resin pulled the plug,
and I was out.

ou've got a tripartite drug economy in Fort Greene nowadays, unfolding within a four-block span and almost nobody the wiser. On the low end are the cats slinging on street corners up and down Myrtle, heads from the projects that bookend the neighborhood on the north side (and best believe the neighborhood does its damnedest to lean the other way, like there really was only one bookend), putting in banker's hours in front of Chinese takeout joints that make ninety percent of their money selling chicken-wing-and-french-fry combos, and whose Mandarin countermen squint at you like "fucking with me, homes?" from behind their bulletproof lazy Susans if you try to order, say, moo goo gai pan, even though there's a huge photograph of the dish right above them on the overhead menu, taken in 1981 from four inches away so that the food looks like a still from a stomach-surgery video.

The project kids sell no-grade bullshit, nickel bags of Mexican brown that smell like ankle-sweat, along with similar sock-stashed qualities and quantities of white and gray. They stay broke and confused and insecure about their business acumen, owing to the fact that they spend all day listening to various rappers brag about the sky-high money-piles they netted through similar means, not realizing that a) rappers are liars, and b) anybody who did stack real paper as a street dealer did so fifteen or twenty years ago, when crack-rock enthusiasts weren't yet a dying and incarcerated breed and people were, on the whole, stupider and had stupider haircuts.

You know that scene in every movie where a BMW full of twitchy Caucazoid teens sporting pastel collar-popped polo shirts rolls into the belly of the ghetto to purchase narcotics from some swaggering, jail-buffed indigene? The last time that actually happened was June 1993. A Connecticut Muffin shop opened on Myrtle a couple of years ago. That's what white people are doing in Fort Greene today: come for the baked goods, stay for the multimillion-dollar brownstones. Even if the new generation of residents were comfortable buying weed on the street from a sixteen-year-old black kid in a do-rag who's saving up to buy an Xbox, there's no way he'd sell to them, because they look like cops to him. Nor would his pesticide-laced dirt engender product loyalty.

Two blocks south of Myrtle, nestled between Dekalb Avenue's French bistros and overbearing black-boho coffeeshops, you've got the intermediate stage of the weed economy, herbgates disguised as businesses a half-step too downscale for what the neighborhood's become: an African hat shop, a video store, a taquería. These aren't like Uptown weed spots—those bodegas with one box of baking soda in the window and two cans of grape soda in the cooler and some scummy, pockmarked dude ignoring you from behind four inches of glass, places only a retarded six-year-old would mistake for legitimate businesses. Your average Fort Greene resident doesn't even know the spots are spots, and the weed they move—passable-to-pretty-good, parceled out in twenties and fifties—probably represents less than half their gross. The video store has a Cult section, which in my opinion is the mark of a decent video store.

Fort Greene is a gourmet market, like my former school, and herbgates of any description are ill equipped to compete in either product or discretion with the dealers cribbed up in quiet garden apartments on the treelined blocks of South Oxford and

Cumberland, Clinton and Lafayette. Needless to say, they're not on the corner with a sock full of nicks. They're sitting in their living rooms, checking their e-mail. And in a steel canister right next to the espresso machine, they've got three different kinds of superbad name-brand designer bud, ranging in price and quality from outrageous to otherworldly. The knuckleheads on Myrtle have no idea these people exist, and neither would I if Karen weren't a weedhead.

Some kids associate a certain perfume with their mothers, or maybe the smell of a homecooked meal. For your boy, it's General Tso's Vegi-Chicken from Kum Kau on Washington Ave and a fruity, trichome-laden Cannabis Cup—winning indica/sativa hybrid called White Widow. And thus, with my first conscious breath I was able to deduce the presence of Wren 209, even before getting a firm handle on where I was.

What I was came easier: hung over like a motherfucker. My head throbbed with a bonerlike intensity; my mouth felt full of cotton. And for good reason: I opened my eyes and found my lips stuck to Dengue's carpet by a gum of drying drool. I attempted to knuckle the crust out of my eyes and learned that my arm was immobile, fast asleep above my head. I groaned, rolled onto my back, and saw Billy and Karen sharing the couch, Fever reclining in his chair. All civilized and shit, like the three of them were about to convene a meeting of their monthly book club.

Karen uncrossed her legs, smoothed her skirt, recrossed them the other way. "Good morning," she said, though it was clearly nothing of the kind unless we were having an eclipse. I dragged myself into a sitting position, leaned back on the arm that wasn't full of pins-and-needles, and beckoned for the herb.

I took a hit, and felt the pressure in my head decrease like somebody inside had spun a wheel. Ain't a hangover been invented that a little White Widow and a greasy plate of diner eggs can't solve.

"What I miss? You kids friends now?"

The upper half of Karen's body bent away from Billy's until she was practically lying sideways across the arm of the couch, a real couples-therapy move. "I wouldn't go that far." She flicked her eyes at him the way a serpent flicks its tongue. "I'm glad he's out of bed," she said, like it was some kind of big-hearted concession, and folded her arms over her chest.

While I was watching her, Fever leaned forward and gangstered the spliff out of my hand. For a fat blind man—well, you know.

"Welcome to Thursday," he said, falling back into his seat. "You've been gone almost twenty-four hours."

"What about you?"

"I outweigh you two to one. I was only out for—what? Twelve?"

"Fourteen."

"Did we see the same things?"

"You saw what you saw," said Billy, staring at me like he knew what I was thinking—which would have been a hell of a trick, since I wasn't sure myself. He was all thawed out now, that much was clear, and something I could not pinpoint shined in his eyes. At first I took it for that worn serenity you sometimes see in people who know they should be dead. Then I realized I'd stopped flexing all the face-muscles in charge of hostility, and he was shining at me. A mild version of that fifteenth-floor threshold nausea gripped me, I guess because I'd just stepped into the present.

"Did you see me?" I asked. "In that hotel room—I felt like you saw me."

"It's possible."

"Actually, it's not."

Karen was chucking eye-daggers at all of us. I seemed to be the only one who noticed.

"That guy, Esteban. How did he . . . ?"

"So you met Esteban." Billy dropped his head. "I wasn't as strong as I thought. That's how."

The last of the joint vanished into Dengue's airplane hangar lungs. "Ay, but you was plenty bumbaclaat strong for a while, bredren. Yuh still 'ave dat obeah wisdom inna yuh head, and now yuh home wi' family an' ready fe mash down di wicked mon once and fe certain, like wi done plan. Di hour fe strike dat blow soon come. Jah-Jah carry yuh back widdin de nick a' time. Take a look at this shit."

The Ambassador rooted through the side-pocket of his chair, brought forth a mangled newspaper. It was the previous week's *New York Straphanger*, a four-page broadsheet published by the MTA. Graffiti writers have been subscribing for years, as a way to stay up on enforcement issues.

"'Coney Tunnels to Be Filled, Sealed,'" I read aloud. "'Transit Authority President Anastacio Bracken announced that the City will fill and seal a number of unused tunnels originating beneath the Coney Island Train Yard and extending north through parts of Brooklyn. These tunnels, originally built in the 1920s and unused since the track reconfigurations of the 1950s, run beneath current train lines. In a statement, Bracken cited 'potential structural issues,' if the tunnels were not dealt with now. 'This is a preventive measure,' he stressed, 'but one best taken immediately. Disruption to normal service will be minimal,' blah blah blah." I folded the paper, chucked it atop the coffee table.

"You know what this means," Dengue declared. I looked to Billy, since the Ambassador obviously wasn't talking to me. But my father just sat there, staring at nothing. It was Karen who reacted.

"I can't believe I'm sitting here listening to this," she said, and stood. "Guess what, guys? It's 2005. 1987 has *been* over. Get a fucking late pass." She glanced around for something to do, somewhere to go. Options were limited. She stalked over to the sink and started washing dishes. Karen can make anything an act of fury.

Nobody spoke. My mother scrubbed and splashed. I wondered what she'd do when she finished, imagined the three of us sitting in silence all night while Karen turned Dengue's lair sparkling clean out of pure ire.

Finally, Fever jerked his thumb toward the sound of running water. "Your wife's objections aside—"

Karen's voice cut through the air the way that one dish soap on the commercial cuts through grease. "I'm not his wife. We were never married."

"Mom, for Christ's sake, can't you come sit down?"

I almost never called her that; it was like pulling out the elephant gun. She dropped the sponge into the sink, dried her hands on her skirt, and took a few steps toward the couch.

"Fine. You can all trade ghost stories. Hold on, I'll build a fucking campfire."

Dengue's palms flashed. "Go ahead, Billy."

My father rubbed his temples with both hands, like the memory was a genie he had to coax forth.

"The night Amuse died," he said, and then looked up, a wince tight on his face. "The night you were born and Amuse died. There was . . . we encountered . . ."

He threw Dengue's gesture back across the room.

"We got chased deep into a tunnel, like I told you," Fever picked up. "Then we climbed into a lower one. We found a ladder—"

"Two ladders. We climbed down two levels."

"Right. Two ladders."

Billy leaned forward, left hand wrapped around his right wrist. "It was one of the first tunnels, for the earliest lines. Much older than the ones Bracken is talking about in the paper. Nobody had disturbed the earth before that, Dondi. Not here. Not in the history of history."

"Motherfucker, why don't you just tell it?"

"No. Sorry. Go ahead."

Dengue scratched at his beard. "Something was down there," he said at last. "Something evil. We were in its house, and it was looking at us. Looking *into* us."

I tried to take that in, and failed. "You *were* on acid."

"Doesn't matter," Billy said. He nodded at Fever. "Tell."

"I dropped in before the rest of them," said the Ambassador.

"And the first thing I noticed was the temperature. Usually, the tunnels get warmer the deeper you go. But this was like a meat locker. And then there was the smell."

Karen spun away from the *W* racer she'd been toying with. "Here we go. Tell him about the smell. Was it sulfur? Brimstone?"

"Strawberry incense," Dengue said.

"Boom. What fuckin' sense does that make? Right?"

"At first it was pitch black," Billy said. "But after a few seconds, we started seeing these faint luminescent streaks, all up and down the tunnel. These forked staffs, like lightning in a photograph. I didn't know what they were then, but I do now: the roots of dead trees. Elders, like El Purga, that the builders destroyed. Their spirits were still lingering there, like ghosts. If they'd been stronger, they would have helped us."

"God*damn*, this is some bullshit."

The Ambassador reconfigured his haunches. "I don't know about spirits and whatnot. That's Billy's department. But there was definitely some kind of misery in there. I could feel it."

Karen reached into the ashtray, tweezered the roach. "And that's when they looked up to see a Native American dude shedding a single tear for the vanished harmony of man and nature."

Billy looked up at her with eyes mooned wide. "Please," he said. "Enough." Karen turned her head, blew her smoke, and buttoned her lip.

Dengue exhaled through his nose and resumed. "Everything went black again, all at once. That was when we heard Bracken's boots on the ladder. And felt . . ."

"The demon," Billy finished.

Dengue's lip twitched at the word, as if he wanted to object but couldn't. "I can't describe it," he said, and a bead of sweat slid past his earlobe. "This . . . *presence* filled the tunnel, Dondi. It was like being set on fire, from the inside. Or no. Pulled open, and stared at. By something looking for parts it could . . . I don't know. Devour."

"Recognize," said Billy. "Recognize and use. Against you."

"That was when Bracken dropped into the tunnel. And lemme tell you, he grabbed that motherfucker's full attention. Fast. They liked each other. They *connected*. We saw this pulse of light, running over his body. I don't know for how long. A few seconds. And we were paralyzed. Not physically—"

"Maybe physically."

"—but because there was nowhere to run. We were trapped between Bracken and the tunnel. And then suddenly the light, the pulse, left Bracken and jumped over to Amuse and lit him the fuck up. As if he had light bulbs inside. And Bracken made this awful noise—a howl that sounded like it was being dragged out of him. Then we heard the gunshots, and saw Amuse fall. Bracken shot him over and over—bam bam bam bam bam, until it was just the empty gun, clicking. And then everything went black again."

"Tell him what happened next." Billy was clutching at himself, squeezing his thighs, his biceps, rocking back and forth. I worried that this was more than he could handle, wondered how little it might take to push him back into dementia.

"Bracken started laughing. It wasn't much different from the howl, and it went on and on. If he knew we were there—"

"And he must have!"

"—he didn't give a shit. I don't know how long we huddled together on the ground, too scared to move. And numb—from the temperature, not just the fear. I swear to god, the tears froze on our faces it was so cold. Sabor was hyperventilating; he wanted to go over and pick up Amuse, but we wouldn't let him."

Billy dug furiously at his scalp, fingers probing the space between two matted vines of hair. "Bracken just stood there, like an animal over his kill. Making that noise. Eventually we walked right past him, and climbed out of there."

Dengue hunched forward, elbows on knees, and opened his milky, vacant eyes. "Shit was never the same, Dondi. Not just because we lost Amuse. We brushed up against something we were never meant to that night, and we've been fucked ever since."

"The curse of the Immortal Five," I said. I didn't believe or doubt it, wasn't ready to commit. The mere existence of answers where there'd only been emptiness had me teetering, off-balance, like the account possessed a physical weight. As if it were a dense, black marble lodged in my brain.

"You goddamn right," Dengue grunted.

"We got cursed," said Billy. "Bracken got blessed, if you can call it that. Every move he's made since—he's not acting alone. That thing's giving him juice."

Dengue palmed his chin. "Shutting off those tunnels, it's gotta be some kind of power move—make sure nobody else can get to whatever's down there. We've gotta do something. Before that motherfucker ends up running the city. The country. The world."

"That didn't go so well last time," said Karen, from the carpet's edge. "Let's pretend for a minute that you're right and the source of Bracken's success *is* some mystical alliance with a demon— because scumbags and murderers never get ahead in politics on their own, right? Let's pretend Bracken didn't just shine a Maglite at Amuse, like I've been saying for eighteen years, and you guys really have been hoodooed by some evil spirit that made *you* go blind, and turned *you* into a fugitive—and an asshole, too, might as well blame it for that. If that's the case, then starting some shit when he's forgotten all about you would be pretty retarded, don't you think? Or are your lives not fucked up enough? You wanna end up dead or in jail like Andy and Sabor and Cloud? And what the hell you smiling at me like that for, Fever?"

"Because I know something you don't."

"Oh yeah? What, how to catch a unicorn?"

The Ambassador interlaced his fingers behind his head. "Cloud comes home tomorrow."

"Get the fuck outta here."

"I'm dead-ass! Everything's coming together, you see what I'm talkin' 'bout? Me, Cloud, this nigga here, together we—"

"Dengue, stop." Billy's palm shook as he lifted it to ward off

Fever's words. "She's right. Look at us." He glanced at me. "I just wanna get to know my son."

Yeah, I know: *aaaawww*. Well, fuck you. I teared up when he said it, shocked us all. Anger is a hard thing, but it's brittle, too. And heavy. I'm not saying I shrugged off a whole life's worth right then and there like James Brown does that cape, but I was ready for easy, for the past to be the past, questions and answers be damned. For the father-son reconciliation montage, the leaf-blown Central Park stroll, the joyous old-haunt watering hole return, the manly basketball-court squeeze around the shoulders, all of it intercut with shots of Karen watching us depart from various windows and doorways and looking decreasingly skeptical until finally the musical score swells and she shakes her head like *oh, heck*, and beckons her man into a big ol' I-forgive-you hug and then you see the three of us cooking lasagna together, laughing our heads off. Then fade to black.

Or fade to Karen, faded off the herb, fading out of sight a quarter-hour later, claiming she had a date (almost certainly untrue) and encouraging me and Billy to spend this and subsequent nights somewhere other than her apartment, since she certainly didn't want to get in the way of all the father-son bonding on which he was so eager to embark. Cut to your boy's overloaded brain and body barking reminders that a state of altered consciousness is not the same as sleep, even if you've got your eyes closed, and shutting the fuck down. I dozed off to the sounds of Billy and Fever's conversation through the bedroom wall, pitched low and serious.

The next morning, I took my father to see his parents. I know I haven't said much about them. Truth is, I'm kind of a shitty grandson. But Joe and Dana are mad cool. I hadn't visited since before Karen threw me out, because I didn't want to put them in the awkward position of having to tell me I couldn't stay there. Although more likely, they'd have broken whatever no-safe-haven promise Karen had extracted from Dana—whom she referred to as her mother-in-law and spoke with at least weekly—and made up the guest room bed.

Even then, I'd have had to powwow at the kitchen table with Big Joe, let the old softie do his best hamfisted sweat-of-my-brow Irish hardass impression while I hung my head and pledged to get my act together, finish high school, go to college. I'd have had to sip chamomile with Dana on the living room couch, endure her cocked-head sympathy and try not to think about how many promising dusky-hued young fuck-ups she'd used her streetsmart-white-lady routine on before me, my mother included. Dana had been Karen's favorite painting teacher at Art and Design, the venerable guitar-strumming Ms. Weissman. Venerable even then, and still teaching now at sixty-nine. Hadn't taken to retirement any more than her husband had.

Joe was a union carpenter when Billy was growing up. In the early nineties he'd gotten hip to the game and started contracting—partnered up with money-men he met along the way whose ambition was to leave no neighborhood in Brooklyn, Harlem, even the Bronx affordable for anybody with a normal job, replace every fifty-cent bodega coffee in the five boroughs with a $4.35 iced mocha latte. He took sweat equity and made a boom-time killing. When I was nine, my grandparents sold their third-floor L.E.S. walkup (worth a grip by then itself) and copped a ninth-floor spread on 94th and West End Ave, where Dana began pretending she wasn't Jewish because the place was overrun with these rich, rabidly pro-Israel Members of the Tribe who voted Republican and made her sick. I take my iced mocha latte with a vanilla flavor shot, by the way, which balances the chocolate lovely.

It seemed wise to keep my father aboveground for now, so I splurged on a cab. For a guy who claimed he just wanted to get to know his son, Billy did a lot of silent window-staring as we crawled the West Side Highway. Sometimes he turned to look longer at a building, a billboard. I didn't ask why. He might've been remembering that the words BRACKEN KILLED AMUSE had once blared from the surface, or just trying to assimilate the current, iced mocha latte New York with the one he'd left behind. The one with neighborhoods where being vanilla-flavored could get you shot. Sorry. I forced that one, I know.

Billy piped up as we passed 50th. "There's nothing else I should know?"

"About *them*?" I said, all broad and italicized, but if he caught it he pretended otherwise, and I let it go. "I don't know. Just that they got old. They're pretty well off now, financially, but they're uncomfortable about it. Whenever the building hires a new doorman, Joe takes the guy aside and tells him, 'When you see me coming, don't get up.'"

Billy ran his hands over his hair, trying to press it down. From a distance, he looked presentable—for a dreadlocked Caucasian, anyway. Up close, my chop job couldn't hide the neglect. There were still twigs and pebbles and shit trapped in there.

"We could hit a barbershop first. Get you a cut."

His hands dropped to his lap, and Billy nodded. Then, remembering: "I have no money."

"That's okay. I got you."

His eyes flashed at me, grateful and ashamed, and we each looked out our windows. Strong wind on the water, little whitecaps. I appraised the distance to Jersey, thinking as I always did that it wasn't so far, that I could swim it if I had to. What circumstances might require me to fling myself into a frigid river strewn with imprudent mobsters was harder to determine. A plague of zombies, perhaps. Zombies hate water.

"You must've had money at some point," I said, breaking my rule. "You made it back here. And got your hands on a lot of paint."

Billy spoke around a thumbnail. "Wish I knew."

He tapped the glass. "There used to be a hardware store right there. Eighty-third and Riverside. The owner was this old Cuban guy, Mr. Jimenez. He kept the back door unlocked for load-ins, so it was real easy to rack paint. Sabor figured it out. One day I walk out the back, and *bam*—Mr. Jimenez hits me in the face with a two-by-four.

"Sabor jets. I'm lying on the ground, blood's pouring from my nose. Mr. Jimenez freaks out. Can't believe what he's done. Thinks he's killed me. He starts yelling for his wife, and she comes down from their apartment with her daughter, and the three of them carry me to a couch in his office. He wants to hand himself over to the cops. I keep saying 'no policía, no policía.'

"After a while, things calm down, and I nod out for a few minutes. When I wake up, Mr. Jimenez is flipping through my blackbook. It's full of outlines, train flicks, color lists—enough evidence to get me locked under the jail. I'm about to make a run for it when he looks up and says, 'You are an artist. You are very good. You should not have to steal.' And he hires me and Sabor to paint a mural on his outside wall. We did it that weekend. The whole time we were painting, he kept coming out and patting us on the back and saying 'No more graffitis for you boys. Only good, honest work, for money.'"

"You should have listened." I rapped on the partition. "Hey, yo, excuse me. Right here is great, thanks."

I'd spotted an old-fashioned barbershop pole, two doors in from the corner of 95th and West End. We passed through the cold, sunny glare of mid-morning Manhattan, then entered the talcum-powder-and-hot-metal warmth of what I quickly realized was the whitest barbershop in New York City.

I don't just mean that no black person had ever crossed the threshold in the three hundred and sixty-seven years they'd been in business, though I was certainly the first. Nor, when I say white, do I mean Polish, or Jewish, or Italian. This place was aggressively nonethnic, in the manner of a successful presidential candidate, or the state of Kansas. I suspected that the only haircuts they offered were The Senator, The Stockbroker, and The Yachtsman—the only difference between the three being the location of the part.

In each of the two barber's chairs sat a well-groomed sexage-narian frowning into the pages of the *New York Post*. The bell over the door clanged when we entered. They stopped frowning, raised their heads, and frowned again.

"Help you?" the bolder one inquired, looking at each of us in turn.

I jutted my chin at Billy, lowered myself into a cracked leather side chair. "Help him."

One thing about these old crackerjacks, they never miss a beat. He was up in a flash, armpitting his paper and spinning the chair toward Billy. "Right this way, sir. Have a seat." Voice smoother than a comb through Ronald Reagan's hair.

The place was musky with propriety; you walked in and suddenly understood that there were correct ways to do things, manly things like applying aftershave or buying cuff links. You didn't know any of the protocols, but these guys did, and that made them better than you in ways they were too genteel to point out. Your only comfort was the knowledge that when you left you'd be a coarse, blundering schmuck with a good haircut, and that would be a vast improvement. All this even though the place was a dump and no member of the ruling class would ever so much as housebreak a pedigreed hunting dog on the *Post*.

Billy clambered into the chair. The barber took a closer look, and experienced the first crisis of his entire life. It was over in three nanoseconds.

"Well. I don't see this every day." He snapped a sheet so that it billowed perfectly over my father. "What shall I do?"

"Cut it off and burn it."

A smile trickled toward his eyes. "I'll cut it off, anyway."

He assembled his tools and went to work. Scissors. Straight razor. Clippers. It was slow going, hypnotic to watch, and this guy was the quietest member of his profession.

A man sitting in a barber's chair is a prisoner of sorts. Nowhere to run, nowhere to hide.

Your boy here? Not a patient dude. Also, I tend to break whatever rules I set myself. Self-discipline's a problem.

"Yo. Billy."

He tried to look over without moving his head.

"Did you ever think about me, all that time you were away? I mean, I know your life was hectic. But were you ever like, 'Damn, Dondi is growing up without a father'?"

"I thought about you all the time."

"Yeah? And how did you *think* I was doing?"

The barber threw me a glance, then pretended to mind his beeswax. Billy sighed, and stared out at the street. "I don't know."

"Well, do you want to know? Because you could ask. That'd be a start."

"Dengue told me some," he said softly.

"Oh yeah? Like what? Because I'm sure Dengue's a *great* source. I'm sure he knows exactly what it was like for me."

Billy turned, and nearly caught a scissor in the eye. "He said you tried to write my name."

I wasn't expecting that—didn't even remember telling Dengue. It had happened on the heels of everything fucked up: Karen just back from the hospital, the ground trembling beneath our feet and fury swirling in the air as thick and green as flare smoke and me desperate for some kind of outlet. I bought a can of Rusto, went down to the Navy Yards. The name that came was his. I put up a lone tag, learned that my handskills were garbage, tossed the paint, and went home more confused than ever.

"Yeah," I said. "Sure, Billy. One time, just to see what it felt like. That's the most irrelevant shit Dengue possibly could have told you." I was doubly heated now, and when he kept quiet, I kept going.

"You fucked us both up, man. Maybe you didn't mean to, but you did, and now you need to man up and face it." I meant me and Karen, not me and him, but whatever, he could take it how it worked.

The barber hit the lever and spun the chair ninety degrees, in concession to our conversation. Then he resumed the business at hand, palmed Billy's head and pushed it down and kept on trimming, *ho-hum, just another morning at the ol' haircuttery.*

Billy looked at me over his brow. "I'm sorry, Dondi. I don't know what else to say."

Something in me unclenched, hearing those words, but Billy didn't need to know it. I felt a tear oozing its way toward the duct and stopped that motherfucker cold, sheer force of will.

"You could have stayed," I said.

"I don't know what your mother's told you, but I couldn't."

"Well, you could've not done the shit that made you have to leave. You could've said 'You know what, fuck it, let me raise my kid instead of leaving him out here to fend for himself, so he can end up in fucking jail.' Which I almost did."

Billy interlaced his hands, beneath the sheet. "I wasn't much older than you are now, Dondi. I did what I thought was right."

I faked a laugh, ran my palms up and down the thighs of my jeans. "Motherfucker, *I* know better and I'm eighteen! You were twenty-four."

I glanced away, trying to chill myself out, and happened to catch a look at a *U.S. News & World Report* topping a stack of magazines. On the cover was George W. Bush, smirking liplessly behind some podium. No sight puts me in a fouler mood.

"Just tell me this, man. How come Amuse was more important to you dead than me and Karen were alive, huh? Were y'all fuckin' or something?"

The chair squeaked as Billy jacked himself out of it. He loomed over me, waiting, but I didn't look up. Little bits of hair slid off the sheet and stuck to the backs of my hands. I ignored those too. He was going to have to lower himself into my field of vision if he wanted to see my eyes.

He didn't.

"I was a soldier," my father said. He turned on his heel, walked back to the barber's chair, sat down. "A soldier. Do you know what that means, Dondi?"

I didn't answer. I couldn't. For a few brief moments, it seemed like a soldier was the only thing worth being in the world.

 don't mean to jerk you around, but Billy's re-union with his parents was sort of boring, so we'll be skipping it. Maybe this is my philoso-phy of life, that the moments you'd think would be important aren't. Or they are with-out managing to be interesting, while the cru-cial ones fall out of the sky like poorly installed air conditioners, and break your neck.

Dana cried, Joe cried, Billy did a lot of mumbling and shrugging and proved generally incapable of answering questions about the past or future. There were turkey sandwiches for lunch. My grand-mother spent the visit trying to gauge whether Billy was well enough to be let back out of the building. I cued our exit around four-thirty, when I saw she was beginning to conclude that he was not. I said we had a party to attend. Which was true.

Cloud 9 had done his bid like a gangster, and he was coming home the same way, with a throwdown that proved his investments had matured more than he had. We could hear the music from three piers away, inside our cab, and by the time we pulled up it was deafening, monumentally obnoxious. Although not compared to the yacht.

Imagine the boat you'd build if you were the richest man in the world, and had the smallest penis. The lower deck was crammed with early-comers, drinks in hand, grooving to techno or one of its infinite, indistinguishable variants, all of which sound to me the way a Eurotrash guy's cologne smells. Hundreds more were lined up on the dock, spilling from the ass-end of a velvet-rope maze. At the front, three bouncer-sized men holding clipboards they never looked at and walkie-talkies they never spoke into beckoned people up the gangway in groups of three and four.

Billy unfolded himself onto the curb and blinked at the commotion. He didn't even have the presence of mind to close the taxi door behind him, just stood there running his palm over his crew-cut again and again. It made him look freshly lobotomized, and his scalp was forty percent lighter than his forehead, but two-toned psych-ward-deserter was an improvement.

"Come on," I said, "we better get in line."

"Like hell."

I turned to look at him, but Billy was already fifteen feet away, and all I could make out was the bob and weave of his shorn dome. At every moment, my father simply occupied the one spot where nobody was; if you shrank the people down to molecules, it would've been the kind of phenomenon a physicist would name after himself. For a second, I wondered if Billy had learned it in the rainforest. Then I realized this was some graffiti-shogun shit.

I tried to follow him, and within seconds found myself as stymied as a spiderwebbed fly. I always imagine Stymie was a real person, by the way, a guy so hapless that his buddies started using his name as a synonym for failure. I turned around and began trying to retrace my long-gone path, then froze when I heard my name over a bullhorn.

"Paging Kilroy Dondi Vance. Mr. Vance, please step to the front of the line."

"Ayo!" I threw my hand up, waved it around. Dozens of older, better-dressed people turned to suck their teeth at the kid acting a fool. "That's me," I announced, and the masses parted grudgingly, salty as the Red Sea. I strutted through a corridor of bodies and joined Billy. A bouncer fastened orange paper bands around our left wrists. "VIP lounge is on the top deck," he said, stepping aside to let us board.

We climbed the gangplank, and both flights of stairs. At the top, another bouncer flicked his eyes at our wrists, then reached for the handle of a smoked-glass door. Weird, I thought, that a dude fresh out the penitentiary would be so into security. Or maybe it wasn't.

I'd never been in any kind of VIP section in my life, but as soon as the frosty air hit me and my eyes adjusted to the pale green hues and ten-watt lighting, I knew I could get used to it. It's a disgusting idea, that a room is worth occupying just because other people aren't allowed to enter. Until you're inside.

Cloud was no longer the lithe, skinny kid I'd seen in photos, his high-top fade unintentionally cropped out of every frame. The first thing I thought when he sprang off the couch was that we'd walked into the wrong room, and the King of Bouncers was going to throw us through the wall and into the right one. The guy looked like a black He-Man action figure somebody had painted a linen suit and a ridiculous jaunty captain's hat on. Before I knew it he had Billy in midair, locked in a bearhug worthy of an actual bear.

"Aaaaaaaaah! Welcome to your welcome home, baby! God*damn*, you a sight for sore eyes."

The guest of honor set my father down, and threw an arm around my shoulders. "Last time I saw *this* cat," he announced, "nigga dookied right through his diaper and ruined my, ha, what was it? One of those silk house shirts with the big Kwame polka dots, I think. Did me a favor. Show some love, dog." My feet didn't leave the ground, but the embrace popped three vertebrae.

Cloud lifted his chin toward yet another bouncer. "All right. Everybody I care about's on board. Tell your man to weigh anchor or whatever the fuck."

"Yes sir." To his lips, with a burst of static, came the walkie-talkie.

"Good. Ay mister DJ, you ready to do the damn thing, or you need another mojito first?"

"I *been* ready," came a voice from the bar in the rear. "This weak shit they playing, it came with the boat or what?"

"Yeah. Got a rule about no live performance till you leave the dock."

At that moment, the ship lurched into motion. I felt it for a few seconds, a horizontal version of that strangely pleasant elevator-drop nutsack-tingle-tug, and then it became so normal that if not for the shrinking Manhattan outside the window, I would have forgotten. There was something very liberating, though, about seeing the skyline fade into miniature, as if New York was loosening its vise-grip on all our lives.

"See you on the dancefloor, party people." The DJ slurped the last of his drink—whatever a mojito was, I wanted one—doled out a few knuckle-bumps, and moseyed toward the door. He had it open when the Ambassador, present despite his agoraphobia, piped up. Perfect timing on the blind man, as usual.

"Naw man, you're for the common folk. We got a special DJ coming for the VIPs. Brother named Doo Wop."

The room galloped with laughter, Cloud's roar leading the charge. The DJ grinned and raised a pair of middle fingers to his chest, then slapped the door back open and was gone.

I sidled up to Karen. At least two dudes, a dread in tinted glasses and a stocky goateed whiteboy, peeped the familiarity of my approach, decided I was her man, and turned their attentions elsewhere.

"Explain."

My mother smiled around the Heineken tipped to her lips.

"That was Kid Capri. You ever heard of him?"

"Sure. But I thought it was pronounced 'Kiiiiid Capri.' That's how he says it on those old mixtapes. I always wanna be like 'we know your name, fool, we bought your joint. Shut up and play the music.'"

She laughed. The green of the bottle matched her dress, which was sleeveless. Whatever she'd rubbed into her skin gave it a glow. For a second I saw what those guys did—or, at least, I noticed how pretty ol' Wren 209 could be when she felt like it.

"He and Doo Wop had this huge battle back in '91, '92, dissing each other on mixtapes. Everybody thought Capri was Puerto Rican until Wop outed him as a whiteboy."

Billy sauntered over from the bar. "His father is Italian, moms is Jewish. Which makes him Jewish. Like me."

Karen plucked the highball glass from his hand. "Name one Jewish holiday, and Chanukah doesn't count. Ew, what is this, rum? Who drinks straight rum?"

"Yom Kippur," said Billy. "Day of Atonement."

"Take your rum." She shoved it at him. "Your father's got a lot of balls, talking to me about atonement."

"You asked him to name a holiday."

Karen's hands fell to her hips, a kind of first-position for her. "So how will you be spending Yom Kippur, Billy? Any plans?"

My father shrugged. Either he didn't get it, or he was doing a brilliant not-getting-it impression. "You're supposed to fast, I guess."

Enter the goateed whiteboy, no longer sweating my mother so as to concentrate on jocking my father. He flanked our perimeter and did a little weight-shifting foot-to-foot two-step, the hip-hop cracker version of a jazz bandleader counting off the tune. When he had his entry timed, he laid a hand on Billy's shoulder.

"Excuse me, dude, but . . . are you Rage?"

My father clanged the ice cubes around in his glass, drizzled the last of the liquor down his throat.

"I used to be."

"No shit? Oh, man, I knew it!" His hand sprang up like it was on hydraulics. "Dregs, TWS—Total Wreck Squad, Toys Won't Survive, whatever. Yo, you were my *man* when I was a kid. Yo—" He reached into his shoulder bag and brought out a hardcover sketchbook plastered with stickers, and a fistful of Sharpies. "Do me the honor?"

Billy accepted the blackbook in slow motion—as if the action were involuntary, the ritual a dim muscle memory. A blackbook was the first thing a writer bought, or stole: diary, guest register and laboratory in one. Billy had probably blessed thousands in his day; style was DNA, and these things spread it the way bees spread pollen. Go to a graffiti gallery opening, and all you'll see is writers bent double, using their knees and one another's backs as drafting tables, a spectacle every bit as orgiastic and aesthetically unpleasant as a million horseshoe crabs propagating the species on a beach.

My father blinked at the selection of writing utensils. It was as if everything were in code for him. Like instead of markers and a blackbook he saw some rekmras and a kablobcok, and was paralyzed until he could unscramble what and why.

He picked a red, uncapped it one-handed, began to write. The Sharpie never broke contact with the page, and I thought of the Japanese black water painters Fever had told me about. They used parchment stretched so thin that any unnatural stroke or interruption to the line, any attempt to correct an error, would destroy the piece. It was supposed to force you to communicate without deliberation. Much as breaking the law did.

Billy's eyes roamed as he wrote. He could have been a doctor signing a prescription pad, a lawyer initialing a page his secretary thrust at him while they marched down a corridor. I looked out the window. We were gliding through open water now, someplace south of the city, and the sun was flirting with the horizon. A drumbeat I vaguely recognized shook the floor, competing with the growling engine.

Billy finished, and me and Dregs and Karen nearly bumped heads leaning in to look. I braced myself for a jumble of mystic symbols, or even BRACKEN KILLED AMUSE. But on the upper right quadrant of the page was a vintage RAGE tag. The hands didn't forget.

Dregs nodded. "Fucking cool, man. Right on."

Billy capped the marker, held it out to him. Karen beat Dregs
to it.

"May I?"

It threw Dregs for a loop, I could tell, but he played it off,
"please, be my guest," and cocked his head to watch. A dude his
age—I put Dregs at twenty-five, old enough to remember seeing
Billy's name fly by but too young to have bombed the lines himself—
probably didn't know a single female writer. I doubt you'll find too
many women dressing up in Union blues and spending their weekends reenacting the battles of the Civil War either, if you get my
meaning.

A hardcore Rage-ophile would've known who had bogarted his
book, or at least had a strong hunch. Dregs wasn't that. When
Karen handed it back, it took him several seconds to decipher the
signature under Billy's—time enough for me to imagine the days
when the 2s and 5s had been my parents' love letters, chugging
from Prospect to Crotona with their names entwined for all to see.
Motherfuck an oak tree and a knife.

"Immortalette 1?"

Karen returned his pen. "A.k.a. Wren 209."

Dregs nodded. "Right on." There's some kind of protocol about
when you explicitly acknowledge knowing who somebody is and when
you don't. I'm not sure which is more respectful or when you do
what, but many an eye's been blackened over such things. Karen's
hands stayed at her sides, so I guessed everything was cool.

Dregs turned back to Billy. "So like, where have you been, dude?
I heard you were dead, heard you were underground, heard you
were doing Pepsi murals in Japan. . . ."

My father rubbed his head, scratched his ear. Rubbed his head
again. Little fragments of scalp fell, dusted Billy's shoulders.

"I've been learning shamanic healing from plant spirits in the
Amazon."

I tried not to laugh as Dregs rifled through his brain for an
appropriate response.

"Right on, right on. Been painting at all?"

All of a sudden, a kind of frenzy seemed to fill Billy, and he grabbed my wrist. "Nobody can know I'm here," he blurted. His eyes bored into Dregs, then into me. "Who is he? Why are we talking to him?"

I put a hand on Billy's back. "It's okay. Relax. He's cool."

Dregs just stood there, looking earnest. "There are some legal issues," I told him, trying to sound offhand.

"My lips are sealed." He performed a pantomime to that effect.

"Right on," I said, filing the phrase under Whiteboy-Ubiquitous, and raised an eyebrow at Karen. "Time for another drink?"

"I think so." She smiled at Dregs. "Nice meeting you."

"You too. Enjoy yourselves."

He was turning to go when Billy lunged, snatched the blackbook out of Dregs's hand, riffled to his page, tore out his name, and stuffed it in his mouth.

Dregs and Karen and I watched Billy's jaw work to break down the nice, thick paper stock. He looked at each of us in turn as he chewed, like the fucking classroom gerbil we had in second grade to teach us about loss and mourning. Spider-Man, we called him, the poor frail bastard.

Billy winced and raised his chin to swallow, Adam's apple bulging against his throat like an overtaxed bass woofer.

"Sorry," he mumbled.

"Can I have my book back?"

Billy obliged.

"I guess we really need that drink now," I said, with the least credible chuckle in the history of fake mirth.

Dregs tucked his book beneath his arm. "Take care of him," he said to me, and walked away.

"I don't need this shit," Karen announced, and followed.

I watched Billy watch her go. About twenty things I could have said came and went, from *don't worry, man, it's gonna be all right* to *how would El Purga feel about you eating a tree* to the punch line to that old Lone Ranger joke, *whatchu mean "we," white man?*

Finally, I just left him standing there. Got myself a mojito from the bar, took it downstairs and checked out chicks and sipped.

Kid Capri was in total control. The crowd trusted him, and from trust follows abandon. Girls get loose, because they aren't subconsciously anticipating the coming of a lame song that will give them cover to hit the bathroom or the bar. Dudes navigate with confidence, knowing they don't have to worry about a musical cock-block, an out-of-left-field switch from dancehall to merengue just when they're getting their swerve on.

Dengue likes to talk about how, back in the day, if the crowd didn't dig a record Afrika Bambaataa played, Bam would bring the needle back and play it again, and then a third time, and a fourth, until the people heard what he did. The party owed its existence to the benevolence and good grace of the DJ; he kept the peace and the pace, controlled the space-time continuum by backspinning beginnings, doubling a moment or erasing it, putting his fingerprints all over history. Today, he's treated like a servant, a human jukebox. Dengue calls that a tragedy, and I tend to agree.

Capri wasn't dishing up alien cuisine, but he wasn't serving the crowd a junk-food diet of new club hits either. He fed us tapas, just big enough to whet the appetite. You got a verse and a chorus, and then he dropped the next song, and the disappointment of goodbye vanished with the ecstasy of hello. He did a lot of teasing, which only works with an educated crowd: let us hear a famous horn fanfare and then pulled back the track just when we were ready to celebrate the blend. During the time it took me to finish my drink, he ran through fifteen minutes of nineties hip-hop, joints I recognized by Main Source and Black Moon, plus a bunch I didn't. Then he segued to reggae of the same era with Super Cat's "Ghetto Red Hot," which was like taking a headcount of Jamaicans, since every last one of them kept a fist raised and swaying throughout the song, even the women.

Cloud stood in the middle of the floor, massive arms molding the air around his dance partner, a blonde whose chest bounced to the music in dizzying doubletime. She and Cloud were trying to carry on a conversation, which I took to be proof that they'd just met. Every few seconds, one would shout something into the other's ear, and they'd both nod or smile.

Guests interrupted them constantly, coming over to offer hugs, congratulations, who knew what—hot tips on cash businesses with lax security, perhaps. Now and then I'd strain to place someone who looked familiar, then realize he wasn't a writer Karen had gotten baked with in our living room, but a bonafide minor celebrity: Fat Joe, Kevin Powell, the fly Latina anchorwoman from New York One, a none-too-sober Dwight Gooden—who I only recognized because, Scout's honor, he was wearing a Mets jersey with his name on it. I even thought I saw Al Sharpton, but it turned out to be some other sunken-eyed old man with processed hair.

It was beautiful, watching this crazy cross section of old-school New York City sweating and swaying in the open air beneath the glinting gold and pink and purple of what was shaping up to be a stunning sunset. Things were okay, I told myself. Shit would work out. We'd get Billy normal. He had friends, and they were not without resources.

At first, nobody paid any mind to the Coast Guard chopper hovering overhead. Capri neutralized the noise by cranking up his decibels, and folks turned back to the business of shaking ass. But minutes passed, and the chopper didn't leave. All at once, the party started to understand that this was not a fly-by, but surveillance.

You know that sensation you get somewhere between your throat and stomach when you notice a cop watching? Doesn't matter if you're in the middle of a crowd; you still feel immediately and intensely alone. Five seconds before, you might've been the mixed martial arts champion of the world, but now you're a gazelle, and the lion has just yawned and lifted his head out of the underbrush.

Maybe white dudes in Dockers who are on some "Hello, Officer, I'm glad you're here, those darn kids have been messing with my lawn again" type shit don't know the feeling. And granted, I walk around with felony amounts of drugs on me, so I might be a little sensitive. But if you're black, you know the feeling. Even Clarence Thomas knows it.

The wave of menace hit us all, and several hundred people who'd been experiencing a rare sense of carefreedom and connection were alone and vulnerable and hate-filled once again. The music seemed suddenly crass, irrelevant. It couldn't save us. It wasn't even trying.

If there's some kind of disc jockey gold medal for skills under pressure, Kid Capri deserves like three. He slowed the record down until it sounded like a dying robot, let it grind to a halt. Silence for one second, two, and then Capri leaned over the mic and shouted, "New York City, make some noooiiiissseee!" and brought in a new jam at a volume that turned the chopper blades into mosquito wings.

When they heard the song, the crowd went bananas, and the stress of the moment exploded in a shrapnel-storm of sound and motion. We were partaking in one of the perfect moments in the history of DJing, and we knew it.

The first time Kool Herc went back-to-back on "Funky Drummer" had to have been one. A prepubescent Grand Wizard Theodore climbing atop a milkcrate to debut the scratch, another. But in terms of pure song selection, which Dengue always touts as ninety percent of the craft, I can't imagine anything more sublime than the rub-a-dub boom of "Police in Helicopter" at that moment and latitude and longitude. Not just for the topical poetry of it, but because if you listen to the lyrics—and I have, many times, because until he went away Abraham Lazarus kept the tune in heavy rotation—you realize that although John Holt sounds like he just smoked a pound of ishen, he's crooning some of the most militant, fuck-the-cops lines ever penned:

> Police in helicopter, a search fi marijuana
> Policeman in the streets, searching for collie weed

Soldiers in the field, burning the collie weed
But if you continue to burn up the herbs
We gonna burn down the cane fields

Everybody seemed to know the words. Capri conducted a massive sing-along, and between our volume and the song's, I thought we might blow the chopper right out of the sky. Which is stupid, I know, but until that day I never had much respect for helicopters. If you see one in an action movie, there's about a sixty percent chance it will go down in flames, and that climbs to ninety if Bruce Willis is around. In real life, too, they seem absurdly flawed: every time you open a newspaper, sixteen Marines have just perished in a crashed Blackhawk for no adequately explained reason.

The craft repositioned itself slightly, and then a door opened and out dropped a coil of rope. We watched it straighten as it fell. The people in its path backed away and it thumped to the ground in front of Cloud, who hadn't moved an inch. He scowled up at the chopper, and I imagined him yanking on the rope and bringing the thing crashing through the deck on some Incredible Hulk shit.

Fastened to the end was a white cardboard box tied up with red ribbon, the kind they put your leftovers in at a nice restaurant. Cloud turned it in his hands. Capri faded the music, and the whirring of the blades turned into a collective heartbeat.

Inside the box was an envelope. Cloud tore it open, removed a card, and read aloud.

> Welcome home, Inmate #44823573.
> Your friends in law enforcement
> will be watching you.
>
> A.B.
> p.s.—I'd ask you for your vote,
> but convicts don't get one.

The chopper swooped toward the deck, and the crowd scattered before it, at velocities ranging from panicked dash to my own casual speed-walk. Cloud held his ground, clenched his fists and tracked the helicopter with his eyes as it came out of its dive thirty feet above us and began easing itself down. At twenty, the doors opened, and out flew dozens of little metal canisters that tumbled to the deck and rolled around, spraying tear gas in every direction.

It's always the personal touches that show how much somebody cares. Like using aerosol dispensers instead of the more common gas grenades.

I wish I could better describe the chaos that came next, but only an omniscient narrator could pull it off—omniscient or goggled. I can tell you that getting gassed feels like rubbing fresh habanero peppers all over your eyes, and that before I had to squeeze mine shut I saw four guys in breathing masks slide down ropes until they reached the deck.

Then my memory becomes a soundtrack, filled with shrieks and smashing glass, charging feet that never get any farther away. There were runners and there were duckers. I was a ducker, and that was a mistake. Within seconds I'd been bowled over, trampled by about six pairs of shoes. I curled double and yelled out, but the people stepping on me could no better pinpoint my voice and body than I could theirs. I scrabbled to my feet, ricocheting off bodies, tripping over limbs, stepping on women I'd probably ogled five minutes before. We were crazed with pain and staggered by fear; we crashed into one another like hot molecules. It was a blind, mindless dance, and the enemy strolled through it, doing as he pleased.

I found the metal staircase leading to the VIP lounge, crouched underneath, and waited. I don't know if it took five minutes or fifteen, but eventually the tear gas started to wear off, and we all blinked our way back to sanity.

The chopper was gone. The ship, trashed. There had been three full bars on board, and not a single bottle had escaped the siege. People were picking diamond-sized shards out of each other's skin, pressing cocktail napkins to flesh and watching streaks of blood soak through. Kid Capri probably would've played a requiem, but his turntables were smashed to shit. Records floated on the surface of the water, like losing hands scattered across a poker table.

The boat was moving at an incredible speed, back toward the dock. The city rose to meet us, magenta reflections still glinting in the highrise windows, and I wished the sun would fucking wrap it up already. Some community-minded black chick was crisscrossing the deck with a champagne bucket, handing out wet washcloths for people to lay over their eyes. Nobody was okay, but nobody was dead, either. I wondered how many of Cloud's four hundred closest homies even knew what A.B. stood for, and whether any who did not intended to find out.

I found him and Rage and Wren slumped shoulder-to-shoulder on a couch in the deserted VIP, and Fever on the matching love-seat. Only one lightbulb still worked. The carpet squished with liquor, and an empty tear-gas canister lolled back and forth across it.

"Hey," I said from the threshold. "Everybody okay?"

Karen beckoned me over for a kiss on the cheek, a double hand-squeeze, some soulful eye contact. Billy glanced up, then right back down. Only Dengue spoke.

"Motherfucker, you know what to do."

"Right."

By the time I got the joint rolled, the yacht was docking. The captain brought us in with a bang that nearly knocked me off my chair; guess he was beyond trying to impress anyone at this point. I stood and peered down at the lower deck. People were pressing toward the exits.

Cloud joined me by the window, leaving a gigantic, Cloud-sized vacancy on the couch. Karen and Billy, who'd been wedged on either side of him, eased into it.

"Fuck them," he said, waving a hand at the throng below. "I got this ship rented for another six hours. Light that shit."

He walked over to the bar, picked up a walkie-talkie, flicked it

on. "Cloud 9 to fucknuts one through six. Come in, fucknuts. Anybody out there?" A staticky voice assented. "All right, listen up, I
need a case of Guinness Stout and about a hundred dollars' worth
of Chinese food up here as soon as possible. I know that might not
fall under y'all's job description, but somehow I don't feel like I've
gotten my money's worth from you Barnum-and-Bailey-ass security
boys, so make it happen. What the fuck, get yourselves some dinner too, it's been a rough night. Cloud 9, over and out. You sparking
that or what, nephew?"

I handed him the joint, the lighter. "Don't you have piss tests?"

Cloud started to laugh, and then *bam*—I was in a headlock, and
he was still roaring. "Nigga, you get here late or something? My
homecoming just got Boston Tea Partied. Drug tests are the least
of my concerns. But thanks for asking." He planted a kiss on the
top of my dome, then shoved me halfway across the room and
shook his head. "Youngblood, he a trip."

Cloud smoked in silence, watching the crowd file down the
gangplank and tapping his foot.

"You'd think they'd fuck me up," he said a half-inch into the
joint. "I mean, why not, right? Long as you're dropping by." He
filled his lungs again, and handed the weed to Karen at arm's
length. "I'll tell you why. Because those dudes didn't know me from
Adam's housecat. Bracken told them to gas the yacht and break
everything, and they were like 'whatever you say, boss,' and that
was that."

"Scary," said Karen, and nodded in agreement with herself.

Cloud spun from the window. "You know what I think about
sometimes?" He spread his arms. "How the whole game could have
turned on a dime. Become a totally different thing. Y'all remember
in '82, when Erni and Pink and them met with the curly-haired
dude from the Transit Authority and offered to give back the
insides?"

"You talking about the scene in *Style Wars*?" I asked, incredulous.

Cloud pumped a finger. "Exactly. The scene in *Style Wars*. I was supposed to be there, but I skipped it to go get some pussy off Giovanna Northrup. It doesn't matter; that dude had no juice anyway. Still, yo, I swear to God, I thought about that meeting every day I was locked up. Right there, everything could have changed."

"What, like if they'd gone for it?"

"Yeah, like if they'd gone for it! Think about it: we stop tagging the insides, because the shit is ugly and stupid and it freaks out the civilians, and in return the MTA gives us the outsides, where all the burners that most regular New Yorkers said they *liked* were popping off. Throw in a couple art scholarships and a press release, and presto-change-o, New York becomes the city that solved its graffiti problem with the most innovative arts program in the country. Next comes x-amount of inspirational news stories about kids from the ghetto making a name for themselves as artists and beautifying their communities at the same time, all thanks to the fuckin' vision of their fuckin' leaders. And we all live happily ever after."

Cloud turned back to the window. The last of the partygoers were filing onto land. "They wouldn't even've had to pay us," he said, almost to himself. "Just left us alone."

Nobody spoke. I looked from one to the next. At Cloud, prison-chiseled shoulders hunched as he watched a parade of people who'd barely entered his life making a U-turn. At mammoth, glue-sniffing, sightless Dengue, the 15's lone standard bearer for all these years, who'd finally left the warren of his apartment only to have paranoia one-upped by reality.

I looked at Karen, saw the timeline of her existence collapsing on itself as she sat here, bruised by life and the elbows of strangers, no longer sure whether she was the abandoned or the abandoner, grieving or aggrieved or just sixteen again.

Finally, I looked at my father. He raised his head to meet my eyes, just as he had in that ravaged hotel room, and we stared at one another until I had to turn away.

The tear gas canister rolled into my foot, and I reared back and kicked it as hard as I could, sent it caroming off the wall.

"Okay. We've got to destroy this guy. Right?"

Nothing.

"Sometimes life gives you a second chance," I announced, finding the courage to look at Billy. Give me my props: it's not easy to talk from your heart and out your ass at the same time.

The faces before me showed no signs of life, and someplace in my memory, a spark fired. I'm not proud to admit this, but your boy here was something of a mock trial whiz back in ninth grade, when I first got to Whoopty Whoo Ivy League We's A Comin' Academy. It was a straightforward case of wanting to compete with the rich kids, and yet confound the expectation that I'd do so on a court rather than in one. I was a fairly nasty two-guard at thirteen, don't know if I've mentioned that, and while Whoopty Whoo didn't technically recruit athletes, my ability to drain an eighteen-footer off the dribble didn't hurt me with the admissions board, you can be sure. Naturally, I refused to suit up once I got there, and also stopped growing. The flyest girl in my English class was on the mock trial squad, so I joined that instead, and spent the year out-arguing the rest of Manhattan's contentious little prep-school jerks.

The judges were always these dour, Easter-Island-statue-looking dudes, impossible to pique. One time a kid from Poly Prep ripped a fart so loud it disrupted radio transmissions in three boroughs, and not one so much as twitched. For some reason, those bloodless sons of bitches brought out the best in me. I'd have the trophies to prove it, if I hadn't chucked them all.

I could almost feel the clip-on tie around my neck now.

"Yo, all due respect? It's time to sack up and play some offense, because if Bracken doesn't go down, you do. All of you. Cloud, this is a man who shows up sixteen years after putting you in jail to wreck your life again, just for the sport of it. Billy, imagine what he'll do when he finds out you're back. And he will find out."

"So what, then?" Cloud demanded, lifting his arms to crucifix height. He stepped in front of me, brought us chest to chest, and for a moment I understood what being terrified of Cloud might feel like—had an ass-puckering flash of the brutal world he'd left behind this morning. Out the corner of my eye, I saw Billy rise to his feet, and realized he couldn't predict his homeboy anymore either.

"You talking murder, youngblood? Or just talking reckless?"

I stared into his eyes—no choice—and realized just how little of a fuck Cloud gave about anything right now. If I was talking murder, he was all ears. And if I was talking reckless, he was getting blue balls.

"Revenge," I said, splitting the difference. "I'm talking revenge. For everything and everybody." I had no idea where I was going, but it beat standing still. "For Amuse, for Sabor, for all the kids whose lives turned to shit because they wrote on trains. Think about it: you guys have troops. You just need to mobilize them."

Cloud's expression seemed to be flickering between a sneer and a smirk. I didn't know which one to root for.

"Mobilize them for what?"

I threw my arms up, imitating him. "What they do. Bomb. Kill everything. Destroy all trains."

Karen was perched on the arm of the couch. "The city doesn't run painted trains anymore, Dondi. You know that."

I spun to face her. "They'd have to, if you hit them all. I'm talking every single car of every single train. The only other option would be to shut the system down, and they *really* can't do that."

"Impossible," said Karen. "Retarded."

Dengue shifted his girth. "I've thought about this," he said. "It's not impossible. With the right personnel, right strategy. Right money."

"How many writers would it take?" I asked.

"Figure fifty."

"Good luck," said Cloud, starting to pace. "Niggas don't know shit about hitting trains no more, B. You'd have to dig up fossils like us. Shit, you shoulda told me a week ago. More subway writers in the beng than out of it. Not that I'm down anyway. Tricks is for kids. I say we lay up in the fuckin' garbage cans outside his little bullshit house in Bay Ridge, wait 'til he comes out, and wedge some hand-guns in some orifices." He tossed a look at Dengue. "Figure two."

"He moved," said Karen. "Lives in midtown now. A doorman building." She glanced away. "I don't even know how I know that."

Cloud considered it for a moment, and when he resumed his voice was slower, sadder. "Look, as far as bombing trains, we been there and done that, and all it got us is here. Hell, Billy killed everything from polar bears to rooftops, and for what?"

"Cloud doesn't know about the tunnel," my father said. He sounded like a scared kid, or what I'd imagine a scared kid sounds like. I probably hadn't heard an actual scared kid since I was him. "Dengue, tell him about the tunnel."

"I look like fuckin' Rosencrantz and Guildenfuck to you? Tell him yourself."

Everybody stared at him.

"It's a Shakespearean reference, goddamnit. You got that, right Dondi?"

"Yup."

Billy walked up to Cloud, put a hand on his shoulder. "Bracken's sealing off the tunnel."

"*The* tunnel?"

"And all points of access."

Cloud scowled, paced a four-step circle that suggested the dimensions of his cell. "And we're sure that's a bad thing? I'm say-ing, if it's sealed . . ."

"Yeah, maybe Bracken's acting for all the right reasons," I said. "Seems like a real Dudley Do-Right to me."

He pursed his lips for a moment. "Has either of you been back down there?"

Billy and Dengue said that they had not.

Cloud snapped his fingers for what was left of the joint. He must have burned his thumb relighting it, if not his lips, but it didn't seem to matter.

"For what it's worth," he croaked, holding in his hit, "I've got a truckload of paint stashed in south Jersey."

You ever have one of those moments when something moves from bullshit to real, but through a side entrance, so you're like *wait, what just happened*? It was a feeling I knew mostly from messing around with females: one second you're play-flirting, or having a jokey theoretical discussion about kissing, and the next you're actually getting busy and you didn't even see it coming, although presumably she did.

This was like that. Cloud tipped back his head and French-inhaled, which looked extremely gangster on him, but I think he did it to hide what had now resolved into a smirk, a challenge.

Dengue rocked back and forth in his chair, obviously hoping this was for real and afraid to jinx it. Billy examined the ground. Karen, her cuticles.

Cloud swung his arms and watched his smoke rise. "Got a ex-cellmate who served in the Gulf War. Dude's up on all types of infrared goggles and smoke bombs and trip wires and shit. Always used to talk about the capers we could pull off with that stuff. Might be useful, I'd imagine."

"How'd he get caught, then?" Karen asked. Her arms weren't crossed over her chest, but if you closed your eyes, it would have sounded like it.

"It was an unrelated charge. You kinda quiet over there, William."

"Just thinking," Billy said into his lap.

We waited.

"It would ruin Bracken, right? If one Monday morning, it was 1982 again?"

"Completely. Forever. He's the goddamn Transit president, and he's campaigning as tough on crime." The Ambassador smiled, cheeks shimmying toward his eyelids. "I notice you said Monday morning. Care to elaborate?"

Billy shrugged, then looked up as if noticing the rest of us for the first time. "Well, you could paint everything laid up in the yards over a weekend, if you worked around the clock. Then, on Monday around four A.M., when the fewest trains are in service, you'd start motioning"—the term means hitting trains in service, when they pause at the end of the line to have their insides cleaned—"and stay in the tunnels until the first ones came back around."

"My thinking exactly."

"Three people per train? Left side, right side, inside? Send teams out to bomb the highways, as a diversion? Call in fake tips?"

"All that, brother. And more."

Cloud wasn't hiding his grin now. He jerked a thumb at Billy, raised an eyebrow at me. "Hear that, youngblood? The monster's stomach is growling."

Karen interlaced her fingers, straightened her elbows, twisted her wrists. Eight knuckles sounded off. "It still two guards per yard?"

Dengue's mouth cleaved into a smile. "It is, sister. It is."

I took a couple of steps toward her. "Thought you didn't believe in any of this stuff."

"I believe in ruining Anastacio Bracken's life. If we compromise some fuckin' ghoul's ability to influence the course of human events in the process, I'm good with that. Mostly, I miss the hell out of bombing."

"You and me both, homegirl." Cloud dropped his roach, ground it into the carpet. "We're gonna need a lot of duct tape," he said. "I'll straight kidnap all of 'em before I hide in the bushes memorizing shift changes. Shit, it's 2005."

There was a knock on the open door, and two bouncers entered, laden with plastic bags.

Cloud raised his arms like he was signaling a field goal. "Fucknuts one and two, my niggas! Is there some General Tso's in there? Yeah? Excellent. You got yourselves something? Of course you did. All right, then. I'll holler when I need more beer."

He dipped into his pocket, brought out a wad of cash, peeled off two hundred-dollar bills. The bouncer who took them looked relieved.

"Close the door behind you, homes."

We huddled over the coffeetable, exhuming carton after greasy carton and passing them around. Cloud opened five Stouts, angling the bottles against the table's lip and chopping down with the heel of his hand to pop the tops.

"Can you imagine," asked Dengue with his mouth full, "the looks on eight million New Yorkers' faces when they wake up to fully bombed trains?"

The rest of us said "mmm" or "uhh" and kept eating. I was pretty sure we were all thinking the same thing: that even if we pulled this off, the Ambassador would still have to imagine it.

Billy took a few bites, then javelined his chopsticks into a carton of lo mein. "There's got to be a meeting. Crew presidents only." He paused. "Are there even enough crews?"

"Crews, sure," said Dengue. "Train-era crews that are still active? Not even close. If we had the dough, we could import some. Chicago has train crews. Rome, Copenhagen. I know some Germans who are sick."

"Don't look at me," said Cloud. "A motherfucker's paper is not all it may appear to be. Especially if Empire Party Rentals expects me to pay for any of this damage, which I'm sure they do." He chewed thoughtfully on a baby corncob. "Might be able to chair the fundraising committee, though. Hold a couple bake sales or whatever." He threw me a wink. It felt like a jab to the throat.

"I might have some thoughts on that," my mother said. "We'll talk about it later."

Before I could wonder what she meant, Billy piped up. "How do you call a meeting these days? I'm assuming there's still enough beef and stupidness that only the right guy can get everybody in the same room."

"Of course. It's still graffiti, B."

"So who's that guy?"

Fever thought about it. "Vexer. Blam 2. Possibly Stoon. Possibly me."

"Nigga," said Cloud. "You kidding me? That guy is Billy Rage. Everybody will come just to lay eyes."

My father shook his head. "I can't. I—I'm just not up to it. Plus, I'm an outlaw. If anybody knew I was back—"

"Billy," the Ambassador interrupted, "*everybody* knows you're back. You went all-city with crazy voodoo symbols in the tunnels, dude. It's only a matter of time before Bracken hears about that—if he hasn't already. The clock is ticking."

The words kind of thudded to the ground. My father ran both hands over his head, then turned to Dengue. "Okay," he said, nodding fast, as if to convince himself it was. "Okay. Just tell me who to call."

 hat night, Karen and I returned to Fort Greene, and Billy bounced to what your man Dick Cheney would call an undisclosed location, just to be on the safe side. Next morning, when I woke up bright and late, my mother was seated at the kitchen table with her coffee and Cloud 9.

"Yo," I managed, waving.

"Yo, yo." He raised his mug in salute.

Karen poured another, sugared it to my specifications. "Sit."

"Can I take a piss first? Maybe brush my teeth?"

"By all means."

I staggered to the bathroom, past the closed door of the guest room. When I reemerged, there were three fat slices of coffee cake on the table. I'd never seen Karen so hostess-y. She slid a folder from her work bag, removed two copies of a manuscript. "Read."

I scanned the first page. It was a cover letter, addressed to Authors' Inc., fairly well written, no red flags, describing a story collection and the sample piece enclosed. It was signed Theo Polhemus.

"Ring a bell?" asked Karen.

"Should it?"

"Read the story."

I turned the page.

CROWN HEIST

Tap tap BOOM. Birds ain't even got their warble on, and my door's shaking off the hinges. I didn't even bother with the peephole. It had to be Isaac Eleazar, the Jewish Rasta, playing that dub bassline on my door.

BOOM. I swung it open and Zar barged in like he was expecting to find the answer to life itself inside. A gust of Egyptian Musk oil and Nature's Blessing dread-balm hit me two seconds after he flew by: Zar stayed rocking that shit like it was some kind of armor. He did a U-turn around my couch, ran his palm across his forehead, wiped the sweat onto his jeans, and came back to the hall.

"I just got fuckin' robbed, bro."

Funny how a dude can cruise the road from neighbor to acquaintance to homeboy without ever coming to a full stop at any of the intersections. Me and Zar, our relationship was like one of those late-night cab rides where the driver hits his rhythm and the green lights stretch forever.

He'd come upstairs and introduced himself the day I moved into his building two years ago. When you're moving four, five pounds of herb a week, you've got to know who you live with. He sized me up, decided I was cool, and told me his door was always open. I didn't really have too much going on then—just a half-time shit job in an office mailroom and a baby daughter Uptown who I never got to see—so before long I was coming by to smoke. If Zar wasn't already puffing one of those big-ass Bob Marley cone spliffs when I walked in, my entrance was always reason enough for him to sweep his locks over his shoulder, hunch down over his coffeetable, and commence to building one.

I called his crib Little Kingston. All the old dreads from the block would be up in there every afternoon, talkin' bout how horse fat an' cow dead, whatever the fuck those bobo Ashanti yahoos do. I never said much to any of them, just passed the dutchie on the left hand side. Zar got much love from the bredren, but a domestically grown nigga like me stayed on the outskirts. Whatever. Later for all that I-n-I bullshit anyway.

I flipped the top lock quick. "What?"

"Motherfucker walked straight into my crib, bro, ski-masked up. Put a fuckin' Glock 9 to my head while I was lying in bed. Ran me for all my herb." His hand shook as he lifted a thumb-and-finger pistol to his temple. Fear or rage; I couldn't tell.

"How many?" I asked. "Who?" In Zar's business, you don't get jacked by strangers. Strictly friends and well-wishers.

"Just one, and he knew where my shit was."

"Even the secret shit?"

"Not the secret shit. I still got that. But the other ten are gone—I just re-upped yesterday. Son of a bitch filled a trash-bag, duct taped me up, and bounced."

"Didn't do a very good job with the tape, did he?"

Zar shook his head. "He was shitting his pants more than I was, T. And that's when you get shot: when a cat doesn't know what the fuck he's doing."

"You want a drink?" I didn't know what else to say.

"You got a joint?"

"Yeah. Yeah. Hold on." I went to the bedroom and grabbed my sack. Zar was sitting on the edge of the couch when I got back, flipping an orange pack of Zig-Zags through his knuckles.

"This might be kinda beside the point right now," I said carefully, settling into the chair across from him, "but it's probably time to dead all that open-door no-gun shit, huh?"

The bottom line was that Eleazar was practically asking to be robbed. He never locked his door, and the only weapon in his crib was the chef's knife he used to chop up ganja for his customers. He had some kind of who-Jah-bless-let-no-man-curse theory about the whole thing. Plus, all the small-timers who copped off him knew that Zar was tight with the old Jamaicans who really ran the neighborhood. And to top it off, Zar was convinced that he looked crazy ill strutting around his apartment with that big blade gleaming in his hand: a wild-minded, six-two, skin-and-bones whiteboy with a spliff dangling from his mouth and hair ropes trailing down his back. Half Lee "Scratch" Perry, half Frank White.

It was an equation that left plenty out—the growling stomachs of every young thug in the area, for starters. A year ago, all Zar's customers had been dimebag-and-bike-peddling yardmen, and everything had been peace. Then the neighborhood boys found out about him. I told Zar he shouldn't even fuck with them. *I know these niggas like I know myself, I said. They're outta control. They trying to be who Jay-Z says he is on records, dude. You don't need that in your life.*

He shrugged me off. *They're babies. I man nah fear no likkle pickney.* Any time Zar started speaking yard, I just left his ass alone. But he should have listened. You could practically see these kids narrowing their eyes every time he turned his back. It had gotten to the point where I'd started locking the door myself whenever I came over.

"It was Jumpshot," Zar said, as smoke twirled up from the three-paper cone he'd rolled. "It had to be."

I leaned forward. "Why Jumpshot?" So-called because he liked to tell folks he was only in the game because genetics had failed to provide him with NBA height. Or WNBA height, for that matter.

"Two reasons." Zar offered me the weed. I shook my head. "Three, actually. One, he sells the most. He's got the most ambition. Two, that shit last month, when he complained and I sonned him."

"Hold up, you did what? You ain' tell me this."

Zar cocked his head at me. "Yes I did, bro. Didn't I? He came by at night, picked up a QP. I was mad tired, plus mad zooted, and I gave him a shitty shake-bag by mistake. So the next morning he shows up with two of his boys, dudes I don't even know, bitching. Little Ja Rule-lookin' cocksucker. I was like, 'okay, cool.' Sat him down, gave him a new bag, took the one he didn't want and threw it on the table. Then I brought out the chalice, like 'now we're gonna see if y'all can really smoke.'"

He had told me this story. It was funny at the time, hearing how Zar had smoked Jump and his boys into oblivion, burned up half Jump's new herb sack before he even got out of the room. The way Zar told it, Jumpshot's crew had passed out, but Jump himself refused to go down; he'd sat there all glassy-eyed, slumped back, barely able to bring the chalice-pipe to his lips, while Zar talked at him for hours like he was the kid's uncle or something—regaled him with old smuggling stories from the island days, gave him advice on females, told him how to eat right, all types of shit.

After a while, Zar said, he'd put this one song on repeat for hours, just to see if Jump would notice. "Herbman Trafficking," by Welton Irie, Zar's theme music: *some a use heroin, some a snort up cocaine/but all I want for Christmas dat a two ganja plane/as one take off the other one land/we load the sin-semilla in one by one/they tell me that it value is a quarter million/me sell it in the sun and a me sell it in the rain/ca' when me get the money me go buy gold chain/me eat caviar and me a drink champagne . . .*

"So what's the third reason?" I asked.

"I recognized that motherfucker's kicks. He got the new Jordans last week." Eleazar stood up. "I gotta send a message. Right?"

I threw up my hands. "I'd say so. Yeah. I mean, you gotta do something."

"Come see Cornelius with me."

"Man, Cornelius doesn't know me."

"You're in there all the time."

"So? I'm just another dude who likes his vegi-fish and corn-bread. Whatchu want me there for, anyway?"

"Cause I'ma go see Jumpshot after that. And I'd like some company, you know what I'm saying?"

"What, you just gonna knock on his door? Say you're the Girl Scouts? Why would he even be home?"

"If he's not home, he's not home. If he is, I'll play it like I'm coming for help, like 'you're the man on the street, find out who jacked me, I'll make it worth your while.'"

Zar looked sharper, more angular, than I'd ever seen him. Like he was coming into focus. "I guess if he wanted to shoot you, he woulda done it half an hour ago," I said.

"Exactly. Now he's gotta play business-as-usual. Besides, I'm known to be unarmed. Now you understand why: so when I do pick up a strap, it's some real out-of-character shit."

"I don't wanna be involved in no craziness, Zar." I said it mostly just to get it on the record. Once you put in a certain number of hours with a cat like Eleazar, you become affiliated.

Obligated. It starts off easy-going: you come over, you chill, you smoke. *Ay T, you hungry? I'm 'bout to order up some food. Put away your money, dog. I got you.* Then it becomes *Yo T, I gotta go out for a hot second. Do me a solid and mind the store, bro.* Or, *Man, I'm mad tired. Can you bring Jamal this package for me? I'll break you off. Good lookin out, T.*

I stood and walked out of the room.

"Fuck you going?" Zar called after me. I could tell from his tone that he was standing with his arms spread wide, like Isaac Hayes as Black Moses.

I came back and shook my duffel bag at him. "Unless you wanna carry those ten bricks back home in your drawers."

"Good call."

We drove to the spot, and I waited in the Cutlass while Zar talked to Cornelius. Most innocent-looking store in Crown Heights: Healthy Living Vegetarian Cafe and Juice Bar. They sold major weight, and only to maybe two or three cats, total. You had to come highly recommended, had to be Jamaican or be Isaac Eleazar.

The funny thing was that Cornelius could cook his ass off. You'd never know his spareribs were made of gluten. All Cornelius's daughters worked in there, too, and every one of them was fine as hell. Different mothers, different shades of lovely. I stopped flirting after Eleazar told me what the place was really about. Started noticing all the scars Cornelius had on his neck and his forearms, too. He was from Trenchtown, Zar said. Marley's neighborhood. You didn't get out of there without a fight.

The metal gate was still down when we arrived, but Cornelius was inside sweeping up. He raised it just enough to let Zar limbo underneath. I watched the face of the barrelchested, teak-skinned man in the white chef's apron darken as the pale, lanky dread bent to whisper in his ear. Then Cornelius laid his broom against a chair and beckoned Zar into the back room.

It wasn't even a minute later when Zar ducked back outside and jumped into the car. He didn't say anything, just fisted the wheel and swung the Cutlass around. His face was blank, like an actor getting into character. I'd always thought his eyes were blue, but now they looked gray, the color of sidewalk cement.

"So what he say?"

I figured he'd probably ignore the question, but I had to ask.

"He said 'Isaac, there are those that hang, and those who do the cutting.' And he gave me what I asked for." Zar opened the left side of his jacket and I saw the handle of a pistol. Looked like a .38. Used to have one of those myself.

"I was hoping Cornelius would tell you he'd take care of it," I said.

Zar shook his head about a millimeter. "Not how it works, T." He made a right onto Jumpshot's block, found a space and backed in—cut the wheel too early and fucked it up and had to start over. There was another car-length of space behind him, but Zar missed on the second try, too. I guess his mind was elsewhere. He nailed it on the third, flicked the key, and turned to me. Surprising how still it suddenly felt in there, with the engine off. How close.

"It's cool if you want to wait in the car, T." Zar said it staring straight ahead.

I ground my teeth together, felt my jaw flare. Mostly just so Zar would feel the weight of the favor. "I'm good."

"You good?"

"I'm good."

"Let's do this."

It was a pretty street. Row houses on either side, and an elementary school with a playground in the middle of the block. I used to live on a school block back Uptown. It'd be crazy loud every day from about noon to three—different classes going to recess, fifty or sixty juiced-up kids zooming all over the place. Basketball, tag, doubledutch. Couldn't be too mad at it, though. It was nice noise.

A thought occurred to me and I turned to Zar, who was trudging along with his hands pocketed and his head buried in his shoulders like a bloodshot, dreadlocked James Dean. "It's too early for a tournament, right?"

That was Jumpshot's other hustle. He had eight or ten TVs set up in his two-room basement crib, each one equipped with a PlayStation. For five or ten bucks, shorties from the neighborhood could sign up and play NBA Live or Madden Football or whatever, winner take all. Even the older kids, the young-thug set, would be up in Jump's crib, balling and smoking and betting. Jumpshot handled all the bookie action, in addition to selling the players beer and weed—at a markup, no less, like the place was a bar. It was kind of brilliant, really.

"Way too early," said Zar.

We stopped in front of Jumpshot's door. "Play it cool," I reminded him.

"We'll see," said Zar, and a little bit of that Brooklyn-Jew accent, that soft, self-assured intonation, surfaced for a second. For the first time, it occurred to me that maybe this wasn't the first time he'd done something like this. Maybe he didn't own a gun because he didn't trust himself with one. I don't know if the thought made me feel better or worse.

"He's got a loose ceiling tile in the bathroom," said Zar. "Right above the toilet." And he pressed the buzzer, hard, for about three seconds.

Static crackled from the intercom and then a grainy voice demanded *Who dat?*

Zar bent to the intercom, hands on his knees, and over-pronounced his words. "Jumpshot, it's Isaac. I've got to talk to you. It's very important."

I tried to catch Zar's eye, wanting to read his thoughts from his face. But his stare was frozen on the door. This much I was sure of: the longer Jumpshot took to open up, the worse for him.

But Jump's face appeared in the crack between door and jamb a second later, bisected by the chain-lock. He flicked his eyes at both of us, then closed the door, slid off the chain, and opened up. He was rocking black basketball shorts, a white wifebeater, and some dirty-ass sweatsocks. If he hadn't been asleep, he sure looked it.

"Fuck time is it?" He rubbed a palm up and down the right side of his face as he followed us inside.

"Early." Next to Jumpshot, Zar looked like a gaunt, ancient giant. "But I been up for hours."

"Yeah?" Jump said, sitting heavily on his unmade bed and bending to pull a pair of sneakers from underneath the frame. "Why's that?"

Eleazar reached into his jacket and pulled out the .38, held it at waist height so that the barrel was pointing right at Jumpshot's grill. "I think you know," he said calmly.

Jump looked up and froze. Just froze. Didn't move, didn't say shit. I gathered he'd never stared into that little black hole before.

Eleazar smiled. "Where's my shit, Jumpshot?" he asked conversationally. I gulped it back fast, but for a sec I thought I might puke. It wasn't the piece, or the fact that Jump suddenly looked like the seventeen-year-old kid he was. It wasn't even the weird fucking sensation of another dude's life passing before my eyes the way Jump's did just then. What turned my stomach was that Eleazar looked more content than I had ever seen him. Like he would do this every day if he could.

Jump opened his mouth, made a noise like *nhh*, and shook his head. I was beginning to feel sorry for him. I'd expected more of the dude. Some stupid Tony Montana bravado, at least: *fuck you, Eleazar. You gonna hafta kill me, nigga.*

"T."

"Yeah, man."

"Go take a look around, huh? I'ma have a little chat with my man here."

"Sure." I headed for the bathroom.

"What are you looking at him for?" I heard behind me. That rabbi voice again. "Look at me. That's better. Now listen carefully, Jumpshot. You listening? Okay. Here's the deal. You give me everything back, right now, no bullshit, and you get a pass. You get to pack your shit up and get the fuck out of dodge." There was a pause, and I could almost see Zar shrugging. "Who knows, maybe a broken leg for good measure. To remind you that stealing is wrong."

Finally, Jumpshot found his voice. It was raspy, clogged, but it cut through the stale air like a dart. "I didn't steal nothing," he said slowly, like if he spoke deliberately enough there was no way Eleazar could not believe him. "I . . . have. . . no . . . idea . . . what you're talking about."

I walked back into the room right on cue, and threw two bricks onto the bed. Jump started like I'd tossed a snake at him. "That was all I could find," I said. Jumpshot's face was a death mask now, so twisted that any lingering trace of sympathy I might have had for him straight vanished.

"Oh, and this." I handed Zar the gun. Jump raised up so fast I thought he might salute.

"I never seen that shit before in my life!" The veins in his neck strained; I could see the blood pumping.

"What, that?" Eleazar pointed at the bricks and raised his eyebrows. "That's weed, Jumpshot. Collie. Ishen. Ganja. Sensi. Goat shit. People smoke it. Gets them high. Or did you mean this?" Zar held up the Glock, and as soon as Jumpshot looked at it, *bam*: Zar swung the gun at him and hit Jump square in the face, the orbit of the eye. Knocked him back onto the bed, bloody. Jump let out a clipped yelp and grabbed his face, and Zar leaned over him, gun in the air, ready to pistol-whip the kid again.

"At least this shit is loaded," Zar said, eyes flashing. "At least you robbed me with a loaded gun. Next time, change your fuckin' shoes." *Bam*. Zar slammed the gun down again— hit Jump on the hand shielding his face. Jump screamed and curled like a millipede, this way and that.

Zar straightened, a gun in each hand, and swiped a forearm across his brow. "Ten minus two leaves eight," he said. "So where's the rest, Jump?"

"Fuck you." Jump said it loud and strong, as if the words came from deep inside him.

"No, Jump," Zar said. "Fuck you." He shoved the guns into his pockets, turned, and pulled the biggest television off its stand, whirled and heaved it toward Jumpshot. Missed. Thing must have been heavy; Zar barely threw it two feet. It landed upright. The screen didn't even break.

Zar glanced over at me, a little embarrassed. "Fuck this," he said. "Sit up, nigger. I'm through fucking with you. Sit up!"

Jumpshot did as he was told. Blood was smeared across his face, clotting over one eye. "Zar—"

"Shut up. Believe me, Jumpshot, I could fuck around and torture you for hours. Trust me, I know how. I even brought my knife. But I don't have time for all that. So I'm going to wait five seconds, and if you don't tell me where the rest of my shit is, I'm going to shoot you in the fucking chest, you understand? Go."

"I don't fucking know, man. You gotta believe me, Isaac, I swear to God I never seen that shit be—"

"Four."

"Please man, I swear on my mother's—"

Eleazar snatched a pillow off the floor and fired through it. Didn't muffle shit. Whole building probably heard the sound. Jump fell back flat. Zar wiped off the Glock and tossed it on the bed. Crossed his arms over his chest and stared down at Jumpshot. The blood was spreading beneath him, saturating the blankets. "What could that motherfucker have done with eight pounds of weed in two hours?"

"Maybe we should talk about that someplace else," I suggested.

"Mmm," said Zar. "That's probably a good idea." But we stood rooted to our spots, like we were observing a moment of silence. I watched Zar's eyes bounce from spot to spot and knew he was wondering if there was anything in the apartment worth taking. Watching him was easier than watching Jumpshot.

"Alright." The moment ended and Zar spun on his heel. We stepped outside. After the dimness of the apartment, the block seemed almost unbearably bright.

We drove back to the crib and ordered breakfast from the Dominican place. Zar had steak and eggs. "Aren't you supposed to be a vegetarian?" I asked. "Usually," he said with his mouth full, swiping a piece of toast through his yolk. He shook his head. "Eight fuckin' pounds."

"Only thing I can come up with is that he took it straight to one of the herbgates on Bedford," I said. "Pump and dump."

Zar nodded. "That's the only thing that makes sense. Anybody else would ask questions. I'll never see that weight again, basically."

"At least it was paid for, right?"

"Half up front, half on the re-up. That's how Cornelius does business." He steepled his hands and tapped his fingertips against his chin. "I'm gonna have to leave town, T. Take what I've got left, go down south, and lay low." He lowered his head, toyed with a lock. "I swore I'd never do the Greyhound thing again. But it's still the safest way to travel."

"How long you talking about?"

Zar shrugged. "A month or so. I'll go see my bredren in North Kack, bubble what I need to bubble, let shit blow over. You can mind the shop, right? Keep the business up and running so the Rastas don't start looking for a new connect?"

"If Cornelius will fuck with me, I can."

"He will. I'll set that up before I go."

"When you gonna bounce?"

Zar reached over and grabbed the duffel with the bricks in it. He walked over to his closet and dumped an armload of clothes inside, then bent down and pulled a floorboard loose. Inside the hollow was a roll of dough and one more brick. He tossed those in, too. I didn't bother to mention that it was my bag he was packing.

"I'm ready now," he said.

Zar took a shower, made a few phone calls. I went up to my crib and did the same, then came back down and rolled us one last spliff. We smoked in silence. Always the best way. When it was over Zar pushed off palms-to-knees, and stood. "Everything is set," he said, and tossed me the keys to the Cutlass. "You might as well get used to driving it."

We were quiet all the way to Times Square. I kept waiting for Zar to start peppering me with instructions, but he just leaned back in the passenger seat, rubbing his eyes. Occasionally, he'd sing a little snippet of a Marley song to himself: *don't let them fool ya/or even try to school ya*. Maybe it was stuck in his head and he just had to let it out, or maybe the song made him feel better. He had a good voice, actually.

I parked the car, walked him up to the ticketing desk and down to the terminal. The bus was already boarding. I offered Zar my hand; he clasped it, then pulled me into a shoulder-bang embrace. "Hey, listen," he said. "That shit with Jump-shot. I'm sorry. I didn't mean to call him a nigger. I was heated. You know I didn't mean anything by it, right?"

"I know," I said.

He leaned in for another soulshake. "Hold it down for me, bro."

"No doubt," I said.

"I'll see you in a month. And I'll call before then."

"Do that."

"Alright, bro. One love."

"Be safe," I said.

"No doubt."

"Peace."

"Peace." He glanced over his shoulder, hefted the duffel bag, and disappeared up the steps.

I walked to the far side of the terminal and checked my watch. Zar's bus was due to depart at 1:15. It was 1:13 when the two DTs I'd tipped off cut the line, flashed their badges at the driver, and boarded.

I didn't wait to see them haul Zar off, just got on the escalator, made my way back to the Cutlass, and rolled to Brooklyn.

Climbed the stairs to my apartment, triple-locked the door, and rolled myself another joint. Slipped on my brand-new Jordans, stacked my eight bricks into a pyramid, and just stared out the window, taking in my domain.

So long, Eleazar, I thought. *I never liked your fake ass anyway. Damn near shit yourself when I put that nine to your dome. Probably serve your whole sentence and never figure out what happened. Probably call me every week from the joint, talking about "What's going on, bro?" Probably expect cats to remember who you are when you get out.*

I turned the story on its back. "I don't know what to say. He barely even bothered to change the names. It's practically a confession. It *is* a confession."

"People write what they know," said Karen. "You ought to see some of the creepy shit that comes in. I forwarded a serial killer story to the cops one time, I was so sure the guy had done it."

"I mean, why change Abraham Lazarus to Isaac Eleazar, but leave Jumpshot's name the same? Because he's dead? Because it's a nickname? What the fuck?"

"Eleazar is Hebrew for Lazarus," Karen said. "I looked it up. And Isaac was Abraham's son. Pretty half-assed. Is Cornelius the dude's real name?"

"Nah, Everton. But he didn't bother to flip the name of the juice bar."

Cloud rolled his copy into a telescope, tapped it against the table. "Lazarus was in the pen with me. Only whiteboy down with the Jamaican Posse. Most niggas make shanks in prison? Those guys scraped cooking pots down into machetes. Hack-through-bone type shit."

I fingered the pages. "Theo Polhemus. I never heard anybody call him anything but T. Dude can write, huh? What do you think his other stories are about?"

"You're wandering a little off the point, youngblood."

"Which is?"

"The raising of funds." Cloud tipped his chair onto its hind legs. "Lazarus got sent up what, more than a year ago? If Polhemus is about his business, he should have three, four hundred K stacked by now."

"He is. From what I've seen, anyway."

"Good enough for me. We'll sting him for a hundred."

"Why not all of it?" asked Karen. "Certain members of the Immortal Five have got to get back on their own two feet."

"We wanna make this a simple decision, something he can live with. Strip a dude naked, you gonna find out more about his true nature than you care to know."

I took a pull of coffee. "You don't seem like the blackmail type, Cloud."

"I prefer the term 'extortion.'" He picked up his coffee cake, crammed half into his mouth.

I figured I had a few seconds before he was able to speak again. "Listen, at the risk of . . . Just for the record . . ."

"Let me guess: you like the nigga." Cake crumbs sprayed the table.

"Yeah, I do. He's a good boss."

But he was more than that. What, exactly, was hard to put into words, not that I would've waxed poetic about the dude to Cloud and Karen anyway. T wasn't my friend. One time he'd let me take home a Chester Himes novel I'd started reading at his crib, but we'd never had a conversation about anything personal. He didn't trust me any more than he trusted anybody, which was to say not at all. And yet, we both knew that I saw something in him which would have been deadly if I'd been anybody else: the fact that his soul wasn't in the drug game. Not to the exclusion of all else, the way the unwritten charter stipulated it should be. He had other plans, ambitions you couldn't weigh on a triple-beam scale, and no degree of acumen or ruthlessness could balance that out. I had no clue what those plans were, had never given it much thought, but I could see it because I recognized it in myself. Anybody could see it in me, of course. But I was just a kid with a paper route. T was supposed to be running the show.

Karen leaned over the table and tapped the manuscript with her forefinger, very TV-cop-interrogating-prisoner. "How can you say that, after reading this?"

"I'm not saying I approve. Just, he's a likable guy. Especially compared to Lazarus. Or Jumpshot, who for the record was a total dipshit."

"That makes it okay to frame him and get him killed?"

"Jesus, Karen. I never said it was okay. Slick, maybe. Elegant. But not okay. Okay?"

"One of Jumpshot's people came at Lazarus in the showers," said Cloud. "A cousin or something."

"And?"

"Jamaicans cut him up."

"Cloud?"

"Youngblood."

"Isn't T going to wonder how you know so much?"

"Nope. Gonna show his dumb ass a copy of this fine literary effort."

"What if he only sent it to Karen's agency? He could track her down."

"There is no her. I'm her."

"Plus, Dondi, nobody gives Authors' Inc. an exclusive look. We're second-tier." She laid her hand over mine. "I'm not worried."

I looked from Karen to Cloud, then back to Karen. "In that case, I need you to do me a favor when this is finished. To even things out."

Cloud brushed the crumbs off his fingers and shot me a look of disgust, or disbelief, or some kind of dis-. "We're already doing this the hard way, out of respect for your employment status."

"What's the easy way?"

Cloud reached out and snatched the remaining coffee cake off my plate. Before he could bring it to his mouth, Karen slapped the slice out of his hand.

"You're not in jail, fool. Act civilized. There's plenty more." She shook her head, and stood to cut him some.

Cloud fingered the corner of my manuscript. "The easy way is selling this information to Everton and walking away."

Karen laid another wedge of cake on the table. "I told him that wasn't an option."

"Thanks. But I still need you to do something."

Cloud snorted, forked his slice in half. "I guess you couldn't have turned out any way *but* stubborn, with these two knuckle-heads for parents."

Karen made a show of ignoring him. "Something such as?"

"Get T a book deal. Shop his manuscript."

"What?" In stereo.

"'Crown Heist' is tight. If the rest are like this, he deserves to be published."

"Shit," Cloud said between bites, "if the rest are like this, I'm gonna be a millionaire."

"You know representing clients isn't part of my job."

"Neither's running a workshop for the lunatic fringe."

She crossed her legs at me. Another gesture Karen had weap-onized.

"It's the least you can do."

"The least I can do is nothing."

"Well, you're not doing nothing. You're extorting my boss, who's been nothing but fair to me."

She hit me with one of her trademark venom-eyed stares, but I was ready: held it, neutralized it, watched it fade, then pounced.

"This is exactly the kind of perverse shit you live for, Karen. And you know I know it."

She sighed, twiddled her spoon, tried to sound petulant.

"Just so you know, the market for debut story collections is fuck-ing abysmal."

ccording to the Ambassador—who, when he's out of glue, has been known to deliver impromptu lectures of considerable scholarship—the underground has not always inspired fear. In ancient times it was safer than topside: the site of mankind's early, womb-like dwellings and the haven to which death would return him. Mining was considered a dirty business when it started, a kind of rape; special rites of absolution were performed at the outset of any expedition. With the rise of science the metaphor changed, and the nurturing mother became a vast brain from whose recesses knowledge had to be extracted in the name of progress. That dovetailed nicely with the needs of industry, and soon the planet was being hollowed out and restocked with sewers and trains, water mains and electrical lines.

The modern city required a level of coordination between its visible and submerged halves that made the idea of people living underground plausible again. But who would populate it, now that the subterrain was so tainted by both the ascendant heaven-and-hell cosmology and the fact that it was full of things we didn't want to see? Laborers and slaves, naturally. And thus the underground came to symbolize the silent oppressed, always threatening to breach the bright surface. Your boy H. G. Wells imagined a future in which mine workers degenerated into a depraved new race; Chuck Dickens and Vic Hugo envisioned sewer-dwelling classes totally severed from the world above, their very existence un-guessed-at.

The mythic journey to the underworld is typically embarked upon alone, but there are exceptions. Like the drunken Athenian duo of Theseus and Pirithous, whose idiotic plan to kidnap Persephone ended in tears. Or my man Odysseus, who brought all his sailors on a roadtrip to the Kingdom of Hades that was more an excuse for Homer to relate the fates of the Greek heroes after Troy than a portrait of hell.

Or me, Billy and Dengue, whose Sunday morning began with a cab ride to the meatpacking district, and continued with a squeeze through a chain-link flap cut from a razor-wire-topped fence. From there, we clambered through a trash-strewn lot, into the alley alongside an abandoned brick building. A wooden door with a dangling padlock opened into a small room. A man slept loudly in one corner, atop a swirl of newspapers and clothes. In another was a jagged hole, chopped through the cement floor. The top rungs of a rusty ladder breached the opening.

We climbed down into a stagnant, pissy near-darkness, and started walking: along the ledge of one train tunnel, then through a service door and down a spiraling flight of metal stairs, into another. Then up to the catwalk.

Billy led the way and I led Dengue, who managed to keep up surprisingly well. What light there was fell in narrow beams, and seemed exhausted from the journey. I'd been forbidden to bring a flashlight. "Cops carry flashlights," the Ambassador had said, and that was that.

Tunnel is one of those concepts you think you understand, but don't—not until you walk through one. We're talking about a goddamn cylinder hollowed out of the rock and dirt that is our planet, and New York City sits atop hundreds of miles' worth, eighteen stories deep in some places and three or four in most. You know

what an ant farm looks like? That's what all our apartment buildings and museums and shit are built on. Forgive me if this is all
obvious to you, or if it sounds like stoner wisdom. If you've never
been down there, you only think you know what I'm talking about.
Whatever, forget it.

Another ladder, me spotting Dengue from below and imagining
the Ambassador losing his footing, taking me down with him, the
two of us shishkabobbed atop a railroad spike for all eternity. And
then we were trudging through a deeper tunnel, tar black and
echoing with the drip of water so that if you weren't too busy waving your hands in front of you and being terrified, you might imagine you were in a cave.

"Couldn't we have done this at a Starbucks?" I asked.

Billy was too far ahead to hear me, Dengue too focused on
drawing breath to respond.

"Or at Fizz's crib. Fizz's office. A church. A synagogue. A mosque.
Maybe not a mosque. Those probably *are* under surveillance."

"Almost there," my father called. I heard him take off running,
then a grunt and a beat of silence and the slap of both his sneakers
hitting the ground at once. "Wait till you see this," he called, sounding like nothing so much as a kid showing off a new Christmas toy.

He was acting pretty goddamn close to normal, and it seemed
clear to me that the idea of revenge was what had nudged him
those final, crucial degrees. Which worried me, a lot: revenge was
what had taken him away, and I knew it could snatch him up again.
And not for nothing? The same obsessive streak or justice-lust or
impulse for self-sabotage ran in my veins, too—had ruled my
thoughts of Billy all those years he was gone, even if I hadn't recognized it as such until now.

"Keep going straight?" I called.

"Hold on, hold on." A tinkling sound, like a wind chime, and
then light flooded the tunnel. Billy stood above us, beneath an
ornate, soot-covered chandelier.

"Voilà. The Parlor."

Four feet up from the tracks, just like a regular subway station, was a huge, semicircular space—not technically a hall, but it felt like one. The ceiling was domed, the fixture suspended precisely in the middle. It was meant to hang much higher off the ground, but the electrical wiring had been yanked loose, presumably so that one might screw in a bulb, as Billy had.

Inlaid mirrors covered the walls, so sixty watts went a long way. There were benches on one side, rows of them lined up like church pews, angled inward so that anyone seated there would have a perfect view of the piano positioned opposite. It was a grand.

Billy's eyes sparkled as he watched me climb up and take in the space. At my expression, I suppose, or the memory of his own first visit. Or the fact that he was sharing this place—hell, sharing anything—with his son.

"Piano still here?" asked the Ambassador, scrabbling over the ledge and brushing himself off.

"Where would it go?" Billy took his arm, just above the elbow. "This way."

"That's all right, I can get there." Billy let go and Dengue bee-lined to it, pulled out the bench, sat down. He fished a tube of airplane glue out of his pocket, rubbed some on the collar of his T-shirt, and treated himself to a big exhilarating-sunrise-on-the-mountaintop breath. "Any requests?"

"Since when do you play the piano?" I asked.

"Shit, if a blind black man can't tinkle the ivories, who can?"

"It's tickle, not tinkle."

"'Straight, No Chaser,'" said Billy. He was seated on a bench, legs crossed at the ankles, smiling wide and calm like all was right with the world.

"Excellent choice." Dengue made claws of his hands, cracking the upper joints of his fingers. "I only know one song," he explained. "But I play the fuck out of it."

The piano was so monstrously out of tune that evaluating the performance was impossible. I walked over and sat behind Billy.

"What is this place?"

He leaned back, spoke over his shoulder. "It was supposed to be the central station of a private train line they built in the thirties. Company went bankrupt. It was never even used."

Dengue murdered Monk for a while, notes ricocheting off the tunnel walls. He'd located an octave in which the keys weren't even connected to their wires. Hitting them produced a thwack that the Ambassador seemed to believe he could employ as percussion.

Billy listened like he was sitting in Symphony Space. I wanted to ask him how he could be so comfortable in one tunnel, and so convinced that a nexus of evil energy dwelled in another. Weren't they all connected? Couldn't this demon move around?

Dengue built to a horrific crescendo, pounding the busted keyboard with iron hands, and then it was over. Billy clapped; I did the same.

I stopped. He stopped. The clapping didn't.

We stood up. Dengue too, so fast he knocked over the piano bench.

"Who's there?"

Into the light strolled a reedy black man, head-to-toed in camouflage like he'd just stepped off a troop transport from Tikrit, patchy beard and all. Only he was pushing fifty: a first-generation writer, a graffiti grandpa. The fact that he was rocking wraparound sunglasses in total blackness confirmed it. All those dudes were bonkers.

"Me." His voice was hoarse, but strong.

"What up, Drum?" from Billy.

Dude swung himself up into the parlor like a gymnast mounting the parallel bars.

"Kill that, kill that. The handle's Supreme Chemistry now. I take that Drum shit as a diss, you know what I'm sayin'?" He gave Billy a pound. "Welcome home, kid. Dengue, what's good, my ninja?"

"Supreme Chem, how you livin'?"

"Yo, ninjas is on some bullshit, B, but what else is new? I been beefin' with this one sucker ninja all week on some message board stupidness. Ninja talkin' greazy 'bout how he invented bubble letters. I'm like, 'Ninja, I been doin' this since '69, where you was at? How come I ain't see no trains with your name on 'em 'til spring '72? If you was at the Writers' Bench so much, why true school ninjas don't even recognize your face?' Not to mention, they ain't even bubble letters, the name is softies. Yo B, I had to break down how much of what the world been jockin' for like the last thirty bullets is just ninjas bitin' Supreme Chem's formulas, from softies to three-Ds to the way I dropped my R behind my D when ninjas was off eatin' Watermelon Now and Laters with Miss Lucy and shit. But let me stop running my mouth. Meanwhile, here come this other ninja, out the woodwork *behind* the woodwork, ain't been heard from in ten, twelve years and now he claimin' he kinged the BMTs in like '77–'78. Shit is crazy, B. Ninjas wanna act all wild west on the interwebs, like they can't get mashed in the face when they step out they little no-windows basement apartment. I call 'em lie-oneers, you know what I'm saying? Origihaters. But let me stop running my mouth. What's the science on this meeting, B? I hope y'all ain't bringin' no ninjas I got beef with."

"That would be practically impossible," said Dengue, giving Supreme Chemistry a pound.

Until the dude smiled, I wouldn't have thought it possible. "True, true. How they say, B? Heavy is the head that wears the crown."

"So that's why I got a headache." Cackles in the darkness, from a direction I hadn't even noticed, and then Nick Fizz and two other dudes emerged.

You know that thing I said earlier about pink-fur-Kangol gay Puerto Rican b-boy flair? I meant it as a figure of speech. But goddamn it if Nick Fizz wasn't rocking an actual pink fur Kangol. Funny thing is, it didn't even look that gay. He had one of those beards you've gotta touch up three times a week at la barberia, same as half of all Boriquan males between fifteen and fifty-five, and the hat was cocked at the classic diddy-bop degree. It matched one of his polo shirt's stripes, sat atop a pair of chunky old-school eyeglasses. By the time you got done looking at him, it seemed totally hetero-plausible.

Cloud and Dengue had squabbled about whether to invite him, Cloud arguing that Fizz had too much to lose to be trusted, and that his old crew, the one he'd have to reunite, was even more scattered than most. Dengue said Nick was solid as ever, and asked Cloud how the fuck he thought he knew anything about anybody after sixteen in the hoosegow, and in this way the matter was resolved.

I gave Fizz a hug and shook hands with the infamous Sambo CFC—who indeed had curly hair, though I'd imagine it had covered far more of his head when he took his nom de plume—and a guy who introduced himself as Stoon BMS, then stepped back a full pace as if expecting me to fall forward onto my face at the thrill of meeting him.

Every few minutes after that, a pair of writers or a trio would step into the light, until I felt like I was watching a kind of reverse play, me standing on stage and the various characters entering from the wings, the aisles. There were twelve people there, plus me, when Dengue sounded a chord on the piano and called the meeting to order. Everybody sprawled on the pews except Supreme Chemistry, who stood behind us like a sentry.

What happened next reminds me of the most boring scene in all of Homer. Just when the action's heating up, my man takes a ten-page time-out to run down every vessel that sailed to Troy, who its captain was, how many battalions of troops he brought, and for what heroic attributes and agricultural products motherfuckers from that particular region of Greece were known. A little later, he provides an equally stupefying catalog of armies on the Trojan side.

How long do you figure it should take a dozen guys who all know each other anyway to introduce themselves? Three minutes, maybe? I'm going to skip the play-by-play—don't say I never did anything for you—but this is how it manages to take fifteen:

"Whaddup, whaddup, good to be here, good to be here, Stoon BMS representing Castle Hill, na'mean, BMS president, na'mean, Bronx Most Shocking, Beat Mad Suckers, Best Motherfuckin' Style, Boogiedown Meets Shaolin, whatever whatever. Original members was myself, Dash 7, who was vice president, um, Ty-Ty 99, Javelin—R.I.P.—and Maser. Then, lemme see, Xerxes and Asap got down in '79, and then Blaze One, Mug, Swag 3, Phast, and Skizz. I also represent 12 Angry Monkeys, 12AM Crew, that's me, Lord Ock, Fed 125 . . ."

And so on. They were a haggard bunch, even taking the dress-down nature of the occasion into account. There was something in their faces, the hang of their skin. They had outlived what they'd invented, and this doomed them to live in the past, and fear the present. That's my half-assed take, anyway.

When it was over, Dengue came around and stood in front of the piano. "I'll get right to it. Y'all speak for the illest subway crews of all time, and we called you here for one reason: because it's time to take back these trains."

His dramatic pause played like an awkward silence. That was punctured by a pudgy, babyfaced Puerto Rican, name of Species, the founder of a comparatively newjack crew from Queens. They'd come late to the party, squeezed in two or three years of intense mayhem as the subway era was winding down. Another contested invite, despite the fact that his squad was the most active on the docket.

"Yo, Dengue, no disrespect? Your man Rage called this meeting, all mysterious, back from the dead and shit. So first things first, a'ight? How we know he ain't five-oh?"

All heads turned to Billy, but before he could respond, the dull thump of a body hitting the ground refocused the collective attention.

Supreme Chemistry stood over Species, blackjack in hand. And I don't mean a face card and an ace.

"No disrespect to you either," he rasped, and raised his eyes— assuming he had some, behind those shades—to the rest of us.

"Those who don't study their history are doomed to be fuckin' stupid forever." He crouched, slipped the blackjack into one of the pockets lining his fatigues, and cracked some smelling salts under his victim's nose. "Rise and shine, ninja." Species twitched and woke. "While you was 'sleep we agreed that Billy ain't no po-po," Supreme Chemistry informed him. "Next time you feel like talking, count to ten first, and then shut the fuck up."

I was beginning to like this guy.

Species rubbed the back of his head, scowled, arranged his limbs to stand. "Yo, what the—"

Supreme Chem pressed four fingertips to Species' chest. "What I just say, B? Check this out: I already forgot your name, but if you on some graffiti shit, then I'm your daddy. You livin' under my roof, ninja. Now show some manners and apologize to Rage."

Species looked around, incredulous that no one was interceding on his behalf. We all waited.

"Okay. I'm sorry." Without a sound, Supreme Chem drifted back to his position in the rear. "I apologize. It's just"—Species looked over both shoulders—"I mean, shit is crazy right now. Vandal Squad is laying fools *out*. Y'all heard what happened to Hades?" Yes-nods, no-nods. "They ran up in his crib last week with search warrants, took his computer. He's got six thousand photos on there, and they're using them as evidence, charging him in four different boroughs. Seven to ten years *each*."

"If he gets convicted, we're all fucked," said Fizz. "That shit will set a precedent."

"What's his defense?" I asked.

Fizz shrugged. "That he stopped writing when his daughter was born, in '93, and anything more recent is copycats. And that of course he has pictures of graffiti on his computer, he publishes books about graffiti, he's a historian."

"Which is why they want him in the first place," said Stoon. "Anybody getting paid off this, Bracken is gunning for."

Another patch of dead air, this one more ruminative than

awkward. Gradually the attention drifted back to Billy, who didn't notice. I once saw a clip of Ronald Reagan standing motionless behind a podium for five minutes, looking like a wax statue. Then somebody shouts, "rolling," and he launches right into a speech. It's chilling. I nudged Billy's foot with mine and he reanimated, Gipper-style.

"Um, so basically, the plan is to bomb every train in the system, all at once. Start Saturday night and work through Monday morning. One crew to a yard. For security reasons, only you guys, the crew presidents, will know the big picture. Everybody else is gonna think they're just taking out a line." He glanced over at Dengue. "There's, you know, a lot of specifics to go over, but we've figured most of it out already. We've got some money, or we're gonna have some money, for supplies and—"

"They watch the paint stores now, Billy." It was a guy called Vexer, a lightskinned Dominicano. His voice was gentle, like your favorite grade school teacher breaking a piece of bad news. "I don't know if you knew that, seeing as you been away. Buying more than five cans is probable cause. They be doin' stop-and-searches."

"I didn't know that. But I wasn't talking about paint. I meant night vision goggles, trip wires, smoke bombs, tranquilizer rifles. Bail bonds. Any information we might have to pay for." With each item Billy ran down, the silence deepened. Words like these breathed life into the enterprise. "We're good on paint already. Cloud 9 is covering that."

Snickers around the Parlor.

"Picking up where he left off, huh?"

"This is an old stash. A truck he jacked back in the day, and put on ice." The Ambassador paused. "Any of y'all happen to attend Cloud's homecoming party?"

A few guys mumbled that they had.

"Then you know the stakes. We're the Committee to Not Elect Anastacio Bracken by Fucking Up His Trains."

"He's ten points behind in the polls," said Fizz.

"Yeah, but he's raised the most dough," countered Stoon. "That's all that counts in politics, watch."

"You crazy, man. In this city, it's union endorsements. Bracken—"

"Fuckin' MacNeil and Lehrer over here," said the Ambassador. "So what's up? Everybody ready to rustle up their people and make history, or do I have to give my big inspirational speech?"

"I know *I* need to be inspired, dog. I was at Cloud's party. Billy ripped his name out of my blackbook and ate it. You saw it, Vex. So did you."

He pointed at me. I guess I forgot to mention that Dregs was in the house.

"Yo, mega, *mega*-respect, Billy, man, but are you sure you're up to this? I mean, you been off in the jungle, just got back, probably haven't, like, totally readjusted yet. . . ."

"Painting that creepy juju shit in the tunnels . . ." Sambo added, under his breath.

"Yeah, yeah, right. I know if it was me, I'd need a year just to get my head straight. I damn sure wouldn't be ready to organize no *Mission: Impossible* shit."

My father smiled indulgently. "I wanted to learn how to defend myself. For when I came home. Those symbols in the tunnels were for spiritual protection—if they're what I think they are, anyway. I, uh . . . don't remember painting them."

The silence this time was tender.

"I heard the shamen taught you how to throw hex," Blam 2 tossed into the void.

"Shamans, ninja. Not shamen. Read a fuckin' book one time in your life."

"Word?" said Vexer. "You on some Obi-Wan Kenobi Gandalf Merlin shit now, Billy?" Grateful laughs. Dregs' was the loudest.

Billy stared into the darkness. "I learned some things," he said. "But this city's no rainforest."

Supreme Chem's throaty voice rose from the back. "Ayo, B, you bring any bazaguanco back with you? I been trying to get my hands on some, but ninjas won't send me any; they all say you gotta come to it, it doesn't come to you."

Billy looked startled. "That's kind of the rule."

Sambo raised his hand, waved it around. "Uh, hello? Hi. What the fuck are we talking about here?"

Supreme Chemistry turned toward him. "Whatchu wanna talk about, Sambo? How your man Shamrock went over me on the 1 train with his little bullshit straight letters and you ain't stop him? 'Cause Kimza told me you was there, ninja."

"I don't give a fuck what Kimza told you, dude. Ask that nigga why he started putting up CFC, when he was never even down for one second."

"Cuz Shamrock's a fuckin' basehead, that's why," called Klutch One, from across the room. "He'll put anybody down who gets him high. Should call that shit the Crack Fiend Crew."

"Yo," said Vexer, rising, "it's kings or better in here, man. Chill. Put it aside."

"Shit, if these ninjas is kings, I *know* I'm an Or Better. I carried the cross on my back for decades, and now these little pisswater ninjas—"

"Fuck this," said Blam 2. "I didn't come down here to reheat twenty-year-old beef."

"Yo, it is what it is, B. Certain shit gotta get rectified, you feel me?"

"No," said Billy, loud enough to turn heads. "I don't feel you. I don't feel any of you."

He walked to the front of the room, paused for a second as if about to speak, and then changed his mind. Stepped down from the Parlor into the gaping nothingness, and was gone.

"Billy!" His name echoed in the tunnel. "Come back, man!"

Dengue pointed after him. "There goes the readiest, downest, *uppest* dude in history. You goddamn . . . *children!*"

He roared the word, and banged his walking stick against the floor for emphasis. Poseidon couldn't have done it any better;

I half-expected a river to gush forth where wood met ground. "We come to you with a plan that can *redeem* all your sorry old asses, make it all *mean* something. But you don't even *see* that, because you don't know what you are."

He turned on his heel and walked away, behind the piano, only to double back. "This should be a New York City thing, strictly. But it's gonna happen, with or without you petty motherfuckers. I got Germans who are down. Niggas from Brazil who *wreck* shit. If you want it to be them who take your trains back, fine." He spun away again. For a couple of seconds, all you could hear was the scuttle of rats.

"Was that your big inspirational speech?" asked Fizz.

Dengue spoke without turning around. "Give or take."

"Not bad. You got it in your pocket in braille or something?"

"Go suck some dick, you fuckin' corporate sellout." But the Ambassador was trying not to smile.

"You know, Fev," said Vexer, "none of us said no."

"Far from it," added Stoon.

"And no doubt, it's gotta be an NYC exclusive," Sambo said. "I think even me and 'Preme can agree on that. Am I right?" He raised his fist into the air, behind his head. Supreme Chemistry came forward, bumped it with his own.

"Yeah, ninja. You right about that, if nothing else."

"Awww. Now hug."

"Fuck you, Fizz," 'Preme and Sambo said together.

Blam 2 tapped me on the knee. "Little Rage, go see if you can catch up with your old man."

Billy stepped into the light. "I'm right here. Let's get down to business."

————

"Yo, ninja, lemme bark at you right quick." Supreme Chemistry loped over, threw an arm around my father's shoulders, glanced over both his own as if to make sure nobody was eavesdropping. Only Dengue, Vexer and I were left; the other writers had melted back into the blackness when the meeting wrapped, minutes before.

"What's up?"

He rubbed his thumb against his nose, sniffed, cracked his neck. "Check the flavor, my ninja. Long as you down here, you best to go see Lou. You know she gonna hear about this, if she ain't already, and you don't need homegirl throwin' salt in the game, on some ol' 'how Billy gon' be in my neighborhood and not pay his respects?' type shit." His arm swung up again, and Supreme Chemistry pushed his shades flush to his cheekbones. "I'm saying, Vex Boogie can take Little Rage and Fever topside, and me and you can dap her up real quick, you feel me?"

Billy goggled at him for what felt like an epoch.

"Lou?"

"Lou, ninja. Don't tell me you don't remember Lou. Who you think kept you alive in these tunnels, gave you paint and fed you track rabbits and shit?"

"The Mole People," said Dengue, strolling over. "Of course." He brightened. "Hey, maybe they'd help. You all could ask."

"Come on," I said. "There's no Mole People. You guys are fucking with me. I saw *C.H.U.D.* That shit was bullshit."

"Rats?" Billy blinked at Supreme Chem. "You're saying I ate rats?"

'Preme turned his head and hocked a snotwad into the abyss. We all watched its majestic arc.

Splat.

"Time's a-wastin', B, and Lou's camp is a hike. We going or what?"

"I guess so," said Billy, slow. "If you guys think I should."

"Yo, Lou got mad people," Vex put in. "If she wanted to help niggas, she could help niggas." He spit through his front teeth, a sleek bullet of saliva that landed without a sound. "Not that she's gonna help niggas."

"I'll go too," I said. "Maybe I can help convince her."

The Ambassador smiled. "Getting a taste for downstairs, huh?"

I shrugged it off, but he was right. Being underground touched some vigorous, neglected part of me that had never stopped wanting to have adventures and explore new lands—the part graffiti channeled when my parents were my age, and nothing channels today, to my generation's great misfortune. No options for a city kid who likes scrabbling up stuff and outgrows jungle gyms, unless you want to go balls-to-the-wall and do that Parkour shit and break your skull. You could join one of those rock-climbing gyms, I guess, but it always smells like farts in there. Besides, scaling some fake wall while a harness hugs your nuts might be good exercise, but it's got nothing to do with freedom.

We said goodbye to Vex and Fever, and got moving. Half an hour of winding, forking tunnel brought us to a flight of metal stairs, and then we were trudging through a series of cavernous rooms separated by grated doors. The ground was littered with lean-tos, sleeping bags, mattresses, fresh human shit—like a foul, Mole version of Central Park during the Great Depression.

"Night camps," Supreme Chemistry explained, covering his nose with his shirt. "Fuckin' trailer parks of the tunnels. You want a ten-dollar suck-off from a foster-care runaway with trackmarks, come back through here in about six hours."

"Thanks, I'll set my watch."

"Oh, Rage-ito got jokes, huh? Let me guess. You're the *funny* black dude up at that hincty-ass school."

"Yeah, something like that."

"Where is everybody?" Billy asked.

"Upstairs hustling. We still close to the surface. These mufuckers come downstairs to crash, but they don't *live* here. Cops bust this up like once a week. The real camps are deeper. Harder to find."

"How do *you* know where?"

"I'm Supreme Chemistry, B. The world is my living room. Here, have a granola bar. I got Peanut Butter Chocolate or Cookies and Cream."

We stopped before a cement wall. "First the doggie door," 'Preme said, and dropped flat to arch himself through a sledgehammered opening. Billy and I followed. On the other side was a narrow ridge, overlooking an abyss, though I use *overlooking* loosely. I couldn't see a thing.

"Now the monkey vine." He reached into the blackness and grabbed a thick cable, like a magician pulling a card out of thin air. Wrapped his legs around it. Vanished.

I went next, and came down a three-count later, atop a layer of trash bags stuffed with clothes—to cushion the drop, Supreme Chem said, but also to make the floor invisible, so that if somebody uninvited made it to the ledge and looked down, he wouldn't risk a jump.

The eyes tricked the brain all kinds of ways down here. You'd catch a flash of light in your periphery, whirl toward it and find nothing, only the darkness spinning itself up around you as punishment for turning your head too fast. Sounds echoed above, in the cubbyholes hollowed from the walls, and you'd look up and see vampiric silhouettes swoop toward you, only to disintegrate an instant before fang found neck. Or your eyes picked out a shape that seemed impossible, and you dismissed it, told yourself no rat could be that big—and then whoosh, the figment brushed against your leg and trundled past like the sale at Macy's was ending in fifteen minutes and you were just one more street-clogging imbecile.

Before long light breached the horizon, cold and pale like it was coming from one of those lamps set toward the bottom of a swimming pool, with none of the flicker or heat of the few campfires we'd passed. I looked away and my eyes seared a bright square blotch onto a charred wall: my own personal Rothko.

"Hold up." Supreme Chemistry stopped short, and I walked into his forearm like it was a turnstile bar.

"Good guests don't show up unannounced." He leaned past me, grabbed a stick propped up against the tunnel wall, and thwanged a pipe running just below the ceiling. A few seconds later, someone on the other end tapped back.

We rounded a final bend, and stepped into an enormous natural cavern, so high and wide that for a moment it seemed we weren't underground at all. Light trickled in through a street grate, bounced off the craggy walls and reached the dwellings speckling the flat ground stripped of warmth, more like moonbeams than sunshine.

Cardboard and bedsheets and black plastic were the primary building materials, plus the occasional beam of salvaged wood. Sounds humble, but some of these structures wound on and on, like the pillow-fort a rich kid with mad couches would build in his living room. There were a few proper tents, too, and as I looked up I saw that every suitable nook and hollow in the high rock walls served as a domicile. Candles threw skittish light on bedding and bookcases; clotheslines sagged with wash. From one of those aeries, a radio wheezed a Bob Dylan song. I'm not sure which one, but Kid Capri wasn't DJing, so it wasn't "Subterranean Homesick Blues," though that is by far the man's best work. Or at least the only joint I found listenable on the *Greatest Hits* CD the Uptown Girl gave me as part of the Advanced Whiteness Studies curriculum that dating her required me to master.

Billy and I just stood there, at the mouth, trying to absorb it all. In front of me, a swarm of kids chased a soccer ball. Behind them, two women cooked over a waist-high metal trashcan, pots balanced on chickenwire, flames oranging their faces.

A sense of peace, of stillness, seemed to permeate the place. That lasted for about thirty seconds, at which point the largest female human being I had ever seen walked straight up to my father, reared back her oven-mitt-sized hand, and slapped Billy across the jaw so hard she turned his head.

"You got a lot of balls, showing up here. And you got a lot bringing him, Drum."

I waited for Supreme Chemistry to tell her his new name.

He didn't.

Billy rubbed his cheek. "You must be Lou." If it sounds like a funny thing to say, it wasn't.

She looked him over. "Heard you were gonna be downstairs. Heard you got your life together."

"You hear a lot," I said.

She snapped a look at me, the kind the pitcher gives the runner on first base, then stepped in close to Billy. "Half these people think you cursed us, man. Come on, before the whole world sees you."

Off she loped. We jogged to keep up. It was like crossing the set of a Civil War movie—you know, the scene where you see the whole bustling battlefield tent city laid out, and then come to the general's quarters, full of crystal decanters and elaborate furniture some battalion of assholes had to lug across four states. Lou's residence was a deep natural recess, a cave within the cave. Cinderblock bookcases lined one wall. The other was a pantry, stocked with cans. Near the entrance, two wooden park benches faced off over a milkcrate coffeetable draped with a piece of coarse African-patterned fabric, the kind you can buy at any street fair. It matched the curtain she'd slapped aside to admit us, and the one obscuring whatever lay farther in.

Billy, Supreme Chemistry and I squeezed onto one bench. Our hostess took up most of the other.

"I didn't curse anyone," my father said. "That wasn't in my training."

"I don't mean you threw a curse, Billy. I mean you are one." Lou leaned forward, elbows on her knees, and used one dreadlock to fasten the rest into a ponytail. "Last week, some real nasty cops started fucking with my people. Asking questions about you."

"Bracken? The one running for mayor?"

"You think I'm living in a goddamn cave so I can follow politics? No pig yet knows how to find my camp, and I don't leave but once a month. A white cop who likes to hurt people, that's all I know. Him and his boys. They been grabbing our runners on the way down. Making threats, and making good on those threats. Look."

Lou pointed halfway up the cavern wall. I squinted and saw a thick pipe jutting from the bedrock. Below it, on the ground, was a toppled stack of white plastic buckets, the kind painters use.

"He made the Tears of Buddha dry up," she said. "Without a water source, this place can't last."

"Maybe the city fixed the leak," I suggested.

"After ten years?" Lou's bench creaked as she sat down. "'Bring him to me, or you'll be drinking each other's piss,' that's what he told my guy. Next morning, dry."

We took that in.

"All your work's been painted over, Billy. You probably wouldn't know where to look, but if you did, you'd see."

"Who?" I asked. "How?"

"The same way your old man had everybody bringing him paint to 'defend' us against demons to begin with." She turned to Supreme Chemistry. "He staggers in a few weeks ago, smelling like year-old ass. No fucking grasp on reality whatsoever, even for down here. Ranting and raving about all type of evil spirits and shit—when he was strong enough to speak at all, which was about an hour a day before these good-hearted, gullible motherfuckers started forcing whatever food they could spare down his throat." She spread her arms across the top slat of the bench and glowered. "Belief is destiny down here. Folks scare easy, and they do what they think they have to. They listened when he told them he needed paint to make us safe from the fuckin' boogeyman, and they listened when the cop said get rid of it or get their legs broke. Busted their tails until everything was gone."

"Wait a sec," I said. "The guy defending you leaves, and you get attacked? You ought to be glad he's back."

"That's some faulty-ass logic."

"I know."

My father stood. "I'm sorry, Lou. I never meant to cause you any trouble. Is there anything we can do to help?"

She eyed Billy from her bench. "Why don't you just tell me what you want, man? I know you didn't drop by to thank me for saving your life, because you haven't."

"No, no, I . . ." My father clasped his hands behind his back, but they only stayed that way a second. "Thank you."

"Don't mention it." Lou raised her eyebrows and treated him to several theatrical blinks.

"We, uh, we were hoping you might . . ."

"Let me guess. Y'all got some fuckin' scheme to paint them trains, and you want my people's help."

"How did—"

"I hear a lot."

"Yeah, you sure do, girl," Supreme Chemistry chimed in. "That's what I always tell ninjas: Don't nothing get by my honey Lou. She the boss of the tunnels and shit, like Don Corleone meets fuckin' . . . fuckin' . . ."

"Save it." She rose, bent, threw a finger in his face. "Don't try to play me, Drum."

He shut his mouth. She wheeled toward Billy.

"You're asking me to put this community at risk, when we're already in crisis. It'd be out of line coming from anybody, but from you it's, I don't know. Preposterous. I've got half a mind to hand you over to that cop myself."

"See, now that's an interesting choice of words," Supreme Chemistry said, and without so much as uncrossing his legs, he extracted from one of his innumerable pockets what I can only describe as a very large, chromey, decidedly modern-looking hand-gun. He didn't point or cock it, just tapped the barrel against his thigh and kept on talking, mad conversational.

"Half a mind's what Nina here would leave you with, if I was to squeeze her off. It's all gravy though, Lou, I know you just voicing some frustration and shit—speaking, how you say, rhetorically right now. Even though I bet fuckin' Eggy and Sikilianos and what-ever other hard bodies you keep around these days is sitting right behind that curtain, waiting on your say-so."

For a moment, nobody spoke. 'Preme jiggled his leg against the ground, real nonchalant, like he was waiting for a bus. Lou tried out four or five different scowls before settling on one she liked, sitting down across from him, and leaning in.

"You ever bring a burner into my home again, I'll shove it up your narrow ass and squeeze the trigger."

They nearly knocked knees, rushing to stand.

"I'm here with love in my heart, girl," 'Preme said, into her neck. The nine still dangled from his hand. "You the one who brought up cops."

"Go!" Lou pushed him as she said it, and 'Preme stumbled back a pace, off-balance and off-guard. Billy darted into the emptiness between them, and raised his arms like a tightrope-walker.

"We're outta here. In peace." He grabbed 'Preme by the elbow, turned him, splayed a hand across his back. 'Preme didn't resist. I scrambled to follow.

"Yeah, *peace*," Lou shouted, the word practically visible as she spit it.

Billy called over his shoulder, without slowing down.

"You'll get your water back, Lou. I promise. We're gonna take him down."

She hipped her hands, rocked on her heels. "Get the fuck on, Billy. Everything you touch turns to shit, you know that? Do you?"

"Yeah," he said through gritted teeth, eyes on the ground before him. "Yeah. I know."

We stepped into the tunnel. It felt like sanctuary. Supreme Chemistry stashed the gun, removed his sunglasses, and pressed a knuckle to each eye.

"I can't believe I used to date that bitch," he muttered, and handed each of us a juice box.

10

ince your punk-ass narrator decided he'd rather dick around in the dark with a bunch of degenerate has-beens than see how real money is made, I suppose it falls to The Party-Rockin Show-Stoppin Pussy-Poppin CLOUD NIZZLE NINE to grab the reins. I *can* write, you know—just cause I stole mad shit and did some time doesn't mean I'm not nice with the pen. Don't forget, those things we used to put on the trains were words. We didn't ramble on with em, either. Said what we had to say and stepped. More than I can say for some of the books I read in the joint. Boring a mufucka locked in an eight-by-ten for years on top of years, now that's a fuckin accomplishment.

One thing, before we get into some gangster shit: you sposed to all-cap a writer's name. Youngblood ain know that, but then what he don't know could fill a warehouse. Haha, I'm just fuckin with you, D. You know you fam, baby. Anyway, don't think I'm yelling every time I say CLOUD 9 or whatever.

In prison you learn that the direct route isn't just the most effective, it's the most satisfying. So while RAGE and FEVER were putting a team together down at the Parlor, I was knocking on Theo Polhemus's door in Crown Heights. Dude lived on floor two of a brownstone, which right away set off my Halfway Crook alarm.

Mad weight coming in and out? Yardbwoys slidin troo fe re-up all the rasclaat time? And you run shop out of a building anyone could just stroll into? Word? I mean, sure, Everton had the neighborhood on lock and everybody knew Polhemus was his guy, but still. There's always crazy niggas, and they always usually got shotguns. You can take that to the bank.

It was eleven-thirty in the morning. I had on shades, an old trick of mine from back in the click-clack days. A mask says you're scared, amateur, expecting to get caught. Sunglasses say you're chill and in control and as long as everybody cooperates things will go by the books. Masks remind people that you don't wanna be recognized, make them start thinking that if they notice something useful, they could be heroes later on. Next thing you know you're getting IDed off your voice, or a real distinctive fuckin nosehair that was sticking out.

On the other side of Polhemus's door, somebody says Who is it.

I say Tap tap BOOM. Birds ain't even got their warble on, and your door's shaking off the hinges.

He says Excuse me? but in a fake way, like a chick would say it when she means Oh no you didn't.

Don't make me repeat myself I tell him. You and me, we need to talk. And then I listen very closely because either he already had a piece when he came to the door, which I put at thirty percent likely, or he's picking one up now. And sure enough, I hear a hand come off the doorframe, followed by the sound of something being lifted off a table. His door is the kind that opens in and to the left, so I wait to hear the last lock move—you gotta count how many there are and then add one for the deadbolt; I forgot to do that once and kicked the door too early and fucked up my whole play—and then I slam my shoulder into it, hard as I can.

As I believe Dondi has mentioned, I'm kinda diesel with mine. So Polhemus is stuck between his door and his wall, gun mashed against his body. Pointed at his own chin, probably.

Drop the burner I say. It's not necessary. All we're gonna do is talk. He drops it and here comes my first game-time decision: obviously I wanna pick it up, but a dude with the right presence of mind could kick the door back at me when I bend over for the weapon. Which is a thirty-eight from the fuckin days of bell bottoms. With Jumpshot's body on it, most likely, making Polhemus an even bigger asshole.

It doesn't make him a dude who will put his life at risk before even hearing what I have to say, though, so I swoop down and grab the gun and drop it in my pocket. Anybody else in here? I ask him, though it doesn't look like it and the place is only three rooms, living room in the front, kitchen in the middle, bedroom in the back, all of them visible over my shoulder.

There's nobody here he says, in a real calm voice I instantly hate because it's fake, the voice of a guy in a movie who's cooler than the guy robbing him. I kick the door closed, tell him Lock it. I'm watching to see how much he fumbles, how nervous he is. He's not. At least, his hands aren't. Or he might be so petrified his body's gone to autopilot, everything smooth and slow. That happens sometimes.

I've got a hand on the small of his back, and I'm checking out the living room for that next little bit of information that might tell me something I need to know about Theo Polhemus. The prison landscape is so boring that you automatically start to dissect the fuck out of everything, on some oh, hey, what an interesting crack in the ceiling, is it wider than a pencil eraser? I felt like one of Dondi's second-rate superheroes out here in the real world, Observant Man and shit.

No TV, no couch to watch it from. Books stacked up in piles on the floor, but no bookcase. Walls bare except a free calendar from the local Chinese restaurant. Hi, come in, take this, gimme that, get out. It's one way to do business.

Over there I said, waving him into the empty room. With my hand—it was better if both of us forgot about the gun.

What do you want?

Don't you think I'm gonna tell you? I said, and smiled to show him how ridiculous he sounded. My script for this shit was: make it feel like two gentlemen coming to a business arrangement. Every nigga out these days wants to feel like a businessman. I blame Jay-Z. Life was easier when hustlers were just hustlers, not the Chief Executive Officers of imaginary criminal empires.

Dondi had done a pretty good job of describing Polhemus to me, which is why I'm only remembering to do it for you now. Dude was nothing special. Five-eight, darkskinned, round rimless glasses. A buttondown-shirt type, coulda played the computer hacker in a crime movie but not the boss. Kind of thick in the chest and arms, like he worked out semi-seriously.

Me, on the other hand, I look like a one hundred percent freak-show with all these jailhouse muscles. I'd never lifted anything heavier than my own dick before I got sent up, but once you're inside you just keep on lifting and getting bigger, lifting and getting bigger, and the next thing you know you're one of these cartoon-biceps-having weightroom dudes. I'm taking it all off as soon as possible. The shit is useless on the outside, if not worse. Attracts the wrong kind of women, lets convicts know you're one of them.

I took a few steps toward Polhemus, spread my legs, and dropped my hands to my belt. Then I slid my copy of his story from my back pocket, unfolded it, and laid it on the table by the door, the one he'd scooped the handgun from.

I'm a literary agent, I told him. I wanna be *your* literary agent. I really think I can sell *Crown Heist*.

I waited a second, then smiled and said To you. Or to Cornelius, if you're not interested. I mean Everton.

He gave me a long stare, his own reflection boomeranging off my shades.

It's all made up, he said. It's like a fantasy. You know what fiction is, don't you?

I sighed.

I was just thinking that I respected you for not trying to hand me any bullshit about fiction. I might have been born on a Friday, Polhemus, but it wasn't last Friday.

He sighed.

Theo I said. There are those that hang and those who do the cutting. It's a good line.

Thanks.

You're welcome. Although it's not really yours, is it?

Polhemus crossed his arms over his chest.

I'm not here to hang you I told him.

That right.

Yes it is. I'm just here to cut you.

The ones who do the cutting means the ones who cut your body down after you're dead Polhemus said.

I know what the fuck it means. Now here's what I mean. I mean you give me a hundred large and I walk out the door. That's a cut. It stings, but it doesn't kill you.

I don't have that kind of money. He dropped his shoulders and shoved his hands in his pockets, which is a typical thing people do when they're soft-selling a lie.

Look, I said, I'm not one of those guys who take it personal when I get lied to. But do you really think I pulled that number out my ass?

I don't—

That number is based on many factors. The type of weight you move. How long you been moving it. What your home-furnishing expenses are. All kinds of shit. It's not how much I think you have. It's how much a nigga who has the amount I *know* you have should give up without even thinking twice to make a nigga like me go away. If he's as smart as he makes himself sound in his fuckin page-turner of a story.

His hand darted out of his pocket, pushed his glasses up the bridge of his nose, then disappeared again. The glasses didn't seem to need pushing. It probably meant he thought he was sweating, even though he wasn't.

How do I know you will?

Will what, Polhemus?

Go away. How do I know you won't come back for more?

That's a fair question. You don't, really. Except that I say so, and because if I wanted to I could take everything right now, all your dough and all your product. Plus unless you're some kind of ill blackbelt, I could kill you with my bare hands in about thirty seconds. And if you are a blackbelt, I could use your gun. I mean Laz's gun.

I took it out. Only then did I think to check the barrel.

Well, I could if it was loaded. I put it back in my pocket. What were we talking about?

How you only want a hundred.

Like I said. I'm a reasonable dude. You're a reasonable dude. I got no reason to ruin your life, or make you decide you need to ruin mine. And a hundred's all I need.

Polhemus slitted his eyes. You did time with Lazarus, didn't you?

That type of question, you should keep in your head. You don't need to get to know me. Now go fetch my dough.

I don't keep money here. I'm not that stupid.

Nigga, if you try to tell me you got a checking account with a thousand-dollar ATM max, I swear I will break your fuckin collarbone.

My mom's, Polhemus said quickly. I use her apartment as a stash house. All I got here's petty cash.

And where does Moms live?

One-forty-fifth and Saint Nick.

Then I guess we're going to Harlem. Still got your boy Abraham's Cutlass?

He nodded.

A fine automobile. Let's roll.

I made him step into the hallway first, then shut the door behind us. We were starting down the stairs when I heard the buzzer go off inside Polhemus's apartment. A moment later, the dude on the front stoop got tired of waiting and tried the door. He discovered, just like I had, that the shit was open.

Yo T, he called when he got inside. Fuck you going? We got an appointment.

I poked Polhemus to let him know he should keep walking. The dude met us halfway. It was dark on the stairs, so even Observant Man didn't really take in much beyond some sloppy cornrows and a broad face lined with scars.

I got something I gotta do, Polhemus told him. I'll catch you tonight, cool?

Hell no it's not cool. I gotta get that thing from you. Come on, turn your ass around, it won't take but a minute. I got the scratch right here.

Polhemus looked to me.

Business is business, I said.

Polhemus slipped past, unlocked his door. As soon as we were all inside he said Terry, shoot this motherfucker.

Terry looked confused, but he pulled a .45 from his waist.

You serious? He held the gun by his side, not ready to aim it.

Yes I'm serious, shoot this motherfucker, he's trying to rob me.

If he's trying to rob you, why y'all leaving together?

Polhemus was in a panic, as if with every second Terry didn't act, the chances slimmed. Terry, on the other hand, seemed perfectly content to take all the time he needed to figure the situation out. Being the only dude with heat gives you that luxury.

Because I keep all my shit at my mother's place, Polhemus yelled. Shoot him!

But all your—oh, I get it. You roll up to your old crib and sic your niggas from around the way on him as soon as y'all step out onto the block, huh?

I think my mouth probably dropped open. When had I turned into such a fuckin moron, about to let this fishcake nigga get me ambushed in another borough? Jail makes you hard in some ways,

softer than baby shit in others. And you might not realize the soft-
ness, the fuckin stupidity, until it's too late or some random-ass cat
figures out your fate before you do. Jesus Christ, I was embarrassed. I'm a man, I can admit that.

Terry looked real pleased with himself. He turned toward me,
the muzzle a little higher now but still directed at the floor. And
just like that, my brain made it up to me, and I realized who Terry
was. And vicey-versey.

I know you from somewhere? he asked.

Yes you do.

He clocked me for a sec, then said We was locked up together.

Yes we were. And let me tell you something. All them scars you
got there for your cousin's sake, this right here's the man you need
to take it up with. That white Rasta might've pulled the trigger, but
it was your boy T who set Jumpshot up, made it look like he robbed
Lazarus.

How you know that?

Terry, don't let him bullshit you! Kill this motherfucker!

I pointed at Polhemus and said He wrote it all down, on some
How I Spent My Summer Vacation shit. It's sitting right there.
Changed a couple names, but not your cousin's. He gets murked on
page ten.

Terry walked over to the table and kind of leafed through the
story with one eye. With the other, and with the gun, he watched
Polhemus. My guess is that homeboy was on the remedial tip,
reading-wise, but I saw his mouth move around the word Jumpshot,
and that seemed to be enough for him.

This shit true?

Of course it's true, I said before Polhemus could deny it. Why
even take me Uptown unless I had some shit on him—some shit
he'd pay a hundred grand to keep quiet?

Terry, Polhemus said. Me and you been doing business for how
long? You gonna believe this?

Terry looked at me, like point-counterpoint. I shrugged.

Believe what makes sense. Or if you want to be sure, take him and these pages over to Everton. He'll probably give you T's job just to say thanks. I ain gotta tell you how tight Lazarus is with those Yardies.

Terry picked the story up and shook it at me.

You came across this how?

I looked at Polhemus, and flashed on his description of Jumpshot's face right before he'd gotten killed. He'd said it was a death mask, that seeing it drained all the sympathy he had for homeboy. Though it couldn't have been much to begin with.

Does it really matter how I came up on it? I said.

Yeah, nigga, to me it does. His grip on the gun tightened. Polhemus saw it too, and took a pointless little half-step back.

I decided to give Terry what he needed. I know you might feel that was reckless, Dondi, but it needed doing. When a situation jumps the shark or the tracks or whatever and you gotta freestyle your way out, sometimes that means throwing your watch and sneakers in the pot like fuck it, all in, I got this. I hope you understand that, youngblood. Wasn't some shit I did light, letting them hear your name.

I pointed my chin at Polhemus, real casual, and said Nigga was dumb enough to send his story to a friend of mine, trying to get a book deal. Turns out her son works for the clown. We were gonna sting him for that hundie and keep it moving. I just got home, you know what I'm saying? Same as you. I need some fresh-start money.

Your friend's kid, what's his name?

Dondi. Young lightskinned cat.

Yeah, I know D. Used to see him up here back when it was Lazarus running the spot.

He looked across his shoulder at me, rocking back and forth on his heels as if he were holding a baby and not a .45, and said He keeps everything under a loose floorboard, under the bed. Take it and go.

Just the hundred, I said. The rest is you. Plus all the product.

He didn't answer. Too busy breathing hard through his nose.

I went back there, tossed the mattress, found the floorboard. Dude had his loot rubberbanded up all neat, in twenty-five or thirty bundles of ten thou. But it was old money, slow money—worn, smelly bills all gussied up like he'd just withdrawn them from his fuckin account in the Caymans. Some people gotta pretend. I threw my cut into my knapsack.

Terry was still pinning Polhemus with the gun when I came out. You kill a motherfucker's kin, he might decide to make your death a real event. Factor in those souvenirs crisscrossing Terry's face, and who knew what this cat was gonna do.

I wiped the .38 clean, laid it back on the table, and opened the door to leave. Then I said Can I make a suggestion? and closed it again.

What?

There's plenty of shit back there for you either way, but if I was in your situation I'd hand him over to Everton. Get straight with them Jamaicans. You gotta live in this neighborhood, right?

We'll see.

Okay then.

I turned the doorknob again, and this time Polhemus twitched, and his eyes jerked over to me. I thought some final words might be in order.

Actually, that's not true at all. No such thing was in order, and the fuckin kid smelled like he'd shitted himself while I was back there digging through his safe deposit box. I should've just left, but I felt like telling the cocksucker a couple of things about himself, so I said Think about this, dude. If you'd been straight with me, I woulda been gone fifteen minutes ago, and all you woulda been's a little light on cash. I'ma drop a Bob Marley quote on you, Polhemus, in the spirit of your fine short story. You can fool some people sometimes, but you can't fool all the people all the time, you fuckin dumb-ass.

I flashed a peace sign. Take it easy, I told Terry. I'm out.

I will, he said, and turned back to Polhemus.

There are a lot of ways to become an old man, but the quickest is to stop caring about new shit—not new ideas, because there's no such thing, but music, technology, fashion. I'm a walking fossil, how you say, a trilobite or a troglodyte or maybe both, and it's not incarceration's fault because some people do manage to stay up on everything from inside. You got cats plugged into iPods and sending e-mails from the library and all that. Whatever mixtapes is on the street, I guarantee they're in the cellblocks the same week, not to mention the fact that so many rap dudes stay coming in and out the joint on gun charges or drugs or whatever stupidness that the most signed-out books are always the rhyming dictionaries. I've seen niggas record whole albums into payphones. What turned me into an old man was that around the time I got sent up, everything started to get wacker and wacker in the real world, especially music, so I just gave up on caring.

All of which is to say that when I stepped outside and saw a Mercedes SUV with government plates and tinted windows idling right in front of Polhemus's building, the two quotes that popped to mind were both from songs that came out in like '88–'89, one from each coast, the two of them together a pretty good snapshot of what hip-hop looked like before everybody started pretending to be a shiny-suit-wearing pimp-thug-golf-pro-actor-murderer.

The Lord giveth and the Lord taketh away is one, from the beginning of A Tribe Called Quest's joint "If The Papes Come," though probably it's from the Bible originally or maybe the Koran, since at least one of those brothers went Muslim.

The other, from the end of some NWA song, was: Oh, it ain't over, motherfuckers.

Indeed.

Down came the back window.

Hello, Adofo.

My government name. Even Ma Dukes has probably blanked on it by now.

Hello, Anastacio.

Step into my office. He opened the door, slid back across the butter cream leather, tapped the seat beside him.

Suck my dick.

He chuckled. Sixteen years earlier, when he'd tried to get me to give him RAGE, they were the only words I said. I said them a lot.

Get in the car before I have the two meatheads in the front seat beat the black off your ass.

The doors opened, and a matching pair of whiteboys in dark suits emerged. Hands on the car, one of them barked, while the other unbuttoned his jacket so I could see the shoulder holster.

He's clean, the barker told Bracken once he'd patted me down. Except for this. He passed my backpack to his boss, then turned to me.

You heard the man. Into the vehicle.

I heard the zipper teeth separate, and then Bracken said Well well Adofo. This is a lot of money.

I climbed into the backseat and checked him out. Word to God, yo—Bracken hadn't aged a day, an hour, a motherfuckin nanosecond. As if while I was humping out my bid all he'd done was go home and take a quick nap and a shower, then cop an expensive haircut and a shoeshine and slip on an Italian suit.

I take good care of myself he said like he could read my mind, and then the cocksucker winked at me, real quick, a little flick of eyelash. Pilates. Works wonders. You should try it.

Yeah, I will. Now what the fuck you want from me?

Bracken flipped one of the money stacks in the air and let it land in his hand. I wonder what I'd find inside that building, he said.

Well I said, if you hurry, you might find a newly paroled ex-con holding a forty-five on a drug dealer who killed his cousin, plus a whole fuckload of weed and money, none of which has shit to do with me, which is why I took what I was owed and left. So how about it? You gonna run your meatheads up to the second floor and stop a homicide, Mr. Tough On Crime?

I saw the driver's eyes dart to the rearview mirror, like he was expecting the order. Bracken caught it. McGrath, Downing, wait outside he said. Leave the air on. The whiteboys did as they were told.

Bracken crossed his legs. Your friend, I hear he's back in town. He studied my face, looking for a tipoff, but I didn't give up shit.

Or maybe under it, Bracken said, trying again.

What friend I said, thinking that before the whiteboys could get to us I might have time to slam either my knee or the heel of my hand into Bracken's nose at an angle that would drive the cartilage into his brain and kill him. I saw it done once, by this smallish Filipino who came into the joint with a rep as some kind of Ultimate Fighting champ and had to prove it every day until word got around.

What friend, Bracken repeated. What friend, he says. It sounds to me like you miss prison, Adofo. Is that it? Cunt just doesn't do it for you anymore, after all that nice tight greasy asshole? Because I could send you back. You make it real easy, strolling out of a drug den with a backpack full of cash.

Who told you he's back? I asked. We had RAGE cribbed up at a real unlikely spot now for safekeeping, two blocks from WREN's pad at an out-of-town neighbor's. Seemed like Bracken's tips were coming late and weak, RAGE topside a week and him just catching a wisp of it now, and for a second I caught a little case of the smugs. Then it occurred to me that Bracken's first move would probably be to send his boys over to the same apartment doors they'd banged on back in '89. He might've been late and weak, but we were only a halfstep earlier, a couple pushups stronger.

Bracken smiled and said How'd you like my gift?

I hear you're down fifteen points in the polls. Maybe you should concentrate on that.

Fifteen last week. It's ten now. But thanks for your concern. He pointed at the backpack, lying open between us like a chick in a skirt with her legs spread.

I could let you have that. What's a little pocket change between friends, right Adofo?

I slipped my hand inside. You sound scared, Bracken. You think my man is gonna take it back to '87, huh? A few thousand BRACKEN KILLED AMUSE tags wouldn't help your numbers, would they?

He pivoted so we were eye to eye. I'm gonna tell you something, you piece of shit. And I want you to tell him. It wasn't me. I didn't kill Stein.

Oh yeah? Who did?

He just stared at me. I just stared back. There was more red in his eyes than any other color.

It wasn't me, he said again. I think you know what I mean.

Like hell I do. Why don't you tell me what happened, if it wasn't you?

Those tunnels I'm closing, Bracken said. It's not something I'm supposed to do. You tell him that. Tell him we want the same thing.

Fuck this bullshit, I said. Tell him yourself. I opened the door. Always a pleasure.

I had one foot on the sidewalk when the whiteboys hustled over and blocked the way.

Boss? the one who'd frisked me said.

I looked back at Bracken. Either arrest me or shoot me or let me go, I said. Because this conversation is over.

The whiteboys stood waiting, like any of those options was cool with them.

I'm going to give you a day to think this through, Bracken said. He reached into his inside jacket pocket, handed me a business card, and crossed his legs again. And to find out what I want to know, just in case you don't know it already. I'll hold on to your money until then. Tomorrow either you give me an address, or I'm going to give you one. One you know real well. In the meantime, like I said, your friends in law enforcement will be watching. Okay, let him go.

The whiteboys stepped out of the way. One closed the door behind me.

McGrath, I said. Downing. See you two bitch-made faggots around.

You could see them straining at their leashes, but they didn't say a word. I sauntered around the corner, then sprinted flat-out for the subway station.

know I haven't really talked about being expelled—sorry, hey, it's me Dondi again—or about the consequences. I haven't talked about a lot of things, because I'm trying to focus on the most interesting shit. So, like, for example during this same time I was also conducting long agonizing breakup-aftershock phone conversations with the Uptown Girl, at the rate of about one per day. Maybe that's an important dimension of the narrative through-line and I should find a way to weave it in, but it was a long slow slog to even live through, and I can't imagine why you'd want to read about it.

The truth is, I'd been lying on my side like a derailed train for months when Billy made the scene. My wheels weren't even spinning anymore. I was smoking more than usual, and for different reasons, worse ones. I had no clue what I was going to do with myself, and each day I felt less able to confront that fact, to shake my head clear and start bouncing on the balls of my feet and throwing jabs and working out a plan.

It was something I'd never really had to do. As different as I felt at Whoopty Whoo, your boy was walking a real conventional path, straight to—wait for it—the Ivy League. I'd applied early-decision to Columbia and they were like *Word, member of a demographically*

*underrepresented minority group with whiteboy-tight grades, which
dorm you wanna live in?*, so by December I was chilling. Nothing
left to do but get my senior slump on, jog a lazy semester-long victory lap around the Whoopty Whoo gymnasium, maybe give some
kind of Ladies-and-gentlemen-I'm-living-proof dinner speech to the
folks who endowed the What the Hell, Let's Give a Clever Young
Colored Boy a Chance to Transcend His Race Scholarship.

I'm not even going to say I fucked up, because the true fucking
up was done by the two halfwit theater dorks who got caught chief-
ing a bowl of my Sour Diesel in the school auditorium before first
period by Mel the janitor. He handed them over to the school dis-
ciplinarian, and the next thing you know my name is in their
mouths like retainers, and then I'm standing in the principal's
office denying and denying and denying.

Meanwhile, good ol' Ironsides Mel is cutting the lock off my
locker, and the office secretary's raising Karen on the phone, and
shortly thereafter Mel rejoins us with the contents of my messenger
bag, and phrases like *zero tolerance policy* and *notify the proper
authorities* start finding their way into the conversation. So when I
walked out of the building expelled but not in police custody, I
considered myself more lucky than not. The feeling didn't last long,
and if Billy hadn't shown up, who knows what I'd be doing now.
Not writing a book, that's for sure. And since sitting down each day
and trying to get this story committed to paper is the main thing I
have going on in my still-beat-to-shit life, I guess I owe him the
same as he owes me.

Anyway, back to it. When we resurfaced aboveground, Billy
made his way to Fever's and I took my ass back to the Fort and
knocked on Karen's door, in deference to my not-officially-living-
there status. No answer. I let myself in, shouted a greeting over the
shower's rush, and began scrubbing tunnel grime from my hands
at the kitchen sink. I'd gotten nowhere when the phone rang.

Cloud. He was out of breath; train brakes screeched behind
him. We needed to meet, he said. The five of us, right now—but no

addresses over the phone, and no names either. We had to make sure not to be followed.

I thought about it for a sec. "You know the building where I found you-know-who? How about the lobby in half an hour, and I'll take us someplace super-private from there?" That worked for Cloud. He told me to set it up, slammed the receiver down.

Why a dude who never left his apartment had a mobile phone instead of a landline, I don't know. Maybe it was cheaper. The Ambassador's voicemail picked up without a ring, and I declared my intention to text him an address that Billy could read and to which they should both skedaddle with maximum celerity. I was typing it into my phone and feeling pretty clever when Karen padded down the hall, her bare feet leaving wet marks on the hardwood and her hair twisted into a yellow bath towel.

"Who called?"

I told her the deal.

"He didn't say whether he had the money?"

"Nope."

"How did he sound?"

"Frantic." I pressed the *send* button, and hoped Billy would be able to figure out text messaging despite having left town when cellies were brick-sized and used primarily on the set of *New Jack City*.

"Frantic, or like he wanted you to *think* he was frantic?"

I stared at her.

Karen shook out her hair. "It's not that I don't trust him. It's just . . ."

"That you don't trust him. That's fucked up. You trusted him enough to let him risk his ass while you slept in."

"Oh, so *I'm* supposed to go shake down a drug dealer?"

"You coulda come to the writers' meeting, at least."

She pointed a finger at me. "I'm going to tell you something I shouldn't have to, Dondi. Money makes people do sick things. Keep that in mind when Cloud tells us whatever he's got to tell us." She turned and walked back toward the bathroom.

"Next you're gonna say that there's no honor among criminals," I called, but Karen was already firing up the blow-dryer. A moment later, my phone buzzed with a message: *K. On r way* ☺. Apparently, a twelve-year-old Korean schoolgirl had taught Billy how to text.

We hopped a cab to Dumbo. I gave the driver a weird, indirect route, sat in the front, used the side mirror to check for a tail. I didn't see one, but I had him drop us around the block from our destination anyway, in front of the yuppie deli. One of them. Karen got coffee. I scanned the street for loiterers. We left through a side door, and when we reached the building I told Karen we were clear.

She stared the other way, into the sun. "That's because nobody followed us to begin with, Columbo."

I was about to reply when some guy with a little emasculating dog pushed open the door. I caught it, ushered my mother inside.

We walked through the lobby and found Cloud slumped on a low, boxy couch, legs kicked out in front of him. We took the armchairs facing it. The space dwarfed the furniture, ridiculed anyone who used it. I felt like a model who'd been hired to demonstrate the comfort of the floor samples at some moderately outrageous design store.

My mother chugged the last of her coffee and deposited the cup on the small lacquered table between our chairs.

"So. What's up?"

Cloud blinked behind his glasses. "Chillin'. What's up with you?"

"Not much." She crossed her legs. "What's up with you?"

"Chillin'." He looked at me. "You reach them?"

"Yeah."

"Then we'll talk when everybody's here."

Karen tossed her coffee cup at Cloud. It landed on his chest, rolled to the floor.

"Stop messing with me, man. You get it or not?"

Cloud snatched up the cup and returned fire. It sailed past Karen's shoulder, landed near a huge vase full of cherry tree branches or some shit.

"Hold your fuckin' horses." He settled even more deeply into the couch, and closed his eyes.

Karen watched him for a few seconds, then rose to pace the lobby. I chased down her coffee cup, found it a trashcan. If we started crapping up the place, the various effete dogwalkers who called this building home were liable to go hire a doorman.

Billy and Fever arrived a few minutes later. Cloud was standing by the time they reached him.

"Where y'all comin' from?"

"My crib," said the Ambassador. "What's left of it." He leaned on his stick with both arms, so heavily that they tremored beneath the weight. "Motherfuckers smashed everything to bits. My sculptures, all the alphabet racers . . ." he trailed off, shook his head at nothing in particular, snorted some snot back up his nose.

"Not all of them," said Billy, grim. "They left the *A* and the *B* alone, on some calling-card shit. Surprised they could even read 'em."

"Damn, Fever, I'm sorry."

He waved me off. "Fuck it. No sense crying over paint and plastic. At least now we know Bracken's still a fucking kick-in-the-door gorilla, even in a suit and tie. If he'd grown a brain, he woulda staked my place out, and Billy would be in bracelets, or worse."

"I can't go home, can I?" asked Karen.

"Nope," said Cloud. "My bad, I shoulda thought to tell you pack a suitcase. I was a little frazzled and shit, on the phone."

"How would you know—"

"Because me and Bracken just had our own little reunion." Cloud tapped me in the chest with the back of his hand. "Lead the way, youngblood."

Billy and Karen did a verbal impression of two people trying to walk through a door at the same time.

"What do you mean, 'lead the way'?" my mother demanded. "Why can't we just talk here?"

"You saw him?" my father asked. "You actually saw him?" But Cloud was following me across the lobby, to the stairwell.

I pushed open the door. "Hope nobody has any pressing commitments for the next twenty-four hours."

"Aaaah," said Dengue. "Smart. Smart." He was the only one I'd told besides my mother, and he'd taken the notion very much in stride. In sit, if you wanna get technical about it.

"Tell me this is a joke. That's your big plan? The magical staircase to tomorrow?"

I ignored her. Nobody seemed to have a problem with that. Not even Karen, really.

"Talk to me," said Cloud, as we began to climb.

"You know that song 'time keeps on slipping, slipping, slipping, into the fuuuuture'?"

"Steve Miller. That's my niggaro."

"Well, this is sort of like that. On the top floor, it's tomorrow. But only if you take the stairs. All of them." I looked over my shoulder at Billy, three steps behind, his hand on Dengue's elbow. "The top floor's where I found you."

My father's eyes narrowed, but all he said was "Huh."

"If you go back down, can—"

"Nope."

Cloud's thousand-yard stare bumped into the wall four feet in front of us. "Weak."

"I find a rip in the fabric of space-time, and all you can say is 'weak'?"

Cloud shrugged. "The shit's weak. All these goddamn stairs for one day? Easier to get drunk and pass out."

"You're right," I said, as we passed the third-floor landing. "It is kind of weak."

"A day is a huge amount of time," said Billy. Nobody paid him any mind. "No portal I've seen gives you anything close to that," he added, and Cloud and I stopped in our tracks. Dengue plowed right into me.

"Say something if you gonna stop walking, boy!"

"Sorry." I faced my father. "How many portals have you seen,

Billy?" Karen crossed her arms, like she was in a rush and we were holding up the line.

"A bunch. The shamans said I had an innate gift for sensing them . . . it was the only thing they said I had an innate gift for, actually. And they considered it pretty useless."

"Guess it's genetic," I said. "I mean, I found this one. We both did."

Billy gave a little tick of a nod. "Usually, a portal only jumps you a few minutes forward. It's always forward. Most of them, you could walk through and not even notice."

"They don't have any buildings this tall, do they?" said Karen. We all looked at her. She dropped her hands to her hips. "In the jungle, I mean. I'm saying, maybe on the ground you only get a couple minutes, but higher up, you could get more. Or whatever."

"That's possible," said Billy. It came out sounding like charity. "A portal has to be approached in a specific way. From a certain direction, a minimum distance. So that part's the same. But a whole day would blow their minds."

We climbed in silence, stopping twice to catch our breath. At last, the door to the fifteenth floor loomed above us. I took the final set of stairs two at a time, threw it open, and paused.

"You know, I've only done this by myself. I never thought about what somebody else would see, if they watched me. Will I just vanish? Will you?"

"Less talk, more walk," said Cloud, and pushed me over the threshold. I stumbled into the penthouse corridor, and when I looked behind me, the stairwell was empty. A moment later, so was my stomach, the rigors of time-travel having caused its contents to perform their usual appearing act.

A few seconds passed, and then Cloud stepped into tomorrow, and a pool of vomit.

"Eeeew, youngblood." He lifted one Timberland and then the other toward his chest, in a modified version of the dance known as the East Coast Stomp.

"Sorry. It always happens."

"Coulda warned me."

I rubbed my temples, then my eyes. "You don't feel sick at all?"

"Nah."

Billy, Fever, and Karen joined us, one after the next. It wasn't much to look at; no shimmering fade into visibility, no sound effect. More like you blinked, and when your eyes reopened, there they were. Minus the blink.

My father and Dengue seemed fine. Karen looked at her phone, doubled over, and waited, cat-style. You ever seen a cat puke? They've got a whole routine they do, like ballplayers at the free throw line. They ratchet themselves into just the right posture, train their eyes on the spot where it's going to land, and hold the pose for maybe a minute, working themselves up to it. If a cat pukes on your rug, it's your fault. You had ample time to move his ass onto the hardwood. Information courtesy of the Uptown Girl, whose brother-sister duo, Gem and Scout, I miss with an embarrassing intensity.

I did the respectful thing and waited until Karen had finished retching to start talking shit.

"There art more things in heaven and on earth than thou dost conceive," I said, mangling a quote I was sure nobody else knew anyway. I offered her a stick of gum. She reached up, snatched it.

"You didn't raise no liar. Next time I tell you some crazy shit, you best believe the kid."

"How 'bout we move down the hall," said Cloud, beckoning for the gum. "Away from y'all's breakfast."

By the time we regrouped under the window, Karen was rejuvenated enough to pick up where she'd left off.

"Start talking."

"Take it down a notch, sis. You got no cause to come at me like that." Cloud paused just long enough to establish narrative authority. "So. Me and Polhemus, we're discussing literature and shit, everything's going good, when Jumpshot's cousin walks in to buy weed. Dude the Jamaicans carved up in prison. Name of Terry."

"Shit, I know Terry."

"Naturally, Terry got a gun and wanna know what's going on. Long story short, I handed Polhemus over to him, took what I came for, and skated. Had to throw your name in the mix, youngblood, because the nigga was nosy about the particulars. But it doesn't matter. Terry doesn't care, and Polhemus ain't been drawing breath for a few hours now."

"A day and a few hours," said Dengue.

"Yeah. Anyway, I walk outside, and there's Bracken, sitting in a whip with two of his guys."

"How'd he get on you?" Karen demanded.

"How the fuck should I know? Think I asked?"

"What did he say?" from Billy.

"You motherfuckers really are the Unnecessary Question Brigade, aren't you? Shut the fuck up for two minutes, and I'll tell you."

"Looks the same, doesn't he?" said Dengue. I saw Billy shiver as he waited for an answer. It came slow.

"Yeah," said Cloud, pawing the ground with one boot, then the other. "Yeah. He does. Like time stood still. Told me he does Pilates."

"What?" said Karen.

"Pilates. It's like a combination of aerobics and weight training."

"I know what Pilates is! What the fuck, you and Bracken gonna be gym buddies now? 'Hey, Anastacio, can I get a spot?' 'Sure, Cloud, how many reps you going for?'" She flung one arm in the air, sort of spastically, and stalked a few steps away.

"You better tell your wife to get a handle, dude."

"I'm not his wife."

"She's not my wife."

I said, "Can we get back to the part where Bracken jacks you for the money?"

Cloud threw some surprise my way.

"He did jack you for the money, didn't he?"

Cloud nodded. "Offered to return it if I brought him Rage."

"And if you don't?" asked Fever.

"Back to jail."

"What else?" said Billy. "He must have said something else."

Cloud started to say something, then changed his mind. "Nothing worth repeating." He pulled a wad of bills out of his pocket, peeled off one or two, and gave the rest to Karen. "Here. This is about two G's. Do what you can with it. I'm out."

"You're *out*? Excuse me?"

"Look, I'm not going back to prison. And this city's too small to hide in. My uncles, they down in Virginia Beach. I don't know what they're doing, but they say they got a good thing going, and there's room for me. I'ma get my ass on a bus and find out. Ain't nothing more I can do here, except bring heat down."

"You know what I think?" asked Karen.

"Mom, chill."

"No, lemme tell you—I think you're full of shit. I think you killed Polhemus yourself, and made up all the rest. And I think you came off with a lot of money. Enough to change your mind about a lot of things."

I expected Cloud to lunge at her or something. I was tensed for it, calves and hands and thighs, wondering if Billy and I could hold him back, if Karen could dart away in time.

But Cloud just looked at her. It was the look Eurydice probably gave Orpheus when dude turned around to make sure it was really his wife he was leading out of Hades: the look on her face as she turned to vapor, doomed by his lack of faith. Right then, I knew Karen was right. Money does make people do sick things.

"That's what you think, huh?" Cloud's eyes swept over us, one by one. "That's what you all think?"

Dengue said no, and so did Billy. But there was a tiny pause, a sliver of air between the call and the response. I said it even slower.

Cloud nodded. Not like he was answering a question, but like he was listening to jazz.

"I got no proof," he said at last. "Just my word. Always been good enough before." He chewed his lower lip. "You could find Terry and ask him, I guess. But you know what? It doesn't matter. Trust is trust, and doubts is doubts."

He walked back to the elevator, pressed the button. It dinged open, and Cloud stepped inside. "I'm the convict, and y'all the ones thinking like criminals. That's fucked up. It's . . . I don't know. It's real fucked up."

The doors shut. We listened to the motors and steel pulleys lowering Cloud to the ground.

"Maybe he'll decide to buy himself another day," I said. "That's what I'd do. We could intercept him on the stairs."

"If Cloud says he's gone, he's gone." Dengue patted himself down for glue, found a tube, and fumbled with the crusted top. It slipped from his hands, fell to the floor. Billy crouched to pick it up.

"You don't trust anybody, do you, Karen?" he asked while he was down there. The way he said it was so sad, so full of pity. I wondered if he realized that it was his fault she didn't. Then I wondered if it was my job to tell him.

My mother sighed. "Don't tell me that story didn't sound shady."

"Maybe," said Billy, rising. "But it's Cloud."

"Exactly. And you all wanna act like he's squeaky clean, when you *know* better. Make me be the bad guy, as usual. Remember Fashion Moda?"

From the expressions on their faces, it appeared they did.

"What happened at Fashion Moda?" I asked. It was a graffiti art gallery in the Bronx; I knew that much.

"It doesn't matter," said Karen.

"Obviously, it does."

"To her, it does," said Billy. "Not to me."

Dengue rubbed a finger-load of glue into the collar of his T-shirt and inhaled the way a young Abraham Lincoln might after stepping out of his log cabin on a crisp autumn morn. "Look, Cloud didn't leave 'cause you insulted him. He left because it was his only play."

"Definitely the only play if you just robbed and killed a drug dealer."

"Mom!"

"I said 'if'!" She threw up her hands, surrender-style. "Okay, it's dropped." She pulled Cloud's wad of money from her back pocket. "Two fuckin' G's."

"We shouldn't have taken it," said Dengue. "That was all he had."

"Well, now it's all we have, and it's barely gonna cover the welding equipment, so I hope one of you bleeding heart assholes has got a Plan B that runs on fuckin' pixie dust and the goodwill of men." Once Karen's aggression reached a certain velocity the brakes stuck, and she veered all over the road until she ran out of gas. Or something like that. I'm from New York, man. I don't drive.

"I might," said Dengue.

"Do tell. And it better not include vans, stun guns, night vision goggles, warehouses, or anything else that costs money."

"Wait a second," I said. "*That* was your fuckin' plan? To kidnap eighty city employees and stash them in a warehouse?"

I know my mother. I can tell when she's tipsy, when she's bluffing at poker, when she's realizing that something she thought made sense is ludicrous.

"I mean, Cloud felt like . . ."

"The same Cloud you just accused of robbing everybody?"

"Yeah, smartass. He said he had the soldiers to make it happen, if we had the dough."

"That's fucking retarded. Dengue, whatchu got? And it better not involve the Mole People."

The Ambassador stroked his chin. "Di bwoy Amuse, 'im 'ave a thought whose time dun come. You all remember that night at the 207th Street yard?"

"Of course," said Karen. "I got arrested. Dumbest shit we ever did."

Dengue wagged a finger. "But it was almost the smartest." He turned to me. "Amuse snuck into the MTA's main office and stole a clipboard with the guards' schedule on it. Then he called the two guys working midnight to eight, and told them their shift was canceled."

Karen rolled her eyes. "We waltzed in at one, thinking it was all good. Never occurred to us that each shift waited to be relieved by the next. Amuse and Drum and these two bozos escaped. Me and Rosa 151 got bagged. That's when I knew chivalry was dead."

"Shoulda run faster. I was no slender reed even back then, and I got away. But check it out: what if there *was* no shift waiting for relief? Wouldn't canceling the next three work?"

Karen drummed her fingers against the pockets of her jeans. "They must use computers now. We'd have to find someone to hack in."

"I could hit up some nerds from my school."

Dengue snorted. "This is the MTA we're talking about. Trust me, they haven't even upgraded their clipboards."

"We'd still need to take out the first shift, and stash them someplace."

"Hold on," I said. "This cuts the workload by seventy-five percent. Why wasn't this plan A?"

Dengue grimaced. "All things being equal, I'd rather know that everybody who could be a problem is tied down for the duration. And that it's all being handled by professionals with hi-tech fly shit."

"They would have been ex-military," Karen put in, still pissy. "Cloud had connects."

"Yeah, whatever. I can read the ads in the back of *Soldier of Fortune* too."

Before my mother could return fire, Billy crossed his ankles, bent his knees, and dropped to the floor, Indian-style.

"I can't do this," he said, the color draining from his face as he shook his head. "I'm sorry. I understand we need these guards out of the way, but I can't be a part of anything violent. Not anymore.

If Bracken was standing in front of me right now, I wouldn't touch him. Except to heal him, if he'd let me."

Karen heaved a sigh. In a cartoon, the word *exasperation* would have floated up out of her mouth. She knelt next to my father, reached into his lap, and took his hand. "You never *were* a part of anything violent, Billy, except getting your ass kicked. You've always been, you know, a pussy. Or a pacifist. Whatever."

He pulled his hand away. "If we start hurting people, we're the same as Bracken."

"Shades of gray, you simple motherfucker."

I looked at Dengue, the only person left at eye level. He didn't appear eager to dive into the middle of a fight between my parents. Which meant, I gathered, that it was my job. I squatted between them, like a preschool teacher about to give a lecture about not throwing the blocks.

"All right, look. Billy, what Karen's trying to say is that a certain amount of physical intervention is probably unavoidable, any way you cut it. Karen, Billy's right that we can't just go around indiscriminately fucking people up. Luckily, I think there's a common answer to both problems. In many ways, it's the answer to all life's problems." I stood.

"Spit it out," said the Ambassador. "Everybody hates coy."

"Drugs. Gnarly, long-lasting drugs that totally obliterate reality. You got anything like that, Billy? I bet you do."

My father's head bobbed from side to side, as if he were listening to the proverbial shoulder-perched angel and devil. I assume they're in a proverb, anyway; I hate when people use proverbial wrong, *I'm losing my proverbial shit* or what have you. That and the misuse of literally, as in, *dude, I was so scared I literally died.* No you didn't, you douchenozzle. But I digress.

"I've got something called cambiafuerza. It's the peyote of the rainforest. You harvest the flowers of this vine that grows on dead logs, grind them into a powder, swallow like a milligram, puke it up, and you're in another world for the next thirty hours. I don't know how I feel about giving it to the guards, though. It's a sacred plant. Only supposed to be used in a few rituals."

"Think of it this way: you'll be guiding them down the path of spiritual enlightenment."

He pondered that awhile, head slumped toward his lap, then nodded loose and sloppy, like a marionette. "We'll have to instruct our people very carefully on how to treat them. Cambiafuerza requires a guide who is attentive and caring. It's very important that the journey feel safe."

"Sure," I said. "Definitely. You can explain it to them yourself."

I clenched my jaw, told myself I wasn't bullshitting Billy, Billy was bullshitting himself. My father knew better than to think anybody could feel safe melting on force-fed psychotropics inside the putrid black guts of the transit system. It was an act of enormous will for him to believe otherwise, and no less willful of me to pretend I didn't know it. In that instant, both of us edged a little closer to obsession, to the kind of labyrinthine rationalization I'd imagine Billy perfected back when he was dissing his family to go paint the town. I flicked my eyes at Karen. She'd seen it too.

"How 'bout we get out of here?" said Dengue. "There's moves to be made, and we already lost a day."

My parents rose. I summoned the elevator. Billy jabbed the lobby button, and the doors slid closed.

Stuck to one of them, with still-warm chewing gum, was Anastacio Bracken's business card. I pulled it off, handed it to Karen. She stared at it a moment, working her own wad with her jaws, then dropped it in her purse.

12

obody designated Vexer's apartment mission control; it just sort of happened. He had the garden and parlor floors of a Clinton Hill brownstone a handful of blocks from Karen's crib—which wasn't trashed when she dipped in that evening to grab us both some clothes, so either Bracken hadn't gotten to it yet or else he'd wised up and thrown a pair of eyeballs on the place. Vex had futons for us refugees, he'd never been on Bracken's radar, and to round out the solid-citizen profile, dude taught ESL at a high school in Sunset Park. Coached fucking volleyball.

When we got there, Stoon and Blam 2 were hunched over the kitchen table, strategizing amidst maps, notepads, falafel crumbs. By the time I crashed out, Sambo and Fizz had joined the huddle, and when I woke up the next morning Supreme Chemistry was making omelettes, decked out in shades, jackboots, and a blue-patterned camouflage ensemble he must have selected to match the wallpaper.

"Dengue needs help getting here," Karen announced, by way of good morning. "He's bringing supplies." She tossed a set of keys. I let them hit me in the shoulder and fall to the floor, just to prove a point.

"Whose are these?"

"Mine," said Blam. "Gray Civic, corner of Willoughby and Grand."

"So you get him."

"He's busy." Karen picked up a clipboard. "You're not. Here's the address." She handed me a slip of paper.

"Since when do I have a license?"

"Cab it, then. Your choice."

I drove, which turned out to be a mistake. You spend your whole life in a city, you think you know your way around. Get behind the wheel, and suddenly you're an idiot. I merged from the wrong lane and ended up on the fucking BQE, Verrazano-bound, instead of the Manhattan Bridge. Next thing I know I'm cruising the Hasidic part of Williamsburg, trying to surface-road-surf my way back to something recognizable. I'll spare you the details, but by the time I reached Dengue, loaded the Civic with a cache of small electronics, wound my way back through the East Vill, endured bridge traffic, found parking, and lugged everything inside, it was mid-afternoon and I was sweatdrenched, starving, and abstractly furious.

"Where the fuck have you been?" Karen asked, opening the door. Before I could answer, she grabbed my arm. "We got the guards' info. We'll make the first round of calls tonight."

"Dope." I dropped onto the couch, next to a passed-out Fizz, and kicked off my shoes. "How?"

"Ate 910," Fizz answered, without opening his eyes. "Old apprentice of mine. Boy works clerical in the main office. Xeroxed the shit, told us what to say, the whole deal."

"Nice." Not a single writer has ever joined the Vandal Squad, but more than a few draw paychecks for track repair, tunnel maintainance, that type of thing. Funny how a passion finds a vector, how a guy who spent his teens destroying trains grows up and realizes he just wants to be around them.

Blam snorted. "'Apprentice,' huh? That what you all are calling it these days?"

"Why?" Fizz asked, his eyes still closed. "Wanna make sure you know your terminology before you hit the bar scene?"

"Man, apprentice yourself to these nuts."

Fizz smiled, and tipped the brim of his Yankees lid lower over his face. "I rest my case."

Billy nudged my shoulder, and when I looked up, he handed me a glass of water.

"Thanks."

"Once an apprentice, always grateful," he said, and walked away.

I nodded, and thought about a speech Dengue liked to give about how professional photographers broke graff's mentor-apprentice backbone, changed the game more than anything short of crack. Before they started taking an interest, burners were only visible for seconds at a time, pulling into the station or blazing along an elevated track, and the only place to learn style was from an older writer. Maybe you started by playing lookout, then advanced to doing fills on his joints. After a few months of that, he'd draw you an outline, help you execute it. Secret recipes stayed that way—passed down, for instance, from Drum One to Dengue to Billy, or Kool Kizer to Cloud 9 to Amuse, or Wildchild 77 to Rosa 151 to Wren 209. Being able to pore over flicks meant you could study and synthesize and improve strangers' styles. Different can of sperms.

A cell phone shimmied across the coffeetable, emitting a tinny rendition of that Average White Band song Eric B. & Rakim sampled for "Microphone Fiend." Dengue leaned forward, scooped it up.

"Dígame, papi. Word. Yeah, yeah, divide it up and cats will meet you at the spot. A'right. One."

He snapped it shut. "Dregs brought back Cloud's paint. Said it's mostly silver, red, flat black, and white. So there's our palette."

"Like the original Jordans," said Stoon. "The butter joints. Remember?"

"You're thinking of the Twos," Fizz corrected from behind his hat. "The Ones were all black, with red piping."

My mother drummed her fingers against her clipboard. "Where was I?" she asked, a little louder than necessary, and I realized she'd been running a meeting or something when Dengue and I arrived. Deny my mother control over one aspect of her life, and she'll choke another into submission every time.

The guys on the chairs and the couch did some shifting, some settling, and Karen cleared her throat and made a show of waiting for their full attention. Vexer finished pouring water into the Mr. Coffee, raised his chin to her. Supreme Chemistry went right on scrutinizing the contents of the refrigerator.

"Okay. As Blam has pointed out, the best way to tie up the Vandal Squad is not by having them chase down fake tips, but by giving them paperwork. So we're gonna feed them some arrests."

"Who?" asked Stoon.

Dengue crossed his hands atop his stomach. "Few young cats with no records who can take one for the team. If the city even bothers prosecuting shit like that, once Monday rolls around."

"Hold on," I said. "Won't asking guys to get arrested tip them off that we're up to more than just bombing a line?"

"Eh. We were stupid to think we could keep our crews in the dark."

"So, what? Everybody knows?"

"More or less."

"Jesus Christ."

"They keeping it close?"

"No doubt."

"What else?" I asked Karen. "How we handling the first shift?"

She glanced at Billy, consulted her clipboard, and changed the subject. "We've got all the fake tips and decoy arrests mapped. Idea being to keep the Vandal Squad spread as thin as possible, and as far from the yards. Blam, you find somebody to phone them in?"

"Yup. Paco BMS is laid up with a broken leg, so he and his girl will make the calls."

"That nigga does mad accents," put in Stoon. "Polish, Israeli, whatever. Dude is straight comedy. We used to have him play a building owner all the time, back in the day."

"We got the welding equipment," Karen continued, refusing to stray from her course. "One set to a team."

"But do they know how to use it?" called Supreme Chem, voice bouncing off the inside of the fridge. "One of these amateur-night ninjas might could mess around and barbecue his hand off."

Karen shrugged. "Guess we'll find out."

"Yo, 'Preme, you hungry?"

"Naw, B, this cold air just feels good on my face."

Stoon smiled. "There's takeout menus in that drawer right there." It was strangely comforting, the way these guys all knew their way around the place.

I raised my hand, waved it at Karen. "Uh, for those of us who came late, what exactly are we welding?"

"Uh, for those of you who came late, this idea goes back days."

"Then why don't I know what you're talking about?"

"Yo, who else want sushi? I'm 'bout to order."

"Get me a dragon roll," said Vexer.

"Billy?"

"Sure."

"What, ninja?"

"I don't know, whatever you're having."

"I fucks with the wild shit, B. Sea urchin, monkfish liver. I don't know if you can hang."

"I've eaten rats. Bring it on."

"You serious, Dondi? You don't remember?"

"I'm telling you, I never knew. And if you're ordering from One Greene, I'll take Sashimi Combo B, extra salmon instead of squid."

"Stoon? Blammo?"

"I'm good."

"Now cipher, god," said Blam. "The god don't fuck with swine."

I turned to him. "How is raw fish swine?"

"Just is."

"What's that, Lesson 121? The secret bonus lesson? You like a six percenter or some shit?"

Blam craned his neck to eyeball Billy. "Yo, your son got jokes."

I glanced over to see how the phrase *your son* hit Rage, found him impassive.

"The welding thing was Cloud's idea," said Karen, looking about half as chagrined as she should have. "In the middle of each train, there's an extra conductor's booth, with a microphone in it. Guys used to break in, turn it on, and talk shit."

"Notably Cloud and Sabor," said Fizz, still pseudo-asleep.

"You crazy, dude? Dash 7 pioneered that."

Everybody started talking at once.

Karen's voice cut through the din. "Later for that shit!" They glared, but they clammed up.

She turned to me. "We're going to record a message, run it on loop, and weld the door shut."

"In every train? We got six hundred and thirty-eight tape players?"

"More like eighty-five."

"How much did that cost?"

"We boosted them from Radio Shack. Tapped out the stock in three boroughs."

"Oh. What's the message?"

Fizz stretched and yawned, deciding to commit to consciousness. "You know the first thing that happens after a terrorist attack, Dondi?"

"Bush and Cheney high-five?"

"After that."

"Condoleezza gives them both slow head?"

"Yo, your son got jokes. Stop playing."

"Somebody claims responsibility."

"Correct."

"And that would be . . . ?"

"Me," said Billy. "Me alone."

I spun to face him. "Who the hell is gonna believe you rocked six hundred and thirty-eight trains all by your lonesome?"

Fizz high-stepped over my legs and headed for the kitchen. "You have to look at it from a marketing perspective," he said, pouring coffee for himself and Vexer. "What's going to capture the public's sympathy? A big conspiracy of spics and niggers uniting to destroy the city's transportation system? Naw. Already tried that. It could play into Bracken's hands, even. Let him style out like he's the candidate criminals are afraid of."

He dumped a heap of sugar into his mug, and then another. "It's gotta be personal. One man, on a righteous quest. To stop the cop who murdered his best friend."

"Talk about 'already been tried.'"

That earned me a withering look of the kind in which Fizz specialized. "There's obviously no comparison."

"Alright, well, answer me this: if Billy did it on his own, why do the trains say all these different names?"

"They don't," said Karen. "They all say the same name. In the same colors."

"You're telling me that fifty some-odd crusty-ass egomaniac writers are all cool with painting *Rage Rage Rage* for forty hours straight?"

"No, I'm telling you they're cool with writing *Amuse Amuse Amuse*."

"Huh. What . . . Huh."

Karen grinned. "My son is speechless. Savor the moment."

"Too late, I remember what I was gonna ask. What happens after Billy takes the weight? Where does that leave him?"

My father raised his mug for Fizz to fill. "No more of an outlaw than I am already."

"What happens when the guards step up and explain that what actually happened was—was what? You still haven't told me how we're dealing with the guards, Wren."

My mother shrugged: one of her fakest gestures, pure misdirection. I knew it well. "Nothing really to tell." She looked everywhere but at Billy. "Just a good old-fashioned bum-rush. We incapacitate them as quick as we can, and feed them Billy's whatever-it's-called. They go on their magical journey of discovery. We babysit. And paint."

I waited for Billy to say something. He didn't. Apparently, his pacifism had suffered a few setbacks. I thought of what Theo Polhemus had said about Laz suddenly looking sharper, like he was coming into focus.

Then I thought about T himself, and a shudder went through me like bad Indian food. A cat I knew and liked—a guy I'd earned with, hustled for, seen weekly—was glued to the floor of his apartment with his own blood, and if the fault wasn't mine it wasn't not-mine either. Had I mourned? Wondered if his mama's phone number was listed? Reckoned with any aspect of the horrible thing that had happened?

No and no and no. I'd completely blocked it out. Compartmentalized that shit, Billy Rage style. Fuck.

Stoon was talking attack formations when I tuned back in. "I'm sayin', we ain' gotta go four-on-two or five-on-two with them. We can all mob out together. Roll like fifteen deep to each yard, handle the guards, leave a team to start painting, move on to the next."

"Except that if anything jumps bad, we lose fifteen dudes instead of four," Vexer pointed out.

Supreme Chemistry lifted himself onto the countertop. "Yo, B, we living in an age of specialization. Me, for instance: I specialize in pioneering super-heavy-duty scientifical Plutonian hot shit, and knocking ninjas the fuck out. What we need to do is put together a, how you say, advance strike team to go in first and mop these clowns. Then, when the smoke clears, everybody can bomb in peace."

A few moments passed, everybody eager to delegate the thug shit to the thugs and nobody willing to admit it. Finally, Karen reached for her clipboard.

"Who would you put on this strike team?"

"Shit, give me Klutch, Maser and Cloud, and these sucker ducks will never even know what happened."

"Cloud's gone," said Blam. "Remember?" He stared out the window. Karen's jaw stiffened, just a little.

"Damn, that's right. Klutch, Maser, Megs and Whyno 151, then."

"I'll call them now," said Dengue, and laid his hand atop his cell. How did the Ambassador operate a phone, you ask? Easy. He had every number he needed memorized, a few hundred of them. Just imagine the brain on that dude, before the modeling glue.

"No guns," said Vexer. "You gotta give your word, 'Preme."

"Man, these are yard bums we talkin' bout. Fuck I need a toolie for? I might just eat some garlic and breathe hard on they ass."

"Don't let Klutch hold, either. Or anybody else."

"Relax, B, I heard you the first time."

I was out cold by the time the sushi arrived, lulled to sleep by an hourlong discussion of escape routes. I woke up in the dark, to an empty living room and a Sashimi Combo missing all the yellowtail and half the tuna.

Karen's note said they'd gone to meet Dregs at some warehouse in Red Hook, to divvy up cans and responsibilities. For the first time in weeks, I was alone. I ate by the light of a *Simpsons* rerun, knowing it was anesthesia and praying another episode would follow. Instead I got Jerry Seinfeld and his merry band, mincing their way through a New York scrubbed Elmer's white. I clicked all the way into the triple digits, but it was too late. I tried to worry about Friday; that wouldn't take either. All I could think about was T, lying lonely in his apartment, and Terry stepping over his body with a sheaf of pages in his back pocket that I'd held in my hands a day before. I reached for Vex's phone, thought the better of it, and threw on my shoes instead.

I didn't even know where to find a payphone, which made me feel old and sad. At twelve, I could have told you the location of every jack in Fort Greene, and whether its coin slot had ever yielded a quarter. To pass without checking would have been sacrilege, despite the minuscule likelihood of anybody forgetting his change in this neighborhood, and the even slimmer chance that some marauding basehead wouldn't beat me to the payday.

I walked all the way to the dry cleaner's on the corner of Lafayette and Cumberland, where Karen took her stuff. There were a couple closer by, but the old lady who ran this one was a church friend of my grandmother's. She'd decided early on, through some private form of divination, that I was going to be a movie star. Every time I saw her, it was *how's the acting going?* The first time I didn't try to correct her, just said *great, great!* had been one of those innocence-sapping moments you never forget.

The night was warm, the receiver cold against my ear. I dialed information, asked for a nonemergency police number in Crown Heights. The operator connected me for free. Who knew?

"Seventy-seventh Precinct. Officer Harris speaking."

"I'm calling to report a dead body. 290 Utica. Second floor."

"Who—"

Click.

It occurred to me that the location of this payphone might be materializing on Officer Harris's computer screen right now, in case he felt like sending a roller screeching over to find out who had made the call. It seemed unlikely, but I set off in search of a different phone. Took me ten minutes of aimless wandering to remember that there was one a block down Lafayette, in front of what had long been a shitty Middle Eastern restaurant—shitty in the literal sense, a surefire constipation cure—and was now a hipster bar, Moe's. Conveniently located across the street from another hipster bar. I'm sorry, *wine* bar.

There's not much to say about gentrification that hasn't been said before. Nor am I one to embark on a there-goes-the-neighborhood whining jag, any more than I plan to boycott the new gourmet cheese shop located two blocks east of Karen's, in what used to be a crack house. I mean, I don't plan to buy anything there either, but bumping into cheese-loving motherfuckers on the street beats running into rock fiends any day of the week. I'm not saying

I want to see my grandma's friend's dry cleaning business fold (haha—fold, get it?) or see folks go for the okey-doke and call one of those "We Buy Houses" companies and take fifty thousand cash-in-hand so the property can get flipped to some Lehman Brothers executive for twenty-seven times that, but I'm also—ah, you know what, forget it, I don't even have the energy.

There were two listings for Polhemus in Manhattan, both in the same building on St. Nicholas Ave. Regina and Rukiya. Clearly, like many women of her generation, Theo's mother had succumbed to a brief bout of Afrocentricity, from which he had escaped but to which his sister would bear testament forever. I wrote Regina's number on my hand, fished some more change from my pocket. Then the magnitude of what I was about to do hit me, and I backed away from the phone.

"Dondi? Is that you?"

I turned. Standing beneath the awning of Moe's, cigarette cocked by her ear, was Joyce Dayton. If my adolescent psyche were a bedroom, Joyce would have been the poster thumbtacked to the ceiling right above the bed. She was my boy Cedric's older sister, four years our senior, exploding into bodaciousness right when I was in seventh grade and it mattered most. I used to stay over at Cedric's just to get a look at Joyce in her bathrobe the next morning, you know what I mean? Shit, a glimpse of her bra lying in the laundry hamper, even.

"Hey, Joyce. Long time no see." I walked over to the waist-high fence, presumably constructed so that patrons wouldn't get any big ideas about strolling across the street to check out the competition, or feel threatened by the occasional late-night hedonist meandering up Lafayette to buy a Heineken and a loosie. That's the true line of demarcation, if you ask me: long as you've still got a bodega that will sell you a single Newport for twenty-five cents, your neighborhood is not yet fully gentrified.

"You got a cigarette for me?" I asked.

"Bummed it from him," Joyce said, indicating one of two

skinny-jeaned, trucker-hatted chuckleheads slouched a few paces away. These weren't Fort Greene hipsters. Fort Greene hipsters wore limited-edition Nikes and bought Jadakiss mixtapes at the Fulton Mall. That was the arrangement: Williamsburg sent us their blue-eyed rapsters, and we sent them our freaky, pierced-the-fuck-up black rock dudes. The fact that these guys were drinking in Fort Greene on a Wednesday night was what Homer would have called a sign of ill portent.

I leaned toward Joyce's benefactor, separating my index and middle fingers at a jaunty, non-threatening angle. "My man, could I possibly bum one too?"

He waved his cancer stick at me. "Sorry, bro. Last one." I was so relieved, I swallowed the "bro." I hate cigarettes. That was Joyce for you. Or rather, that was me in Joyce's presence.

She tapped the ash from hers with a manicured nail, and handed it over. A sweetheart all the way.

"So where have you been hiding?"

I brought the filter to my lips, turning toward the street to hide my fake-inhale.

"I've been around. What's up with you? Getting ready to graduate?"

"I wish. One more semester, if I take five classes. *And* write a thesis."

"How's your brother?" A sad story, Cedric. Got to high school, made the football team, turned into a full-blown jackass.

"The same." She knew it as well as I did. Better. Joyce still lived at home.

"He playing ball?"

She nodded around her final drag, then dropped the butt and eliminated the threat of wildfire with a practiced ankle-twist.

"I'm bartending a few nights a week at a place called Sleet, over on Twelfth Street and Sixth Ave. You should come by sometime. We've got pretty good DJs on the weekends."

"Yeah," I said. "Cool. That'd be fun." I was feeling very weird, all of a sudden. This conversation was like a page torn from a normal life, and it was making me realize just how isolated and bizarre my shit had become. Not since February had I hung out with a friend, somebody my own age, and I couldn't tell you the last time I'd seen a movie, or gone to a party that wasn't teargassed by a chopper.

It had been months since I'd even worried about anything a regular person could relate to. What did I have to say to Joyce, whom I'd adored since before any of these bars were bars, who lived eight blocks away, who studied urban planning and danced capoeira, who'd told me I had pretty eyes when I was ten? At what coordinates did my existence meet hers? Where had I been hiding? What was I up to? I couldn't answer those questions without exposing myself as a fuckup of Olympian proportions, and making her an accessory to crimes so numerous and elaborate I wasn't even sure how they'd be charged.

Hell, the only reason I was even outside was to make a couple of phone calls I didn't want traced. Oh, hey Joyce—damn, girl, you're looking fine as usual, gimme one second, I've just gotta ring this slain drug dealer's mama and break the news real quick, and then I'd love to buy you a drink. But just one, I gotta get to bed early, I'm kinda beat because I just spent half of yesterday down in the tunnels planning a conspiracy and talking to the chief of the Mole People, at gunpoint. And I really need my rest, 'cause this weekend we're gonna bomb every train in the city and force-feed psychedelic drugs to a bunch of security guards, so as to bring down a mayoral candidate who murked a homeboy of my parents' back in the day, although actually a demon might have made him do it. So, what are you drinking?

Fuck.

We chatted a while longer, but my heart wasn't in it. Joyce had to go back inside; her friend Tamika was waiting. I had no ID anyway, and getting denied in front of Joyce would've been too much to bear, even on the best of nights. We hugged goodbye. It seemed full of promise, hug-as-rain-check, and that made me feel worse. Like I was deceiving her, somehow.

I watched the door to Moe's swing shut, then walked straight past the payphone and back up the block. What had I been thinking? What in the world did I imagine I'd say to Regina Polhemus? What speck of morality did I hope to salvage?

An asshole, that's what I was. I knew it then, I knew it as I pulled out my phone, and I knew it as I pressed speed dial and watched the Uptown Girl's number blink onto the screen.

"Hello?" It was a thing she always did, pretending not to know who was calling despite the name and number spelled out before her. I'd never asked why. It was sort of charming. Old-timey.

"Kirsten," I said, that being her name. Kirsten Kennedy. No joke.

"Hold on, let me step outside." That meant she was at home, and so were her parents. As far as they knew, we weren't speaking. "Outside" was a private roof deck larger than most apartments in my zip code.

"What's up?" she asked.

"I don't know. It's getting so I can't tell up from down."

It was the kind of thing I'd been saying to her lately: vague, melodramatic, pithy. I don't think I was looking for sympathy. More like envy. If the Uptown Girl had one complaint about her life (and to her credit, she knew even that many was pushing it), it was that nothing exciting ever popped off.

"Why? Did something happen?" I could see her arching her back, sliding the flat of her hand into the back pocket of her jeans.

"It's about to. Monday morning, go check out the trains."

"Yeah? Really? Which line?"

Which line. Thatagirl. I'd schooled her a little, you know.

"All of them."

"What?"

If you're feeling an urge to wince and slap your forehead, you can relax. This isn't some big plot pivot where I spill the beans and she throws a monkey wrench, out of some misguided sense of concern. That's not how the Uptown Girl was built.

"I know. Crazy, right? It was my idea."

"Holy shit. Dondi."

A pause. Maybe she'd brought her wineglass and was sipping. The Uptown Girl's family usually popped a bottle with their gourmet takeout. Monstrously pricey stuff, in glasses so enormous I thought it was a joke the first time I ate over. And yes, I was a frequent dinner guest. Bill and Alexandra loved my ass until it got thrown out of school. The fact that their daughter was dating a black guy proved to them that they'd raised her right, nice and colorblind. Until I showed my true colors, anyway.

You know, I never thought before about the fact that my father and the Uptown Girl's share a first name. Maybe the differences in our lives can be traced to what they chose to call themselves, these two men christened William. Vast distances are wrapped up in that semivowel. Sometimes-Y should have been Rage's nickname.

"What for?" asked the Uptown Girl.

I thought about it.

"For Billy."

This time, I was sure I heard her take a sip. A nice, long one. She was no doubt savoring the subtle overlays of anise and cranberry, the slight intimations of walnut, the almost autumnal shades of the bouquet.

"So, yeah, Yale," she said.

"Wait, what?"

"I got in."

"Holy shit. When did you find out?"

"Two days ago. I left you a message. I thought that's why you were calling."

"If I'd checked my voicemail, it would've been. Congratulations."

"Thanks." She drained the glass. "So what are you going to do, Dondi?"

I was walking in little circles, in front of Vex's building. "Make history, for starters. Nobody's ever pulled something like this off."

"Okay. I mean, great. And then?"

"Ask me on Tuesday."

Awkward pause.

"Your dad must be ecstatic," I said, "daughter following in his footsteps and everything. You know, Skull and Bones is co-ed now. You could join. Find out if the head of Geronimo that Preston Bush stole from that museum really has magic powers, like they say."

She sighed. "Dondi . . ."

"Yeah?"

"Nothing. It's Prescott Bush. Not Preston."

"See? You're halfway there already. Just promise you'll teach me the secret handshake, the one Dubya gave Kerry before the last debate."

I was under no illusion that I was making sense. Nor, probably, was the Uptown Girl. This was her cue to tell me she had to go, that she was in the middle of dinner. I could feel it coming.

Wrong.

"I spoke to Moya today."

My peer mentor. Remember? Studying art history at Columbia?

"Oh, yeah?"

"She's friendly with a guy who works in the admissions office."

I let it hang there for about a five-count. A courtesy of sorts, like giving somebody a head start before you throw a rock at them.

"So?"

"Maybe there's—"

"I already got in, Kirsten. The fuck is Moya's friend gonna do?"

"I just thought—"

"Yeah, well, think again. Better yet, don't. Fuck college. I don't even wanna go anymore. That shit's for losers."

"Thanks."

"Sorry."

"Whatever."

"Look, I gotta go. Me and my parents, we've got a reservation at Nobu."

"Really?"

"Fuck no."

"You don't have to be an asshole, Dondi. It's not my fault."

"What? What's not your fault?"

Here came the shrug. She had a great shrug. Excellent clavicles.

"Anything."

"I never said it was."

I watched the old lady two buildings down carry her garbage to the curb, a little parcel tied up so neatly it could've been a present for her grandkids.

"Fine."

"Fine. Congratulations, again. My best to Bill and Alexandra."

Meaning: plenty of shit's your fault. You let your parents run your life. You let them break us up.

"Fuck Bill and Alexandra," the Uptown Girl replied, and we proceeded to goodnights.

Vexer was playing the couch when I entered, a lit blunt in his hand.

He threw me a chin-nod. "Ay."

"Hey. Everybody else go home?"

He nodded. "I'ma crash soon myself." As in, I'm not trying to mack your mom.

In walked Karen, a beer in each hand. She didn't look like she expected him to toddle off to bed. But she didn't look like she understood that he might linger for reasons unrelated to smoke or strategy, either. Same old Karen.

"We got the paint," she told me, handing Vex his bottle.

"Great. I'm going to sleep."

"What? It's only nine-thirty. We're just about to start calling the first guard shift, the twelve-to-eight boys."

"Yeah, well, what can I tell you? It's been a long day. See you tomorrow."

I hit the futon full of dread and resignation, expecting to toss and turn and think. But as it happened, I caught a break: conked out within minutes and slept like I was getting paid to do it. Sometimes the body pulls rank.

ur crew had two hundred and twenty-nine cans of paint, four army rucksacks, eight hands, six working eyes, a bag of sandwiches, a bunch of water. Two Maglites, a welding torch and goggles, ten portable tape players, five prespun joints, two small ladders, a roll of toilet paper, three cell phones, one thing of pepper spray, one set of bolt-cutters, a shitload of extra batteries. Two watches, mine and Karen's, both of which read 4:37 P.M.

We were sitting in a van outside the Coney Island Train Yard. Inside, Mop And Go, as Supreme Chemistry's advance strike team had come to be known, was getting acquainted with the guards who'd recently clocked in for their Saturday evening shift. The other nine crews were in position around the city, waiting their turns. We were shorthanded, so we were first.

Dengue, of course, would not be painting. Instead, he was running point for the whole operation, cell phone tricked out with a walkie-talkie feature that turned it into something like a CB radio. Each crew had one. Hitting the trains was up to Wren and Rage and me. Wren and Rage mostly, since fills and the occasional spot of light welding were the only things I was qualified to do, and in both cases *qualified* was pure speculation.

If we fell behind schedule, the plan called for Mop And Go to augment us after they finished their duties, but Billy and Karen scoffed at the idea that we'd need bailing out. The two of them were cockier and more buddy-buddy than I'd ever seen, talking shit all morning about how they we were going to finish so early they'd be able to paint a whole train's worth of burners.

That was the reward speed won you: knock out your allotted cars with time to burn, and you got time to burn, a chance to cap your marathon of simple blockbuster straight letters with a bona fide wildstyle or two. Who was going to rock the illest AMUSE piece was a subject of much discussion. At this very moment, everybody was probably sitting around sketching the outline they hoped to execute.

Even if Mop And Go mopped and went smoothly, some crews might not be working until eight or nine. There was a lot of grumbling about that, but not so much that a single squad opted to handle the guards themselves rather than avail themselves of M.A.G.'s talents. A felony assault charge—with a deadly weapon, maybe, never mind what the D.A. might slap on you for trickling cambiafuerza down a card-carrying, union-dues-paying city employee's throat—was not something guys were willing to risk.

Except for the guys who were thrilled to risk it, that is. M.A.G. was gelling into a real band of brothers. Supreme Chem had outfitted his squad in fatigues and black facemasks—I swear, the dude must've run an army surplus store on the low—and as if that weren't enough, they were all done up with war paint *underneath* the masks, à la Martin Sheen shortly before he hacks up Marlon Brando. The horror, et cetera.

Mop And Go was being chauffeured from one yard to the next by a cat named Zebno, long-dormant founder of the Crazy Fresh Crew. He painted houses now, out in Queens, owned a van that seated fifteen uncomfortably, and had agreed to pull transpo duty throughout the weekend. Coffee runs, high-speed getaways, whatever.

A burst of static erupted over Dengue's phone. Flaw in the technology; it happened whenever someone was about to speak.

"Yo, Fev, y'all niggas still waiting?"

The Ambassador lifted the mic until it brushed his lips. "'Y'all niggas still waiting,' *what*?"

"My bad, my bad. Are you still waiting, over?"

"Affirmative. Over."

"The fuck is taking M.A.G. so long, man? You think they got a problem? Over."

"No. Stay off the line unless it's important. Over."

"Yeah, yeah, yeah. Over. I mean, out. Over and out, good buddy."

Dengue shook his head. "Give 'em radios, they gotta act all *Dukes of Hazzard* and shit."

"Here we go," said Karen, and tapped the window. Somebody, Klutch One I think, was jogging toward us.

"They look like a postapocalyptic boy band," I said. I'd been saving it. Nobody laughed.

The masked man beckoned. "Let's go." We grabbed our gear and followed. He yanked back the flap they'd cut into the fence, motioned us past.

Karen glared. "What are you doing? Didn't you take their keys?"

"This is faster."

"Money, I asked you a question. You're supposed to take their keys. You want one of these assholes locking himself in the booth? You take the radios, at least?"

It's easier than you'd think to read somebody's expression through a mask.

"Yeah, yeah, we got the radios. But look, once you see these dudes, you'll understand. Ain't no way they fitting no keys to no locks."

We followed him inside—a misnomer, since inside was still outside, a massive open-air holding pen topped with coils of razor wire. There were two guards' booths, one by the tunnels that opened into the yard and one halfway across the lot. The only other buildings were a few scattered maintenance sheds, where workers stored their equipment and maybe watched a little TV if they had some downtime.

Otherwise, it was all trains. Rows of them, stored end to end and side by side. A sea of steel, pristine and glistening. I was probably the only person there without a hard-on.

To move through the yard, you had to find the gap between the front of one train and the back of the next. They were parked haphazardly, so it was a matter of instinct, whether a left turn or a right was faster. And the alleys between them were so narrow that you could extend your arms and touch two trains at once.

"Any problems?" asked Billy.

"Nah, easy. We all got these." He pulled a blackjack from his pocket, held it up. "Guards were in their booths, so we just creeped up and banged 'em."

"You knocked them out." Billy sounded grim, as if he knew he was asking questions to which he wouldn't like the answers.

"Knocked 'em out, gave 'em the stuff, got 'em both inside a train. Waited twenty minutes for it to kick in, like you said, then gave 'em the smelling salts."

"They throw up?"

"*Did* they."

"And now?"

We took a right, and stopped before the lead car of an F. "See for yourself."

The doors were open. Two paunchy, middle-aged white men in guards' uniforms lay on the floor, eyes pinwheeling in their skulls.

"I don't see any puke."

"We moved them."

"These guys shouldn't be alone." Billy spoke in his thinking-out-loud voice. "What they're seeing is very powerful."

"Aah," said Karen. "Forget about it. They're fine. Happy as pigs in shit." She looked around. "Where'd everybody go?"

Her answer was a vigorous *clicka-clacka* from the other side of the train.

"Tryna help you ninjas out!" somebody called—Supreme Chem's word, but not his voice. We all stepped over to the other side of the train. There stood the rest of M.A.G., one man to a car, paint cans in motion.

Until that moment, I'd never really thought about spraypainting—the act itself, the kinetics. I'd never seen it live. Just lots of sped-up, Charlie Chaplin–looking videos of legal murals being produced, and maybe a few minutes' worth of hazy footage from the yards.

In real time, it's mesmerizing. Like tai chi or something. The paint-hand is the focal point, but the entire body's involved. Each movement is deliberate, calibrated, fluid. The knees bend. The toes point. The shoulders roll. Form follows form; the writer dances the word onto the surface. Paint arcs only as wide as the arm holding it, a line breaks only when the rhythm is ruptured. And that rupture is built into the design, the same way it's hardwired into everything my parents' generation of New Yorkers invented. They expected to get fucked with, so they wove interruption into their art, embraced it, made it fly, from the b-boy's freeze to the DJ's backspin.

I couldn't even see what the four of them were painting, because of my angle, but it didn't matter. Billy and Karen and I just stood and watched for about a minute. Dengue, he listened. Each writer had a distinct physical style, covered space at a different rate, made of himself a unique paintbrush. But they all seemed to move together, like dancers in the same ballet. The matching costumes helped.

Karen snapped out of it first. "You all better get the fuck on."

Nobody answered, but the duress wrought an instant change in the lines of their limbs, the speed of their movements. I wondered how many gears a writer had, and which one this was.

Supreme Chemistry finished first, stepped back, nodded at his piece the way you'd acknowledge an acquaintance from across the street. The can dropped into a pocket.

"One-minute warning," he called, and sauntered over to us. "Brothers needed a taste. Gotta keep your troops happy." He handed me a roll of duct tape. "Here. In case those guards give you any problems. Dengue, where we at with canceling the next shift?"

"Eighteen down. Still can't reach the last two. We'll keep trying."

"A'ight, well, keep me posted."

"Will do. And hey, nice work."

"Much obliged." He lifted his arm, and made an all-in motion. "Posse up, yo. Time to roll." The arm dropped, then rose to elbow Billy in the ribs. "Don't forget to have fun, ninja." And M.A.G. was out. The Immortal Five controlled the yard.

"Follow me," my father said. "I've got a job for you." He glanced down the line at Karen. She was already painting. He frowned.

"We really shouldn't leave them alone."

"Dengue can watch them. Fever, what are you doing, making calls?"

"Yeah."

"Can you do it in the car with the guards?"

"Guess so."

"Need help getting there?"

"I'll find it."

I turned to Billy. "There. Done."

The worry didn't leave his face, but he pulled three cans from the rucksack by his feet, and offered me a silver. We trudged over to the next train, stood before the last car.

"Okay, what you're going to do is just paint over all the windows." He took the can, removed the nozzle, replaced it with a fatcap. Climbed the train's undercarriage, reached up, and covered the window in one continuous motion, left to right and back again.

"Nice and easy, like that." He shook the can, handed it over.

"That's it?"

"The train's already silver, right? So if you cover the windows, I can do top-to-bottoms with just an outline. Watch." He fatcapped a red, tested it with three short blasts into the air. A wind I couldn't feel grabbed the paint particles, carried them a few feet, made them disappear.

Billy squared up to the train, crouched, and brought a line of color into existence along the baseline. He swept it up into a swirl that fell back over itself like an ocean wave, then left it alone, straightened, leaned across himself, began something else. Finished, raised his arm above his head, painted a third thing. This letter was being built in sections, in a manner utterly contrary to the way I would have thought to do it. The connections came last, bottom to middle, middle to top—and suddenly this collection of flamboyant lines had coalesced into a rakish capital *E* nearly the height of the train, leaning back against a field of silver like a pimp behind the wheel.

It had taken Billy all of thirty seconds. I felt like I was watching one of those cooking shows where they mix up all the ingredients, put the pan in the oven, and take out a finished version at the same time.

They say a great chef can make the simplest dish revelatory. Cereal with milk—reimagined, reinvented, better than it's ever been.

The letter *E*—nasty as fuck, ready to scrap. And this was just a straight-letter. No bars, no bits, no arrows, legible to even the squarest civilian. Its attitude was a matter of minutiae, of math.

"See? Now a few highlights."

He switched cans and doubled the inside curves in white, the line emerging thin and sharp. Shifted a few paces to the left, and embarked on his *S.*

I'd been trying to figure out what Billy's painting stance reminded me of, and now it hit me: fencing. I'd taken one class, during the blink-and-you-missed-it try-new-things phase that marked my first semester at Whoopty Whoo Ivy League We's A Comin' Academy, and I remember the teacher demonstrating the correct posture, telling us it allowed the quickest, longest reach. By the end of the hour I'd determined that while the sport might fulfill my gym requirement, an hour a week crossing blades with a coterie of greasy-faced Dungeons & Dragons types was not going to turn me into the dude from *Legend of the Liquid Sword,* so that was that.

"Go paint," Billy said over his shoulder. "And don't try to climb the train. Use the ladder."

"Yes sir." It felt good to address my father as *sir*, to be under his command. I grabbed the ladder, set it up below the next window over, and quickly realized that was the wrong place for it. Climbed back down, moved it a few feet to the left so I could paint without being in my own way, reascended. *Clicka-clacka, psshht, psssht, clicka-clacka, psshht.* Descend, grab ladder, reposition, climb, repeat.

I have this tendency to suspect that anything I've never done before, I might just be a natural at, a prodigy. The one time I went to the driving range with Andy Simpkins in tenth grade to "hit a few buckets," I could already see the lead paragraph of the *Sports Illustrated* profile as I was renting my club. The first ball I hit was going to soar whatever an astronomical distance was in golf. Inside of two weeks I'd be inking Tag Heuer endorsement deals, bagging Swedish broads, and denying I was black.

I was mistaken, naturally, just as I had been about tennis, chess, sexual intercourse, and billiards. But graffiti? Shit, aptitude had to be inscribed on both sides of the double helix; that eighth-grade misadventure was too small a sample size to be scientifically significant. As I moved from window to window, I spun a fantasy about sneaking down a few rows and quietly rocking a ridiculous burner— but not just ridiculous, revolutionary: the letterforms pulsing with a style nobody had ever thought of, so daring and iconoclastic that only a brilliant neophyte could have conceived it. I'd be adding the finishing touches when Karen and Billy happened by, and . . .

And, my fucking arm felt like it was going to fall off. My hand was cramping up, to the point where I had to switch my grip, press the nozzle with my thumb. I'd painted a grand total of eleven windows. Badly. Billy had covered the glass and nothing but, whereas my lack of can control yielded a kind of lipsticked-clown effect. It didn't matter, of course. Except to me.

My father was halfway through his second top-to-bottom. I paused to watch.

"Come on, come on, back to work," he ordered, without looking up. I climbed my ladder, raised my arm. *Clicka-clacka. Psshht.*

This was a waste of time, I found myself thinking. Why couldn't he do window-downs? The obvious answer, *because whole cars are iller*, I pretended not to know. *Clicka-clacka. Psshht.* I switched arms, painted with my left. The quality of the work didn't suffer.

I was two windows short of done—with that side of that train, anyway—when Dengue bellowed.

"Yo! Billy! Little help! It's fuckin' Wild Kingdom in here!"

I jumped off my ladder and ran. The Ambassador stood outside the car, back pressed against its center doors. I peered inside. One guard sat balled beneath a corner seat. The other lay wrapped around a pole. The sound coming from their mouths was animal in the purest sense, an expression of a pain experienced in the eternal now. If there was a hell, that's what the residents' wails would sound like, if you lowered the volume on the Black Eyed Peas CD enough to hear them.

"I don't know what happened," said Fever. "One minute every-thing was quiet, and then bam, freakout city."

"Fuck it," said Karen. She and Billy had both arrived while my back was turned. "There's nobody around. Let 'em go nuts."

Billy didn't even bother to answer, just pried open the doors and climbed inside.

"Oh, for God's sake." My mother ran through a greatest hits medley of pissed-off poses—arms crossed, hands hipped, chin lifted to commiserate with God, body angled away from the offender—performed in such swift succession that it looked like something you might see the Pips do behind Gladys. Then she clambered up into the train herself and crouched opposite my father, on the other side of the guard he was trying to soothe.

"We're on a schedule, Billy."

"Give me a minute." He held the guy's palm in both his hands, doing acupressure or something. The screams were coming at intervals now.

"We don't have a minute."

Billy knelt over the guard, and began whispering into his ear.

Karen bent lower. "Billy. Listen to me."

Yeah, right. He finished whatever he was telling dude, leapt up, and headed for the other one.

Karen stood. "Fever? Dondi? Care to weigh in here?"

Guard number two wouldn't budge. He kicked at Billy, from his fortress beneath the bench, and howled bloody homicide. My father reached out to him over and over, repeating low, calm words I couldn't quite make out.

I stuck my head inside. "Dad?"

Billy's head jerked up. "Get me my bag."

"Listen, we've really gotta—"

"I'm not leaving them like this. I can't." He turned back to the guard.

Karen watched for a few seconds, then jumped off the train.

"You know what your father's problem is? He says 'can't' when he means 'won't.' Fuck this, and fuck him. I'm going back to work." And off she stalked.

Dengue's walkie-talkie crackled. "Yo, Fever, you there?"

"This is Fever. Go ahead. Over."

"We're in. Rock and roll, baby."

"Sambo's in," the Ambassador called. "Yo, Wren! You hear me? Sambo's in. We're up in three yards, going on four!"

"Yeah, great." She didn't turn around. "I guess I'll just paint all these fucking trains myself."

Clicka-clacka, psshht.

Your boy? I did as I was told. By the time I came back with Billy's bag, guard number two wasn't cowering in the corner anymore. He'd graduated to wild spasms, torso bucking and limbs whipping out like jellyfish tentacles, and he seemed hellbent on murdering his coworker; Billy and a total lack of bodily control conspired to stop him. Twenty feet away, the prospective murderee moaned with operatic gusto, clutching the base of the pole like a stripper with a stomach virus.

I tossed the bag into the car, and climbed in after it. "You got an antidote in there?"

Billy pulled open the zipper, and removed a bottle of water. I took it as a no.

"Talk to him," my father instructed, as he daubed the madman's face with a wet rag. "Tell him not to fight it. Be calming. You can even hum."

I knelt over guard number one, realized dude had shit himself, and backed away in a hurry.

"Sorry, Billy. I've got trains to paint."

I found Karen doing window-down throw-ups, red and black, four to a car. She slung a can at me the way a whiteboy in a high school sex comedy slings his buddy a beer from the cooler, and taught me to do fills.

Our collaboration was a three-part, two-color process. First, my mother sketched the letters. Then I stepped up, tried to color inside her lines. It was easier with my feet on the ground, not the rungs of a ladder. When I finished, she painted a real outline, thick and black: erased the mistakes, solidified the form, imposed the style. We knocked off three cars in silence, trying to ignore the waxing and waning of the guards' screams, before Karen stepped back, cocked her elbow, and read her watch.

"This isn't gonna fly. Get Fever."

"Why?"

"He's gotta paint."

"Don't be ridiculous."

She pointed a spraycan in his general direction. "That's Ambassador Dengue Fever, okay? One of the all-time greats. He can paint."

"Karen, he's blind."

"Ah, that's a crock of shit. It's all in his head. Hurry your black ass up."

I found the Ambassador at the gates of Billy's makeshift mental hospital, debating the head nurse. They both wore their T-shirts hooked over their noses, to mitigate the stench. I leaned around them, got an angle on the car. One guard lay atop a row of seats, curled toward the wall, arms shielding his face. He was quiet. The other, the bowel-voider, sprawled on the floor, eyes closed. If you listened hard, you could discern a low, quivery moan.

"Looks like you've got it under control in there," I said. "Come paint."

"I can't. Their journey will take many turns. You know what it's like. So do you, Dengue. Please, you've gotta call Zebno."

"Call him for what?"

The Ambassador's face was grim. "Blam, Fizz, Dregs and Species have all got psychotic guards on their hands, too."

"So, everybody who's in."

"Except Stoon and Vexer. Both Vex's guys are cool. Stoon, it's too early to tell."

"We've got to get them here," said Billy. "All of them. They could be permanently damaged, without guidance." He stared balefully at the ground. "This was wrong. I should have known better. I *did* know better. I fooled myself into believing . . ."

He shook his head inside the T-shirt. It made a frictive sound, against his stubble.

"Get them here, Dengue. Please. I don't care what it takes. And don't say another word to me about the trains, either of you. These are human beings."

The "I don't care what it takes" was my tip-off. That's a movie line. I couldn't tell you which movie—all of them. If you utter that phrase in real life, a part of you is acting, whether you know it or not. I'm not saying Billy wasn't sincere. Just that this situation had begun to serve a second purpose as a stand-in, a do-over, a shadow version of previous dramas.

Certainly, my father had plenty to reprise. And I could see how, in his mind, going off-mission to help the guards might feel like refusing to repeat the mistakes of the past. Like compassion was finally trumping graff and justice and revenge.

Except for one thing: that so-called compassion was every bit as misplaced as it had always been. He was still helping the wrong people and turning his back on the ones who mattered. Still waving a flag of sanctimonious morality to justify it all. Same tired-ass hero-on-a-quest man-apart narcissism.

I reached out, grabbed his shirt, jerked it off his nose.

"You know what that stink is, Billy? That's your fucking bullshit. I been smelling it my whole life, but here I am—talk about *should have known better*. Talk about *let myself believe*. And what do I get for it? I get fucked over again—we all get fucked over again—and *you* get to act like you're doing the right thing. Selflessly."

I was right up in his face. He didn't even blink. A second ticked past.

"Dondi . . ."

"Stay out of this, Fever."

I poked Billy in the shoulder with two fingers. "Don't you *dare* look at me all serene. Go ahead, say you have no choice. Right?"

My father leaned back against the train—all passive, like if I wanted to push him he'd comply and retreat. But it wasn't that. He wanted to make a show of sizing me up. As if the additional two feet had given him perspective.

"You haven't forgiven me," he said, slow and pained, like he was reading the words off an eye chart he had to squint to make out. "Not really. I understand. I should have known."

It was true and false at the same time, and it threw me for a loop, scrambled my circuitry. Was it possible that I was wildly off base, and Billy was indeed acting out of moral necessity—acting like the father he'd never been while I, in turn, acted like the father he *had* been, blind to everything beyond the mission?

I've been wondering ever since. This, however, was not the time.

"What kind of slick shit is that? Don't be psychoanalyzing me, motherfucker—that's first of all. Second, whether or not I've forgiven you is fucking irrelevant. And third, I *have* forgiven you. But I won't again. So you need to decide what's important right now: feeding your ego, or playing your part? Doing right by them, or doing right by us?"

Billy raised up to his full height. "I am playing my part. I'm sorry you don't—"

"Yeah? Fucking one-man show, huh?"

"Think whatever you want."

His eyes flashed and his face went hard, and I knew Billy had finished listening. It was impossible not to picture him doing the same thing eighteen years earlier. I doubted my father had ever really listened to anybody.

From inside the train came a wail, and then another. The journey, apparently, had taken another turn. Billy boosted himself up and in.

"Call Zebno, Fever."

The Ambassador raised the phone to his ear as if it were a gun, and paced off.

Billy looked down at me.

"You were such a beautiful baby," he said. "So smart. So fucking smart. We couldn't believe how smart you were, Dondi. I missed you so much."

"What the fuck does—"

But he'd already vanished into the car's interior.

I caught up with Dengue just as he was finishing his convo.

"You gotta come with me," I told him.

"For what?"

"A bunch of reasons. But mostly because I'm not gonna be the one who tells Wren we're about to be running a funny farm."

"I got business to attend to, Dondi."

"I'm sure you do." I took him by the elbow.

Karen looked up when we turned her corner. "Finally," she said. "Fever, sack up and paint. We're way behind."

She tossed him a can. It bounced off his stomach.

"Ouch. The fuck is wrong with you?"

"You really have to ask? The train is two feet to your right. Get cracking. That was black. Here's silver." She chucked another can. Dengue managed to catch the rebound off his chest. Karen shot me a triumphant look. I ignored her.

"It's not as bad as it seems," said Dengue.

My mother snorted. "It's quarter past nine, and we've finished one train."

"Yeah, but this is just one yard. Everybody else is rocking, or will be within the hour. Worst comes to worst, we'll bust the windows, so they can't put these puppies in service."

"Yeah, right—and live *that* down for the rest of my life? I'm a writer, not some fucking . . . vandal."

Both of them were quiet. It was a double fault; breaking windows was a borderline-dishonorable solution, and mentioning bragging rights was just as bad. Treating the word *vandal* with such contempt wasn't cool, either. Writers had always embraced it.

I seized the chance for diplomacy. "Mom, you haven't written for eighteen years. Stop throwing paint and calm down. Dengue, enough with the silver linings. Tell her."

"When this is over, your ass is fucking grounded, talking to me like that. Tell me what, fat man?"

"I figured when this was over, I'd go back to being kicked out."

"I'll ground you *and* kick you out." Which made no sense, obviously, but that's where Karen's head was at. Maybe telling her wasn't such a good idea. She'd find out soon enough.

The Ambassador sighed. "The rest of the guards are flipping out, and Zebno's bringing them here. Billy's orders. Says this is what he's trained for."

"No way. Tell Zebno to dump them in Brownsville or some shit."

Brownsville: I had to smile at that. One thing about my mother, ol' girl is consistent. No sudden fits of morality. Fuck 'em today, fuck 'em tomorrow, fuck 'em for all time.

"Come on, Wren. You know that's not going to happen."

"Since when is Billy giving orders around here?"

"These are human beings."

"No, Dengue, these are *transit guards*. God, is everybody having a crisis of confidence around here? You wanna make an omelette, you gotta fuck some people up!" She handed me a can of silver. "I hope you've learned a thing or two about your precious father."

"Crisis of conscience," I said.

Karen frowned. "What?"

"You said crisis of confidence, but you meant crisis of conscience."

She pointed at the train. "Go do your fills."

For the next ninety minutes I shadowed my mother, concentrated on coloring her hollow shapes and let my fury simmer, unattended. As for Karen, anger seemed to improve her work. She'd been painting by rote before, in keeping with the philosophy behind throw-ups: they're supposed to be mass-produced, easy to assemble, attractive in repetition. Now, though, each outline was a little wilder than the last. The *A*'s crossbar sprouted flares, the horizontals on the *E* whipped skyward with greater and greater insouciance, the *S* hit puberty and started dressing sexy. It was like those evolutionary charts you sometimes see, monkey to a caveman to a dude in a suit. The outlines were getting harder to fill, but I was getting better at it, even as dusk turned to night and we had to work by the light of the moon and the far-off streetlamps.

If it comes as a surprise that Dengue was indeed capable of painting, then you haven't been paying attention, to either the litany of tasks the blind man managed to manage or the implications of my recent statements concerning dance and fencing and martial arts. If a ballerina loses her eyesight, the ability to bust pirouettes and whatnot doesn't vanish, right? If somebody King Lears one of those ponytailed dudes you see doing qigong in Fort Greene Park, can he no longer embarrass himself in public?

So yes, Fever picked up a can and did his thing. In the Immortal era, he'd strictly been a wildstylist, not the uppest dude but one who upped the ante, whose pieces advanced and disseminated aerosol theory each time one rolled out. Asking him to do throw-ups was like asking one of those super-freaky free jazz intellectuals to play a wedding, *hey, excuse me Anthony Braxton, can you give us a few choruses of "I Can't Help Falling in Love with You" before we cut the cake?* Dengue did his best to keep it swift and simple, but his letters couldn't help shattering into segments, growing connections, masking themselves with camouflage. Eyes or no eyes, the Ambassador's sense of space was impeccable. Occasionally he was off by a few inches, overlapped something he didn't mean to or vice versa. But the style made it work, at least to me.

We worked in silence, the vibe poisonous. When Zebno called to announce his approach and Dengue sent me to meet him at the gate, the prospect of overseeing a nine hundred percent spike in cambiafuerza-deranged security guards actually cheered me up.

I jogged over in time to see the van lurch to the curb. Supreme Chemistry and two other M.A.G. men threw open the doors, leapt out, and started hauling forth passengers. There were sixteen of them—every guard but Vexer's, both of whom remained the picture of tranquillity. Perhaps it was due to previous familiarity with hallucinogens, or sympathetic brain chemistry. But what were the chances that a matched pair would groove on the dose while everybody else was bugging? The walkie-talkie chatter was heavy on Vex-as-guru jokes, though he insisted the only amenity he'd provided was a transistor radio tuned to the oldies station he always left on for his cats.

The rules of the van ride, apparently, had been that anybody who got loud got duct-taped. That was all of them. And, of course, securing a sovereign individual's pie-hole is pointless if he retains the use of his hands, so what anybody watching would have seen was three masked men in camouflage yanking a series of bound, gagged, uniformed hostages from an unmarked van and dragging the disoriented, flailing victims through a flap in a fence and into the blackness beyond like it was just another evening at Guantánamo Bay.

"You gonna help or what, ninja?" Supreme Chemistry called.

The truth was, I could barely move. Watching people get tossed around like luggage made me sick, and I just stood there, knuckles whitening around the portion of chain-link I'd pulled back. The last time I'd felt this way I'd been wedged into that window seat, watching Knowledge Born and Twenty-Twenty swing the bats.

It was an ugly business, there was no getting around it. But then again, so was whapping people unconscious with a blackjack and force-feeding them rainforest peyote, and I hadn't objected to that, had I? On the contrary, I'd dreamed it up, believed it necessary— and if it was, why wasn't this? Maybe the only difference lay in the relationship between the act and my eyeballs, and I was confusing moral repugnance with being a pussy.

"Make yourself useful," 'Preme said, and shoved one of the guards at me.

I caught her in my arms. She was a mousy, bony thing, looked like some Irish cop's frailest daughter. Her clothes were sweat-drenched. There was vomit in her hair. The eyelids fluttered open, then closed. Homegirl was a million miles away.

I draped one of her arms over my shoulder, grabbed her by the waist, and started walking. Supreme Chem followed, pushing two guards ahead of him, one hand fisted around each of their belts.

"You better untape them before we reach Billy," I said. "If he sees this, he's going to freak out."

To my surprise, 'Preme accepted that. He stopped, and I heard the flick of a switchblade, the fibrous rip of tape. As the other prisoners passed into the yard, he cut their bonds as well. Some screamed when the adhesive was peeled from their mouths. Others babbled nonsense. Mine stayed quiet. I wondered if Karen and Dengue were still painting, or if they'd stopped to listen.

Sustaining verticality was more than most of the guards could handle, but M.A.G. didn't seem to care. They shoved and yelled and threatened, determined to advance the whole group at once, as if we were taking sniper fire.

"Look, they don't get it, okay? You doing *this*"—I pushed Megs in the shoulder, or maybe it was Maser—"means nothing in cambiafuerza-land. Their brains are too busy frying to translate *this*"—I pushed him again; I would have liked to punch him in the mask—"and even if they did, it wouldn't make them stand up and walk. It'd be like when you're dreaming, and the alarm clock goes off, so you start dreaming about fire engines. You understand?"

Some kind of bootleg soldier mentality had really set in on these guys. As long as you acted like an authority, somebody further up the chain of command, they responded with deference.

"What should we do?" asked the guy I'd been pushing.

"Carry them."

M.A.G. dropped guard after guard on Billy's threshold like so many sacks of flour, jumped back in the van, and peeled off to go deal with the next catastrophe: it was past ten, and two of the guards working midnight-to-eight still couldn't been reached, one guy's cell going straight to voicemail and the other's landline disconnected.

Mop And Go was short on time. They had to gamble. The guy who hadn't paid his phone bill lived in the Bronx but was reporting to a yard in Queens, and the guy with the cell lived in Brooklyn but was pulling his shift in the Bronx. The plan was to roll to the Boogie Down, ambush Cellie on his way into the yard and grab Landline outside his house. If he was home.

I saw them off, then backtracked to the loony bin and lingered outside. I needed to see Billy in action. My revulsion at the guards' treatment hadn't softened me any toward him—okay, maybe five percent, but five percent doesn't get much done; ask Clarence 13X. I suppose I was curious whether he could do them any good. Mostly, though, I wanted the satisfaction of a glimpse inside the hell Billy had built himself.

To say that the patients had taken over the asylum, as the expression goes, does the situation little justice. *Taken over* implies some kind of agenda: inmates take over prisons, the state takes over management of failing schools. This wasn't even a frenzy; this was eighteen separate frenzies. Billy dashed from one shrieking, thrashing victim to the next, constantly forced to decide which of these people was the most desperate, when to abandon one for another. The noise exploding through the cracked-open doors was unbearable, least of all for being ear-splitting. The smell made my eyes water like a punch in the nose.

My father never wavered. No breaks, no breakdowns, focused and purposeful. *In the moment*, as some of my fake-Buddhist fuckhead customers are fond of saying. It was like he could diagnose the particulars of each agony, and ease it—with words, with touch, with his very proximity. Had Billy been able to devote himself to any one person, I'm sure he could have steered him back toward enlightenment—and I had no doubt that cambiafuerza could take a motherfucker there, for the simple reason that something had to lie opposite of this.

I stood and watched for five or ten minutes, the spectacle hypnotic in its horror. If Billy noticed me, he didn't let on. I paid special attention to my guard. She was one of the quietest, but when she did open her mouth, it was to loose a scream so sharp it cut a swath straight through the general cacophony—which then crested, as if the sound had actually penetrated their brains, folded itself into their nightmares.

The sound of rapid, labored breathing wrenched me away. It wasn't particularly loud, but it was coming from the wrong direction. I stepped away from Billy's hospital and prowled the corridor between the trains, straining to home in on the source.

It was a guard. He lay on his back beneath the train, chest heaving so hard it nearly touched the undercarriage. I dropped down and tried to grab him, but the poor schmuck was too far in. I ran around to the other side, but he was out of reach from there as well. I'd have to get down and push. He was a big guy, one of three Megs and Maser had carried in together. No way I could do this without someone on the other side to catch hold of a limb and pull.

I found Karen and Dengue two rows away, slouched inside a half-painted car. Static poured from the walkie-talkie. They were sharing a joint.

"What the hell is this?"

"We're on break," my mother croaked. "It's fucking hopeless, Dondi."

"Yeah, if you sit around getting high it is."

"Don't be an asshole. We've been working nonstop until five minutes ago. But two people can't bomb a yard. It's impossible."

She passed Fever the joint, now doubling as a conversational baton.

"I'm slow," he announced, and pulled some weed into his lungs. "Fat, blind and slow. And stupid." He passed it back.

"It's not just us," Karen explained. "Everybody's behind."

"How behind?"

"Enough that all of this could be for nothing. The MTA's only gonna run bombed trains if there's no other option. We leave even a quarter of them clean, and they'll have one."

"So we break windows."

"I already tried. They're made of fiberglass or something now. Not like the old days."

"We should have reached out to more people," Dengue said. "Active people. That was a mistake." He shook his head. "Blam's crew just lost forty minutes, to a patrol car. Turned out some drunk was smashing bottles outside the yard, and a neighbor called in a complaint. But they had to hide until the cops bounced. Shit like that will kill us."

"M.A.G. will help out here," I offered.

"M.A.G. is in up to their asses," Karen replied, and shut her eyes.

The walkie-talkie static swelled, and then a voice came on. "Yo, it's Paco. I just got word, they're booking the boy Frog, up in Harlem. He made them chase him for like half an hour, before he got caught. Fucking A-plus work, right?"

Dengue picked it up, and pressed a button. "Good. How many's that?"

"Uh . . . two, dude. The juvie over on Staten, and now Frog. I'm spacing it out, just like you said."

A new voice crackled through the speaker. "Fever, you okay, money?"

The Ambassador put his phone down.

"What's up with Cool Rage-ski?" a third writer chimed in. "He chilled them niggas out, or what?"

"Ha ha. Probably got 'em doing fills!"

"Yo Species, how many trains you rocked, kid? Spe? You there?"

"Smoke break's over," I said. "Karen, I need a hand with one of these guards."

She crossed her legs. "I'm here to paint. You want to play Mother Teresa with your father, that's on you."

"I've got a fucking guy lying underneath a train, Karen. I can't get him out alone."

"So ask—"

"He's busy."

"Yeah, well, so am I. Doing his job. As usual. And yours."

She grabbed the pole and swung to her feet, eyes blazing. My mother in full I-dare-you-to-speak mode was terrible to behold, like when the Greek gods revealed their true forms to mortals.

I sighed. "The guy is *trapped under a train*, Wren."

She glared at me awhile longer, as if suspecting it was a trick. "Fine." She turned to Dengue. "I'll be right back."

The guard was just as I'd left him. "You want to crawl under and push, or stay here and pull?" I asked Karen, who didn't deem the question worthy of a response. I dropped to my stomach, dragged myself forward on my elbows.

The bulk of the train blocked outside noise; by the time I reached him, the guard's breath was all I could hear. He sounded like a small animal having a heart attack. Puke glinted in his mustache, trailed down his uniform. At his side lay a pair of eyeglasses, the kind you buy off a drugstore rack. One lens was smashed.

I braced my feet against the metal track, and shoved him as hard as I could. He shifted a few inches. I crept forward, did it again.

"One more," called Karen. "I can almost reach his leg."

I couldn't find a decent foothold. I tried pushing him anyway, but it was me who slid. Finally, I got him close enough for Karen to grab, and we did the old ready-on-three routine until the beam of her Maglite shone full on his face.

I came around, and we both looked down at the dude like he was something we'd just hit with our car.

"Well, that was fun. I'm going back to work."

"Hold on, Karen. We gotta get your man here back inside."

My mother rolled her eyes, but she bent over him, hands dangling by her ankles.

"Grab him under the knees. Ready? And . . . lift." I staggered slightly, struggling to control his weight, feeling the sweat burst out of me.

"Got him?"

"Uh huh. Let's go."

We turned and began the fifty-foot journey to the nuthouse door, both of us walking sideways, leg crossing over leg.

We never made it. Directly in front of us stood five men, their faces cast in shadow, their bodies silhouetted in the moonlight.

14

ell, well, well. So it is true, after all." A deep voice, clipped and accented. He crossed his arms over his chest. I looked at Karen. She was frozen in place, elbows still locked around the guard's knees.

"Did we come at a bad time?" the man inquired. His companions chuckled.

I lowered my half of the guard to the ground. Karen followed suit. Slowly, together, we straightened.

"That depends," I said. "Who the fuck are you?"

More low laughter. "We are from Denmark. Copenhagen."

"Yeah? You lost or something?"

He stepped forward, into the light, and extended his hand. From the look on Karen's face, you would have thought it was a dog turd on a stick. He dropped it to his side.

"Trash, FTP. Fuck The Police, or Fame Then Power. These, I can introduce, are the rest of my crew."

Karen pulled the pepper spray from her back pocket. "This some kind of joke?"

Trash slid a giant canvas rucksack off his back, took a knee before it, and undid the latch. It was crammed with cans.

"We heard NYC was gonna be the spot this weekend. So we came."

"Where'd you hear that?" Karen's tone evinced little of her trademark warmth. But she'd put away her weapon.

Trash stroked his chin. "Where *did* we hear?" He stood, and turned to his boys. "Was it from Edom?"

"I heard from Nalgas and Tyko, when they came over from Barcelona," one volunteered. "But I don't know, Edom might have told them."

"Who the fuck's Edom?" demanded Karen.

I stepped in front of her. "Who cares? Welcome to New York. You have no idea how glad we are to see you. I'm Dondi. This is Wren 209."

Practically in unison, they gave that writer-nod that meant they'd heard of her. I shook Trash's hand, then everybody else's. Their names went in one ear and out the other, except for one dude who called himself Fuck. Catchy.

"Edom, from Paris?" Trash said to Karen, when the introductions were complete. "He's one of Europe's most famous writers."

Trash might as well have said the dude was one of Indonesia's best-groomed mastodons. I could tell he was taken aback that she didn't know. Though not as taken aback as Karen looked, to learn that dudes in France and Spain and Denmark had their ears to our ground.

"So y'all motherfuckers just figured you'd show up and surprise us?" My mother's aggression was giving way to incredulity. Beyond that, on the other side of a treacherous mountain pass, lay jubilation. Getting there, for Karen, took time.

Trash shifted his weight. "Yes, I guess so. I try to come to New York every year, anyway. I usually stay with Hades? Come to think of it, maybe he's the one who told me."

"Fuckin' Hades," Karen muttered.

They all looked absolutely scared to death of her. I scrambled for a way to make them feel welcome. Then it dawned on me that Karen's shenanigans might not be as discomforting as the muffled wails of dementia coming from behind the silvered-over windows of the nearest train. Or the unconscious, puke-slathered guard who lay between us even now.

"You guys look ready to paint," I said.

"Yeah, man."

"Awesome. Follow me, and I'll take you to headquarters. Which is wherever Dengue's at. You guys know Dengue Fever?" I started to walk. I felt like skipping.

"The Ambassador," said one of the guys whose names I'd forgotten. "I bought a sculpture from him when I was here in '98. I haven't spoken with him since."

"Trust me, he's gonna be fucking ecstatic to see you guys."

Trash was on my right, struggling to keep up. "Yeah, so . . . is everything cool?" he asked, with a backward glance at the various atrocities we'd left behind.

"I don't even know where to start."

We found Dengue pacing between trains, phone pressed to his head. From the sound of the conversation, he was trying to get a report on M.A.G., and failing.

"Yo, Fev! Fev! You're not going to believe this, B! The fuckin' cavalry just arrived."

"Hold on, Fizz, K.D.'s calling me. I'll hit you back." He spun with what could almost be called grace, and grinned hugely.

"Cómo están, pendejos? Ustedes han llegado en el justo de tiempo, en la hora mas desesperado. Hay muchos trenes para pintar, y necesitamos sus ayuda like a motherfucker, ¿me entienden? Pues, ¿dónde está mi gran amigo, Gotch Uno?"

Silence, except for the sound of brows furrowing.

"Uh, Fever? Why are you speaking Spanish?"

"It's not Matamos Todos Crew, from Mexico City?"

"FTP, from Copenhagen."

"Oh, *shit*!" He flung open his arms. "Bring your asses over here and give me a hug! Ha ha! Dondi, get these motherfuckers a sandwich, or a joint, or *something*!"

One by one, they filed up to Dengue, and were swallowed in his arms. It was pretty funny, watching them trying to tell him their names while he cackled with delight and rocked them back and forth. The Danes couldn't get enough. After Karen's welcome, they deserved it.

"I'm going to assume these Mexican guys are coming too, then?"

"We got cats showing up from fuckin' everywhere, K.D.! Berlin, London, Chicago. Two guys from Stockholm just strolled into the Ghost Yard, fifteen minutes ago. Almost gave Fizz a heart attack."

"Tobias and Jacob," said Trash, nodding. "They told me they would try to make it."

"Everybody wants to be a part of history," Fuck added. "To bring the New York trains back to life, that is, what would you say, the ultimate."

"So how come nobody bothered to let us know they were coming?" I asked.

Trash looked as if he'd suddenly found a strange-tasting object in his mouth. "There are no RSVPs in graffiti," he said.

"Well, how come everybody's showing up at the same time? Y'all coordinate this shit or something?"

Even as I said it, I felt like an ass. Here's this guy old enough to be a twenty-year vet, comes to New York every year, probably famous in his own right—like his boy Edom, who we're too provincial to be impressed by—and instead of offering grub and weed I'm peppering him with pointless, vaguely suspicious-sounding questions.

I bet you're wondering too, though. Right?

"In Europe, we would never dream of going out before midnight. I've never painted earlier than that here, either."

"Oh." I looked at my watch. Quarter past twelve.

All of a sudden, it dawned on me that we'd forgotten all about that guard. I rushed back to the spot. No sign of him. I busted a U-turn and headed to Billy's car, to break the news and wash my hands of the whole affair.

First thing I saw, through the cracked-open corner doors? My mother, crouching over the female guard, two fingers pressed to her wrist, the other hand cocked so Karen could read her watch. A bandana covered her nose and mouth.

"Normal," she called.

"Good," Billy called back, from the other side of the car. "Massage the pressure points a little."

I stole away. Found Dengue chilling in a train car as FTP unpacked outside it, and sat down beside him.

"I just saw something that kind of blew my mind."

"Speak on it, nephew."

"My mother, she's in there helping Billy."

"Sure. Was only a matter of time. You got to overstand, K.D. Wren? She loves that fool. She's *always* had his back."

"Not when she threw him out."

The Ambassador snorted. "Never happened. She woulda rolled all the way to Mexico with him, if he'd let her—she sure as hell tried. I'm telling you, underneath all her bullshit, your mother's a rider. Till the wheels fall off. And underneath all his, your father's—"

"A cold-hearted bastard."

Dengue smiled. "Big-hearted. He's a big-hearted bastard."

"Yeah, well. You say potato, I say fuck that motherfucker."

"Got to accept the man for who he is, boy."

"And who's that?"

He pulled a glue tube. "Billy Rage, nigga."

Outside, Trash and his boys were organizing their cans by color, leaning together over sketches, chatting in their own language.

"They know the rules, right?" I asked. "Amuse throws only?"

"I told them. They said they didn't come all this way to do throws, they came to burn. I think it'll be okay. Europeans paint fast. And we're gonna have crazy manpower soon, so fuck it, you know? Either the tide's turned, or we all drown." He cracked his glue.

"What's up with M.A.G., and those two guards?"

"Been wondering that myself. But neither of them showed up for work, so . . ." The Ambassador shrugged.

"I could use a nap," I said, and immediately realized I'd never be able to sleep. Your boy here was a snarl of jangled nerves, dead on my feet but still in panic mode. I told Dengue I was going to take a stroll, appraise our progress.

The Scandahoovians had fanned out, one man to a car, and donned gasmasks. Give motherfuckers a little free health care and all of a sudden they're too good to inhale toxic fumes, I guess. They'd barely gotten going, but it was obvious these dudes had technique: the shapes of their outlines were sharp and decisive, and they painted with a kind of compact efficiency, as if each move was preprogrammed—not just the strokes, but the swapping of one can for another, the periodic step-back evaluations.

I took up position behind Trash, and soon found myself lulled into a meditative wooziness by the stretch-and-bend of his limbs. He clocked my presence over a shoulder, ignored me until his outline was complete. When he finally spoke, I jumped.

"It seems perhaps wrong to be using fancy German paint, and this thing," he said, tapping the breathing apparatus that hung loose around his neck now. "If not for that, I could pretend it's 1984 and this is *Style Wars*."

"You'd have to pretend to be thirteen, too. Most of those kids retired from writing as soon as they could be prosecuted as adults. Or tried to." I knew it was a dickhead answer as soon as I heard myself say it. Something in me felt proprietary toward these Europeans, wanted to remind them just whose shit this was. Not that it was mine.

Trash didn't notice, or he didn't care. "That's how old I was when I saw it. In Copenhagen, it played in the cinema."

"Huh. No shit."

He hefted a yellow in each hand, gave them a synchronized shake, then straightened both arms—the left above his head and the right below it, as if showing me what six o'clock looked like—and started on his fill. "My mother saw it first," he said. "She was a hippie, I guess you would say. The next day, she bought me a bunch of spraypaint, and told me 'you are going to write graffiti.'"

The empty vessel of his *A* filled up with color, and Trash dropped the yellows like a shooter would a pair of empty handguns. He crouched over his cans, sprang up with a mint green and a royal blue, and started detailing the interior. That threw me for a loop. To finish one letter before embarking on the next was like gutting your apartment, then remodeling the kitchen down to the oven mitts before you even put a toilet in the bathroom.

"*Style Wars* disappeared after a week. By then, every kid in Copenhagen wanted to bomb." Trash snickered. "We were somewhat confused in the beginning. The way to get props was to be the best at biting Broadway style, or Computer Rock. Many crews named themselves after the NYC ones. Very embarrassing shit, to look back on."

A strangled wail rang out from Billy's infirmary, several rows away, then faded like an ambulance siren tearing off through traffic. Trash froze, hearing it, paintcans cocked and index fingers hovering. I sensed a question working its way from his brain to his lips, and the thought of having to explain reminded me just how exhausted I was.

"So did it play all over Europe?" I asked, before he could change the subject to torture and kidnapping.

Trash snapped back to painting. "I know in Sweden, they showed it on TV for one night. There were only two channels back then, so basically half the country saw it. Next day it was like, hello Tunnelbanan trains, very nice to meet you."

I watched him rock his *M*, eased off, and walked on. Matamos Todos had indeed arrived; I found the four of them holding down an outer corner of the yard, speaking low, ultrafast Spanish as they collaborated on a double whole car. A scattered mess of bits and chips and fragments covered the train; the shit looked more like an exploded architectural diagram of some complex machine than a burner. If Trash was remodeling a kitchen, these motherfuckers were Amish farmers putting up a barn; nothing to see but piles of lumber, dudes pounding nails, and then bam, here come four whole goddamn walls swooping heavenward—from spare parts to structural coherence in a single, grand gesture. I could tell the moment was coming, but I didn't have the patience to wait.

That turned out to be a template for the next five hours of my night. I told myself I was a sentry, crisscrossing the yard on high alert, but really I was that dude at a party darting his eyes at the next conversational cluster, convinced he could be having a better time. I flitted and roamed, useless as a teacher patrolling the rows of a study hall humming with productivity. Every half hour or so, it would hit me anew that this thing was actually happening, and I'd have these heart-surges of elation and want to find Dengue or Karen and try to put it into words, get it corroborated. But Karen was with Billy, and I wasn't going anywhere near that fucking car. Speaking might have jinxed it anyway; those bursts of giddiness disrupted a foreboding thick enough to choke on.

I looked at my watch incessantly, and at the sky. Somehow, daylight seemed to promise safety—writers were nocturnal creatures, after all, and the Vandal Squad knew that—or at least an infusion of energy. Spraycan sounds and snatches of shoptalk still floated over the tops of trains as I museum-strolled the predawn aisles, but dudes were flagging, slowing down. By the time sunrise finally rolled around, not even the horizon's deep pinks could scrub the pallor from everybody's grill, and I was adding stamina to my laundry list of worries. All at once, an overwhelming fatigue hit me. I climbed into a train car, threw my feet up on a seat, shut my eyes and tried to rub away the ache with a thumb and forefinger.

Then a cheer went up, somewhere close by.

"Breakfast is served, ninjas."

I jumped down and followed the sound to the next row. There stood Supreme Chemistry, his mask and war paint gone. In one hand, he carried a cardboard box of coffee, the plastic-nozzle kind that serves twenty. In the other, a stack of cups. Karen and several dudes I'd never seen before stood before him, spraycans abandoned by their feet, clamoring for refreshment.

Dengue lumbered into view behind 'Preme, and sniffed elaborately at the air. "Do I smell what I think I smell? Why, can it be . . . is it really . . . Supreme motherfucking Chemistry?" I used the laughter as cover and sidled up to Karen, just as she reached the front of the line.

"Hey. Hook me up." I handed her my empty cup. She traded me her full one, and I cream-and-sugared it.

"You get any rest?"

"Hell no." I stifled a yawn. "You been with Billy all night?"

"On and off. There's a dude here from Boston who works in a hospital, and another from Mexico who's an EMT or something. We've been taking turns."

"Has Billy had a break?"

"He left for a half hour, tried to sleep but couldn't. Did a piece instead. The guards are 'much deeper inside the experience' "—she slashed quotation marks around the phrase—"so it's calmed down some. But your father says that's deceptive."

She turned to Supreme Chemistry. "So where in the fuck you been, son? Your boy Klutch dropped off his guard at one. Said they left you in front of the other dude's house around eleven, and hadn't heard a word since."

All the writers within earshot put their conversations on pause, wanting to hear the answer. Supreme Chemistry blew out his cheeks, wiped imaginary sweat from his brow with the inside of a wrist.

"Y'all kids tucked in? 'Cause heeeeere we go."

The Slick Rick reference was lost on no one. A couple of guys sat down on the ground at 'Preme's feet, literalizing his view of the world. The rest of us spread our legs a little wider, and sipped our steaming drinks.

"So. This ninja's name is Dudley Yarborough, and the address we have for him is a row house up in my old neighborhood, few blocks from my PJs. I tell Zebno creep past. We see the lights on, folks is home, so boom, I tell M.A.G. drop me off, I got this. I leave the mask in the ride, scrub off the paint. I'm figuring I'll play the block on some incognegro shit until the ninja comes out, which should be any minute now if he's gonna make it to Queens before his shift starts. He's gotta be driving, or he woulda *been* gone.

"So I jump out, and they break north to go handle theirs. I post up underneath this ninja's window. Which is open. The ninja's inside arguing with his old lady. Sounds like both of them have been drinking. I can hear every word. It's one of those arguments you can listen to and still not know what the fuck it's about, because it didn't start tonight, it started like fifteen or twenty years ago, you dig?

"After a while, Yarborough says something like 'Enough of your shit, woman, I gotta go make the money that keeps this goddamn roof over your head,' and he slams the door and comes on out. I'm by the curb, thinking I'll follow the ninja to his car and take advantage of the split second of concentration it takes him to insert a key into his door. From the sound of his voice, Yarborough is pushing up on sixty, and nobody that old got a whip with keyless entry, you feel me? Old men drive old-man cars.

"He comes out, and my fuckin' heart falls out of my chest and starts rolling away down the alley. It's Coupe DeVille. I'd know the ninja anywhere. He was president of the Vicious Knives when I was a kid. Y'all too young to remember the gang days, except maybe you Fever, but them times was *mean*. Sixties into the early seventies, boy. You couldn't go nowhere in the Boogie Down unless the ninjas that controlled that neighborhood let you pass."

"Right," said Dengue.

"You got to a certain age, you couldn't even walk in your *own* neighborhood unless you was affiliated—never mind going someplace else. You walked into another territory, you were supposed to have permission, and take your colors off to show respect. Otherwise, they'd take 'em off your back and whip that ass, maybe bring out some chains or some bats. And every few blocks, it was a different gang. The shit was real structured, B. Every gang had a president, a VP, and a warlord. Plus, they had junior divisions, for the kids too young to join the main one—like, the Vicious Knives had the Young Knives, the Baby Knives, and the Lady Knives, for the girlfriends. The shit was crazy.

"So anyway, Coupe DeVille was the *man*. He was a hustler, a car thief, always smooth, always looked good, always had girls around him, had this butterfly knife he was always flipping around in his hand. He founded the Vicious Knives, and every little kid in the PJs wanted to be him. The Knives did a lot of good, too; they weren't just thugs. We cared about our neighborhoods back then. Tried to keep things clean. You sold heroin, they'd throw you off a rooftop, you know what I mean?

"Me, I was in the Young Knives. My job was to write the name all over the neighborhood, mark the territory. This is even before graff jumped off, B. I'm talkin' 'bout, they gave me a bucket and a brush, and told me to write that shit on all the abandoned buildings and make sure I spelled it right. This is '67, '68, when I'm like eleven, twelve. I don't even count those years on my graffiti résumé, 'cause it wasn't that. It was gang shit.

"First, though, I had to get jumped in by the older guys. What they did was take you into the clubhouse, which was an abandoned building, and they put on a forty-five and took turns beating your ass. And if you stayed on your feet until the record was over, you were in."

"What was the record?" I asked.

"It was a James Brown record. 'Cold Sweat.' And that's a long motherfucker, too, believe me. I'll never forget, I'm getting my ass kicked, but I'm handling it. I'm protecting my face, I'm hitting back when I can. The song ends, and Coupe DeVille waits about two seconds, then punches me dead in the mouth, knocks out two teeth. Just to show everybody he could do whatever he wanted.

"Nowadays, he's an old, broken-down man. But still, I couldn't yoke this ninja up. I couldn't lay him out. It'd be like laying out my father. Laying out God. I'm watching him come toward me, and I decide, you know what, fuck it, I'm going to show the proper respect. The ninja's drunk, he just finished squabbling with his wife, he doesn't wanna go to work. So let me do the right thing here. And I just walk straight up to him and say 'Coupe DeVille. You wouldn't remember me, but I was a Junior Knife back in the day, and you were my hero. I'd know you anywhere, even all these years later. Come on, man, lemme buy you a drink on a Friday night.'

"He looks at me with those drunk-man eyeballs, and says 'I gotta go to work.'

"And I say, 'Listen, brother, I'm going to level with you. There's something jumping off tonight at that trainyard in Corona that you want to stay as far away from as possible. All you gotta tell them when they ask is that you got a phone call saying your shift's been canceled, and you won't get in any trouble. You dig? I know you dig, shit, you're Coupe DeVille. Now come on, drinks on me.'

"I took him to this titty bar a little ways Uptown. Real skanky place. He loved it, boy. Who knows how long since he'd had a night? I'm ordering round after round of Hennessy, and he's living it up, talking all kinds of shit to these off-brand dancers. Then he starts in with the back-in-the-day stories, bringing up all kinds of names I haven't heard in thirty-some-odd years. Fights, parties—his mind is crystal clear. We're having a ball."

Supreme Chemistry massaged his eyes, as if just realizing what a toll the night had taken. "Me and DeVille kept drinking until the club shut down," he said, "then I took him home in a cab, and hit up Dunkin' Donuts for you ninjas. And here I am. Ready to paint. Oh, yeah, almost forgot. Boom." From his shoulder bag, Supreme Chemistry produced three sizable sacks of baked goods. Then, true to his word, he wandered off to put in work.

The writers scattered a few minutes later, high on sugar and caffeine, ready to burn. Dengue and I repaired to his command center and made doughnuts disappear. The occasional progress report trickled in, via walkie-talkie. All was well in the train yards of New York City, now host to a global graffiti reunion, an Amuse burner contest, and the steady forward march of the greatest achievement in the artform's history. The impending shift-change would be without calamity; every guard scheduled to work dozed blissfully in his bed. Closer to home, their psychotropically subdued colleagues explored new vistas of discovery, or at least plunged through the terrors of their inner worlds in relative quiet.

"This is ridiculous," I told Dengue.

"I know."

"I keep waiting for—"

"I know." He groped for the waxpaper bag. "Anything good left?"

"Not really." I poked around. "Half a blueberry crunch?"

"Sold." I handed it over. We listened to the hum of the yard for a while, and then I had my best idea ever.

"We should buy one of those little hibachi joints, do some burgers and dogs. Show folks a little hospitality. What do you think?"

"I'm embarrassed I didn't come up with it first."

We fired up the grill at noon, and kept it blazing through the night. Different cats hoofed to the nearest supermarket, which was none too close, whenever we needed to resupply. For lunch, we rocked everything from kielbasa to veggie links. Then Trash copped skewers of marinated shrimp and tuna (the euro, apparently, is kicking the dollar's ass), and took the whole thing to another level. In retaliation, Enrique from Matamos Todos disappeared for two hours, located a Mexican carnicería, and returned with some type of spice-rubbed pork good enough to call Judaism and Islam into profound question.

Cats ate and drank and painted. They pulled out cameras, called in friends. Our numbers multiplied. *Clicka-clacka, psshht.* By midnight every car was painted, and motherfuckers had invoked The Rules and started going over yesterday's rushed throw-ups with fresh burners. I museum-strolled the aisles, turning my head left and right, AMUSE AMUSE AMUSE AMUSE AMUSE in every hand and style and color scheme. Jutting, monochromatic pieces so convincingly three-dimensional they might have been laser-hewn granite sculptures ran next to classic battle-ready wildstyles, arrows licking out like tongues of flame or hooking inward to suggest a power so unstable that the piece might self-destruct. Playful, soft-edged letters leaned together like off-kilter drunks, floating atop pastel puddles of melted Popsicle. Classic b-boy characters speckled the trains, shelltoed and Cazaled, tracksuited and Kangoled: tour guides directing your attention with jutting forefingers or cocked thumbs. There were throwback pieces, shouting out the early days by way of primitive patterned fills, flat regimented fields of stars, spindly-legged letters clumsy as baby giraffes. Some random cat from Far Rockaway even recreated Amuse's most famous joint stroke-for-stroke, a Duchampian collage of silver-turquoise-scarlet panes and shards that looked like a stained glass window the instant after a wrecking ball hit it.

At three A.M., the motioning began. Every twenty minutes, a train parked just past the end of the line so the conductors could walk through and pick up garbage, and we had eight to make sure it pulled out fully bombed. Dengue was right; the Danes were masters of that shit. Every one of them was ambidextrous, with a wingspan like a hawk, and they knocked out pieces like fucking snow angels; all you'd see was a body plastered against the train, a series of furious gyrations, and then the dude would walk away and bam, there'd be a burner in his wake.

At five, the yard would begin to empty of trains in anticipation of the morning commute, so three o'clock was also the welding hour. Any earlier, and we'd have been wasting too much of the tape players' batteries. I demoted myself to assistant, and did Supreme Chem's prep work: opened the booth, set up the tape, made sure the mic and the PA were on, then stepped back and watched the sparks fly.

Billy's message was short and to the point, repeated six times so as to fill both sides of a five-minute cassette. Writing credits went to

Fizz, who'd also coached Billy on delivery, and made him record so many takes that his voice had a slight robotic quality. The careful listener—the one who had to hear the tape all the way from Brooklyn to the Bronx, for instance—might discern a faint cry of "I got crack for sale" a minute and twenty-nine seconds into side two, courtesy of Rockwell, who'd been wandering Vexer's block during what had otherwise been Billy's sharpest take.

Hello, New York. My name is Billy Vance. I was born on the Lower East Side, and I've lived my whole life in this great city. I spent the weekend painting my best friend Andrew Stein's nickname, Amuse, on every single subway train there is. Andrew was killed on July second, 1987. He was shot to death in cold blood, and I saw it. I saw it with my own two eyes. So did three of my friends. The man who killed him was a police officer. He made it look like an accident, and he was never arrested. Now, that man is running for mayor. His name is Anastacio Bracken. I don't think he'd make a very good mayor. For one thing, he's a murderer. And for another, he's the president of the MTA, which means that his job is to make sure nobody writes graffiti on the subway trains. As you can see, Anastacio Bracken is not very good at his job. I'm asking you to do two things today, New York. I'm asking you to remember my friend Andrew, who didn't deserve to die. And I'm asking you not to make Anastacio Bracken your mayor. That's all. I hope you enjoy my paintings. Have a nice ride.

By four, the welding was done, and by quarter past cats were popping bottles of the cheap champagne Fuck and Gotch Uno had brought back on the last supermarket run. Except for the tumor of trepidation metastasizing in my chest, it was all sublime. The vibe was beautiful, everybody giddy with the knowledge of what we were pulling off. Dengue's radio crackled with extensions of those feelings, from all over the city. It felt like all across the world.

At 4:25, Karen was pulling Billy through the yard by his hand. I looked up, saw them coming toward me, and hid as much of my face as possible behind an upturned beer bottle.

"Time for a toast." She beckoned for the six-pack in my hand, popped a couple, handed one to Billy.

"I don't think Dondi wants to drink with me," he said.

"I'm surprised you have time. Isn't there a treed kitten you should be off rescuing or something?"

"Knock it off," said Karen. "Drink." She raised her bottle. I looked across her at Billy, saw my expression mirrored on his face. Slowly, we both lifted our Coronas, clinked, and drank.

At 4:28, the shouts started.

"Five-oh! Five-oh!"

Karen dropped her bottle. I heard it break as if the ground were a mile away, as if she'd dropped it down a well. Trash tore past, his long form shattered into blurred parts like a cubist painting: elbows, knees, neck, fingertips. A pack of bodies followed in his wake. Karen joined it.

My father stared at the approaching stampede and did not move. I grabbed his arm, jerked. Nothing doing. I knew it as soon as I touched him, as if the knowledge had passed from his skin to mine: Billy would not be denied a look. I prayed it would be brief, and distant.

Then I ran.

The options were the same as they'd ever been. Tunnel. Fence flap. Hide. My first assumption was that only hiding was viable: if the cops knew, they knew everything, and if they knew everything they'd brought as many bodies as they could muster, covered every exit, parked wagons outside the gate to load us all aboard.

I was wrong. An instant later, Billy got his glimpse: five men dashing toward us down the passageway between the trains, guns in their hands, light beaming wildly from their fists. That was all of them. I knew it on sight, twisting backward toward the sound: this was no departmental matter, no detachment of officers responding to a radio call. This was as personal on one side as it was on the other. This was Bracken and his flunkies, the quartet from the helicopter. Cops who did whatever he said, played by no rules but his, played to the death. They were young and fast, and they were leaving their boss in the dust, the V-formation elongating with every step.

Three members of Matamos Todos ran before them, losing ground fast. All at once, two broke left and the other right, into parallel aisles. I could see the indecision in the lead cops' hips. Bracken bellowed at them from behind, voice thick with phlegm.

"Ignore them! Get Vance! There he goes!"

I heard the cops accelerate behind me, their boots falling harder and more frequently. I imagined them straining to achieve top speed: the grimaces, the peeled-back lips, the extra tension in the calves and thighs as the stride lengthened. The burst of sweat, the thinning of the air—not that I needed to imagine any of it, because I was experiencing every bit myself.

Before me loomed the tunnel's wide black mouth. I didn't want to go in, but I knew the yard. Far off, the chain-link rattled as someone yanked back the flap, escaped as we could not.

Ahead of me, Karen raced through the foyer of pale light the moon managed to throw inside the tunnel, and the darkness swallowed her whole. I followed, then turned in time to see Billy hesitate, lingering in that pool of luminescence.

"Come on!" my mother shouted, and he sprinted to her, to us. The next sound was the clatter of the cops' boots as they came to an abrupt stop, there at that place that was tunnel but was not yet underground. Their flashlights darted left and right, but could not pick us out. They were perhaps fifty feet away, but this darkness would not be penetrated. It was too deep, too suffocating. Like swimming in some viscous liquid.

If we ran, they would hear us. If they heard us, we were dead. And so there we stood, invisible and paralyzed—and shivering. Maybe it was me; maybe it was fear. But I could hear Billy and Karen shaking too, gripped by the same bone-deep chill.

For a moment, I thought it was keeping Bracken's boys at bay, that they were too scared to advance. Then I realized they were waiting for orders.

Bracken caught up, pushed through their ranks and passed into the darkness smoothly, like he was a piece of it being restored. His footfalls crunched over the gravel, as if with each step he were crushing the skulls of tiny animals. The sounds came slow. Bracken was strolling.

"There's nowhere to go," he said in a low, even voice that reverberated off the walls and came back hard, metallic. "You know that, Billy."

I felt Karen's fury rising from her like heat, reached out and clamped my hand around her wrist.

More footfalls. Slower. A voice coiled tense as braided steel.

"You and me have got to talk, Billy. It doesn't have to be like before. That's up to you."

I realized this was our chance. His men couldn't fire, not with Bracken standing between us and them. That left only his gun to elude.

His gun, and the abyss ahead.

I tugged my parents close, cupped my hands, spoke almost soundlessly. "They don't have a clear shot. We've got to run. Now."

The air moved slightly as Billy shook his head. His whisper was too loud. "I can't do this again."

"I'm giving you five seconds, Billy. We can help each other. We have a common—"

I never heard the last word.

Shots rang out in a long, tight cluster, and I dove to the ground. I couldn't feel Billy or Karen, didn't hear their bodies fall beside mine. The noise was deafening, seemed to go on and on. I groped until I found my mother's hand. I squeezed; she squeezed back. Twice. I knew it meant that she was touching Billy, that he had not been lost.

Finally, the air was still. I raised my head a few inches, saw that the bodies blocking the entrance were gone. I strained to see Bracken, but he had been hidden all along. My chest was pressed against the iron train track, heart pumping so hard I was afraid it would betray my location. I had no idea what the fuck had just happened.

Footsteps broke the silence—footsteps coming closer.

Closer.

Stopping just above my head. The legs adjusting, planting themselves wider.

I held my breath. There was a click. I heard it in slow motion. It had four parts. The nearly inaudible application of pressure to metal by rough hands. The sound of metal sliding into metal. The backfire of its withdrawal. The jagged, slicing echo.

I knew it was a shotgun.

My lungs began to ache, to beg for air. Then came the moist thud of a heavy object meeting ground.

To not see is frightening. To know that you are seen is terror.

A voice.

"Y'all motherfuckers didn't really think I'd miss this shit, did you?"

A far less sophisticated click, and light beamed down upon us. I turned over, sat up, stared into it. Karen was already on her feet, pulling Billy to his.

Cloud 9 leaned against his shotgun, sixty watts radiating from his forehead.

"Howdy, youngblood. You like that shit?"

I took my time standing. My legs quaked.

"Uh, yeah," I managed.

My mother threw herself at him. Cloud caught her with one arm. Her face was buried so deep in his chest that it took me a moment to understand that she was sobbing.

"That my apology?" he asked.

Karen sniffled, nodded.

"Accepted." Cloud lifted his head, directed the miner's light at Billy. "How come I always gotta *ask* you for a hug, nigga?"

Billy walked over and joined Karen in his arms. The light moved when Cloud did, and as he shifted to grab my father the beam passed over Bracken, sprawled motionless on his side with his gun in his hand. I started. He was almost close enough to touch. I caught a quick glimpse of another cop, laid out behind him. He wasn't moving, either.

"You killed them?" I heard myself say. "Cloud, you *killed them!*"

"Relax, youngblood. Nobody's dead. I spent my money wisely."

"What money?"

"The hundred grand I got back from Bracken, when I told him where he could find Rage."

"What?"

"Yeah, dog. I was like halfway to Virginia when I decided, you know what, fuck this, I'm not running from a motherfucker dumber than me."

He raised his voice, and his chin. "That's right, Bracky-Brack, I'm talking about you! So I got off that bus, and caught another one. Been back in the city since Tuesday, making my little plans. On Wednesday, I called up shithead here, told him I'd had some revelations about what friendship was really worth. Had me a lovely little rendezvous with Officers McGrath and Downing over there on Thursday—whaddup, McGrath? How you feeling, homey? Downing, my nigga! You holding it down over there, partner? All right, then! Do you, baby!"

Cloud turned back to us. "I told them Billy had a plan to sneak a couple BRACKEN KILLED AMUSE cars into service around four in the morning, here where all of us have so much history. Then, I hired me some goons. Goons, meet Rage, Wren and Dondi. Rage, Wren, Dondi, these are my goons."

Three headlamps flickered on, along the walls of the tunnel.

"Hello, goons," I said.

"Mufuckers is top-notch, the best money can buy. Got a couple more stationed out there in the yard, but I was pretty sure it'd go down here. All right, fellas, back on alert." The lights vanished.

"And finally, I bought a bunch of hi-tech fly shit, you know what I mean? All the stuff we talked about. Got me some infrared goggles, some laser scopes. And that old cellmate of mine, the Gulf War cat? He hooked me up with these tranquilizer rounds. The army uses them for interrogation and shit, to fuck with niggas' heads. They leave you fully conscious, but they knock out your whole nervous system for like twelve hours, from the brain down. Mufuckers can't move, can't talk, but they can see and they can think. I'ma get Bracken settled in at the old Writers' Bench up on Grand Concourse, so he can appreciate the many fine burners you all took the time to paint. Speaking of which, I hope there's some space left, 'cause you know me—I *will* cross somebody the fuck out if I have to."

hat do you do when the mission is over? Most of the guys, local and imported alike, wanted only to find themselves a clear vantage point, sit down, and watch the trains go by. A bench at an elevated station, an apartment window looking out onto the tracks, a milkcrate outside a bodega with a view of an overpass, whatever: savor the sight, burn it into your brain, squeeze off some flicks, bug out.

Dengue had gotten on the horn and cautioned everybody against drawing attention to themselves. When the story broke, the city was going to be embarrassed and desperate—to disprove Billy's claims, and to find somebody they could parade past the cameras in bracelets. There was a good chance they'd sweep up all the writers they could find—for questioning, and for appearances' sake. The smart play was to make yourself scarce, sleep at your girl's house for a few nights, train-watch in groups of three or fewer and keep the pointing and backslapping to a minimum, the technical analysis and newly minted war stories under wraps or at least your breath.

After some debate, Cloud was prevailed upon not to install Bracken at the Writers' Bench, that being the first place the Vandal Squad would look for celebrants. Better that the MTA president remain mysteriously unavailable for comment while the story swirled into enormity. That he only emerge hours later, with a fantastic, unbelievable account of his whereabouts, one that raised more questions than it answered. If he dared to tell it at all.

Various poetically just options were put forth, and rejected: let Bracken and his men ride the trains, have them locked up for vagrancy, and, naturally, Karen's go-to, dump everybody in Brownsville (what fate she believed awaited anyone who set foot there, I can only imagine; yeah, it's a grimy neighborhood, but it's not like mortar rounds rain from the sky). In the end, function trumped form and we decided to install the five of them in one of Times Square's few remaining round-the-clock porno theaters, where the risk that they would be discovered before the tranq-pellets wore off was nil, and they might even make a few new friends.

Despite Billy's wishes, the guards were not laid gently on the welcome mats outside their apartment doors. Even Zebno, who'd been a fucking Viking, didn't have the patience for that. He offered to return them to their yards of origin, where they could sleep away the final hours in the comfort of the worksheds. Billy decided to be okay with that, though he insisted on coming along to supervise. If he'd had business cards, he probably would have slipped one into each of their pockets, in case they needed post-cambiafuerza counseling. I watched him climb into the van's shotgun seat, jabbering like an asshole about how a violent trip was often a transformative one, and perhaps these people we'd assaulted and drugged and gagged and imprisoned would rejoin the flow of reality changed, healed, opened. Zebno threw him a look that suggested he thought it was Billy who needed to rejoin the flow of reality, and mashed the gas.

My own postmission inclination tended toward a scalding shower, a hearty, carbohydrating breakfast, and a nap of epic duration. There was something depressing about the notion that in addition to making history, we also had to sit and bear witness to it. Surely, riding off into the sunset was a classier move.

I said as much to Dengue. He assured me I was a fool, and asked if I knew what he would give to watch just one train burst from the 116th Street tunnel, climb the bridge to 125th and Broadway, and slide to a blazing, rainbow halt along a platform teeming with commuters and schoolchildren. I told him I did not, but that it would be my pleasure to stand next to him and describe the experience in vivid detail.

Cloud's goons piled Bracken and company into a van of their own, and I do mean pile. Karen, Dengue and I hitched a ride to 42nd and 7th, hopped out in front of a street vendor just opening his cart. Cloud got off with us, entrusting the porn-theater placement to his underlings, and we copped coffee and bagels and stood beside the stairs to New York's biggest subway station, chewing and slurping, postponing our gratification, letting the anticipation build. It was that time of day when the city always seems fresh and clean and slightly desolate, and you feel as though you share a strange, vague secret with every other person walking the streets at such an uncivilized hour. And also that you have a secret *from* them, the secret of what you're doing awake.

At seven on the dot, we shuffled down the steps and saw our particular secret transformed into a proclamation. An Uptown-bound 1 Local was just pulling in; it was the train we needed to get to 125th Street, but getting on board would have required a fight. People stood three and four deep, from one end of the platform to the other, jockeying for a look. One tiny flash of light after another, everybody snapping photos, crappy cell phone cameras raised above their heads. Motherfuckers balanced atop the benches for a clearer look—and I'm talking guys in business suits, en route from their houses in Montclair to their jobs on Wall Street. Parents squiring their kids to school lifted the tots onto their shoulders, oohing and pointing. There was less noise than you would have expected, as if the commuters were ogling some rare wild animal that had just wandered onto their front lawns.

The hush burned off fast. Before the 1 even opened its doors, a downtown 2 Express arrived on the opposite track. Everybody whirled, saw that it was equally bombed, and started New Yorking it up. Across the way, the people coming off the 2 did the same. One train covered end-to-end with burners was an oddity you mentioned to your coworkers. Two, and you turned on the news to find out what the fuck was going on.

"I'm telling you, they're all like this," I heard a guy say, as the four of us strolled slowly through the din. It all sounded like one big conversation, though of course it was a hundred small ones. Dengue had a look on his face like he was listening to a symphony. And getting a blow job.

"I can't read that one, but that one says 'Amuse.'"

"Yo, they *all* say Amuse! That nigga kilt it!"

"Daddy, I want one."

"One what, sweetheart?"

"Whatever they're selling."

"This takes me back to the bad old days, when this city was falling apart."

"Let's wait for a clean one."

"What's Amuse?"

"It's that new PDA I was telling you about."

"My son got mixed up in this graffiti business when he was a kid. Thank God he straightened out."

"How many trains you think they did?"

"This shit is crazy!"

"No, Amuse is some guy's name."

"It's a fuckin' disgrace, that's what it is."

"It's gotta be an ad campaign."

"My cousin told me it has something to do with that MTA guy who's running for mayor."

"What does it say?"

"Yo, quick, get a flick of *that* one, down there."

"Amuse was this kid got himself killed writing graffiti."

"I hope they arrested whoever did this."

"Lord have mercy, I haven't seen anything like this in thirty years. Back then, New York had *character*."

"Why don't they take these trains out and wash them?"

"How come graffiti disappeared from off the trains, anyway?"

"You know what this makes me think of? Terrorism. If they can do this to our subways, think how vulnerable we are."

"I don't know if it's all of them, but it's a lot. I took the C from Brooklyn, and it was all graffitied up, too."

"It can't be just one guy."

"Yo, yo, c'mere, c'mere! This one down here is sick!"

"The Q was just like this. Amuse, Amuse, Amuse."

"They should lock him *under* the jail."

"Okay, I admit it, I'm Amuse."

"You stupid, Jerome."

"No, no, listen. It was a guy named Billy. He recorded a tape on the D train, I just heard it like five hundred times. Amuse was his friend, and he says that guy who's running for mayor killed him. Shot him, or something. Bracken, the MTA guy. So he did this to tell people don't vote for Bracken."

"How'd he get a tape on the train?"

"Same way he did all this."

"Way better than those stupid NBC Thursday Night Line-Up ads inside the train."

"*That*, we used to call a burner, and *that*, we used to call a throw-up."

"Eewww, why'd you call it that, Uncle Bernard?"

One after the other, the trains pulled out, leaving the crowd on either platform halved. Seeing the trains behave like trains, running just as if they had not been transformed into a moving art gallery, was an odd thing—a stark illustration of just how absurd this "war" had always been, with its nine-figure budgets, its "bombing" and "killing" and "kings." The subways' job was to move people around the city, and they performed it equally well whether or not they carried a few extra coats of paint. That much couldn't be debated, and for a moment it thrust all the rest into the realm of the absurd.

But the majesty of what we'd done refused to stay tamped down. I glanced up the line at the Ambassador. He'd found a seat on one of the benches, and was slumped there with his hands folded over his stomach. Karen stood behind him. I thought of all the hours they'd spent camped out at subway stations, waiting to see last night's burner once more, pining for a sixty-second fling with that one car out of thousands. Such a strange fidelity. And now, after two decades of abstinence, to know that whatever pulled in next was sure to be yours? I could hardly imagine the feeling. It would be like walking the streets, knowing you'd had sex with every single girl you passed.

Or maybe it would be nothing like that. It occurred to me that I should be wondering what I was feeling, not what they were. The answer was, a little hollow. At first, I attributed it to simple letdown, postpartum depression. Then I found myself thinking about *The Great Gatsby*, eighth grade, fall semester, and that scene where Gatsby (I think) says to whatshisname, the narrator (I think), something like, "You know who that was? That was the man who fixed the World Series." They meet the guy in a bar—old F-Dot, not exactly a regular contributor to the B'nai B'rith, describes him as vile and hook-nosed—and then a few minutes later, it's like the Wizard of Oz in reverse: this nothing-looking old fart sitting there eating his sandwich or whatever is revealed to be a criminal mastermind who once knocked the entire country on its ass. My memory of the book is pretty much limited to this one astonishing moment in which the world distorts, fills up with mystery.

It came to mind now, I realized, because it was precisely what I craved: to be pointed at, whispered about. I only wanted to be the man behind the scenes, the invisible mastermind, if everybody knew it. It was so silly and selfish, it made me want to slap myself in the back of the head.

I did the next best thing and sidled up to Cloud. He was leaning against a support beam, smoking a cigarette like he didn't give one single solitary fuck about any law, rule or regulation on the books.

An Uptown 2 was docking. We turned to stare at it.

"Thing of beauty, eh youngblood?"

"I feel like getting a bullhorn and telling everybody it was me. I mean, us."

He brought the cigarette to his mouth, index finger hooked around the top, and nodded as he took a pull. "Yeah, I remember that feeling."

I waited.

"Vexer," he said, nodding at a panel piece. "Or somebody biting him. Nobody else does *E*s like that, with the arrows all coming back in on themselves. You see?"

The doors closed, reopened, closed again. As if the train were clapping its hands.

"You were saying, you remember that feeling . . . ?"

"Yeah, man. You gotta think about it like this: only fly niggas appreciate fly shit. And they gonna find out on their own. For everybody else, fame is the opposite of fame."

"I'm not following."

He flicked his cigarette onto the tracks, and cocked his head enough to look at me. "The way you think about fame, like an accomplishment? Some shit to pursue? That's how you should think about not being famous."

I mulled that over, while Cloud smoked another one. My mother joined the Ambassador on the bench. I took it we were in no rush to get Uptown.

"Cloud?"

"Something else on your mind, youngblood?"

I wanted to ask him about T. Whether everything had gone down as he'd claimed, whether he'd left anything out. Whether it was all intricately concocted bullshit, and he'd just walked into the apartment and lit the man up. I couldn't, of course.

"What happened with you and my mother at Fashion Moda?"

He squinted at me. "Say what?"

"Nothing. Forget it."

"Naw, why, she said something happened?"

"Forget it."

"What she say, that I bogarted the opening, and it's my fault nobody else sold their little bullshit canvases?"

"I seriously have no idea."

Cloud shook his head. "Fuckin' Wren, boy."

My phone rang. I took it from my pocket, looked at the screen. It was the Uptown Girl.

"Yo."

"Are you there? I can't see you!"

"Am I where?"

"With your father, on TV!"

"What? Where?"

"He's giving a press conference. Turn to New York One."

"Hold on, hold on, I gotta get to a TV. What's he saying?"

"What is it?" Cloud demanded.

"Billy's on TV," I told him, and took off toward the stairs. "Kirsten, you still there?"

"You're breaking up. Where are you?"

I jackknifed my way through the flow of downward traffic, dashed toward the turnstiles. "Kirsten? Can you hear me? What's he saying?"

"It just started. He's standing next to that gay guy we had lunch with that one time."

"Nick? Nick Fizz?"

Static dissected her response. People were lined up behind the turnstiles, waiting to swipe and pass. It's a stupid fucking system, if you think about it, making the entrance and the exit the same.

"Coming through! Emergency!" I shouted, and ran toward one of the turnstiles, figuring I'd back down whoever stood opposite. It was an old lady, clutching her Metrocard in a bony hand. She paid no attention, backed me down, brushed past muttering aspersions.

I tried again, got shoulder-banged by a beefy businessman. Broke
through on the third try, reached the street, and spun around looking for an electronics store. There were a half dozen within blocks,
but none in sight. I picked a direction and lit out, doing that
stressed-out top-speed too-cool-to-run New Yorker walk.

"Kirsten? What's happening?"

"He's about to read a statement."

"Can you turn it up for me?"

"Yeah, sure."

She cranked the dial. Billy was reading the message he'd
recorded for the trains.

"Why is he doing this?" the Uptown Girl asked. "What about the
cops?"

"I don't know. He didn't tell us anything." I saw a store across
the street, JP Discount Electronics, and cut toward it, dodging
through four lanes of crawling traffic.

An Indian guy in a cheap suit greeted me at the front door.
"Hello, my friend. What can I do for you?"

"Just looking." The TVs were in the back. I found the channel
just as Billy was reaching the end of the statement. The reporters
seemed to know it—maybe they'd already gotten ahold of the tape.
I could hear them outside the frame, shouting for his attention.

How did Billy look? I believe the expression is "preternaturally
calm," and it's usually applied to psychopaths and athletes. The
shot was tight on his head and shoulders, making it impossible to
tell where he was. If he hadn't been squinting, I might not have
known he was outside. Fizz was behind him, hands folded behind
his back, his stance that of a bodyguard or a manager.

Billy looked up, into the cameras. From the way one shoulder
rose, he appeared to be shoving the paper into his back pocket. A
flurry of shrill questions filled the pause. Billy ran his eyes back
and forth over the throng—trying to find one he felt like answering, maybe. It made him look as if he were reading a teleprompter.
Even in the sunlight, you could see the flashbulbs going off. I guess

in news photography school, they teach you to catch your subject with his mouth closed. Then he opened it, and the reporters fell silent.

"I figured maybe people needed to see my face. So they could look into my eyes, and believe me."

There was no clamor this time. They waited. My palms started to sweat, and the thought of vomiting crossed my mind.

"You look like him," the Uptown Girl said in my ear.

I'd forgotten we were still on the phone. Remember how when you're thirteen or fourteen, just falling in love for the first time and too young to go out on a school night, you spend hours and hours on the phone with your girlfriend every evening? The two of you might watch a whole movie together on the phone, talking and not talking, might even fall asleep listening to one another breathe.

"I guess I do, a little," I mumbled back.

The reporters stopped waiting. One did, anyway, and the others, caught flatfooted, didn't try to compete.

"Billy, you've been a wanted man for sixteen years. You were convicted on multiple charges of felony vandalism, and fined two million dollars. Where have you—"

"Graffiti was the only voice I had then," my father said, "and it's the only voice I have now. I tried to tell people the truth about Bracken—that he's a murderer, that he killed my friend. Nobody listened. So I'm trying again."

"This is crazy," said the Uptown Girl. "He's got to get out of there."

"He will," I croaked, suddenly understanding. "He's leaving. He's doing it again."

It was his eyes that told me. There was something heavy and defeated in them, something incongruous with the victory all around. He looked like a man who was bowing out. A man preparing to live with his decisions, and live with them alone.

"Not like this," I whispered, a hot sadness welling in me. "Please. We need more time."

He took another question.

"All due respect, Mr. Vance, you expect us to believe you did this by yourself? With no help?"

Billy blinked a couple of times. "I'm a master painter. One of the best in the world."

The media exploded into chaos, and for a moment Billy stood still, staring into their lenses.

"I'm not going to tell you my secrets, but look: I've been gone for many years, and in that time I've studied with some of the wisest men in the world, and learned how to do things most Westerners would think are impossible. The whole time, I was preparing for this. To come back and do this. So don't be too quick to think you know what's possible. You'll see what I mean when the cops get here."

"Oh my God," said the Uptown Girl. "Dondi, what's he talking about? He sounds crazy. Is that the point? Is he going to plead insanity?"

Before the reporters could recover, my father resumed.

"That reminds me, has anybody heard from Bracken? A statement? Anything? Not like the candidate to be so quiet, is it?"

The briefest flicker of a smile crossed his face, and I felt myself tear up.

"Will you turn yourself in, Billy?"

"Where did you go when you left New York?"

"Can you elaborate on what you studied, and with whom?"

But Billy was looking past the cameras now, tracking something farther away.

"Oh, shit," I said. "Go. Go."

The cameramen were no dummies. They turned to capture whatever was distracting Billy. Four police cars, regular city rollers, skidded to a halt at the curb. The doors flew open, and out poured the uniforms.

I recognized the block.

Hardy-har, we live in a flying elephant.

"He's gone," I told the Uptown Girl. "He's gone, or he's dead."

The cameras swung back toward Billy.

"I'm sorry, Dondi," he said. "I wish—"

His eyes darted to the street, and Billy turned and ran. Threw open the front door, sprinted through the lobby. Fizz was right behind him.

Thank God for a free and independent press, hellbent on getting the scoop. The reporters chased Billy. The cameramen chased the reporters. The cops had to fight their way through all of them.

The New York One team led the pack. Their cameraman got a shot of Billy and Fizz slipping into the stairwell, plus some nice audio: the distinct click of the door closing, and then a sound that probably mystified the majority of those watching at home, the Uptown Girl included.

"He's welding it shut," I told her.

"What's the point of that? He's got nowhere to go! He's trapped! They'll search every apartment!"

I was too anxious to respond. There are no fresh metaphors left in the English language to describe an overtaxed tickbox, or any of the physical sensations endemic to extreme duress, but you can probably imagine the state your boy was in. If motherfuckers had to feel that way all the time, human life expectancy would be like ten, fifteen minutes.

The cops got there thirty seconds later, charged through the newspeople and started throwing their shoulders at the door. I figured Billy could climb a flight every ten seconds—the first few, at least. That put him on the fourth floor by the time they turned their attention to the elevator. It would have been half that, but these guys were determined to take the door. They looked like idiots: seven or eight boys in blue hulking around, trying to appear useful, while two young bucks, the first to arrive, slammed themselves against the ungiving metal again and again.

When they did think to find an alternate means of pursuit, it took the po-pos another minute to realize that the elevator was stalled on the second floor—Fizz and Billy must have taken care of that before they called the press. If there's anything that looks dumber on TV than a bunch of New York's finest outsmarted by a door, it's those same ten guys jabbing at a button again and again, as if they think the problem is that they haven't pushed it hard enough. I could almost see the commissioner throwing shit around his office as he watched this.

"Five minutes," I muttered. "Five minutes, that's all he needs." It had been three and change. The Uptown Girl didn't ask what I meant. I think she was too busy willing Billy to make it, even if she couldn't imagine how.

"Crowbar!" shouted the cop in charge. An eighteen-second dash to the patrol car and back. Ten more for one of the disgraced young bucks to redeem himself and pry open the door.

"Richards, second floor—unstick that elevator! Ufland, third floor, search every apartment! Donnelly, four, Wilson, five, Cabrera, six. The rest of you, take the elevator to fifteen, and work your way down! He's here somewhere!"

Four minutes. I decided to revise my estimate. Four was plenty. My father was gone.

As for that sentence he never finished, it hasn't kept me up as many nights as you might think. There are only a few basic directions it could have taken: *I wish I was different, I wish you were different, I wish things were.* I agree with all of them.

You never know it's too late until it's too late. That's what makes it too late, I guess.

he end. Basically.

By that evening, a chemical death bath had washed the burners from the trains. You could almost hear them screaming as they melted into Day-Glo puddles.

But trains are easier to buff than reputations. Losing a guy in an apartment building on live television when you've got half the police force camped out in the lobby is hard to explain. Especially when he's just confessed to the splashiest and slickest crime in city history. That's not me bragging; that's a quote from *The New York Times*. Okay, a paraphrase.

The story went global. Interstellar, probably. I've got no interest in cataloguing the particulars of the coverage. Fame wasn't why we did it, and besides, there are plenty of other places you can go to read about that.

I will tell you about Bracken, though.

Credit where credit is due: he played it smart. I suspect one of those high-priced public relations firms that specialize in crisis management was calling the shots, but I'm just guessing. If that is the case, though, they earned their fee without working up much of a sweat. On Tuesday morning, Bracken released a statement to the press. Then he walked straight off the map, disappeared as utterly as Billy.

I'm not talking unavailable for comment, or disgraced and reclusive. I'm talking Abominable Snowman, Serengeti Yeti, some cryptozoological shit. The crowd of reporters outside his apartment dwindled every day, with the holdouts from the retard networks abandoning their vigils on Friday. Maybe he sent somebody for his personal effects, or maybe he left everything behind.

His statement was the tersest, most inscrutable document in the history of printed matter. It didn't address Billy's accusations, neither accepted nor dodged the blame for Amuse-A-Thon 2005, offered nary a clue as to his whereabouts for the previous twenty-four hours. He suspended his campaign and resigned from his job, effective immediately, "in light of recent events." That was all. Didn't even bother to endorse a candidate.

Naturally, the disappearance of both hero and villain only gave the story legs. Funny how everybody wants closure, and nobody realizes they already got it.

Karen and I unplugged the phone, and put on a show of acting normal—for ourselves and each other and whoever else was watching. Fizz had a PR guy issue a statement on our behalf, a Bracken-esque two-liner saying that we were estranged from Billy and hadn't even known he was back in New York, much less what he'd been plotting or where he was now, and we asked the media to respect our privacy and our total lack of connection to recent events. What a fantastic phrase, *recent events*. It adds so much, yet says so little.

We spent Tuesday waiting for the NYPD to show up and search the apartment, but it never happened. They were in spectacular disarray, seemed like, between the Bracken press release and the Billy fiasco, and if they raided us and came up empty, it would have been an embarrassment trifecta. Which is exactly what would have happened, because we'd dumped all the maps and notepads and shit on Sunday night, even moved Karen's old blackbooks and photo albums to her homegirl's place. They would've sulked back out with nothing but a twenty-year-old jean jacket covered in tags. And we would have made damn sure the press was there to see it all.

On Wednesday, Karen went to work, and I went to Theo Polhemus's funeral. It was at a chapel in Harlem, and the service was in
French. Turns out the dude was Haitian. I played the back, paid my
respects from a distance. The casket was closed, and probably
empty, considering how much time had passed since his death. I'd
been to a couple of funerals for young people before—a girl I went
to elementary school with died of cancer, awful thing, and a guy
I'd played on summer league ball teams with caught a stray bullet
last year, which is no fun either. Worst thing in the world, burying
a kid. You can't say the person lived a full life, or it was his time to
go, or any of that. All the rules of decorum are suspended: people
wail. But T's was not the funeral of a young person. It was the
funeral of a gangster. His mom, his sister, everybody was blank-
faced, like the only surprise was that he'd lived this long.

On Thursday morning, I schlepped out to Staten Island, and
took a cab to the Arthur Kill Correctional Facility. Signed in, followed a series of increasingly authoritarian signs to the visiting
room, sat down before five inches of grimecaked duroplastic,
picked up the phone. Wiped away the condensation of sharp, cheap
aftershave, the spit flecks of the previous conversationalist. Waited.

Abraham Lazarus loped into the room. His eyelids rose slightly
when he saw me, from half-mast to three-quarters. His dreadlocks
were tied into a massive beehive at the back of his head. It wobbled
as he walked over, stabilized as he sat down. With an arm scarcely
thicker than the stray ropes of hair falling over his shoulders, he
reached across himself and grabbed the receiver.

"Dondi. What's up, bro?"

I'd expected a little more effusion, or surprise, or something.
But I guess when you're in prison, you pretty much just take things
as they come.

"Not much, man. How you doing?"

Lazarus shrugged, and slid lower in his chair. "Getting by."

"Right, right." I nodded. Lazarus tapped his thumb against the
phone and waited for me to explain my presence. For some reason,

I didn't want to come right to it. But I couldn't think of anything else to say that wasn't totally inane.

"You heard about T?"

"I heard he got shot."

"Heard why?"

Lazarus studied me a moment. His eyes were the color of prison. "Nobody knows."

Which was what I'd figured. Terry would have had to be a whole different type of dude to go see Everton.

"I do. T put you in here, man. We found out, and did what had to be done."

"*We* who?"

"Me and one of my partners, dude name of Cloud 9." I unfolded my "Crown Heist" printout, pressed the first page against the glass. "You know my mom's a literary agent, right? Well, T wrote the whole thing down, and sent it in. He set Jumpshot up, got you popped, took your connect, and went into business for himself."

Truth be told, I wasn't entirely sure what I was doing. But I figured the gratitude of Abraham Lazarus was a good card to hold, whether I ever played it or not. For Cloud, too. Sooner or later, both of us were going to need sources of income. No sense leaving lemons rotting on the ground when you've got sugar and water and a pitcher full of ice.

I watched Lazarus's eyes scan the text and thought of Billy's on TV, flitting across the throng of reporters.

"Turn the page."

I did. He worked his way down.

"Turn."

No cobwebs on Lazarus. He finished the story in five minutes, then sat back and stroked his chin.

"So . . . what?" Lazarus asked softly. I half heard him and half read his lips: a bad connection to three feet away. "You tryna come up in the game, K.D.?"

"I don't know. Kind of weighing my options right now."

Which was true, but that wasn't why I said it. Naked ambition from the guy who took out the guy smart enough to play your ass into a cell without you even knowing what had happened seemed ill advised.

"I got kicked out of school," I went on. Lazarus knew me as a college-bound kid dabbling in the bougiest and lowest-risk sector of customer service; some serious explanation was in order if he was to believe I'd started blasting on drug bosses. Desperation seemed like a plausible motive, and if I cut it with loyalty, I figured it would go down smooth. "School and my mom's crib both. I'm not sure what comes next."

The moment I said those words, they became untrue. Funny how that works, right? You declare yourself tired and snap alert, or reply that no, thanks, you're not hungry, and feel your stomach growl.

I was going to write a motherfucking book. Obviously.

Not obviously like, *because you're holding it in your hands right now!*, which is lame, but like, of course. I had to do something, and somebody had to do this. It felt right, by which I mean the idea was chaperoned by a convoy of endorphins: the body's way of applauding a decision it can get behind. Or maybe it's the body's way of whisking you past the complicated crannies, the second thoughts, *I have no idea how to write a book, what are the legal ramifications of said project, is this one of those pretentious An Artist I Shall Be epiphanies you read about in boring old-timey novels*, etc. It beats me. I don't really know that much about endogenous opioid polypeptide compounds.

The immediate result of my revelation or whatever was that the conversation I was having with Lazarus became meaningless. There he sat, playing Kingpin on Lockdown—which is the kind of role you could fuck around and score a Best Supporting Actor nomination for, if you really kill it, but most likely it doesn't even get your name mentioned in the reviews—while your boy here, more excited than I'd been all week, was busy composing first sentences in my head and spending my advance.

"You always been a smart dude," Lazarus said, slitting his eyes in what he probably considered a savvy look of appraisal. Hilarious, right? I mean, how savvy could dude have felt, just then? How savvy could I have believed him to be?

"You and your boy, you showed some real initiative, bredren. I like that. My people like that."

I nodded my head, and let him steal his scene. Trust me, it's not worth running down in any further detail. You've already seen that movie. Walked out on it, maybe. Suffice to say that by the time we parted with a fists-pressed-to-the-Plexiglas pound, Gangster Movie Cliché #234, a future I didn't want was mine for the taking. And for Cloud, the door to Healthy Living Vegetarian Café and Juice Bar had swung wide. It was a portal through which he would soon pass, and reemerge from five pounds heavier for reasons that had nothing to do with cuisine.

On Saturday morning, I had brunch with the Uptown Girl. She talked about my future. I refrained from asking why she cared, since she clearly didn't intend to be a part of it, and told her I was writing a book. It became realer the moment the words hit the air, so I said it a couple more times. Then I told her I had to go to the bathroom, and paid for our meal at the register in back, before they could bring the check to the table and she could make a show of grabbing it.

I got back to my building around three, unlocked the door, and held it open for a guy on his way out. There was something furtive to him. Probably visiting shady-ass Hector and them up on the top floor, I thought, not giving a shit. Then I caught a whiff of the smell he left in his wake. Campfire.

I charged up the stairs in a panic, and stopped short in front of Karen's door. Sitting on the welcome mat was a two-liter plastic bottle, smudged with black fingerprints and full of rust-tinged water. A card dangled from the neck, attached with a piece of string.

Thanks, it read, in its entirety.

Nice gesture, Lou.

That night, I went to Sleet. Joyce got me drunk, and I learned two important lessons: carrying on a conversation with a busy bartendress is impossible, and trying makes you look like a sucker and a lush. I woke up with a hangover, and chilled all motherfucking Sunday, as the Good Lord intended, me and Karen and dumb movies on TV, neither of us saying much that didn't involve pizza toppings. On Monday, I found a proper café, with power outlets and no Wi-Fi, and started writing—though not really, because it was all too raw, and I was too stupid to wait, and thus I didn't produce so much as a usable paragraph for the first month and a half, and depression at my newfound inability formed an alliance with all the numbness and lethargy and panic and fury of losing my father and my future, and together they nearly beat my ambition into a coma. But that's a different story and besides, I'm better now. Fake it till you make it, as they say. Keep sitting in that chair.

The end. Except for one last thing.

A few weeks ago, when I was working on chapter 7, Cloud's homecoming, I had a visitor. I'd stepped up my café game by then, was rotating between one in Park Slope with sexy-ass baristas but not enough light, one around my way that was cool until lunchtime and too crowded afterward, and one in Carroll Gardens that was always peaceful because the coffee and the food both sucked. That afternoon, I was at the Park Slope spot, two espressos deep, wrestling with the teargas sequence and having all sorts of problems. I was in a zone. Not a productive zone, but a zone nonetheless. I didn't see him come in, didn't look up until I heard a body settle into the chair across from mine.

"You're Billy's kid."

I slapped my laptop shut. He looked as if he'd aged two decades in two months. Gaunt cheeks beneath an unkempt salt-and-pepper beard, red sunken eyes, skin loose and gray. Clothes filthy and random: a too-big Oakland Raiders sweatshirt, acid-washed jeans, a baseball cap bearing the logo of a failed brokerage firm.

"You don't have to be scared of me." He laid his hands on the table. "There's nothing I could do to you now, even if I wanted. Your father and his friends took care of that."

"The ones who are still alive," I said.

Bracken stared into his lap. The smell was slow in coming off him, bound to his body by a shroud of grime. I knew it well. It was the stench of the underground, of depth and blackness, fire and fear.

You can't walk off one map without walking onto another.

He raised his eyes to me. "I have to see Billy."

"That's a good one."

"Please. I need his help." Bracken's lips trembled. He started to speak, changed his mind, leaned back. Changed it again, bent over the table, and hissed the words.

"I need to be *free*."

"From what?"

Long pause. Slow dissolve into silence.

"You know something, Bracken? He'd probably give it if he could. I want you to think on that. *Billy Rage would help you if he could.*"

Behind the counter, the barista and the café's owner were conferring in hushed, agitated tones. It seemed like a good bet that We Reserve the Right to Refuse Service to Anyone would be invoked shortly, if Bracken stayed.

"I need his help," he said again, and slumped lower in his chair.

"I have no idea where my father is. He could be anywhere. He could be dead."

We stared at each other for about a minute, and then his eyelids started drooping, lower and lower, until at last they closed. His head lolled with an agonizing slowness that ended when chin met chest. Anastacio Bracken had passed out. Of all the goddamn things. I packed my shit and bounced.

My father *could* be anywhere, I guess. I tell myself that. But there's only one place I can imagine Billy going, and that's back to the jungle. The thought terrifies me. I can't dwell on it for long, or I start feeling sick. At the same time, though, I understand. I get why. I get him. I didn't have that before.

I try to hold that close.

ACKNOWLEDGMENTS

hanks to the following writers, without whose vast understanding of graff history and practice this book could not have been written: KET, LORD SCOTCH, TRUE MATH, BOM 5, ZEPHYR, PART ONE, FABEL, UPSKI, Jacob Kimvall and Tobias Barenthin Lindblad. I'm doubly thankful to KEO, a font of knowledge with a knowledge of fonts who drew the jacket and the illuminated letters that begin each chapter. I'm grateful to Daniel Alarcón, Vinnie Wilhelm, Theo Gangi and Alain Maridueña for their invaluable notes on the manuscript, to Eugene Cho for his design expertise, to Joel "J.PERIOD" Astman for proofreading and mixology, and to Victoria Häggblom and Vivien Mansbach for their love and support throughout the writing process. I'm also indebted to my agent, Richard Abate, and my editors at Viking, Amber Qureshi and Liz Van Hoose.